WHO COULD THEY TRUST?

Hazardous materials technician Brie Williams
had been trained to spot danger, and Linc Tanner,
her handsome new partner, seemed to be it.
Was he going to protect her from the threats
she'd been receiving? Or did he constitute
the biggest threat of all?

**"Lindsay McKenna continues
to leave her distinctive mark
on the romance genre with...timeless tales
about the healing power of love."**
—*Affaire de Coeur*

Agent Nick Romero was hired to protect
schoolteacher Addy McConnell from a potential
kidnapper. With him guarding her, Addy was quite
sure she was safe from the outside risk.
But what about the danger *within?*

**"Ms. Barton masterfully delivers excitement,
adventure and romance...sheer delight."**
—*Romantic Times*

D0836998

LINDSAY McKENNA

A homeopathic educator, Lindsay teaches at the Desert Institute of Classical Homeopathy in Phoenix, Arizona. When she isn't teaching alternative medicine, she is writing books about love. She feels love is the single greatest healer in the world and hopes that her books touch her readers on that level. Coming from an Eastern Cherokee medicine family, Lindsay was taught ceremony and healing ways from the time she was nine years old. She creates flower and gem essences in accordance with nature and remains closely in touch with her Native American roots and upbringing.

BEVERLY BARTON

has been in love with romance since her grandfather gave her an illustrated book of *Beauty and the Beast*. An avid reader since childhood, Beverly wrote her first book at the age of nine. After marriage to her own "hero," and the births of her daughter and son, Beverly chose to be a full-time homemaker, aka wife, mother, friend and volunteer. The author of over thirty books, Beverly is a member of Romance Writers of America, and helped found the Heart of Dixie chapter in Alabama. She has won numerous awards and made the Waldenbooks and *USA Today* bestseller lists.

BEVERLY BARTON

LINDSAY McKENNA

BENEATH HIS SHIELD

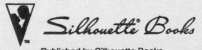

Silhouette Books

Published by Silhouette Books

America's Publisher of Contemporary Romance

 SILHOUETTE BOOKS

ISBN 0-373-21730-7

by Request

BENEATH HIS SHIELD

Copyright © 2002 by Harlequin Books S.A.

The publisher acknowledges the copyright holders of the individual works as follows:

COME GENTLE THE DAWN
Copyright © 1989 by Lindsay McKenna

PALADIN'S WOMAN
Copyright © 1993 by Beverly Beaver

This edition published by arrangement with Harlequin Books S.A.

® and TM are trademarks of Harlequin Books S.A., used under license. Trademarks indicated with ® are registered in the United States Patent and Trademark Office, the Canadian Trade Marks Office and in other countries.

Visit Silhouette at www.eHarlequin.com

Printed in U.S.A.

CONTENTS

Dear Reader,

Come Gentle the Dawn was written around the time I was in the West Point, Ohio, Volunteer Fire Department. I was the only woman in a twenty-person fire department—and their first woman. I took some training in hazardous materials from the Ohio Fire Academy down in Reynoldsburg, Ohio, to help supplement my knowledge of this area, which firefighters are confronted with in one form or another almost every day. I loved being educated about the "mop and glow boys," as we call 'em—though I should rephrase that and say, "the mop and glow girls and boys"!

This book was my first attempt to create a mystery within the context of a romance, and my knowledge of hazard materials, or haz-mat as we call it, was a must in order to write authoritatively and accurately. And since I was in the second most active haz-mat spot in the USA, I had plenty of experience to supplement that knowledge. Much of what the heroine does in this book, I did. Nothing like translating firsthand knowledge.

The other aspect of this book, which is even more poignant now in the wake of the bombing by terrorists of our Pentagon and the World Trade Towers, is the emotions that emerge in the aftermath of trauma. Firefighters are no less affected by traumatic experience than civilians are. The heroine mirrors these emotions as she recovers from the loss of her partner and is healed by the hero's love.

I hope you enjoy the romance and the intrigue in this story!

Happy reading!

Lindsay McKenna

COME GENTLE THE DAWN

THE DAWN

Lindsay McKenna

To my sisters
Ruth Gent, René Anderson, Ann Roher,
Betsy Lammerding, Cinda Garland, Linda Dubnicka
and Karen Mylnar.

And to our Mother, the Earth,
who needs our protection.

Chapter One

"There's no way in hell I'm working with a woman in hazardous material," Linc said. He got up from the leather chair and faced his superior, Brent Cramer, who sat behind the massive oak desk. The scowl on Linc's lean face deepened as he gauged Cramer's unruffled reaction to his caustic statement. He didn't care. He was bone tired from his last assignment and hadn't been given enough time to recoup before Cramer had decided to throw him on another one.

"She knows what she's doing, Linc." Cramer lifted his narrow shoulders beneath the three-piece gray pin-striped suit. "I'm getting plenty of heat from the senator from Ohio to do something about this pronto. The Hazardous Material Bureau is his pride and joy politically. He can't have haz-mat people being blown away with no suspects. It won't look good to the voters in that state. And he's up for reelection soon."

Linc Tanner stopped pacing and threw his hands tensely on his lean hips. He glared out the window through the venetian blinds. He stared unseeing at the other government buildings surrounding them. I need rest. I don't need a damn broad who's fingered to be blown apart, he thought savagely. He twisted his head in Cramer's direction and, with barely veiled anger, said, "I don't care about the senator's voting problem in Ohio. My job and his politics don't mix."

Cramer calmly steepled his fingers. "I know you could care less about politics. That's my job. Yours is to go into the field and assume an identity. I chose you for this assignment because you're the best, Linc."

Tanner shot him a venomous look out of the corner of his eye. "Spare me the platitudes, Cramer. Chances are, if I look at the roster, I'm the *only* available agent for this mess."

A hint of a smile curled Cramer's thin mouth. Ever since Linc had joined the Bureau of Alcohol, Tobacco and Firearms, he had been considered a master of sorts. Of sorts, he reminded himself sourly. A few well-chosen adjectives summed him up: acerbic, a loner and damn good at his job. He knew it was the last reason that kept Cramer from firing him outright for his constant insubordination.

"You're probably right," Cramer acknowledged. "Now, let's talk about this problem with the haz-mat team in Ohio."

Linc tensed. "I just got off a heavy assignment. I want a couple of weeks' rest. I almost got exposed on this last one, and you want me to stick my neck out a week later. This time I'm saying no."

Cramer unsteepled his slender hands and leaned forward, a crafty gleam in his gray eyes. "You take this one, Linc, and it will earn you that desk job you've been wanting for some time. Think for a moment. Six years out in the field as an ATF agent is a long time. You crack this case, and I'll get it for you. Anywhere in the United States, Linc.''

Linc studied his boss in the taut silence. It wasn't like Cramer to promise him a plum just like that. No, Cramer was a politically savvy animal on the Hill who manipulated others as easily as puppets. But Cramer had never promised him something and not delivered. He rubbed his square jaw, considering and weighing the offer. Finally, he sat down opposite Cramer.

''One of two things has happened. Either this is a hell of a lot bigger than both of us or you're getting political pressure even you can't control.''

''A little of both. The senator from Ohio just happens to be on the Appropriations Committee, which holds the purse strings to our budget. We've got some big requests coming up before them soon. If I don't give him what he wants, he could turn on us. We're strung out too thin in the field and we need to hire more agents.''

''Tell me about it. I'm so used to leading a double life my real one was destroyed years ago.''

Cramer nodded, looking grim. ''I know.''

''You've got my attention,'' Linc muttered. ''Go on.''

''You'll take the assignment?''

''I didn't say that. I want to hear the details,'' Linc countered.

Cramer smiled and opened the file beneath his hands. ''The players involved are the Ohio State Fire Marshal's office, the Hazardous Material Bureau, one murdered hazmat tech, one suspicious explosion—and no answers.''

Linc scowled. ''A murder?'' Who would want to blow away a haz-mat tech?

''Yes. A man by the name of John Holcomb, who'd

been employed by the FM's office for five years, bought it. His partner nearly went with him, but she managed to pull through and is now back on the job.''

''Who's playing rough?''

''No leads. Your guess is as good as mine.''

''You said 'she.' Was that Holcomb's partner before he died?''

''Yes.'' Cramer pulled out a large black and white photograph and handed it to Tanner. ''Meet Brie Williams, the unknown quantity in this puzzle. She's a qualified hazmat tech. Been working for the FM's office for the past three years. Report is, she's very good at her job.''

Linc studied the photo intently, missing nothing. It showed a tall woman in a one-piece dark uniform directing several fire fighters toward what appeared to be a haz-mat accident involving a derailed tank car. Linc looked closer. Brie Williams was not what he'd call a beautiful woman. Her face was square, holding large, expressive eyes, an aquiline nose, full lips and a mildly stubborn chin. The high cheekbones emphasized her eyes, which were her best feature, in his opinion. Her hair was dark and short. Linc halted a smile, thinking that with the baseball cap on her head, she could almost pass for a man. Except for her rounded breasts. Her shapely rear and hips would also persuade any man that she was definitely female. His gaze came back to her face, and he waited for his gut impression, which had never led him astray and had often saved his life. Despite the tension in her face, the intentness reflected in her eyes and thinned lips, she didn't seem all that tough. Maybe on the outside, but Linc would bet his life she was vulnerable beneath that exterior. He fervently hoped so or there wouldn't be a prayer for them working together as a team.

"How did a woman get that high up in the state on something as specialized as haz-mat?" he asked.

Cramer pulled out another paper and held it out to him. "Here's Williams's bio. Read it and you'll see why."

"She was a fire fighter for five years?" Linc muttered in disbelief. Another rarity. Out of one million, three hundred thousand fire fighters in the United States, only one percent were women.

"Williams has paid her dues," Cramer defended. "When the FM's office hired her on, she was a lieutenant with her fire department up near Litton, Ohio."

Another unique quality, Linc thought. What were the odds of a woman fire fighter becoming an officer? One in a hundred thousand. She was sure beating a lot of odds. Tiredly, Linc rubbed his face, tossing the papers on the desk. "That's all I need: a woman who's in male territory."

Cramer's eyes grew hard. "Look, I know you think all women belong barefoot and pregnant, but this one time, you'd better put your opinions aside. Williams has nothing but commendations in her file."

Linc raised his chin. "Is she a suspect then? A pawn? The next victim? What?"

"We don't know. That's what you're going to find out and tell us. Her partner was murdered, judging from all the evidence that was gathered. Although officially, it's being soft-pedaled as an accident with an ongoing investigation."

"So?" Linc challenged. "Did she walk away from it and let Holcomb get killed or what?"

"No. She was going back to the haz-mat truck to get some tools when the explosives detonated. Williams was in the hospital for three months afterward."

It wasn't making sense to Linc. Either he was as tired

as his thirty-three-year-old body felt or Cramer was being handed a royal gift that could blow up in several directions. And he didn't feel like teaming up with a woman who might be a suspect herself, and becoming a target in the bargain. "For all we know, she could have had Holcomb fingered. Maybe they were lovers. Maybe she got scorned and blew him away."

Cramer's mouth tightened. "Always the woman's fault, isn't it?"

Linc glared at him. "That's been my experience."

"The odds point to her innocence. According to the FM, she's a possible target, too. They don't want to lose their highly skilled people, Linc, regardless of whether they're males or females. I know it makes a big difference to you, but that's tough. If you take this assignment, you're going in to protect Brie Williams."

He snorted. "More than likely, from herself. She'll probably get me killed screwing up a detonation."

"Well, now, that's your problem. You're the explosives expert. I'm sure you'd speak up and let her know if she was doing something wrong."

"You bet I would. Women have screwed up too much of my life already. I'm not going to let another one finish off the job and get me killed."

Cramer held his angry stare. "So you'll take it?"

"Do I have a choice?"

"Realistically, no."

Linc rose. "Protect Super Woman, huh? Okay, I can do that. The price is high, Cramer. You'd better come through with that desk job or else."

Cramer grinned. Linc knew the older man was used to his bark, which was generally much worse than his bite. "You name the city and state, and you'll have your desk job, Tanner. Now go home and shave, will you? You look like hell.''

Linc picked up the folder marked Williams and tucked it beneath his arm. He'd get home to his dingy, rarely used apartment, shave, take a hot shower and read her file. No, on second thought, he'd catch up on sleep first, then read the file. He didn't want any nightmares.

"You what?" Brie stammered in disbelief.

Chief Craig Saxon obviously girded himself internally. He must have known without a doubt that there was going to be a minor explosion in his large, well-appointed haz-mat office. He nodded his craggy head, the silver in his hair giving his bulldog face a saintliness it didn't deserve. "Calm down, Brie," he soothed in his gravelly voice.

"Calm down!" Brie repeated, whirling and planting her hands on her hips. "You call giving me a *second* rookie nothing? What are you trying to do to me, Chief?" There was an odd catch in her voice. "I've got one trainee right now. Jeff is coming along fine, but he won't be fully qualified for another month. Why a second trainee? Give the guy to Jim McPeak over in Quadrant Two. He's got the nice, quiet sector of Ohio." She ran her fingers through her sable-brown hair. Saxon had requested her to come down from Canton for a meeting on her only day off that week. Brie had arrived in a peach-colored dress of silk instead of her haz-mat uniform.

"Sit down, Brie," Saxon tried again. "Come on," he entreated, giving her that fatherly look that always got to her.

Brie's green eyes narrowed speculatively on her superior's face. Saxon was like a father to her in one way. Ever since she had been hired by him three years ago, she had never made him sorry for that decision. Brie recalled the furor that had hit the newspapers over the appointment of a woman to the haz-mat team. There wasn't a fire chief interviewed around the state who didn't parrot the same tired old spiel: she was a woman, she couldn't do a man's job. Well, she had proven them all wrong. Just as she had when she had been one of the few female fire fighters in the state.

Reluctantly, she acquiesced to Saxon's plea. "Okay," she said, sitting down and smoothing the silk over her long thighs.

Saxon smiled benignly. "I'm sorry to have to call you down here to the Fire Academy on your day off, Brie. I know it's a three-hour drive one way. But I've received orders directly from the FM to assign—" he raised the official-looking paper, squinting at it through his bifocals "—Linc Tanner to you."

Brie digested the information, feeling as if she were being torn apart. She knotted her cold hands in her lap, the knuckles whitening, as she tried to control the fear eating away at her. Few people saw Brie Williams down and out, but for the good of all, she had to level with the chief.

"Ever since the—" Brie choked and lowered her gaze. Blinding tears stabbed her eyes. Her voice had been low and unsteady, which wasn't at all usual. Groping for control Brie sat silent a long time before she spoke again. "What are you trying to do? Pressure me out of my job, Chief? Because if you are, I'll hand in my resignation now. I can't take—"

"No," Saxon uttered in astonishment, his gray eyebrows raising in alarm. "My God, no!" He got to his feet, pushing the chair back.

Brie winced beneath his whiplash tone. Neither of them was overtly emotional, but ever since the—accident? murder?—of John Holcomb, she had been riding a daily roller coaster of vitriolic emotions. She knew the Chief felt responsible for John's loss almost as much as she. But not quite. At least Saxon could sleep at night. She couldn't. Desperate to regain some calmness, Brie forced words out. "Look, you pushed a green kid on me one week after I got out of the burn unit up in Cleveland and you asked me to train him to be my partner to replace…John." She paused, still fraught with recent pain and nightmarish memories. "So, in the past three months I've trained him. Now you're telling me Jeff isn't going to be John's replacement. Jeff's going to the southeast quadrant. And this—this…"

"Tanner," Saxon provided softly. "Linc Tanner is his name."

Brie jerked her head up and looked across the desk at Saxon. "He could be the archangel Gabriel and I wouldn't care, Chief!" She tried to still her rising temper. Licking her lips, Brie concentrated on breathing more slowly before she went on. "Jeff's doing fine. He's enthusiastic and he learns fast. I need someone up in the northeast quadrant who's quick and alert. I don't need a rookie to babysit again."

Saxon looked down at the file on Tanner. "Brie," he murmured apologetically, "this one is out of my hands. If it were my decision, Jeff would stay. You've been through hell. I can see you need more time to recover, but it simply isn't possible under the circumstances. I need you and your experience back up there now."

"Since when does the FM stick his nose into our business? You've always had total control of haz-mat. Why now? I could understand if things were getting worse up there, but they aren't. Since you created this unit three years ago, Chief, we've accomplished so much."

Saxon gave her a sad smile. "The FM feels you need

someone with better credentials than what Jeff possesses. Tanner has a BS in chemistry like yourself. He's got six years with a fire department as an officer—''

''Paid or volunteer?''

''Paid. Does it make a difference to you?''

Brie grimaced. ''You know it does. Paid fire fighters always think they're better than volunteers.'' She was unable to sit any longer and began to pace the length of the office in her low-heeled sandals. ''That will be just one more hurdle I'll have to deal with him on. Once Tanner finds out I came up through the volunteer ranks, he'll challenge me.'' She turned. ''Paids hate volunteers. It's pounded into their thick, Neanderthal skulls.''

''Well, the way you're talking, you sound a bit prejudiced yourself, Brie.''

A sour smile touched her lips, and she halted. ''Guess I do, don't I?''

''It's commonly referred to as a chip on the shoulder, I think.''

Her mood lightened momentarily at Saxon's gentle teasing. ''Touché. I'd better look at myself first before I start hurling hand grenades at others.''

''Perhaps, perhaps.''

''Chief, why does the FM feel we need Tanner over Jeff, aside from the degree he holds?''

''They want the best for Quadrant One, Brie. Things are heating up. You know that,'' he answered quietly.

Her green eyes narrowed. ''Because of John's murder?''

''We don't know if it was a murder yet, Brie. At least not officially.''

''That's a bunch of—''

''Facts, Brie, facts. Until we have proof from that ongoing investigation, John's death has been officially listed as accidental.''

"That call we answered was rigged! I saw the photographs that were taken right after John got killed. Freshly painted fifty-gallon drums sitting by an old warehouse in Cleveland where only rats lived is suspicious. You'd expect rusted drums instead. I saw those wires leading to the drums, Chief. It was murder." She took a deep, ragged breath. "Is that it? Tanner's older, more mature? They don't want someone of Jeff's age with me. They want me to defer important decisions to the man?"

Saxon must have heard the edge to her voice because he frowned. "If you remember nothing else from this conversation, Brie, remember this: *You* are in charge. Tanner is a rookie, as far as I'm concerned. The moment he disobeys you, he's done." He opened the file. "And I intend to make that particular point very clear to him, believe me. I won't have you hassled in any way."

Her shoulders sagged, and suddenly feeling the stress of the last three months, Brie wearily sat down. "You don't deserve my anger or frustration over this whole thing."

"It's all right," Saxon admitted unhappily, also sitting. "At sixty-five, maybe I'm getting too old to handle this job any more. It used to be that a haz-mat spill was bread and butter. Now, with a probable murder of one of my best people, the rules of the game are changing. I feel like a fish out of water." He folded his hands and gave her a sober look. "I was a fire chief for thirty-nine years, Brie, not a cop. And with this situation, we need law-enforcement direction. Fire fighters aren't policemen. John Holcomb's death has proven that." He released a long sigh and sought out her intelligent gaze.

"Look, Tanner comes with top recommendations. Maybe the FM's right: you need a more mature, older partner. John was three years younger than you, Jeff is four. Tanner is thirty-three to your twenty-nine. He's been around. Here, take a look at his file.''

Brie reluctantly took the file and settled back in the chair. She groaned, giving Saxon an I-don't-believe-it-look. ''Ex-Marine lieutenant? Oh, wonderful, Chief. Now I know he'll be a male chauvinist hunting for me!''

''He was a mine and explosives expert in the service, though,'' Saxon pointed out, but that angle didn't soothe her distress.

Brie gave him a flat look. ''There's no war going on, Chief. We aren't hunting bangalores, land mines or rockets. Just hazardous material.''

She knew Saxon wasn't so sure with the powerful criminal element in the Youngstown-Cleveland area, which was part of her territory to protect and cover. And despite all her objections, she could see Saxon only wanted her safe at any cost. After the explosion in Cleveland, Brie had been in a coma for nearly five days before becoming conscious. Saxon must have seen with brutal clarity the third-degree burns that had scarred her back, right shoulder and arm. She had also suffered internal injuries and had spent three months recovering in a hospital.

Brie couldn't hide from Saxon the emotional scars that had resulted from the incident. He'd felt it best to get her a new partner in order to take her mind off the horror. Jeff Laughlin's youth, idealism and lack of chauvinism had helped her get back on her feet. Still, she knew the chief worried.

''Tanner does have a good background,'' Brie grudgingly admitted, handing the file to him. The initial resentment in her voice had disappeared.

Saxon breathed a sigh of relief. ''If it makes you feel any better, Brie, I know how hard it's going to be on you dealing with two trainees at once.'' He spread his hands in a gesture of futility. "I tried to reason with the FM on this assignment, but he's made up his mind."

With a grimace, Brie leaned back in the chair. "Instead of sixty hours a week, it will now be seventy," she uttered tiredly.

"Maybe after the first month, you can get a couple of days off and let Jeff run the show with Tanner."

Brie pursed her lips. "By that time, I'll probably need it." She cast him a grin, rising to her five feet, eight inches. "So when do I meet Superman?"

Saxon opened his appointment book and peered at it through his bifocals. "Next week. Tuesday to be exact. Meet us over at Lock 24 Restaurant for lunch at noon, and I'll introduce him to you."

"You buying?"

He matched her grin. "Sure."

"I think I'm gonna have a cardiac arrest. This Tanner must really be important or you'd never spring for lunch, Chief."

Saxon escorted Brie to the door and opened it for her. "Now you've went and hurt my feelings. I occasionally buy you lunch when you get down our way.

Brie was barely able to suppress her growing smile. She felt her tension dissolving in the good-natured teasing. "Okay, I'll see you next Tuesday. Fair enough?"

"Fair enough."

Brie swung her white leather purse strap across her shoulder. At this time of year, when the May weather was turning mild and sunny, Brie usually wore pretty sundresses that showed off her shoulders and back. But since the explosion, she never wore anything that might expose her scars. She knew she'd retreated into a shell. Would she ever emerge?

As she began to walk away, Chief Saxon called out, "Hey, be careful out there."

"Yes, sir, boss," she said, throwing him a mock salute and a halfhearted smile. The smile disappeared almost immediately as she stepped through the air-conditioned modern building that included the Ohio State Fire Academy and the FM's office. Brie gave the place a tender look. She had taken her two hundred hours of fire training here. She had loved every minute of the grueling and demanding classes that turned her into a fire fighter. That was so many years ago.

She went out into the sunny afternoon, and a breeze ruffled her hair. Her mind swung to Linc Tanner. She formed his name on her lips, saying it softly. She could often get a feel for the individual by rolling the name off her tongue. His was a strong name, one that had no obvious weak facets, not like her name or how she felt presently. The murder of John had destroyed so much of her confidence. She wished she could change her name to connote a stronger facade. Maybe Gertrude. Now that was a strong, immovable name. Or Dagmar, another name that vibrated with strength. A gleam came to her eyes as she opened the door to her silver Toyota. At least her sense of humor had survived the explosion.

She slid in and closed the door, hungering for the warmth the sun provided. She dug the sunglasses from her purse and put them on. The headache throbbing in her temples was increasing: another gift from the explosion, she groused to herself, starting up the Toyota then backing out.

It was a long drive to her small house near the outskirts of Canton, and as Brie pulled into traffic, she wondered what kind of man Linc Tanner was. She prayed he had a streak of humanity in him because if he didn't, she wouldn't be able to cope with him.

Linc looked discreetly at his wristwatch. He had learned a long time ago to mask his impatience. Chief Saxon sat next to him at a table for four in a sunny corner of the restaurant. He gave Linc an apologetic look.

"Brie must be running a bit late," he said.

Like every woman I've ever known, Linc countered silently. "I think it's part of the female mystique."

Saxon's gray brows drew downward slightly. "Brie is normally on time to the second."

Strike one, Linc warned himself. He had met the grizzled, white-haired chief only a half hour ago, and he wasn't sure where Saxon stood on the subject of women in men's careers. It appeared Saxon was not a chauvinist, despite his age. Folding his hands and leaning his elbows on the table, Linc tried to cover his tracks. If Williams wasn't going to show up on time, he might as well buttonhole Saxon and find out the lay of the land a little more.

"It must make things a little more interesting having a woman in the ranks, chief."

"In what way, Mr. Tanner?"

Careful. Linc shrugged his broad shoulders beneath his red polo shirt. He was damned if he was going to climb into a business suit to meet Williams. He wore a suit to impress his date, not his boss. "I would imagine Ms. Williams adds a different perspective to things around here."

"Oh." Saxon grunted, reducing his defensiveness. "Brie gets along with everyone. The men in the haz-mat unit treat her like a sister." Saxon chuckled. "To her, they're like brothers." His voice lowered. "Do me a favor, Mr. Tanner?"

"What?" Linc never promised anything before hearing what the request was.

"Don't mention John Holcomb's death to her. I know you and the FM had a closed-door meeting earlier, and I don't know what was discussed, but Brie is still very sensitive to John's death."

I wonder why? Was she his lover? Linc mentally cataloged all the possibilities. A woman didn't grieve like that without it having a sexual angle. "All right," Linc agreed slowly.

"If she brings it up, fine. But don't hit her on it. Frankly, I'm worried about Brie. I'm afraid you're meeting her at the worst possible time, and that's not fair to either of you. Brie is—well, how do I put it? She's a confident person with plenty of experience to back her up in the haz-mat area. There are few who can equal her savvy, enthusiasm and dogged adherence to principle."

Linc's brows fell. "What principle, Chief Saxon?"

Saxon watched the door, waiting to see Brie appear. "Northeast Ohio is the armpit of toxic waste problems mainly because it's the most industrialized part of the state. A lot of steel mills, chemical companies and tankers transporting the stuff make it a highly active area. Three years ago when she agreed to head up that quadrant, she made a promise to me. Brie knew of the waste disposal problems and the cheating that goes on up there by many of the companies. She wanted to clean them up."

Wonderful, now I have a raving fanatic on my hands to boot. "Go on."

"She and John made a great inroad on that promise. She has a list of chemical companies and facilities that use chemicals that she visits every month. Of course, none of the officials for any company are going to deny her access to their records because she can get a court order at the drop of a hat and force them to show her their files. They're running scared of her now. It used to be that some of these companies would send out their trucks loaded with toxic waste and order the drivers to dump then in some unsuspecting farmer's field, a roadside ditch or in a stream in the middle of the night. Reports of that kind of activity have fallen off almost seventy-five percent since Brie has put the pressure on these companies to produce records of when a truck hauling toxic waste is sent out and where its destination is, and then checking that destination to make sure it arrived and dispensed with the chemicals on its bill of lading.'' He smiled grimly. ''Brie has handed out a hell of a lot of citations, and the attorney general of the state has backed her to the hilt and prosecuted these companies. The fines these companies have had to pay run into the millions, and now they're wising up and deciding to play by the law and not get caught dumping illegally. They can't afford it anymore.''

Linc rubbed his jaw. ''Maybe that's what got Holcomb killed.''

Saxon gave him an unhappy look. ''There are over a hundred people whom she's had heavily fined. Holcomb's death could have been an act of revenge, a warning, who knows? She's too valuable to our continuing efforts to clean up waste disposal and toxic substances in our state. Oh, here's Brie now,'' Saxon said, and rose.

Linc tried to mask his surprise as a tall, slender woman made her way through the heavy noontime trade of the popular restaurant. Her sable-colored hair gleamed with gold highlights; wispy bangs barely brushed her brows. The one-piece uniform of dark blue sporting patches on both arms, a gold badge over her left breast pocket and gold name tag over the right one made her look like some-one in authority, Linc decided. His gaze moved up to her face, and he decided to modify his first opinion. Although Brie had a square face and that stubborn-looking chin, he found himself staring into her huge dark green eyes, which appeared almost catlike. And when his gaze dropped to her delicious mouth, he felt his body tighten with unexpected heat.

Shocked at his initial response to her, Linc maintained an unreadable expression on his face. What a mouth, he thought: full, corners softly curved upward and lushly red. When he realized she wore no makeup and that was the natural color of her lips, he gave himself an internal shake. He'd thought there wasn't a female alive who didn't plaster herself with foundation, gobs of mascara for almost nonexistent eyelashes, rouge for cheeks and lipstick. Brie had a natural flush on her cheeks, which emphasized her large eyes. And her lashes were so thick and long that at first Linc would have sworn they were false. But they weren't. Brie Williams wasn't like other women, he grudgingly admitted, and grimaced, displeased with his physical reaction to her. There wasn't much not to like about her upon first meeting: nice body, attractive in an arresting fashion, and she moved like a gazelle. What the hell was she doing to him?

Brie risked a glance at the tall, ruggedly built man in a red polo shirt and faded, well-worn jeans that emphasized his superb build. He was scowling at her, and she tried to gird herself against his obvious dislike of her. She turned her attention to Saxon.

"Hi, Chief," she said breathlessly, "I'm sorry I'm late. There was a tanker on I-76 without placards indicating what chemicals he was hauling, and I pulled him over."

Saxon patted her hand. "See, Mr. Tanner? I told you there would be a reason our Brie was late."

Linc slowly inclined his head toward her. He saw a great

deal in her suddenly darkened eyes: distrust, wariness and fear. Why fear? Did he look like an ogre to her? More than likely. He managed a sour smile. "So you did, Chief Saxon, so you did."

Brie matched his scowl, immediately on guard against the insinuation in Tanner's carefully modulated voice. Had he accused her of being late because she was a woman? Brie felt anger surge through her, and she swallowed hard, holding his dark blue gaze.

"Brie, I'd like you to meet Linc Tanner, your new partner. Linc, this is Brie Williams."

Linc extended his long, tapered fingers. "Ms. Williams."

Brie slid her damp hand into his, very aware of his blatant maleness. "Mr. Tanner."

The waitress came up, shattering the icy tension. "Something to drink?" she asked them, smiling warmly at Linc.

"Coffee for me," he said.

Brie hadn't missed the waitress's moon-eyed reaction to Tanner. He wasn't pretty-boy handsome. No, his face had been molded by experience. Harsh experience, she would bet. There were deep lines at the corners of his eyes and grooves on either side of his well-shaped mouth. Despite his unshakable arrogance, Brie found herself liking Tanner's mouth because it wasn't as hard as the rest of his rugged features, which could have been hewn out of stone. "I'll have a vodka gimlet," she told the woman. It was one of the few times that she would use alcohol to settle her taut nerves. One look at Tanner's disapproving look and her stomach automatically knotted.

"Drinking on the job?" he queried softly.

"It's my day off, Mr. Tanner. Do you object?"

Linc heard the warning in her husky voice. Strike two.

"I'm not your keeper, Ms. Williams. You drink whenever you feel the need."

Brie gave him a sizzling glare, locking with his cobalt eyes. The arrogant bastard. He was gunning for her. And right in front of the chief. Pulling the napkin into her lap, she fixed a brittle smile on her lips. "I'm glad we agree on one thing, Mr. Tanner."

"So am I, Ms. Williams." He wanted to kick himself. He had stepped into it with her and he hadn't meant to. Most women wouldn't have challenged his innuendo. But she had. A part of him admired her gutsiness. Not many women—or for that matter, men—took him on.

Saxon cleared his throat, thanking the waitress when she returned with their drinks and the menus. He gave Tanner a warning that spoke volumes. "Brie works fifty to sixty hours a week, Linc. It's rare she gets a day off. And when she does, she's on twenty-four-hour call for haz-mat accidents up in her quadrant. She made a special trip down here today to pick you up and take you to Canton to start looking for an apartment."

Linc inclined his head, a hint of amusement in his eyes. "I owe the lady an apology then, plus thanks for going an extra yard on my benefit." The car he had driven from the East Coast had developed transmission trouble. The garage said it would take at least a week to repair, leaving Linc without any transportation. An auspicious start, he thought, to the whole assignment.

He saw her eyes widen momentarily, as if shocked by his sudden good manners. Good God, he wasn't an animal! And when Brie quickly averted her gaze and picked up her drink to take a healthy gulp, Linc felt a tinge of guilt. He missed nothing from being an agent for so many years. The fact that her long fingers trembled made him feel like a heel. He was supposed to protect her, get her confidence, not make life rough for her. If Cramer saw how he was behaving, he'd yank him off the case. Fortunately, Cramer wasn't around to see his spectacular hoof-and-mouth act, and Saxon didn't know his true identity, so he was safe. This time.

They ordered lunch, and Linc noticed Brie wanted nothing but a salad. The uniform she wore hung loosely on her, telling him she had lost weight. Of course, if he had been nearly killed, he wouldn't have much of an appetite, either. There were hints of shadows beneath Brie's eyes. She didn't get much sleep. Was it due to the trauma or just the fact that Saxon was working his people to death?

Linc folded his hands, resting his chin on them. "Fifty or sixty hours a week is a lot," he said to no one in particular.

"It doesn't do much for your personal life, either," Brie said, sipping her drink and hoping he would take her comment as a joke, which would ease the tension between them.

He met and held her nervous gaze. "Do you have one?"

He was taking her seriously! "If I did, it wouldn't be your concern, Mr. Tanner."

"Call me Linc. I don't like standing on formality any more than necessary."

"I would think with your military training, you'd enjoy it."

He picked up his cup, holding it to his lips. Saucy, aren't you? He took a sip of coffee. "What I learned in the military can't be applied too much in civilian life, Ms. Williams." Linc waited for her to drop her guard and ask him to call her by her first name just as he had done. But she didn't.

"That's what I told the chief: you can't apply war games to haz-mat."

Tanner smiled slightly. Okay, I'll let you play with me. I spat and hissed first, so now you get your turn. I'll take my lumps before the chief has a cardiac arrest in front of us. "From what I understand, haz-mat is taking on certain aspects of war."

Brie stiffened at his inference, her spine going rigid. "I hope you left your Marine Corps training where it belongs, in the past."

"I try to. But sometimes, in some situations, it comes in handy."

"One thing is in your favor for being in service, Mr. Tanner."

"What's that?" he asked amiably, deciding a friendlier tone might have a soothing effect on her.

"You know how to take orders."

His blue eyes gleamed as he held her gaze. "I also know when to question them, Ms. Williams. I don't just blindly walk into a situation without first assessing it properly."

Brie was stung. Was Tanner hinting that she hadn't properly analyzed the situation in Cleveland that had gotten John killed?

Chapter Two

Halfway through lunch, Chief Saxon's emergency beeper went off. He gave Brie and Linc an apologetic look and went to find a phone.

Linc leaped at the opportunity. Since his last idiotic comment, Brie had sat there pale and shaken. The fork she used to push the salad around in her bowl trembled from time to time.

"Listen, Brie," he said, using her first name deliberately, "I do owe you an apology. We got off on the wrong foot." He gave her a lopsided grin, trying to figure out how to dissolve the fear he saw in the depths of her jade-green eyes. "I think we've both had a pretty rough week, and we're a little more sensitive and jumpy than usual." He raised his hand, holding it out to her. "Forgiven?"

Brie stared at his large, well-shaped callused hand. The nails were short and blunt, the fingers beautifully tapered. Searching his pensive face, Brie tried to see if this was all a game with him. There was some undefinable nuance about him that made her instincts go on guard. Was it the look in Tanner's eyes? The glint in them told her on a gut level there was more to him than what he presented. He was a man of secrets. But what secrets? He made Brie uncomfortable. "You've got a razor for a tongue."

Linc winced. "Yeah, I know I do. Usually it gets me out of trouble, not into it. When I'm tired, I get crabby. My ex-wife would gladly tell you that." He kept his hand extended. "Well? Am I forgiven? Can we shake hands and start over?"

Some of her terror began to disintegrate, and she firmly shook Linc's hand. "Forgiven," she said, quickly retrieving her fingers. Had he noticed how damp and cold her skin was? If he did, he said nothing.

"But not forgotten," he added.

"I'd like to forget everything," Brie said, "and settle in for a long, hot bath and ten hours of uninterrupted sleep."

A glimmer came to his eyes. "Is that an invitation?"

Brie gave him a flat stare. It took her a few seconds to realize he was baiting her and wasn't serious. At least she didn't think he was. "Like I said before: you join haz-mat and you have no personal life to speak of, Mr. Tanner. It's probably just as well you're divorced because your wife wouldn't be seeing much of you anyway except late at night and in bed."

Linc speared a few French fries with his fork, his gaze never leaving Brie's. She was an open book, he realized. There was a translucence to her every expression, and her lovely eyes reflected everything she was feeling. That was good. He wouldn't have to work at prying things out of Brie. All he had to do was drop a verbal bomb, and she'd react plenty. "Is there anything more important than a night in bed? I could live with that."

"I'm sure you could, Mr. Tanner."

"You're beginning to sound like a prude, Ms. Williams. I didn't realize there were any left."

"I'm hardly a prude. What happens between two people should be private, not a topic for a luncheon meeting."

Linc grinned. "I've been told I have a terrible case of hoof-and-mouth disease. Think there's any truth to it?"

The man was impossible! But Brie found a grudging smile inching across her lips. "I don't mean to sound like I'm perfect, Mr. Tanner. I know I've got my share of faults, maybe not as obvious as some of yours."

Linc gave her a long, appraising look. "You look pretty perfect to me." When he saw the color rise in her cheeks, something wrenched inside his heavily guarded heart. Didn't men compliment her on her good looks? Not according to her reaction. "Bet you had to chase the boys away from your door when you were in college."

Brie managed a shy smile. "Being an honor student through four years in chemistry didn't leave me much time for anything else."

Linc rubbed his jaw, his smile warmer. Brie had a nice trait of being unassuming, which was a plus in his book. "Ouch. I barely scraped through."

"I imagine because you had the girls knocking down your door to get to you."

His laughter was free and rolling. How good it felt to laugh again. "What are you? A mind reader?"

Brie shook her head, her shoulders slowly relaxing. Maybe Tanner wasn't so arrogant after all. More than anything, Brie wanted to believe that he was just tired and out of sorts from his long trip from Washington. "With your good looks, it's pretty easy to figure out."

"Logic in a woman. A rare find," he murmured.

"A lot of women have logic, Mr. Tanner," she said stiffly, some of her defenses moving into place.

Careful, Linc. "Most of the women I've been around have little ability to add up one and one and make two. It's not an insult. Just an observation."

Brie toyed with her glass, enjoying the beaded coolness on her fingertips. "In this business, we go by the numbers and by the rules," she put in with an edge of warning. "I'm not going to automatically assume you have that capability, Mr. Tanner. Just because you're a man and men are supposed to be logical won't wash with me. You'll have to prove that out in the field to me before I believe it."

Linc sat up, frowning heavily. "I'll stack my logic up against yours anytime, Ms. Williams."

Brie gave him a tight grin. There was something within her that loved challenge and competition. And Linc Tanner had just triggered it. "Fair enough, Mr. Tanner. Just as I'll be assessing your abilities day in and day out, you can do the same to me." She leaned forward, all business. "With one major difference: the final decision rests with me, not you. Jeff Laughlin, the other rookie, will tell you that I openly encourage your input and observations, but in the end, the responsibility is mine."

He didn't know whether to be angry with her or admire her. Now she was talking like a hard-nosed businessman, and not a woman. "That's damn democratic of you, boss."

She held his stormy gaze calmly. "I'll give you the chance you deserve, Mr. Tanner. I only hope you'll extend that same courtesy to me and try to overlook the fact I'm a woman."

"That's going to be hard to do."

"You haven't worked around many women, have you?"

Linc was unsettled by her insight into him. "I never mix business with pleasure. Anything wrong with that?" he drawled.

Brie colored beneath his digging inspection. "In this case, yes. I'm a woman dealing with you in a business function. Something that I'm sure has never happened to you before, since you were a fire fighter and there are few women in the ranks."

"Right again, Ms. Williams. But in your case, I see no reason we can't mix a little business and pleasure."

"Am I supposed to be flattered, Mr. Tanner?"

Linc gave her a disarming smile. "I would hope so."

Brie saw Chief Saxon returning, his face serious. She blotted her mouth with her napkin. "I would never have thought you were a dreamer, Mr. Tanner."

He shrugged his broad shoulders. "Who knows? I like to learn from every new situation. Maybe I'll find out logic and fantasy do mix."

Brie shot him a withering look meant to deflate his ego. "Now who's being illogical?"

Linc was about to answer when he caught Saxon out of the corner of his eye. The chief sat down and directed his conversation to Brie.

"Looks like McPeak has a good one going down near Dayton."

Brie was relieved to get back to what she knew best: haz-mat. In that area, she felt safe and secure. Or she had before the explosion. Still, it was an escape from Linc Tanner's challenging blue gaze and the dangerous parrying with him. "Oh?"

"Yeah, train derailment. Seems a couple of tank cars carrying some nasty chemical combinations have overturned and are burning. Jim's having to call in quite a few of the surrounding fire departments to help coordinate a mass evacuation near Englewood where it occurred."

"Sounds pretty serious. Any loss of life?"

Saxon blotted his forehead with his handkerchief. "None so far, thank God."

Brie gave Tanner a glance. "Well, there goes the rest of my day off."

"What do you mean?" Linc asked.

She patted the beeper that was hanging from her right pocket. "When McPeak gets a bad haz-mat incident, we get one, too. Don't ask me why. It just seems to happen that way."

"Better not," Saxon said gruffly, handing the check and some bills to the waitress.

"Why?" Linc wanted to know.

Brie rose and slipped the strap of the purse across her shoulder. "Because Jeff's over in Pennsylvania visiting his folks until Sunday afternoon. That would leave just me to handle the call. Chief Saxon believes in two heads being better than one in handling a haz-mat incident, and I agree." She held up crossed fingers. "Chief, let's hope McPeak's curse doesn't land on us like the bluebird of happiness."

Saxon grinned, putting his hand on her shoulder. "Is that like cows flying, Brie?"

Her laugh was full. "One and the same, Chief. Thanks for lunch. I'll get Mr. Tanner's gear, and we'll head for Canton."

They emerged from the restaurant and found the sunlight blinding and the bright blue Ohio sky sporting a few puffy clouds. Linc followed a bit behind Brie, openly admiring her. She was built more like a cat than a gazelle, he decided. There was definitely a feline grace to her walk and a nice, easy movement to her swaying hips. Maybe this assignment wasn't going to be as horrendous as he had first thought. Despite her defensiveness, Brie had a decent sense of humor. And she looked like an ingenue of twenty-three, not twenty-nine.

"Well, here's your home away from home, Tanner." Brie stopped and gestured to the large white van sporting huge red letters on each side that said: Fire Marshal's Office, Hazardous Material Team. "This van is affectionately called the white whale because it looks like one." She looked up at his serious face.

"Any relation to Moby Dick?"

She smiled. "I hope not. We don't need haz-mat trucks gobbling up people. Is your gear at the Fire Academy?"

"Yeah. With my car in for repair, the chief let me put my suitcases at the dormitory."

Brie unlocked the passenger side door and opened it for him. She saw him grin. "Chauvinism is dead, Tanner. You might as well get used to it."

He chuckled indulgently. "If you say so, Ms. Williams."

Brie ignored his irreverent humor and climbed into the driver's seat. She put on the safety belt and started up the van, all the while noticing that Tanner was looking over the various supplies inside. She headed out of the parking lot.

"Impressive," he murmured, gesturing toward the rear. "Air packs, holding drums for toxic waste, gas suits. I can see no expense was spared to put this baby together."

"When you realize Ohio is number two in the nation for toxic spills, you know why, Tanner. Chief Saxon single-handedly created the concept of splitting the state up into four quadrants, manning each one with a truck and two haz-mat techs to protect our people." She pulled out into the lazy Saturday traffic, heading for the Fire Academy, which was located only a few miles away.

Linc faced front, and his gaze swept across the complex radio equipment that had been installed in the dashboard. There were special radios for the state police and for sheriff and fire departments. "There must be twenty thousand dollars wrapped up in this equipment alone," he said, whistling.

"Close to it. If we have a full-scale haz-mat incident, it's imperative we be able to get hold of all agencies in order to help evacuate the people who might be harmed by a spill."

He nodded. "I'm impressed as hell."

A slight smile appeared on Brie's mouth. "Wait," she told him softly, catching his glance. "There's a natural high you get from coordinating such a massive effort. Not that I wish for those sorts of spills, but I like the knowledge that from this truck, we can mobilize an entire county, if need be, from Disaster Services right up to the Red Cross in a matter of minutes."

Linc digested her fervor. She loved her job. It was obvious from the luminous quality that had suddenly sprung to life in her bleak-looking eyes. "I can tell you've handled a few of those."

"A few. And so far, my record is clean. Well, almost," Brie said, stumbling.

"What do you mean?"

"Before John was murdered, in every call we answered in the past three years, there had been no loss of life." Her voice dropped to a whisper. Brie hadn't meant to discuss John with Tanner, but her enthusiasm for her job opened the guarded door to her grieving heart.

"I'm sorry it happened, Brie."

She trembled; his husky voice was like thick, golden honey soothing her aching heart. "Thanks, Tanner."

"Don't you think we can begin to act civil with one another and call each other by our first names?"

He was right, Brie realized. She had been deliberately holding him at arm's length because of the red flag her instincts had waved in front of her face. There was a searching quality to his voice. He wanted to smooth the waters between them, too. "Okay," Brie agreed reluctantly. "Call me anything you want as long as it isn't derogatory."

"How about if it's provocative?"

She glanced at him, again aware of the amusement in his eyes. With a laugh she said, "You're incorrigible, Linc Tanner."

He settled back in the seat, a pleased expression on his face. "So I've been told, Ms. Brie Williams, so I've been told."

Brie stifled a yawn. The interstate stretched long and boringly in front of her as she drove the haz-mat truck toward Canton.

"Want me to take over for a while?" Linc asked, realizing how tired Brie was becoming. Those faint shadows beneath her eyes were darkening.

She shook her head. "No, thanks. We've only got little over an hour to go. Why don't you get us some coffee from that thermos down there. I filled it before meeting you at the restaurant."

Linc picked up the battered aluminum thermos, noting its quart size. "Who drinks this much coffee?" he asked, twisting off the cap.

"Me. There have been times when all I've lived on for three or four days were coffee and nerves." She looked at him, offering him a slight smile. "Comes with the territory."

"Saxon didn't warn me about that," Linc groused good-naturedly, handing her half a cup of the steaming coffee.

"Thanks," Brie said. "He probably didn't tell you too much for fear you'd turn down the job."

"Then you weren't stretching the truth about putting in sixty hours a week."

"Stick around and find out."

He rested one booted foot on the dash. "I intend to do just that."

"Real masochist, aren't you?"

"Nah, I'm a red-blooded American man who believes in Mom, apple pie and Corvettes."

"Corvettes?"

He gave her an innocent look. "Sure."

"Expensive taste."

"Superb," he agreed contentedly, pouring himself a cup of coffee then recapping the thermos.

"Bet you've never eaten any humble pie."

His grin tore at her senses.

"I said apple pie, not humble pie."

She joined his laughter, sensing that Tanner's arrogance shielded a solid layer of confidence. She fervently hoped so. Maybe Chief Saxon had been right. She needed a partner who was more mature than her own twenty-nine years. Still, Tanner wasn't exactly the answer to her dreams. He was a chauvinist of the first order, and she knew they would butt heads on just who was the boss. He was a man with secrets, possibly. She'd have to sit back, use her considerable patience and watch. With time, he'd reveal parts of his real self.

"I can tell you from lots of experience that humble pie isn't as good as apple pie," Brie said.

"I don't see you eating too much of that."

She shrugged, gazing at the rolling green countryside of Ohio. She always enjoyed the drive to and from Canton; most of it was comprised of farms, silos, dairy herds and hundreds of acres of corn. "A long time ago, when I joined the fire department in Litton out of college, I used to think I was really something."

"What happened to change your mind about that part of yourself?"

Brie was pleased with his interest in her as a person. "Anyone ever accuse you of asking good questions?"

Linc sipped his coffee. "Not recently. Ask my ex-wife, JoAnne, that, and she'll give you a very different answer."

"That's the second time you've mentioned your divorce. It must be pretty fresh."

"Am I that obvious?"

"Mack trucks usually are," Brie said, giving him a warm smile meant to take any sting from her comment.

"Guess I drove into that one, didn't I?" Linc returned, thinking her whole face became breathtakingly beautiful when she genuinely smiled. He saw a glimmer of light in her eyes and for no reason, it made him feel good, even if the joke had been at his expense. *Where are your claws, little cat? You're a woman, and I know you have a set.*

"Just shows you aren't perfect, that's all."

He feigned a hurt look. "Most women think I am."

"All except JoAnne, remember?"

Giving her a sober glance, Linc agreed. "In all honesty, it wasn't Jo's fault. I was gone too much of the time."

"The fire service is tough on marriages," Brie agreed.

Linc said nothing. In the bio given to Chief Saxon, he had been a lieutenant in a fire department for the past six years, with specialization in the field of hazardous material. For some reason, he didn't like lying to Brie. There was a freshness to her that he'd never encountered in a woman before, and he didn't want her to think negatively of him. At some point in the future, she would eventually be told who he really was and his reason for being with her. Linc studied her profile for several minutes, wondering how Brie would take that information. Would she hate him? Distrust him?

And then he pulled himself up short. Why should he care what she thought of him after this case was out in the open and solved? One look at her and those soft lips curved gently upward and Linc knew why but refused to acknowledge the answer.

"Tell me, what's a marshmallow like you doing in a job like this? It's got to be tough on you emotionally."

Brie pushed her fingers though her short hair, giving Linc an unsettled look. "You calling me a marshmallow?"

Linc sat back, arms across his chest. "It's not an insult, you know. I pride myself in knowing people pretty well on first meeting. Despite your tough act, you're basically a pretty gentle woman. The two don't mix chemistrywise with a job like this."

Now he was playing amateur psychologist, Brie thought, a bit of panic racing through her. No one had ever been able to see the real her beneath her uniform and title. She had never allowed anyone that privilege. And now, Linc Tanner had peeled her open, and she didn't like it. "Even if I was that so-called marshmallow you accuse me of being, who said it matters?"

Linc treaded carefully, hearing the challenge in her voice. "Far be it from me to say a marshmallow can't be effective in a job."

Brie cast him a look. "That's big of you, Tanner."

"So you are a marshmallow."

"I didn't say that."

He grinned widely, which made him look boyish suddenly, instead of hard. "If the shoe fits, wear it. In this case, you practically admitted you're a marshmallow."

Disgruntled, Brie pulled a map of Canton from the side pocket on her seat and handed it to him. "If you want something to do, open this up and take a look at it. It's a map of Canton. You have to decide where you want to look for an apartment or house."

Unfolding the map, Linc was still grinning. "What's wrong with being a marshmallow? Did I say there was anything wrong with them? I happen to like marshmallows. They're all soft inside. And sweet—"

"One more word out of you, Tanner, and—"

He gave her an innocent look, realizing how delightful she was to tease. "Okay, boss lady, I'll read the map." He pretended to study it, then after a few minutes he lifted his head and murmured, "I like hot dogs roasted over an open fire. Nothing like a few well-toasted marshmallows for dessert—"

"Tanner, you're really bucking the odds."

He met her flashing green eyes. "If I say I'm sorry, would that count?"

"No, because you wouldn't mean it."

Linc suddenly laughed. "Has anyone told you, Ms. Williams, that you're fun to tease?"

"On second thought, you're not a masochist. You're a sadist."

He had the good sense to bury his head in the map, giving Brie the space she needed from his unmerciful prodding.

Quiet settled into the van, and occasionally Brie would steal a glance at Linc. He had scrunched his well-built frame down into the seat, one foot resting lazily against the dash. She liked his ability to be laid back, and hoped that he would apply the same easygoing attitude to his dealing with haz-mat incidents.

Her heart beat hard when Linc turned his head and met her gaze with a heated look. Embarrassed that he had caught her inspecting him, Brie looked away. He could have needled her about it, but he said nothing, thank God. When had she ever met such a self-assured male? Never, her heart whispered. Somehow, that knowledge steadied her brittle confidence.

Over the years, Brie had met many fire fighters. Some of them had that unique confidence that emanated like a beacon from Linc. But Linc's strength, or whatever it was, was deeper, and her womanly instincts knew that. Brie smiled. She could just imagine what Tanner would say if he knew how she relied more on her gut instinct than on her so-called logic. That was all right, he'd find out soon enough. In the past three months, she'd gotten Jeff to switch to that life-saving internal equipment each person possessed.

Sadness engulfed her as Brie recalled with aching clarity that her gut instincts were screaming at her the day she and John approached the drums sitting just outside the abandoned warehouse on the seedy side of Cleveland. When the call had come in, her stomach had knotted instantly, which wasn't normal. John had smiled, shrugging it off.

"We'll be more careful," he had told Brie. And they had been, parking the haz-mat truck farther away than usual and using binoculars to size up the situation. When it didn't look dangerous, they decided to cautiously approach the freshly painted drums. Unconsciously, Brie rubbed her stomach, trying to shake off the dread that had nearly suffocated her as they walked toward them. It was only when they had changed the angle of their approach that she had spotted several red and gray wires coming out of the bottom of the center drum. The wires disappeared beneath the corrugated aluminum wall of the warehouse wall. She had pulled John to a halt, pointing toward the wires.

They had stood there staring at the drums that were still a good hundred feet away, talking over and assessing the new development. Her stomach was knotted so hard that Brie was in pain. Her heart was galloping in her breast, and her throat was constricted.

"What's your gut say?" John had asked softly, his hand coming to rest on her upper arm, as if preparing to pull her away from the drums.

"To get out of here. It's not right, John. I feel real bad."

"Okay, Brie. I'm going to keep the same distance from them and see if I can spot where those wires lead while you go back to the truck and get the nonsparking tools. This might be a job for the Cleveland bomb squad, not us. But we're going to have to get closer to find out."

"John, why don't you come with me? I don't feel good about this at all. Let's call the police instead and let them investigate it."

"I won't get any closer. I promise. Now go on. Get that box of tools for us."

Brie closed her eyes for a second, dragging in a ragged breath. Her insides felt like quivering jelly, and she broke out into a sweat.

"Brie?"

She jerked her head in Linc's direction, hearing the concern in his voice. The normal hardness was not in his face as he silently met and held her gaze. For a second, Brie wanted to cry. The feeling caught her off guard: she hadn't cried since getting out of the hospital. She had cried for John. She had cried for his wife, Carol, and their two-year-old girl, Susie. But she had never cried for herself. Hot, blinding tears stung her eyes, and Brie swiveled her head to face front. Trying to concentrate on the task of driving, she was mortified that Tanner had caught her with her guard down. What would he think if she suddenly burst into tears? He'd grumble something about it always being just like a woman to cry at the drop of the hat or some such garbage. Her fingers tightened on the wheel until her knuckles whitened.

Linc rested the map on his lap, directing all his attention to her. He had glanced over moments before and saw Brie visibly pale and a light film of perspiration glaze her flesh. What had triggered that kind of reaction? At first, he thought he had caused it by teasing her too much. But when he had softly called her name and she had swung toward him like a startled doe caught in a hunter's cross hairs, he knew differently. He saw genuine terror in the pools of her luminous eyes. He was no stranger to terror himself and recognized that whatever Brie carried within her was tragic and profound because it was affecting her physically.

He watched her expressive face close up and become unreadable. If he hadn't seen the transformation, Linc would never have believed it. Was this another facet to Brie? The embattled veteran of one too many horrifying accidents? Linc had seen fire fighters gradually lose their nerve to fight fires or peel injured or dead people out of gruesome auto wrecks. He recognized that same look in Brie's eyes, and his throat tightened with sudden emotion. The urge to reach out and place his hand on her tense shoulder and tell her everything was going to be all right nearly overpowered him. It took a supreme effort for him to sit quietly.

"I—I'm all right," she forced out in a low, strained voice.

He gave her a gentle smile meant to support her. "I don't know about you, but I could use another cup of coffee. Want some?" He held up the thermos. His ploy worked—he saw the terror slowly drain from her eyes, and her shoulders dropped to their normal position.

"That sounds like a good idea, thanks."

You're pretty cool, aren't you? You're in a lot of pain, but you hold your own. Linc's mouth tightened as he mulled over how Brie was able to shift gears quickly, from being frightened by something inside her to being calm and returning to the outer world, where she had to continue to function. That was good. Was her terror due to the accident? John Holcomb's death? He handed her the coffee, their fingers briefly touching. He felt how cold hers were, and again, to his own disbelief, he felt the urge to hold her in his arms and protect her.

You're getting old, Tanner. Let a woman with big, beautiful green eyes that are marred with pain come near you, and you want to protect her. What's gotten into you? Separate, pal, separate. She's supposed to be protected from a possible criminal element. No involvement. It will screw up your reflexes, and that won't be good for her or you if someone's gunning for her.

Linc settled back, sipping the hot coffee. He repeated the litany in his head several times before all those new feelings Brie had brought to life in him had been erased.

The silence in the truck was broken by a call coming over one of the radios. Which one? Linc wasn't sure until Brie reached for the mike closest to the driver's seat.

"Remind me to kill McPeak the next time we see him," she muttered, switching one of the dials to a new position.

Linc sat up. "Why?"

"This is the Ohio state police calling. The only time they contact us is when there's a haz-mat accident on our turf."

He listened with interest to the radio conversation. Without being told to, he picked up the small clipboard that swung from a hook on the dash, and wrote down the location of the accident, the types of chemicals involved and the numbers on the truck placards.

Brie's scowl deepened as the trooper read off the numbers.

"FM 26, he's got two placards. One is 1050 and the other is 9161."

Linc started to reach for a small manual entitled Hazardous Materials Emergency Response Guidebook to find out what the numbers meant. But before he even opened the booklet, Brie was saying, "Sergeant, that's anhydrous hydrochloric acid and zinc sulfate."

"What kind of danger does that present?"

Plenty, Brie wanted to answer. Instead, she kept her voice impersonal and calm. "What's the status on the tanker carrying the chemicals?"

"It's resting on its side along the berm."

"From your position, can you see any of the contents leaking out?"

"Not that I can see. I have the driver with me. He escaped injury and ran from the truck."

Brie turned to Linc. "I would, too." She switched the mike on. "We'll be on scene with you in—" she glanced at her watch "—twenty minutes, Sergeant D'Onofrio. Until then, block that entire stretch of road one-half mile away on either side of the actual accident. If there is a leak, the fumes from the hydrochloric acid, if breathed in, can kill. Alert the nearest fire department and have them on the scene and standing by."

"Roger, FM 26. We'll be looking for you shortly."

Grimly, Brie hung up the mike. "Well, you wanted some excitement, Tanner, you've got it."

Linc held up his hands in a gesture of surrender. "Hey, this is McPeak's fault, not mine."

Brie managed a slight smile, dividing her attention between driving and rustling through a series of manuals between the chairs. "Cross your fingers that tanker hasn't sprung any leaks. If it hasn't, clean up can go pretty smoothly and quickly."

He reached for the manual she placed her hand on. "How quick? I'm beat."

"It's five o'clock now. If we're lucky, maybe three or four hours. Take this manual and look up those two chemicals. Acquaint yourself with the safety procedures regarding each of them."

"You know them by heart, don't you?"

"Backward and forward, but that isn't going to help train you. We've got time before we arrive on scene, so bone up, Tanner."

He began paging through the thick index of more than a thousand chemicals. "Yes, ma'am," he drawled.

Brie reached up to a panel overhead and flipped on a switch. The red and white light bar came on, whirling brightly above the cab. She pressed more firmly on the accelerator, making the van move at a brisk sixty-five miles an hour. Time was of the essence.

Silence settled into the cab again, but Brie's mind was working at a feverish rate. Her heart was pumping hard. The very thought that the serious accident could erupt into a full-scale explosion and loss of life shook her deeply. Before John's death, Brie had never felt worried like this. Now, her hands were damp and sweaty and her breathing came fast with each call. She was scared. Swallowing against the burgeoning fear, Brie forced herself to focus on the contingency plans that might have to be initiated once they arrived.

Linc watched Brie change like a chameleon before him as they drew up next to several white state police cars that blocked the two-lane highway. Troopers in gray uniforms were directing traffic to turn around. In the distance, Linc could see an eighteen-wheeler tipped over, its elliptical tank rusty looking. Not a good sign, he thought, climbing out of the truck with Brie.

Brie met Linc at the back of the van. As she unlocked the rear doors, she said, "Stick close, watch and listen."

He nodded, settling his hands on his hips, noticing the crowds of interested spectators who had pulled their cars over to look at the accident. "Any other way I can help?"

"I wish," Brie answered fervently, pulling the doors open and slipping a pair of high-powered binoculars out of their case. She gave him a quick look. "Thanks just the same."

"I feel like a three-legged dog—useless."

A bare hint of a smile touched her mouth as they walked toward the four state troopers. "I happen to like dogs. They're good companions."

He looked down, openly admiring Brie's demeanor. With a job like this and all kinds of pressures on her, she could have been cold, huffy or defensive. Instead, she was trying to put him at ease and make him feel needed! Grudgingly, Linc admitted that was a good sign of leadership, something he hadn't ever seen in a woman before. With that new lesson, Linc decided to relax slightly and learn from her. Sergeant D'Onofrio gave Brie a look of relief as she approached him. Did Brie have that kind of effect on all men? he wondered, suddenly a bit jealous.

Brie gave the sergeant a nod. She listened gravely to his report, all the while scanning the tanker through her powerful binoculars. Above all the confusion, the crowd and the blaring radios, she was wildly aware of Linc beside her. Some of her fear abated because she felt an overwhelming sense of protectiveness emanating from him. How was that possible? They had known each other only three or four hours. Unable to give the thought more attention, Brie tucked it away for a later time when she would be able to examine the discovery more closely.

She handed Linc the binoculars. "From all signs, I don't see any cracks in the tanker's skin, and the lid on top looks secure. Sometimes they get sprung, and that's where most leaks will occur."

Linc scanned the wreckage. He was flattered that Brie gave him the binoculars. That implied a certain amount of trust, and he was at once surprised and pleased. Another sign of a good leader—make your people feel involved and important to the total effort. How could a woman know so much about leadership?

Brie stared at Linc, watching his mouth purse as he studied the tanker. Now she would see how he responded under actual working conditions. If anything, he had grown quieter and calmer. A good sign. "Do you see anything?"

"Nothing," he said, handing her the binoculars, "but that tanker is old and rusty. I wouldn't trust it."

"Right." She turned to the trucker who stood nearby. "Have you contacted the tanker's company?"

"Yes, ma'am, I have. They're sending out another tanker from a local company to come and drain the contents from the truck when you give the word."

"Are the cables leading to that truck battery still attached?"

"Yes, ma'am, they are." He was a short man with an

ample belly beneath his white T-shirt. "Ordinarily, I'd cut them, but I didn't know if the sparks might set the chemicals on fire if there was a leak," he apologized.

Brie nodded. She'd have to go in with the nonsparking tool kit and cut the wires leading to the battery, or a fire could occur if conditions were right. "Fine," she answered absently. "We'll take care of it. Linc, let's go."

Linc followed her to the rear of the haz-mat truck. She climbed into the back—she was almost able to stand up in it—and took a silver suit with a hood from the wall.

"What are you doing?" he demanded, scowling.

"I'm going to get suited up and go in there to cut the cables, then inspect the tank."

"Well, where's my suit?"

She sat down on the bumper, nudging off her low-heeled shoes and slipping her long legs into the attached boots of the one-piece suit. "You don't have one yet. Your measurements were taken only today. It's still on order for you."

"What about that suit?" he protested, pointing to a second one hanging on the wall.

Brie shook her head, sitting again. "That's Jeff's, and it won't fit you. You're too big for it, Tanner. Here, help me get the air pack over my shoulders."

Muttering a curse under his breath, Linc lifted the forty-pound air pack off its holder and spread the array of nylon straps aside so that Brie could struggle into it. "I don't like this, Brie. You shouldn't be going in there without a partner. That's the law of fire fighting: you always work on the buddy system."

She felt the weight of the air pack on her shoulders and pulled the nylon straps to tighten them. She snapped the latches closed across her breast and stomach, then shrugged a few times to settle the tank comfortably against her. "Normally, I'd agree with you. But I can't allow you to go near that tanker without being properly protected. You might breath in hydrochloric acid or step in it, or it might explode. You need the safety this suit offers."

Running his fingers through his hair, Linc said, "Let me put on an air pack and go in with you." No woman could handle a task like that alone. How could she recognize battery cables from other cables in a huge truck engine?

Brie was grateful for his help in getting the bulky suit up and over the air pack. The silver-colored material of the gear glared in the dying rays of the sun hovering on the western horizon. She closed the crotch-to-throat Velcro and tested her breathing apparatus. Everything worked fine. Linc held the silver hood in his hands. "I appreciate your concern, but it's impossible." Her voice turned grim. "I've already had one partner die, and I'll be damned if you'll be the second because I overlooked a point of safety." She slipped on the oxygen mask, which fitted over most of her face. She tightened the rubber straps on either side until it was sealed, keeping her from breathing any poisonous fumes.

Linc suspended his protests, realizing this wasn't the time or place to argue. Brie needed his support, not his dissension in the face of a crisis. He lowered the hood and sealed it to her shoulders. A large glass plate showed her beautiful green eyes and thick lashes and nose behind the clear plastic of her oxygen mask. "How can I communicate with you?" he demanded, raising his voice.

Brie pointed to a small radio inside her suit and to a similar one on Jeff's. "Just put on the headpiece and take Jeff's radio off his suit," she shouted, her voice muffled.

At least he'd have radio contact with her! Linc slipped on the slender headpiece with the mike close to his lips.

She picked up the toolbox, and he followed her around the van.

"Are you sure you know where the battery cables are located at the back of that truck?"

Brie almost laughed but had the good sense not to. "Yes, I know where they're at."

Linc rubbed his jaw, giving her a dubious look. "You sure?"

"Look, I know by now you don't think women are of much use beyond the bedroom."

"I didn't say that."

"Yes, you did." She met and held his cobalt gaze. "Put your prejudice aside and maybe you'll find out that women can understand mechanical and electrical things, too."

Linc clamped his teeth together, his jaw rigid. The looks she received from the bystanders made him want to laugh: the people were reacting as if a Martian had landed. The bulky silver suit did resemble something from outer space. Brie walked with surprising agility in the cumbersome outfit, but then, she was a feline.

Linc went with her as far as the troopers' cars. He gripped her arm, gently swinging her around. "You be careful out there, kitten. You get into trouble, you call me. Understand?"

Brie's eyes widened momentarily as his raspy voice came through the headset she wore. A heady warmth suddenly blanketed her, and she felt an exquisite sensation at his concern. A tiny shiver of pleasure raced up her spine when his voice dropped intimately at the word kitten. "I will, Linc. And thanks." She smiled. "See, even three-legged dogs are valuable."

That was her last contact with him for the next ten minutes. Linc paced back and forth, watching as Brie made her way toward the tanker with the small toolbox in her left gloved hand. When she finally reached the rusty, battered truck and leaned into the truck engine and cut the cable wires, his heart began a slow, uneven pounding. He stood, legs apart, binoculars to his eyes, watching her every move. Brie, be careful! he told her silently. The what ifs overwhelmed him. What if there was a leak in some unknown place? What if there was a spark if she cut the wrong cable and it caught fire? She could easily be killed in the resulting explosion. What if her air pack suddenly stopped working? She could suffocate in minutes if she couldn't get out of that suit to fresh air. What if the breathing apparatus developed a leak and she breathed in some of those deadly fumes? She could be dead before he would be able to race that half a mile to rescue her.

Muttering another curse, Linc swore violently that this would be the last time Brie would ever go anywhere by herself. She needed a man around in case anything happened! She wasn't able to handle a situation like this by herself! He punched down the radio button. "Talk to me, Brie. What's going on? What do you see?" His voice came out in a low growl of impatience.

Brie felt immediate relief when she heard Linc's voice. Talking used too much oxygen. If she were breathing lightly and evenly, she would have twenty-five minutes of air. If, like today, her breathing was choppy and erratic, she had perhaps twenty minutes. She climbed down from the rear of the truck and approached the tanker. Her eyes narrowed as she quickly took in the condition of the rusted tanker. "I don't see anything yet. I'll let you know, Linc. Got to conserve my air. Out."

With painstaking care, Brie examined every square inch of the overturned tanker. The tank was badly dented, and she got down on her hands and knees to slide her gloved

hand along the area where the tank rested on the berm. If
there was any leak, the dirt would be dark and damp.

Brie knew that it was possible the entire truck might
shift down unexpectedly. If it did, her fingers, if not her
entire hand or lower arm, would be caught and crushed.
Then she could be trapped, and in far greater danger.
Sweat trickled down her brows and into her eyes. She shut
them tightly, then blinked a few times. The sun was still
warm even at six o'clock, and sweat was running freely
down her body. The suit acted like a sauna. It was a great
way to lose five pounds in a half hour's time. Except she
needed to gain weight, not lose it.

As she neared the top of the tank, she stood up and
minutely inspected the hatch and shoring mechanism, making sure it wasn't sprung. The lid was plenty tight. Brie
got back down on her hands and knees, continuing her
inspection. Finding no change in the dirt, she went to the
other side of the truck and crawled in between the huge
tires and axles, hunting for leaks. Her breath was coming
in ragged gasps. She had to be careful not to tear her suit
on the jagged metal sticking out at odd angles from the
truck. If there was a leak, one tear could be her death.
Chemicals were quickly breathed in by the pores of the
skin, and that could kill her just as though she had breathed
them in through her mouth and nose.

"Brie?"

Linc's voice was quietly furious. He's probably lost
sight of me, she thought, making her way toward the cab
of the truck on all fours. "Nothing so far. Lid's secure."

"You've got five minutes of air left." That wasn't a
comment, it was an order for her to get away from the
truck.

Brie smiled and slowly made her way out of the tangle of wheels and torn truck cables and stood near the cab. "Roger. On my way out now. Tell Sergeant D'Onofrio that the truck's secure. There's no danger of a leak."

Chapter Three

Linc's eyes were burning with obvious concern as he walked the last hundred yards from the barricade of police cars and met her. Without a word, he helped her out of the hood. The fresh air felt heavenly, and Brie closed her eyes as she loosened the rubber straps of her face mask. She pulled it over her head, breathed in deeply, then gave him a welcoming smile.

"I never lose the wonder of taking the first deep breath after wearing this gear."

Linc's mouth was a thin line as he walked at her side toward the van. "You may be the boss, lady, but that's the *last* time you ever go into a situation by yourself." He still didn't believe she had been able to cut the battery cables by herself, much less make sure there was no leak.

Brie gave him an understanding look. "If it makes you feel any better, I didn't like the idea of going in alone, either."

He tried to ignore the natural warmth that emanated from her. The crisis had brought them together as a team, and he found himself reacting like a team member. "Like I said, it's the last time that's going to happen. So many things could have gone wrong." His jaw tightened and his mouth worked as he wrestled with emotions he refused to share with her.

"They'll have a suit for you by next week, Linc," she soothed. "Chief Saxon will give us a call when it's ready."

Partly mollified, Linc nodded. "For whatever it's worth, you really bring out my protective side, lady."

She smiled, amusement in her dark jade eyes. "Don't look so distraught over it happening, Tanner. It's not a disease, you know."

Linc didn't have time to respond to her obvious teasing. Brie was hounded by a television camera crew and two local newspaper reporters the moment she stepped beyond the line of state police cars. He hated reporters with passion and stepped in front of her to protect her from their rabid charge, placing his bulk between them like a wall. Brie gave him a silent thank-you and escaped to the rear of the van to change. The reporters were behaving like spoiled children because he was an unknown who had broken up their charge.

"Hey, buddy," one freckle-faced reporter with carrot-red hair called, "who do you think you are? We have a right to interview Ms. Williams!"

Linc stood with his arms crossed. Sergeant D'Onofrio joined him, looking equally menacing.

"You'll get your interview when we're done coordinating this haz-mat cleanup," Linc growled back.

"If you're with the haz-mat people, why aren't you in uniform?"

Linc glared at the pushy little reporter. "It was my day off. Now do us all a favor and stand back. When we're done, you'll get to talk to Ms. Williams. But not now."

"But," the television reporter cried out, "I've got to make the eleven o'clock news!"

"You're breaking my heart. When are you reporters going to learn you can't interfere in a crisis like this? You wait your turn."

The trooper at his shoulder allowed a hint of a grin to appear as they watched the newspeople reluctantly disperse.

"Couldn't have said it better myself, Mr. Tanner. If I did that, my post would get accused of being uncooperative with the news media."

Linc snorted, dropping his hands to his sides. "I hate those people, if you can call them that. They're always underfoot."

The sergeant smiled, looking past Linc. He spotted the tanker that had been dispatched to come and pump the contents from the damaged one making its way slowly toward them. "I've worked a couple of times with Brie, and it's my opinion she allows those reporters too much time. She gives in to their demands."

"She won't any more," Linc promised, turning and walking to the back of the van. Brie was putting on her shoes when he rounded the corner. Her hair was dark with sweat and plastered against her head, the bangs hanging limply over her eyebrows. The heavy, protective gear, had made her perspire, and her one-piece uniform clung to her body as a result. He appreciated her slender lines.

"Do me a favor?" Brie asked, lifting her head as she tied her shoelaces.

"Name it."

"In the front, between the seats, is a jug of water. I'm dying of thirst. Can you—"

"I'll get it. You just sit there and rest for a minute."

Brie swallowed her smile, aware of Linc's exaggerated protectiveness. John had given her a similar, although not as powerful, sense of care. Jeff didn't, but perhaps that was because of his age. Linc came back and handed her a plastic glass. The water was lukewarm but it tasted wonderful anyway. She drank three glasses before her thirst was sated. Thanking him, she stood and touched her hair. With a grimace, she tried to tame the wet strands into some order, then gave up.

"You look beautiful just the way you are," Linc said.

"You have strange taste, then."

He shared her smile, watching the golden flecks of life in her eyes. "I have good taste, though. Does that count, Ms. Williams?" he asked her in a gritty tone.

Brie's heart thumped at the sudden intimacy between them. She felt heat flooding her cheeks, and avoided his intense blue stare. "The tanker's here," she stammered, avoiding his question altogether. "Come on, I want to talk with the driver before the troopers allow him through."

Linc followed, keeping an eye on the restless band of reporters nearby. Good, they were staying out of the way—for once. Brie spoke at length with the driver, and Linc found himself in awe of her knowledge of the equipment to be used, of pumping procedures and of how to safely take the chemicals out of the overturned vehicle. No woman could know that much about mechanics!

Climbing into the van, Brie motioned for him to come inside. She was allowing him to go with her! Then he decided since they were going to the overturned truck, he'd personally check for leaks, not trusting Brie's inspection. The women he knew always glossed over situations, and Brie could have, too.

Floodlights provided by a nearby volunteer fire department illuminated the transfer of chemicals. Linc looked at his watch and realized it was nearly nine o'clock. The day had died in a crimson sunset earlier. He had suspiciously checked the tanker for leaks. To his chagrin and relief, he didn't find any. Brie had caught him at it and broke into a grin, making him feel foolish. And it needled him further that she had said nothing and merely turned away to leave him to complete his personal inspection.

Linc made sure all the equipment was hung up in the van afterward. He said little as the tanker carrying the noxious chemicals slowly drove away. In the floodlights, Brie's features were washed out and taut with exhaustion. He wanted to urge her to forget the reporters, but she doggedly shook her head and went over to them. She answered their barrage of questions for nearly twenty minutes. He breathed a sigh of relief when she finally ended the press conference and walked to the van.

"Why'd you go out of your way to talk to those idiots?" he asked, shoving his hands into the pockets of his jeans.

"Because the people of Ohio need to be informed on what we do. Every little scrap of information through the media to them may help us do our job in the long run, Linc. It helps everyone if we can teach the public to check tankers as they pass them on the highway, see if they have any leaks, then report them, if there are." She stopped near the van, giving him the keys. "You drive, I'm getting tired."

He opened the door for her and saw a shadow of a

smile lurking at the corners of her glorious mouth. "Chauvinism is *not* dead," he informed her silkily.

She climbed in. "Does that mean you'll put my seat belt on, too?"

Linc hesitated, very aware that she looked so vulnerable because of her fatigue. "Just say the word. Nothing's too good for you, lady. Not after the way you handled this haz-mat situation."

Brie met his dark eyes, realizing he respected her for the first time. "Get in. I'm not so weak that I can't buckle up. Will I need to put on a crash helmet with you at the wheel?"

Linc shut the door and grinned. "My good friends always called me Captain Crash."

Brie chortled and waited until he climbed into the van before saying, "Is that short for Captain Crash and Dash?"

"Yeah. How'd you know?"

"That's an old fire fighter's pet name for those who crash through a burning structure's door, then fall through the floor into the basement. We never thought much of the crash and dashes in our department, or any other, for that matter. They risk other people's lives with their inability to think coolly under stress."

He got the van on the road and they headed toward Canton. "I'm not that kind," he protested.

Brie slumped into her seat, relaxing and closing her eyes. He wasn't a reckless driver, and she smiled slightly. "So, how many pumpers or tankers did you wreck then? There had to be a reason for the nickname."

He glanced at Brie, alarmed by the faraway tone in her soft voice. Darkness shadowed her features, relieved only by the lights of passing vehicles. "The name Captain

Crash was given to me because in certain situations I just lower my head like a bull and charge.''

"Wonderful. Now you tell me. What did you do, bully those poor reporters earlier? They didn't have many nice things to say about your handling of them.''

His brows drew down. "Tough. I'll never let them at you when you're exhausted or busy coordinating an incident.''

Sleep tugged at Brie, and she wanted to give in to it. "Linc, I'm going to knock off for a while. It's still an hour until we get home. Wake me up when you hit the outskirts of Canton, okay?''

Again, Linc was struck by Brie's exhaustion. Didn't she ever get a decent night's sleep? "Are you all right?'' Concern was obvious in his voice, and he saw her look at him through her lowered lashes.

"I'm fine. Don't worry, I didn't breathe in any of that stuff at the site. I'm just beat, that's all.''

"Okay. Sleep for a while.''

"Sure? It's been a long, hard day for you, too.''

He liked her sensitivity and regard for others. "Go to sleep, kitten. I'll wake you when it's time,'' he told her in a husky voice. Linc tried to tell himself that the care he extended toward Brie was part of his cover, not real concern.

Pleasantly wrapped in the melting honey of his tone, Brie went to sleep. She spiraled quickly into an abyss where nothing except peace existed.

When she awoke, it was to the caress of strong fingers gently massaging her shoulder. Wanting to remain in the arms of sleep, she nuzzled the hand, which she discovered had wiry hairs across it. When it slowly dawned on her whose hand it was, she jerked awake and sat up.

"We're near Canton," Linc said quietly, giving her a worried look.

"What time is it?" she asked groggily, rubbing her eyes.

"A little after ten. How do you feel?"

"Like I've been hit by a Mack truck," she muttered, sitting up. "My neck feels like it has knots in it." She began to rub it gently. Her hair had dried and was mussed, giving her a fragile look that Linc found hard to ignore.

He wondered what it would be like to make love to Brie. She was so responsive, like a hot, spirited thoroughbred. He had spent the past hour mulling over many facets of Brie, making a checklist of what he did or did not like about her. In the minus column, she was his boss. She was either a target or had set up Holcomb to be murdered. Which was it? Linc wanted to discount that Brie was capable of having her partner blown away, but he couldn't that easily. Then again, if she was the culprit why did she risk injury as she did? He had only a few answers, and there were still so many pieces of the puzzle that didn't fit. A plan had formed in his mind as she slept, and now he was going to spring it on her.

"Listen, I've been thinking, Brie."

"Uh-oh, that could be dangerous," she said, digging for the thermos.

"Are you always a tart when you wake up?"

She sat up, the thermos between her hands. "Just with your kind, Tanner. Want some?"

"No, thanks. What do you mean, my kind?"

Brie poured herself a cup of coffee, capped the thermos and sat back, enjoying Linc and her just awakening state. "Your kind meaning the guys in the fire service who are all macho and given to rooster crowing and strutting. They always have a line for the women who come around. Actually, I should thank all those guys I spent my fire fighting years with. They helped me handle some-one like you.'' She glanced out of the corners of her eyes to see how he was taking her teasing.

"You can really dish it out, can't you, Ms. Williams?"

She grinned, placing both feet on the dash. "That's right, any time, day or night. I'm on twenty-four-hour call, Tanner."

"I'm impressed as hell. When I wake up, I'm not sharp at all."

"No? Pity. Here I thought all you ever did was parry your way through life."

He slid her a warning look laced with humor. "Only with smart mouths like you, Williams. Satisfied?"

"Immensely. Now, what did you want to talk about?"

Saucy little cat. I'll corner you someday and then we'll see just how fast you can try and talk your way out of me kissing you. Linc wondered where that thought had come from. "How about if I crash and burn on your couch? We're both beat. There's no sense in driving all over Canton to find a motel open at this time of night. Besides, if you are called out, you'll have to come and pick me up, wasting valuable time."

Brie's good humor disappeared abruptly. She put her cup down, rested her hands on her knees and pondered his suggestion. Panic riffled through her. She didn't want Linc at her house. She had no way of knowing when she would have another nightmare and she'd awake scream-ing. No, she couldn't risk her image with Tanner like that. She wanted no one to see that weakened side of herself at any cost.

"I think you'll be more comfortable at a motel, Linc."

"I don't sleep well in motels. There's just something about a home that puts me at ease." He glanced at her, seeing the set of her lips. What was going on inside that head of hers? Was she hiding something at her house she wanted no one to see? "I promise I'll stay on the couch. No cute stuff. Okay?"

Brie rubbed her brow, feeling a headache coming on. Great, he didn't sleep well at motels. Neither did she. "It's a small couch. You wouldn't be comfortable on it. Take my word."

Linc softened his features and gave what he hoped was his best puppy-dog look. "We had a rough start. How about if we both get a good night's sleep to put us in good stead for tomorrow?"

She wasn't prepared for the sudden pleading look in Linc's eyes and felt like a heel for trying to turn him down. "Oh, okay," she grumbled. "But I warn you, Tanner, I won't be your cook or bottle washer. Tomorrow's Sunday, our day off. I don't want to have to jump out of bed and feed your growing-boy appetite in the morning."

Linc tried to look properly grateful. "No problem. All I like in the morning is coffee, anyway."

Brie shot him a disparaging look. "At least we agree on that."

Allowing a bit of a friendly smile, he murmured, "Not bad for two people who are opposites, eh? I'm impressed, too."

"Well, just don't expect the Ritz, Tanner. You make up your own bed on that lumpy couch. I'm going to grab the shower first, then hit the sack. You're going to have to wait your turn. I'm dead on my feet."

"No problem," he said. "Ladies first, anyway."

Brie wrinkled her nose, trying to figure out how to short-circuit the nightmares that stalked her. She still had some sleeping pills left from her stay in the hospital. But what if there was a haz-mat call? She wouldn't be able to function properly in that groggy state, and Jeff wouldn't be returning until tomorrow afternoon. Groaning, Brie shut her eyes, trying to think clearly and not succeeding.

Following her directions, Linc found her small white home with green trim on the outskirts of North Canton. The one-story house was hidden by a long gravel driveway lined with oaks, elms and maples. A large overhead sulfur lamp lit the entire front of the house, which was embraced by blossoming white and purple lilac bushes. They stood window-height in some places. Tulips, daffodils and hyacinths were in full bloom in front of the shrubs.

"Nice place," Linc murmured as he shut off the engine. He'd meant it.

"This is Camelot, the place where I go and hide when the world gets too much to take," Brie said, climbing out. She fished for the key from her purse and opened the door.

"Come on in," she invited Linc, who was hanging back. Was it her imagination or was he looking around the entire area as if he were an investigator? Brie shook her head, not caring. Throwing her purse on the Formica counter in the small kitchen, she headed for the linen closet in the hall near the bathroom. She found sheets, a pillow and a blanket, and put them in Linc's waiting arms. "The living room is that way," she said, pointing. "I'm getting my shower then going to bed."

He gave her a nod. "Sounds good. Good night. And thanks"

Brie barely responded, going to the kitchen to pour herself a glass of chablis instead of downing a sleeping pill. In the bathroom, she shed her clothes, dying for a bath, but it was too soon after her burn injuries to subject her tender, still healing flesh to it. With a sigh, she stepped into the warm shower and scrubbed her hair and body. By the time she finished, she was so groggy she could barely stand. After she slipped into a pale apricot silk nightgown that brushed her slender ankles, Brie opened the bathroom door and padded down the carpeted hall to her bedroom. Before the accident, she had always worn gowns that showed off her shoulders. Since then, because of the terrible scars, she wore only gowns with high necklines that hid the telltale scars. Some of them were still visible, but a robe would hide them from her eyes as well as Linc's curious, always penetrating gaze.

Bed had never looked so inviting as she quietly shut the door. Moonlight streamed in through the floor-to-ceiling windows on the east side of the room; the pale ivory sheer curtains lent a radiance to the scene. But Brie couldn't appreciate any of it tonight. The instant she snuggled beneath the quilt her grandmother had made for her, she was asleep.

Linc took a shower and stepped into his light blue pajama bottoms. He tightened the drawstring and opened the door, waiting and listening. Damp dark hair clung to his brow, and he tamed it into place with his fingers. It had been nearly a half hour since Brie had gone to bed. He turned off the hall light, stepped up to her door and carefully turned the brass knob. The door opened without a creak. He waited a few more seconds, listening. Then, he pushed the door open just enough to see. There, lying on one side of the brass bed, was Brie sleeping soundly, the moonlight outlining her form.

Her face was almost radiant and was without a trace of the previous tension around her full, sensual lips or eyes. His heart beat harder, and he took a deep, steadying breath, his body going rigid with need of her. She looked

soft and warm, vulnerable and incredibly feminine. With
a shake of his head, Linc slowly closed the door. It must
be moon madness, he thought wryly. No woman made
his head spin like that.

Padding to the living room, which, in his opinion, had
so many plants it bordered on being a jungle, Linc went
directly to the massive cherry rolltop desk. He turned on
the Tiffany stained-glass lamp and, with painstaking thoroughness, he began his investigation. He found a stack
of letters and committed the names of the correspondents
to memory. If he had time, he'd read the contents of each
later. Another small drawer yielded several color photos.
In one, Brie was smiling brilliantly, her arm around a man
in a haz-mat uniform. He had to be John Holcomb. Linc
felt the stirrings of envy as he absorbed the happiness
evident in Brie's face. Her eyes were like dead embers
now compared to the photo. He pushed aside his personal
feelings and noted that Brie was at least fifteen pounds
heavier in the photo, and sported a golden tan. Her beautiful sable brown hair was curling richly around her
shoulders. Had her hair been burned off in the explosion?
More than likely, and he was suddenly sad that had happened, because she was lovely with dark hair framing her
face. His throat constricted with emotion as he gazed at
her. Where her cheek had once been filled out with a rosy
bloom, it was nothing but flesh over bone now.

He cradled the picture between his hands, lifting his
head and staring into the darkness toward the bedroom.
The trauma of the explosion had devastated Brie much
more than he had first realized. No one looked like a
prisoner of war as she did now without the ravages still
inside her, still eating her up. His forehead furrowed
deeply as he stared down at Brie. The report on her had
said she suffered internal injuries and burns. Had she

sought therapy afterward to cope with the trauma? More than likely not. Who of them did? Linc recalled her every move at the haz-mat scene. Brie had been professional, like a man would have been. She hadn't lost her touch. So how was the trauma affecting her?

Having more questions than answers, Linc continued his search of the desk. There were several photos of Brie with Holcomb, his wife and child celebrating Christmas, Easter, birthdays and other holidays. Linc got the impression that Brie was part of Holcomb's family.

Going back to the letters, he opened the one with the latest postmark, which was only a few days ago. It was from Carol Holcomb.

Dear Brie,
How can Susie and I thank you for the lovely flowers? They were such a wonderful surprise and they brightened our day. Susie loves the balloons that came with the bouquet and has them in her room. And whenever I'm down, I go smell the flowers, and it makes me feel better.

By the way, Susie asks me every day, when is Aunt Brie coming over again, Mommy?

We miss you, Brie. And I know how busy you are. Just know we pray for you nightly.

Love,
Carol and Susie

Linc folded the note and put it into the pink envelope. *Aunt Brie.* You endear yourself to everyone pretty quickly, don't you? What is it about you that makes people want to reach out and become a part of your existence?

The next letter was from Steve, her brother.

Dear Fighting Tiger,

How's my ace sister doing? When you gonna come to my base and visit me? I haven't seen you since visiting you in the hospital. Knowing you like I do, you're licking your own wounds by yourself, as usual. Come on! I may be your kid brother, but I have a pretty broad shoulder that you can lean on if you want.

And, also knowing you, you haven't cried much lately (you'd get more blood out of a turnip) and I'm pretty good at sitting and listening, why not try me? How come you haven't been calling me once a month like you usually do? I know you're busy, but the state of Ohio can't have blown up that much. It's been three months since you got out of the burn unit, and I haven't heard from you.

If I don't hear soon, I'm going to go A.W.O.L. from the Air Force and fly back to see you. How's that for a threat, Big Sis? Seriously, call or write. I'll even accept a collect call from you, Tiger.

Love,
your strong, intelligent, handsome brother Steve

So you've locked yourself up since the accident.

He glanced at the names on the next letter—Mr. and Mrs. Vernon Williams. Her parents.

Dear Sweetheart:

How are you doing? Dad and I are so worried about you. Please come home for a visit. I just have this feeling you need someone, Brie. You and John were so close. And I know he was like the big brother you never had, honey.

Why don't you take some of that vacation you've

earned? You haven't had one in over a year. I know you love your job and you believe in what you're accomplishing, but everyone needs a rest now and then. If you'll come home Dad's promised you can help around the farm. You always loved plowing the fields in the spring. He says your favorite old John Deere tractor has been tuned up and is waiting for you.

Of course, if you don't want to work, you don't have to. We just need to see you again, honey. After that awful three months in the hospital and seeing what it did to you, we both think that right now, you need a little T.L.C. Please, Brie, you give so much to others. Don't you think it's time you came home to get some for yourself?

If you can't afford the plane ticket, Dad says we'll spring for it. Let us know soon. We love you, honey.

Love,
Mom and Dad

Linc's mouth twisted as he put the letter in the stack. He stared down at six others. Were they all from friends and family who were worried? Driven to find out and rationalizing that his decision to read them was for the purpose of his investigation and not his personal need to know, Linc spent another twenty minutes perusing them. By the time he was done, his face was grim. The other six letters were from members of the haz-mat team. Some had sent funny cards; others more serious, but they all contained one message: Brie was special, respected and cared for by her family of coworkers. He sat back in the chair, the Tiffany lamp casting light and making deep shadows around him.

Everywhere he looked, Linc saw life. Huge ficus trees,

almost as tall as the eight-foot ceiling, graced two corners of the pale green living room. Behind the bamboo couch with fluffy ivory colored pillows were two tall, slender palms, adding a wild touch to the room. He liked it, realizing he was privy to another facet of Brie's existence. The room throbbed with vibrancy. She had embraced life in ways he had seen few people able to do.

Linc stared at the stack of unanswered mail and returned the letters to their drawer. Framed pictures of lions, cheetahs and other animals graced the walls. Was that how Brie felt? Was she a wild lioness who demanded freedom? He smiled. He hadn't missed the mark on her after all—she was feline...

Why are you running from everyone's offer of help? Is there something they don't know? Are you mixed up with a criminal element and afraid to talk for fear they'll blow the whistle on you, too? Or maybe you really were secretly in love with John Holcomb and are afraid to admit that to anyone. Rubbing his face, Linc got up, running his hand across his chest where an ache had centered.

Brie moaned and tossed violently, throwing the quilt off her. She lay floating between sleep and wakefulness, aware that her nightgown was sticky against her flesh. Her breath came in ragged gasps as she saw herself turning from John to head to the haz-mat van. She felt her heart start a hammer of warning. No! Oh, God, please, no! she screamed silently. Come back, John! Come back! Helplessly, Brie watched the unfolding drama before her.

Just as before, Brie heard the powerful explosion, felt the blast of annihilating heat. Then blackness overcame her as she was slammed to the concrete surface. A scream tore from her lips when she regained consciousness. She rolled over on her back. Her ribs hurt, and she gripped her right side as she sat up. Warm liquid was running down her face, blinding her. A metallic taste was in her mouth, and her nose was bleeding heavily. Brie felt another scream building deep inside her, clawing up through her like a caged animal that had to free itself. She lifted her chin to look at the drums. The raw cry finally tore from her. Brie sprang up, fighting pain and dizziness as she lurched forward, trying to get to where John lay facedown three hundred feet away.

Brie jerked upright in bed, burying her face in her hands, her shoulders hunched and broken. She barely heard the door being torn open; she was not aware of the light being turned on.

Linc froze, one hand on the doorknob, the other on the light switch. Brie was breathing hard, her gasps hoarse. She sat on the edge of the bed as if she were prepared to leap off it. He had heard her scream and thought that someone had slipped into her bedroom and attacked her. His wide eyes traveled from the closed windows to Brie. Without thinking, he started toward her out of some instinct to comfort her. His mouth opened then closed. He tasted the bitterness of bile as he stared at her heavily scarred right shoulder. The upper buttons of the gown were open and moved aside enough for him to see some of her injury. Twisted pink flesh clearly showed the path of destruction the explosion had collected from Brie.

He knelt on one knee and raised his hands to settle them on her shaking shoulders. She was in so much pain that unexpected tears came to his eyes.

"Brie? Kitten?" he began haltingly. Linc berated himself. He was so damn good in a dangerous situation. Why couldn't he be just as good when it came to a genuine human crisis? His hands wavered inches from her shoulders, and he didn't know whether to touch her or not. JoAnne had always accused him of being incapable of expressing emotions openly, of always hiding behind his image as a cool, collected agent. Linc swallowed hard, then called Brie's name again and again until she responded.

The need to touch her, to soothe away some of her pain forced him to settle his hands gently on her shoulders. Her skin was clammy. The moment he made contact with her, she reacted violently, pushing him away, her eyes wide and unseeing. Linc slowly got up, holding out his hand toward her, talking to her in a low, unsteady voice.

"Brie, it's all right, take a deep breath. You're here, in your bedroom. The explosion is past. You're safe now. Take slow breaths…"

Her face was contorted. For several long, agonizing seconds she stared at him. Her breasts rose and fell beneath her nightgown; her hands dug convulsively into the mattress.

"That's it," Linc whispered, seeing her eyes begin to lose their terrified look. "Slow your breathing down. I'm here, and you're safe."

Brie wanted to cry, but no tears would come out! The need to cry was like a knife thrusting deeply inside her, but no tears would come! Linc's face wavered like a mirage before her, conflicting with the image of the warehouse and the flames roaring around her as she tried to get to John. Disoriented, Brie raised her hand. "John… John?" she cried hoarsely.

Linc winced and shut his eyes momentarily. "No, kitten, I'm not John. Come on, pull from the grip of that nightmare. You're at home, and I'm Linc. Linc Tanner. Remember? Brie, keep taking deep breaths."

She staggered and fell, the jolt ripping through her. For a moment, she felt blackness swallowing her. Reaching out with her left hand, Brie crawled forward across the blackened concrete toward John. He had to be alive, he just had to be—and yet, the voice she was hearing wasn't John's. Fighting to shake off the powerful nightmare, Brie closed her eyes and concentrated on listening to the instructions to control hyperventilation. When she opened her eyes some minutes later, she found herself staring directly into Linc's tortured features.

Licking her dry lips, she croaked, "What are you doing here?"

Relief flickered in his blue eyes. "Thank God," he whispered. "You had a bad dream, Brie. And you screamed." He looked toward the windows. "I thought someone had broken in and was attacking you, so I practically took your door off the hinges getting in here."

Brie turned slowly to look at the door. It hung by one hinge. She buried her face in her hands because she couldn't stand the look of pity written across his face. "Just leave," she said brokenly.

"Are you sure? I mean—"

"Please!"

Linc started for the door. "Are you sure, Brie?"

Tears struck her eyes. Maybe it was because of the unexpected tenderness in Linc's voice. Or his protectiveness. Brie wasn't sure. She felt embarrassed. With a trembling hand, she pulled the throat of the gown closed. He had seen her ugly burns and seen her down. Not even her own family had seen the extent of her injuries yet, only the doctor. And more than anything, Brie didn't want to be alone. She felt him close to her and lifted her chin. He hadn't left, and old hurt tore loose from her heart. Linc looked exhausted and ravaged.

"M-maybe some water…please?"

"Sure. Just stay put. I'll be back in a minute," he promised.

Brie shakily reached for her apricot robe at the foot of the bed, pulling it haphazardly across her shoulders to hide her burns. The shame of being seen weakened washed over her. Unable to cope with what he probably thought of her now, Brie simply sat there until Linc returned. He shut off the lamp when he entered the room, the moon giving them enough light. Gratefully, Brie took the glass of water he offered her. Linc knelt beside her, one callused hand resting lightly against her elbow. She drank the contents and handed the glass to him.

"Thank you," she whispered, her voice raw.

Linc set the glass on the bed stand. "It's the least I could do. Listen, let's get you back into bed and covered up. You're pretty sweaty, and this cool air isn't going to do you much good."

His voice was like balm, and numbly, Brie did as he directed. As she allowed him to pull up the quilt, she closed her eyes.

"I wish I could have a bath," she murmured, her voice slurring with exhaustion.

Linc stood there, puzzled. "I can fix it for you if you want, Brie."

A broken smile faded from her lips. "Can't...yet...my burns...time, the doctors say it will take time before I can take one. I miss the bath so much. I can relax in it..."

He gently sat on the edge of the bed and took her hand. She had curled up on her side. "You can relax now, Brie," he soothed quietly. "Just hold my hand and you'll relax."

Her fingers tightened slightly around his hand. "I'm so scared," she whispered, "so scared..."

"Shh, that will go away, Brie. Go to sleep, kitten. I'll just sit here and hold your hand so you can sleep. You'll be safe now. No more bad dreams."

The tension began to dissolve from her face, the soft corners of her mouth relaxing. Linc continued to talk in a low monotone to her, speaking from a heart he didn't realize existed within him. He spoke in words meant to heal and take away her pain. He willed her anguish into his hand so that she could sleep in a dreamless world where only peace existed, instead of grief. Within half an hour, her fingers uncurled from his hand; Brie had found an edge of peace in the torn fabric of her universe. Linc wanted to stay with her, but he fought the desire. He could take her into his arms and hold her...and protect her.

As Linc sat there, watching the slow rise and fall of her breast beneath the rainbow quilt, he was able to put all the letters together. Brie had no one she could reach to for solace or healing. Even he knew that at times he needed someone in order to heal himself. Of course, Linc thought with a bitter laugh, he was the pot calling the kettle black. He was just as bad as Brie in that instance. Except he had channeled out all his traumas and cleansed himself, and Brie had not.

Sadness overwhelmed Linc as he reluctantly stood. He leaned over, tucking the quilt behind her back, and noticed Brie had thrown the robe across her shoulders—to hide her scars from him. Against his better judgment, he reached down, barely stroking the crown of her sable hair. It was as soft and silken as he had imagined it would be. That small discovery pleased him as much as if he had taken her to bed and made love to her. True, he hadn't known her very long, but that didn't matter. Just having the privilege of being near her, sharing the haz-mat incident and now sharing her tragedy, had melded him like hot, molten steel to her. The forge of trauma had cast them into one. They held an indestructible link to one another whether they wanted it. He tried to break that emotional bond, because she was still a prime suspect. Brie could be a killer, and he reminded himself he was an investigator, not her haz-mat partner.

Linc forced himself to leave her bedroom, and he left the door hanging at a sad angle. He wanted it open in case Brie started having nightmares again.

Chapter Four

The morning sun was warm against her back, the soil moist between her hands. Kneeling, Brie lifted her head momentarily, allowing the sun to caress her face. The birds, mostly robins, some sparrows and a pair of noisy blue jays, provided the music that surrounded her in the small garden behind the house. Brie took the hoe and got to her feet. She dug a shallow trench from one end of the plot to the other, the freshly turned soil like a dark scar against the lighter, drier earth.

That's how she felt—stripped. She was cold inside. Her stomach had knotted soon after she had awakened this morning. She tried to concentrate on planting her garden and pushing last night's memories away. But it was impossible. As she knelt and opened her first packet of peas, a flood of embarrassment washed over her. Not only had Linc seen her stripped of all control over her emotions, he'd probably seen a portion of the massive scarring caused by the burns on her back. She gently nestled three peas every few feet until the entire row had been sown. The lulling songs of the birds quelled her screaming nerves, and Brie devoted her complete attention to one of her favorite pastimes of the year—spring planting.

Glancing at the watch on her wrist, Brie saw it was almost eleven o'clock. She risked a glance toward the house. Linc was still sleeping soundly, thank God. She didn't want to have to meet him face to face after last night, but she knew it was inevitable. Her gut had told her not to allow him to stay overnight, and now she was going to pay dearly for ignoring her instincts. Linc was the kind of man who would hold last night against her. More than likely, he'd throw it up in her face at a critical moment, questioning her authority.

Lips compressed, Brie pushed the right amount of soil over the peas and gently pressed it in place with the palm of her hand. Jeff was supposed to arrive around noon. If only he would arrive before Linc woke up. That was almost an impossibility, Brie realized. No one slept until noon. She was surprised Linc had slept this long. Perhaps her screams had unsettled him more than she realized, and he hadn't been able to get back to sleep for a long time afterward. A ragged sigh escaped her as she got up and made another shallow row with the hoe.

Time melted away with the joy of caressing and molding the soil of the earth between her hands. Brie's back was to the house, and she was kneeling near a row in which she was dropping beans, when a slight noise startled her. She twisted her head around.

"Good morning," Linc greeted quietly. He stood there with a cup of coffee in each hand, dressed in a navy blue polo shirt that emphasized the clean, powerful lines of his chest, shoulders and hard stomach. Worn jeans hugged his narrow hips and long thighs like an intimate lover. Brie's lips parted, and her heart banged at the base of her throat. Her hands froze in midair as she forced herself to look at him. She melted beneath his sleepy inspection. If his face had been hard and unforgiving, as it usually was, she would have died a little inside. As Brie took in his drowsy features, her heart wrenched with compassion. She recalled Linc telling her he didn't wake up quickly in the morning. Right now, he looked like a little boy with his hair softly mussed, eyes sleep-ridden and his features vulnerable to her inspection.

Brie returned her attention to the planting, averting her gaze from the tender flame that sparked in his half-closed eyes. "Good morning," she muttered.

Linc looked around. The back yard was embraced on all sides by towering trees and, a strong shaft of morning sunlight brightened the lawn and garden. His gaze moved to Brie, who was doggedly paying a great deal more attention to her planting activities than to him. Could he blame her? Although he was still groggy, he noticed the high flush to her cheeks when he had spoken to her. He sat down on the grass a few feet from where Brie worked, and put down the coffee cups.

"When did you get up?" he asked, his voice gravelly. He rubbed his face wearily.

Brie shrugged. "A couple hours ago." Please don't let him start asking me about last night. Please don't! She didn't know what she would do if Linc did. Even now, she could feel tears pricking her eyes, and she was stunned that Linc would bring out that kind of response in her.

Linc sipped the coffee. "You make good coffee."

"I'm glad you like it."

He realized Brie's cool, clipped manner was to protect herself from last night's ordeal, and he tried to steer delicately clear of anything having to do with the episode. "I'm used to concrete, condos and people all jammed together. Not trees, birds and quiet."

She managed a slight smile, continuing down the row. Why wouldn't Linc just get up and leave? If only she could will him to go into the house. "Canton's a nice middle-size city. Large enough to offer you anything a big one has, but small enough to afford the luxury of trees and privacy, if that's what you want."

Linc gazed at the two acres of neatly kept lawn that was guarded by trees. "I think you wanted your privacy."

"I did."

He sipped more coffee, a feeling of contentment filling him. There was something almost maternal in the way Brie was running her fingers through the soil, planting the seeds then patting the soil into place. Dirt had lodged beneath her short nails, her hands were stained with the color of the earth she was lovingly tending, and a small smudge streaked her right cheek. But that didn't detour him from thinking how beautiful she was this morning. Dressed in a long-sleeved pale pink blouse and a pair of loose-fitting jeans, she looked as if she belonged with the land. When he remembered her parents' letter and the fact that they farmed for a living, it all made sense. At least he hadn't caught her in a lie…yet.

"This place must have cost you a bundle. Two acres in D.C. would equal our paychecks combined for the next ten years."

Brie took a tiny breath of relief. Was Linc going to have the sensitivity not to mention last night? She got to her feet, retrieved the hoe and began another shallow row. "It didn't cost that much, but it has put a definite strain on my budget."

"Why aren't you like every other modern woman I know who owns an apartment closer to the city?"

Brie gave him an irritated look, then resumed her hoeing. "Modern woman? Is that your concept of one? She owns a condo and parties in town?"

"Sounds good," he mumbled.

"Are you always a comedian in the morning?"

"Hey, slow down, you're getting too far ahead of me. Remember, I'm the one who staggers around after getting up."

She relented, stealing a glance at Linc. There was something about his groping and stumbling demeanor that endeared him to her. He was more open now than she had ever seen him. Still, that alert glint was in his eyes, always making her think he was a wolf stalking a quarry. And that red flag of warning was screaming at her again. She wrestled with the clash between her gut feeling and Linc's vulnerability. He invited her trust, and his actions thus far made it easy for her to trust him. So why was the alarm going off inside her head? "Then refrain from those chauvinistic remarks."

"Ouch." He gave her a boyish smile meant to defuse her abruptness. "Just ignore me, okay? I'm not much good the first hour."

"That's an understatement," Brie murmured, trying to curb her slight smile. She put the hoe down and went through her collection of seeds yet to be planted, trying to decide what should go next to her green beans.

"You're a country gal."

"Yes. I love the land," she admitted softly.

"Is that why you got into haz-mat? To protect the earth? A lot of chemicals are buried in the earth, ruining it for years if not decades to come."

She was pleased with his insight and sat back on her

heels, a package of bush beans in her hand. "Being a city boy, you'd laugh if I told you the truth."

Linc crossed his legs Indian fashion, the cup resting on one knee. "No, I wouldn't. Besides, it will help me understand you."

Brie wrinkled her nose and tore the top off the seed packet. "That's what I'm afraid of."

"Isn't it natural for people to want to get to know each other?" Part of him wanted to know because of the assignment. Another part of him wanted to know for personal reasons. Linc was disgusted with his indecisiveness regarding Brie. To hell with it. He wanted to know her more intimately because she was a suspect, he rationalized.

She shrugged and crawled up to the head of the row, carefully putting the seeds into it. "Up to a point," she parried.

"You know, you're like this place of yours: hidden, guarded and mysterious."

"I like it that way."

"Why? What's wrong if someone knows you?"

Brie shifted uncomfortably. The coffee he was drinking must be waking him up; he was sharper and more focused. "Technically, nothing. I'm just a private person by nature. I don't feel it's anyone's right to know all about me."

Linc absorbed the stubborn set of her face. This morning, there was a fragility to Brie. He couldn't put his finger on exactly what made him sense that. The nightmare had left her devastated and wide open to attack. That was why she was behaving defensively with him, he reasoned. Desperate to establish some sort of beachhead of trust with her, Linc shifted the conversation to himself.

"When I was a kid growing up in the city, I often wished I could just pack up and head for the country. I guess it's like that old saying—the grass is always greener on the other side of the hill.''

Brie closed her eyes for a moment, thankful Linc was talking about himself instead of trying to needle her. She resumed the planting, needing the warmth of the earth in her hands to soothe her frayed nerves. ''Didn't your parents ever take you to the country?''

Linc drank the last of the coffee, then set down the cup and rested his hands on his thighs. ''I grew up between foster homes and orphanages in New York City, so I saw a lot of skyscrapers, glass, steel and concrete.'' At least that part of his life wasn't a lie. Linc laughed at himself. Why should he care? Brie had a soft side, and he wanted to cultivate it in order to make her trust him. Ordinarily, he never spoke about his childhood to anyone.

Brie lifted her chin, her eyes dark with compassion as she met and held his blue gaze. ''Orphanages?'' she uttered, a catch in her voice.

''Now don't go getting soft on me,'' he warned. ''Plenty of brats got dumped by mothers who didn't want them, and they ended up kicking between foster homes or an orphanage. It's no big deal.''

Her hands stilled on her thighs. She could imagine him as a dark-haired, blue-eyed little boy who strutted around pretending he was tough and could take anything. Perhaps that was why he came across like that now. It was the only way he knew how to protect the vulnerable inner core of himself. ''I—I had no idea...''

''Come on, Brie, it wasn't a life sentence. Quit giving me that sad, soulful look. You aren't going to cry on me, are you?''

The right blend of sarcasm laced with disbelief effectively tamped her flow of feelings toward him. He was still that tough little boy, she thought, her heart wrenching in her breast. And somehow, knowing that about Linc made him less of a threat to her. But she'd never tell him that. "No," she whispered, "I won't cry." She never cried, and she needed to. The tears might crowd into her eyes, but they'd never quite spill out and release the pent-up grief that she carried within.

"Good," he said.

She went back to planting. "So you were raised in the city in a series of foster homes?"

"Yeah. I lived in a jungle, too. But it wasn't like the jungle you have inside your house or surrounding you out here."

"I see. A concrete jungle?"

"Something like that."

Brie compressed her lips. "What parts of New York City did you grow up in?"

"The Bronx. A good blue-collar community that's been eaten away by street gangs."

She heard the disgust in his voice. "Did you belong to one of those gangs?"

"Yeah. If you were anybody, you were part of a gang."

"And you wanted to belong…" Brie said gently, meeting his eyes.

He shrugged. "I was bored. The Panthers gave me someplace to go and something to do."

"What did your foster parents have to say about that?"

Again a shrug. "Let's put it this way, Brie. One set of foster parents took in brats like me to get the money. They really didn't give a damn about us. All they wanted was the monthly allotment check."

Her heart twisted. Linc had been rejected from the day of his birth. My God, how would she have felt if that had happened to her? Brie's hands stilled over the warm earth. Her voice was almost inaudible. "My growing up years were very different. I have wonderful parents. They have a three-hundred-acre farm in Iowa.'' She gave him a wry look. "I grew up working alongside Dad and my younger brother, Steve, fixing tractors, hay balers, wind rowers and trucks. We didn't have the money to send them to a garage in town to be fixed, so we did all the repairs ourselves.''

Linc gave her a sour look. "So that's why you knew where the battery cables were located on that truck yesterday?''

Brie swallowed a smile. "Yes.''

He gave her a disgruntled look. Brie could have rubbed his face in it with that piece of information, but she continued to plant her beans. Linc knew more than a few people who would be delighted to make a first-class fool of him if they had the opportunity. But Brie hadn't. His brows drew together.

"You're a strange bird, Ms. Williams.''

She rose, dusting off her knees. "I could say the same of you, Mr. Tanner. Well, do you feel up to seeing a truly strange bird?''

Linc enjoyed looking at Brie, at the way the sunlight made her hair a brown halo laced with strands of gold. He had touched that hair last night and felt how silky it was. Emotions woven with desire deluged him as he absorbed her in those fleeting seconds. Somehow, with dirt-stained hands, her hair loose and free, standing in a pair of patched jeans, she looked beautiful. Was she like Ceres, the mother of the earth from Roman mythology, giving life to everything she touched? Linc thought so, responding to the wry smile on her full, provocative lips.

"What surprise do you have for me,'' he asked, rising to his full height.

Brie's eyes glimmered with mirth as she stepped carefully between the rows and walked toward the house. "Come on, and I'll show you."

After removing her tennis shoes at the door, Brie stepped inside and led Linc down the hall. The moment she opened the door to the right of the bathroom, an excited whistling sound emerged. Frowning, Linc followed Brie into the room. He saw a sewing machine in one corner with some peach-colored fabric that resembled a blouse. Turning toward the whistling sound, he saw a small gray bird flapping its wings madly in its cage on a desk across the room.

"What's that?" he asked.

Brie smiled, sat on a chair and opened the cage. "This is Homely Homer, an orphaned baby pigeon the kids down the street brought to me two weeks ago. Apparently Homer fell out of her nest, and they couldn't get her back into it." She gently picked up the pigeon, which had no feathers on her breast. Looking at Linc, she could see his scowl deepening. "Come on over here. You wanted to see what it's like to live in the country, now you're going to find out."

Linc came and stood near the desk. "He's the ugliest-looking thing I've ever seen."

Homer perched on Brie's finger, flapping her wings and whistling shrilly. Brie laughed and stroked Homer's few feathers, which were beginning to grow out on her back. "Homer's a she. Don't insult her like that, Linc. Here, sit down. You can let her perch on your finger while I get her the baby food."

"Baby food?" he echoed, not sure at all that he wanted that ugly-looking, buck-naked bird with its long, oddly shaped beak on *his* finger.

Brie motioned for him to sit on the edge of the desk,

which he did with great reluctance. "Hold out your finger," she urged.

"What if—what if that thing decides to take a dump on me?" he protested.

She chuckled. "I have papers spread over the desk. Just hold Homer away from you. She'll be a lady and sit nicely on your finger." Without waiting for him to say no, Brie placed the squab on his finger. She turned and headed for the door.

"Hey! Wait a minute. Where are you going?"

"To the fridge to get Homer's breakfast. I'll be right back."

Linc's face fell. "But—what if—"

"I'll be back in a moment," she promised airily, disappearing. He scowled at the pigeon. "You're ugly," he growled at the bird. Homer blinked her big brown eyes at him, whistled through the nostrils of her long beak and gently flapped her gray and black feathered wings, as if to dispute his comment. Linc sat there uncomfortably. What had he gotten himself into? He glared at the bird. Relief rushed through him when Brie came back minutes later.

"Here, take this thing," he growled. "I'm no good with animals."

She placed the small jar of baby food on the desk and twisted off the lid. "That's only because you haven't been around animals much, Linc. You're doing just fine. Look at Homer, she's very contented on your finger. You can tell she's happy because she barely flutters her wings and she's talking to you in that soft whistle of hers. She's accepting you as her parent."

"The whistle is driving me crazy," he said tightly. "And I'm not going to be some bird's foster parent."

"You'll get used to it after a while. Okay, I'll take her now. Thanks."

Grudgingly, Linc watched. He was fascinated with Brie's understanding of so many things—first battery cables, then a garden, now a pigeon. Who had that kind of broad spectrum of knowledge? No one he knew. He saw her in a new light and decided she was like a well of unfathomable and unknown depth.

For the next fifteen minutes, Linc was taught a lesson of interaction between a human and an animal. He'd seen nothing like it. Brie talked and chatted with Homer as if the bird were human, and occasionally reached out and petted the pigeon's back or short, stubby tail. The bird dived into the jar of baby food, flapping her wings wildly, whistling shrilly, dancing around it as she gobbled down the food and had a great time. Linc crossed his arms against his chest, sourly admitting he was enjoying the odd spectacle. More than anything, he saw Brie's pale features glow with a breathtaking radiance as she communicated with the orphaned bird through voice and touch. Linc actually felt a bit envious. What also fascinated him was that a pigeon was responding to Brie with joy because of the attention.

There was a heavy knock at the back door, and Brie's face registered relief. "That's probably Jeff," she told Linc. "Come on in," she called, raising her voice.

Linc scowled. "You always just tell someone to come in without first finding out who it is?"

"I always know who's coming here. Why should I leave Homer half fed and go find out?"

"Look, this place is in the sticks, Brie. What if it was a burglar? Or someone else up to no good?"

She shook her head, confused by the sudden tension in his body and voice. Again, her instincts begged her to be on guard toward him. Linc's reaction was ridiculous under the circumstances. "I've lived here three years, and nothing has ever happened."

He was about to give her a lecture on the topic when a string bean of a man with a narrow face appeared before them. Linc's scowl remained as he sized up Jeff Laughlin. String bean was a good word to describe him, Linc decided irritably. Laughlin was his height and a third his weight. Dark brown hair lay neatly against his skull, emphasizing his large, twinkling eyes of the same color. There was a relaxed quality to the twenty-five-year old man, and Linc decided the haz-mat tech wasn't darkly handsome enough to interest Brie. That particular thought surprised him because he didn't normally assess another male in that manner. And on the heels of that thought came a bizarre realization: he didn't want Brie to have any romantic relationships right now.

"Hey, Brie!" Jeff greeted, throwing her a wave.

"Hi, Jeff. I'd like you to meet our second trainee, Linc Tanner. Linc, this was going to be my partner, Jeff Laughlin."

Linc shook the smiling man's slender hand. "Nice meeting you," he said. Liar.

"Same here. Welcome aboard, Linc." Jeff leaned over Brie's shoulder. "You feeding the Bottomless Pit again?"

She laughed fully. "Remember what I told you. Homer is sensitive. What if I called you the Bottomless Pit? How would you feel?"

"But it's the truth! I keep trying to fill out and look like Linc here to impress the women, but it just doesn't happen."

Brie's jade eyes lightened with genuine happiness. "Maybe you ought to start eating baby food and see what happens."

"Ugh!"

Linc sat there for the next ten minutes listening to the easy banter between them. And he was uncomfortably jealous of Jeff Laughlin. Brie's lovely green eyes were sparkling with happiness. He had begun to wonder if she was always in a serious state, but now he knew differently. And he didn't like it each time Jeff reached out and touched her arm or shoulder. Brie didn't seem to mind it, but Linc did. She and Jeff sounded like the best of friends, and Linc's scowl deepened.

"Listen, Jeff, I've got a favor to ask of you," Brie said, gently placing Homely Homer in her cage.

"Name it. I'm yours forever anyway."

"You've got problems then. Seriously…"

Jeff grinned lopsidedly and rocked on his heels, his hands resting on his narrow hips. "I'm always serious where you're concerned, Brie. You know that."

"Oh, go practice those lines on the women you're stalking, and not on me!"

He had the good grace to blush slightly. "I'm still too chicken to go after Elaine down at the FM's office. Gotta keep polishing my lines until they sound genuine and not like a line," he complained.

Brie rested her hand on Jeff's shoulder, giving him a playful shake. "I'm sure Linc can help you in that department. Listen, I want you to take Linc around Canton and help him find an apartment or house this afternoon. Will you do that for me? I've got a lot of paperwork to catch up on here while you're gone."

Jeff cast Linc a conspiratorial look. "Now we've got her where we want her," he said in a dramatic stage whisper.

"What are you mumbling about, Jeff?" she demanded, placing the lid on the baby-food jar.

"Linc, tell Brie that if she doesn't have her world-famous chicken barbecue ready tonight when we get back, we aren't going anywhere. We'll just sit here underfoot all day and drive her buggy.''

Brie groaned. "Jeff!"

"I want an apartment, not chicken barbecue.''

"Man, do you have lousy taste. Anyway,'' Jeff said archly, centering all his attention on Brie, "no chicken barbecue, no driver for Linc.''

"Laughlin, you're such a—''

"Yeah, I know. And you love me anyway, don't you?''

With a shake of her head, Brie slipped past him. "All right! You're such an arm twister, Laughlin.''

Jeff leaned against the doorjamb, watching her move down the hall. He turned to Linc, a loose smile on his face. "I'll tell you what, Linc. You got the best person in the world to train you. Brie is one of a kind. She's special. Actually, I'm envious you're getting her for a partner and I'm not.''

Linc remained sitting lazily on the desk, hands resting against his thighs. "Luck of the draw, I guess,'' he said in a neutral tone. Brie reappeared, drying her hands on a towel. It struck him deeply how domesticated she really was, and that knowledge sent a ribbon of warmth through him.

"Hey, Brie, what happened to your bedroom door?'' Jeff asked. "Did you run into it last night?''

Brie froze, all the happiness slipping from her eyes, her face draining of color. She flashed a pleading look at Linc.

"When we got home last night it was stuck shut,'' Linc lied in an off-the-cuff tone, rising to his feet. "I used a little too much force unsticking it and nearly took it off the bottom hinge.''

Jeff nodded, standing. "This is an old house. I told Brie

one day it would start shifting on its foundation and then the windows and doors would start jamming.''

Linc saw relief flood Brie's waxen features. Obviously, Jeff knew nothing of her emotional problems from the explosion. He reached out, guiding Jeff out of the room and away from the sore spot of conversation. Brie didn't need any more stress than was already hanging over her head like a scimitar. ''Look, there's the Sunday paper on top of that rolltop desk in the living room. Would you mind getting it for me?'' Linc asked Jeff.

''Sure. Tell you what. My pickup is parked out front. I'll get the paper and meet you out there so we can start your house hunt.'' Jeff leaned over, kissing Brie's cheek. ''See you later, doll face.''

Brie barely nodded, her dark eyes centered on Linc as they stood in the dim hall. How easily Linc had lied for her benefit. And if she hadn't known it was a lie, she would have accepted his explanation without questioning it. Uneasy, Brie tried to shake the feeling of wariness toward Linc.

Linc forced a grin. ''That's not a good line to pull on the ladies today, in case you wanted to know,'' he told Jeff.

''Oh?'' Crestfallen, Jeff shrugged. ''Well, cross that one off my list. How about if I run them all by you this afternoon? You can tell me which ones are in and which ones are out.''

''You've got a deal,'' Linc agreed amiably. He waited until Jeff disappeared before turning toward Brie. She tried to slip by him, the towel clutched in her hand.

''Wait a minute,'' he called to her softly, gripping her upper arm and bringing her to a halt. He saw the terror in her eyes as he swung her around. ''Look,'' he began, ''I know this isn't the time or place to talk about what happened last night, but—''

"Please, Linc," she begged, her voice strained, "not now. Not ever." She tried to shore up her dissolving defenses, barely able to hold his compassionate blue gaze. "Thanks for not telling Jeff the truth. He…doesn't know."

No, and neither does anyone else, little cat. But somehow, someway, you've got to let go of all that hell you're carrying around inside of you. Linc was aware of the softness of her flesh and gentled his grip on her arm. He kept his voice low and quiet. "Will you be all right here by yourself this afternoon?"

Brie gave him a shocked look. "Of course. Why?"

He gave her a slight smile. "I'm just being protective of you after what happened, Brie. You're more affected by this incident than I had realized."

Tears ached in her throat, and Brie tore herself away from Linc, blindly moving past him to escape. "I'll be okay. Now just get out of here and find a place to live."

Linc digested the desperation and pain in Brie's tone. He wanted to stay and hash out the nightmare that stayed with her. But another, wiser part of him stemmed this inclination. He would have to get Brie's trust before he could try to defuse that mass of terror she carried. Time, he told himself, heading toward the front door. Time and patience.

Brie tried her best to hide her agitation when they returned. She was in the back yard with the barbecue. Jeff waved to her. What a difference between them, Brie thought. Linc walked with long, deliberate strides, his gaze restlessly scanning right, left then toward her. He was always looking around, checking things out. That wasn't normal for most people, and Brie tried to explain his alertness on his Marine Corps experience. She felt heat move into her cheeks and avoided his intense eyes. Thank God, he wouldn't be staying with her tonight.

"Hey, guess what, Brie?" Jeff said, coming up to inspect the eight chicken breasts that were close to being done over the coals of the barbecue.

"What?" she asked dryly, barely raising her head to acknowledge Linc's presence. Her heart was thundering away at a gallop.

"Linc found a real nice apartment only two blocks from here. Man, we must have gone to at least fifteen places before he found this one."

"Two blocks?" she repeated stupidly. Only two blocks? What kind of bad luck was following her?

"Just one hitch," Jeff said, reaching out and tasting the sauce in the bowl beside the chicken. He licked his lips and smiled. "Man, you make the best sauce."

Brie stared at Linc, but his face was unreadable. "What hitch?" she ground out.

Jeff sat at the wooden picnic table nearby, spreading out the plates, utensils and napkins. "He can't move in for a week. They're still painting it and stuff." Jeff turned. "I'd offer Linc my place, but you know I live up in the attic and it's a one-room studio. I told Linc how you let me stay with you that week when I was trying to find a place to live. So I figured you'd make him the same offer." He gave her a sheepish smile. "Hope you didn't mind me telling him it was okay if he uses your couch for the rest of the week."

The brush trembled in her hand. Had Linc put Jeff up to it? He was capable of that. First anger then despair flooded her. Numbly, Brie brushed the last coating of sauce on the chicken, then started to pick the pieces up with the tongs. If she tried to back out, Jeff would be embarrassed, not to mention herself. Linc wouldn't care. He'd taken a few on the nose before and survived. But one look into Jeff's animated face and Brie lost the heart to chastise him for his decision. Wasn't she trying to teach him good leadership? He had accurately assessed the situation and come up with what he thought was a good solution. Technically, it was. Emotionally, Brie felt a clawing sensation moving up through her, and she wanted to scream. She knew Linc would corner her sooner or later about her nightmares. And what if she had them again while he was there? She never knew when they would hit.

"No, it's okay," she said in a barely audible voice.

Jeff frowned, getting up and taking the platter of chicken.

"Sure? You're looking might peaked, Brie."

Linc was watching Brie closely from where he had sat down. The tension sizzled palpably around them. He knew and she knew. Jeff was floundering, realizing he had done something wrong, but he didn't know quite what. Linc felt his heart wrench as he met and held Brie's bleak stare, then he savagely destroyed the emotion. Brie was hiding something, and he wanted to get to the bottom of it.

Jeff waved goodbye from his truck and disappeared around the corner, swallowed up by the line of trees. Linc stood on the front porch, hands on his hips. The sun had set and the sky was a lush pink, reminding Linc of the color of Brie's cheeks. She had eaten little of the meal and had kept silent except when spoken to directly. He felt like a first-class jerk for camping under her roof. But it was necessary. It would give him the time he needed to thoroughly investigate her and the premises and, he hoped, come up with some clues on who had killed John Holcomb. He pushed several dark strands of hair off his brow, turning and going inside the house.

Brie was busy in the kitchen, an apron tied around her slender waist. She was up to her elbows in soapsuds, and Linc wandered over. He picked up a towel and began drying the dishes in the drainer.

"If word ever got back to my ex-wife that I'm helping do dishes, she'd die," he said, trying to relieve the tension between them.

"A woman's work is in the kitchen, is that it?"

He nodded amiably, giving her a warm smile meant to get her to relax. It didn't work. "Yeah, something like that."

"I suppose you wanted her barefoot and pregnant, too?"

His grin was genuine. Brie's sense of humor was still intact, thank God. "Maybe at one time."

She scrubbed the bowl hard, obviously trying to hide her nervousness. "Did you want kids?" she asked.

"No."

"Why?"

"I don't know. Maybe because I had such a rotten childhood that I never wanted to see another kid have to scratch and claw like I did to make it."

Brie raised her chin, her jade eyes meeting his. "Your child wouldn't have. He or she would have had you and your wife for parents."

"I was never home because of my job," he grumbled. Well, Linc reasoned, she was responding, and some of the terror was draining from her face. He never discussed his personal life on an assignment. He always fabricated a cover. But if it was going to get Brie to trust him, then it was worth opening up.

"I see," she said.

"I really don't dislike kids."

"I know."

He stopped wiping a plate as he stared at her. "How?"

"At noon, when I fed Homely Homer, I could tell you were enjoying her despite your protests. The look in your face, I guess."

He resumed drying the dishes with a snort. "I'm just a sucker for orphans, is all."

"I like that about you," she said softly.

A shaft of pleasure and shock hit him simultaneously. He was surprised at how happy he was over her admission. "That wasn't a line?" he teased.

Brie shook her head, pulling the sink stopper out so the suds and water could drain. "Jeff is the one practicing the lines, not me," she said, trying to smile. Maybe Linc wasn't going to bring up the nightmare. God, please don't let him do it.

"That's something I like about you. You're honest as the day is long."

Brie met his smiling eyes, sinking into his warmth and absorbing it. "What's the matter, don't you think women aren't normally honest?"

He completed drying the dishes and hung the towel over the handle of one of the drawers. "In my experience, women say one thing and mean another." And as an agent, honesty wasn't his policy. It could get him killed. Still, his conscience nudged him a bit because Brie seemed incapable of lying or being dishonest—so far.

She turned to him, wiping her lower arms. "And I suppose you never do, Tanner?"

Picking up her challenge, Linc reached out, his fingers outlining her cheek and delicate jaw line. He saw shock in her eyes, and her lips parted beneath his unexpected action. "That's one thing you'll find out about me—I'm honest. The truth may hurt, but it's better than the alternative." Guilt pricked at him. Containing the unexpected feeling Brie brought out in him made him scowl. Suspects shouldn't get under his skin, but somehow, Brie had.

He reluctantly dropped his hand to his side. Brie's flesh was soft and pliable, and he ached to continue his featherlight exploration of her. His body was going rigid at just that fleeting touch. The look in her eyes melted his professional intent, and he no longer tried to deny his building hunger for her. "Like now," he said, his voice dark like thick honey. "I've been wanting to reach out and touch you all day. To tell you that everything is going to work out. I don't like what I see in your eyes, Brie." His brows fell. "And I wish there was some way I could help you…" What the hell was happening? Linc caught himself and pulled back.

Brie lifted her fingers, resting them against her cheek where he had caressed it with his work-worn hand. A new ache throbbed to life deep within her, and she recognized the heady warmth that enveloped her. Linc was affecting her, and she didn't have time to sort out anything. She took a step away from him, folding the towel with deliberate movements. "Sometimes you have to go through a particular experience alone, Linc."

He shook his craggy head, holding her brittle eyes, which were marred with confusion. "Listen to me, Brie. In my thirty-three years of life, I've faced just about every kind of traumatic situation you want to name, including the losing of my partner. I was able to work through some of them by myself. On others, I needed help. Emotional support." His voice grew husky. "Don't shut yourself off from people who love and respect you. They can help in their own way if you let them…"

He had said enough. More than enough, judging by her startled reaction. Thoroughly disgusted with himself and his lapse of being on guard, Linc excused himself and went to the living room. He turned on the television. The overpowering urge to reach out, to drag Brie into his arms and hold her was eating him up alive. When had any woman affected him as Brie did? Never. With a grimace, he sat on the couch, idly watching the show on television, his mind on anything but that.

For an hour Linc sat there, embroiled in an emotional quandary. Restless, he got up. He wandered into the kitchen. It was empty. He looked out the window toward the back yard. Brie wasn't there. Getting concerned, he ambled toward the hall. Her bedroom was dark, with the door still ajar. There was a light beneath the closed door of Homely Homer's room, and he walked quietly up to it. Homer was whistling softly and Linc smiled, remembering what Brie had told him earlier—the little bird was happy. He knocked softly at the door, then opened it.

Brie was sitting in an overstuffed chair opposite the door, pocket book in hand. She tried to give him a slight smile.

"This is where I do my reading," she explained.

Linc noted how Brie looked calmer and less out of sorts. "I just got worried about where you might be."

She placed the novel in her lap, her lips curving. "Tell me something, Tanner. Are you a great big watchdog the chief has sent to hover over me?"

He felt heat in his cheeks. If only she knew how close to the truth she was. Linc ruefully shoved his hands into the pockets of his jeans. "Nah, just my normal protective mechanism coming out. Why? Does it bother you?"

Brie shifted position, curling her long legs beneath her. "It just feels strange. I'm not used to having someone care openly about me, that's all."

Linc went over to the large bookshelf that dominated the back wall. Most of the books were on chemistry, hazardous material or fire sciences. He leaned down to the bottom shelf. "What's this? Romance novels?" His mouth quirked, and he slid a glance in Brie's direction. She arched one brow.

"That's what I happen to be reading right now."

His grin increased as he straightened. "I'd never have believed it. You, of all people."

"Now what kind of crack is that? I happen to enjoy a few really good writers, and they just happen to write for a particular category."

"Are we getting defensive?"

"Not in the least," Brie shot back, relaxing beneath his banter. "You'd be surprised to know that these books can educate."

His cobalt eyes darkened with mirth. "Yeah, I'll bet they do."

"You're such a pervert on top of being a chauvinist, Tanner."

He held up his hands, enjoying their exchange. When Brie wasn't on guard, she was delightful, making him feel lighter and happier than he'd felt in a long time. "Guilty as charged, I suppose." He walked over and took the book from her hands, studying it. "Look at this cover. And you call me perverted? With two people in a clinch like that, I'd think *you're* the pervert." He handed the novel back to her.

Brie gave him a bored look. "Typical male. You're so good at casting stones at something you haven't even made the effort to research first." She waved a hand toward the bookcase. "Read one before you hand me your assessment. I hope you don't analyze haz-mat situations in the same haphazard fashion, Tanner, or we're all in trouble."

Saucy little cat, I like your style. "That's logical of you." He went to the bookcase and squatted, perusing the section containing the romance novels. "Okay, for a first-time reader of these things, which one do you suggest?"

Brie gave him a stunned look. "You're serious?"

"Yeah. We'll discuss the issue of romance novels tomorrow morning over coffee."

A smile glimmered in her eyes. "You? Alert at breakfast? This I have to see."

He ignored her jab. "Okay, which author?"

She uncurled like a cat and came to join him, their shoulders almost touching as she knelt beside him. "Let's see...there's one author here whose books can be read by a man or a woman. You'll probably like her style. She has a lot of adventure and suspense in her books." Brie pulled one off the shelf. "This one is about test pilots. Even my brother, Steve, who's a first lieutenant in the Air Force, enjoyed it." She put the book in his awaiting hand.

Linc slowly rose. "Was your brother a doubting Thomas about these things like I am?"

"Dyed-in-the-wool doubter," she agreed, going to the chair. "He now reads the books by this author that I send to him. Religiously." She sat, watching Linc as he stared at the cover then read the back-cover blurb.

"Give me the keys to the white whale," he said.

Brie frowned. The haz-mat truck was always locked when they weren't using it. "Whatever for?"

"I'm going to take some of the tools from the kit and repair that bedroom door for you."

Her heart dropped, and she stared at him. She could find no trace of any emotion in his face. "Well, I could repair it," she managed to say.

"No. I did it, so I'll fix it." Then he added a smile that reached his eyes, making her feel warm all over. "And I know you can probably repair it just as well if not better than me, but you're busy."

There was so much Linc could have said to wound her or to probe more deeply into the wounds within her, but he didn't. He was keeping the conversation light for her benefit. "I don't call reading for pleasure busy. I'll just—"

Linc leaned down, pressing his hand firmly against her shoulder so she couldn't rise. "I said I'll do it. Just tell me where the keys are."

Brie avoided his gaze. "On a hook over the sink." She was wildly aware of his hand, her flesh burning beneath his touch. For an instant, Brie wanted to drop her book, lift her arms, slide them around his neck and draw him close to her.

Removing his hand, Linc nodded. "Okay. Just stay here and rest."

"But—"

"Damn, woman, do you always have to have the last word?" he asked, moving to the door.

Brie watched Linc's easy gait. He was a broad-shouldered man sculpted with muscle. She felt buoyant beneath his teasing. "I guess I don't." His returning smile devastated her screamingly aware senses.

"That's more like it. I always like to see a woman who knows her place."

"Linc Tanner! You get out of here before I throw this book at you!"

Chuckling, he closed the door quietly behind him. He stopped smiling and felt worry churning within him. So, he had the ability to lift her out of her quagmire. And she was responding beautifully, like a purring cat who loved his touch. Disgruntled, Linc came to the realization that he was attracted to Brie on a personal level. This wasn't supposed to happen. He had to rise above his needs, which Brie had effortlessly tapped into. Had she done it on purpose? Or was she innocent, responding to him because she needed a little support? Linc firmly rejected the possibility that Brie was genuinely drawn to him, man to woman. Tossing the romance novel on the kitchen table, he went to the haz-mat truck and got the toolbox.

It was nearly ten o'clock when he finished repairing the bottom hinge on Brie's bedroom door. She hadn't emerged from the other room all that time, and Linc suspected she was too uncomfortable about the situation to be up and about. Later, around eleven, Linc went to the room and gave a soft knock. Receiving no answer, he gently opened the door.

Linc's heart began a slow pound as he stepped inside the room. Brie was curled up and asleep in the chair, her head resting against the overstuffed fabric, the novel barely held between her long fingers. Linc removed the book from her grip and laid it on top of the bookcase. He placed his hand on her arm. He felt the texture of the cotton blouse and her supple flesh beneath it.

"Brie?"

She stirred slightly.

Linc watched her for several moments. He didn't have the heart to wake her. Let her sleep. He slipped his hands beneath her back and legs and lifted her easily. She weighed next to nothing, he thought in alarm. Her head lolled against his jaw and he absorbed the soft curves of her womanly form against him. He was aware of the sandalwood scent to her skin and inhaled it deeply. Was it perfume? He felt her stir, her hands coming to rest against his chest.

"It's all right, Brie," he told her quietly. "I'm taking you to bed."

"Bed?" she slurred.

Linc pushed the door open with his foot. "That's right, bed." He heard Brie mumble something, but he was unable to understand it. She relaxed totally within his arms, and it made him feel good. Trust was being established.

He laid her on the bed and drew the quilt over her. Another shield enclosing his heart melted away as he watched her slide into the embrace of sleep. The urge to lean down and lightly brush her full, parted lips was excruciating. Linc pushed his fingers through his hair, agitated with all the feelings Brie was bringing to life in him. He walked to the door and left it ajar. If she was going to have any nightmares, he wanted to be able to reach her quickly. Good night, he told her silently. How he wished he was beside her....

Chapter Five

Brie awoke, feeling at peace. She stretched, uncoiling from her position, vaguely aware of dawn light peeking through the windows. What time was it? Turning her head, she stared at the luminous dials of the clock on the bed stand. Six-fifteen. Time to get up. As she sat up and realized she was still dressed, Brie frowned. Then the events of the night before returned to her. She remembered being carried by Linc. She recalled his low, vibrating voice, the strength of his chest that her hands had rested upon and a delicious feeling of being cared for.

Care? Her jade eyes narrowed as she considered where that word had come from. Closing her eyes, Brie allowed all the feelings that had come to her as Linc carried her to appear. She didn't remember all their conversation, only that she felt warm and lovingly cared for. Ridiculous, she told herself. She was old enough to know the difference between love and sexual attraction. And Linc was definitely sensual. It was nothing more than physical attraction, she told herself sternly. Besides, her instincts still shouted a warning to her, and until that feeling was explained, she could never fully trust him. Rubbing her face, Brie got to her feet and went to the closet to select a clean uniform. She tried to sidestep the fact that yesterday, her opinion of Linc had altered drastically. Linc was a loner because he had never been wanted. Yet he still had the ability to reach out and try to help her. That spoke of his sensitivity and unselfishness as a human being.

The lukewarm shower helped awaken her. Brie towel dried, splashed on her favorite perfume, then dressed. She continued to dwell on her budding emotional fusion with Linc. The feelings were there, whether she wanted to admit it or not. Looking at herself in the steamy mirror, Brie wondered what he saw in her. She had mouse-brown hair, now short because it had been burned off by the explosion. There was nothing exceptional about her face except for her eyes. Her mother had always told her she had lovely eyes. She wasn't built like a voluptuous woman. Instead, her breasts were small and her hips and rear only vaguely hinted that she was a woman.

"You're not a prize, Williams," she told herself out loud. "But you have other assets." She smiled because she was content to be herself and not a raving beauty depicted in so many magazines.

Brie halted at the entrance to the living room. Linc lay on the couch, too long for it, his knees drawn up beneath the pale yellow quilt, which barely covered his lower body. Her gaze moved to his naked torso, dark-haired chest and broad shoulders. Last night, she had lain on that magnificent chest. In sleep, Linc looked vulnerable, and an ache seized her. His beard shadowed his features, making his cheeks more hollow than they actually were. The dark growth gave him a powerful look, and she trembled. Brie longed to walk over, kneel down and gently trace each of those lines that life had etched in his face. She suddenly wanted to talk at length with him and ask about each one, and how it had gotten there. She wanted to know him better.

With a shake of her head, Brie wondered if moon madness was upon her. Never had any man shaken her to the core as Linc did whenever he looked at her with those thoughtful blue eyes of his. Each time, Brie felt as if he was gazing past all the walls she had erected and was clearly seeing her. But there was something else in those eyes that held secrets, and it bothered her. Tucking all those warm and disturbing thoughts away about Linc, Brie forced herself to switch to work mode. Much had to be done today—and that wasn't including possible haz-mat calls. First, coffee. And then she'd get Linc up.

The aromatic smell of coffee pulled Linc from his sound sleep. He grimaced, his back in a knot because of the lumpy cushions he slept upon. He barely opened his eyes. At first, he didn't believe what he saw. Then he forced himself to concentrate. Brie was standing in front of him, a welcoming smile on her lips, holding out a cup of coffee to him. He stared through his spiky lashes at her soft, pliant mouth, and a stab of yearning surged through him. He wanted to kiss her, to feel just how lush her red, inviting lips really were. His brain fogged and he blinked again.

"There's no secret to how a woman gets you to wake up," she said, placing the mug of coffee on the lamp table near his head. "It's six-forty, Linc. Time to get up."

Linc watched her turn with that feline grace that fed his hunger for her. She looked so damned good in that dark blue one-piece uniform. How did any man she worked with keep his hands or his eyes to himself? The scent of the coffee delighted his nostrils, and he inhaled deeply. Brie sure knew how to cater to him. For no particular reason, a lopsided smile tugged at the corners of his mouth as he levered himself into a sitting position. He pushed unruly strands of hair off his brow and gratefully took the mug in his hands, cradling it reverently. He owed Brie one for her thoughtfulness.

After an eye-opening cold shower and shave, Linc felt semihuman. For the first time, he wore the dark blue one-piece haz-mat uniform. Last night, he had sewn on the required patches with needle and thread he found near the sewing machine. Of course, the red thread didn't match, but he didn't care. The silver name tag went over his right breast pocket and the silver badge over the left one. Linc felt strange when he stared at himself in the mirror. In reality, he was a government agent and had his real badge stashed away in his apartment in D.C. It was odd to be undercover and assuming a law-enforcement identity. It didn't dissolve the fact that Brie believed in what he was, and the misrepresentation ate at him. Maybe on another case, where there was clear demarcation between himself and those committing an obvious crime, it wouldn't bother him at all. Today it did, in a very deep and disturbing way. Brie could be a killer. He had to erect those guards to protect his life and continue to play the game with her. But where did the game begin and end? The lines were blurred, and Linc felt uneasy.

He ambled to the kitchen, cup in hand. Brie was sitting at the table, chin resting in the palm of one hand, studying a clipboard before her. Soft waves of hair caressed her brow and framed her cheeks. He thought she looked beautiful, but he kept his heated, simmering comments to himself.

"Good morning," he said, heading to the coffeepot on the counter.

Brie met his greeting with a crooked smile. "I keep wondering what you'll be like when you have to take a call in the middle of the night."

He snorted as he poured himself another cup. He turned, saw that her cup was empty and poured her another one. Settling himself at the table near her elbow, he drank in Brie's radiant face. "You'd better have that quart thermos filled to the hilt with coffee before we leave or we'll both be in big trouble," he joked. Linc couldn't hold back the compliments that he wanted to give her. It seemed the more personal he became, the more she dropped the walls she hid behind.

"I never realized a woman could look so good without makeup," he told her in a husky voice.

Brie stared in shock for just a second, caught off guard. "Why, thank you."

His smile tore at her senses. "You're welcome. This coffee sure hits the spot. You make a good cup, lady."

She colored prettily and pretended to concentrate on the task before her. "Strictly self-preservation, believe me. I can't seem to get started without it, either."

He rubbed his jaw, content to share the quiet of the morning with her. "I wonder if it has anything to do with the stress of our jobs? High stress means a lot of adrenaline flowing. Coffee's a natural upper when you're running low on adrenaline."

"Makes sense. Trauma junkies always have their fix of coffee or cigarettes," Brie observed.

He gave her a wry look, thinking how much a good night's sleep had erased the shadows beneath those lovely green eyes of hers that glimmered with flecks of gold. "Healthwise, coffee is the lesser of two evils."

"Amen," Brie agreed fervently.

"You sleep okay last night?" he asked after a few moments.

She nodded, her heart picking up. "Yes. Thank you for tucking me in last night. I was dead to the world."

"It was a pleasure, believe me," Linc said, meaning it. He saw her cheeks turn pinker, and smiled more broadly.

"Stop enjoying my discomfort so much, Tanner. Few people get to see me sacked out on a chair."

"I thought you looked kind of nice sleeping in it." He slid her a wicked glance. "I had considered waking you up like Sleeping Beauty."

Brie pursed her full lips and barely held his gaze. How many times had she wondered what it would be like to feel his strong mouth against hers? Brie tried to ignore the yearning in her body. The man carried secrets. Until he showed all of himself to her, Brie had to try to combat her attraction to him. "The day I'm Sleeping Beauty is the day Miss Piggy will win the Miss America contest," she told him archly.

Linc started to laugh but stopped when he realized she was serious. "Well," he drawled, "guess I'll have to prove to you that in my eyes, you're a Sleeping Beauty and not bacon on the hoof."

Brie rose, unable to stand his closeness. She went to the counter, hoping to hide her nervousness. "Jeff should be here any minute now."

"You start at seven every morning?"

She automatically went through the motions of making beef sandwiches for three people. She had to do something, anything, to quell her nerves. "Take a look at the clipboard. It's a list of companies we've got to check. At the bottom are the classes Jeff and I will be giving to the various fire departments in our quadrant this week."

He dragged the clipboard over to him. The number of companies listed was staggering. "I was wondering what you did with your spare time," he groused.

She put a sandwich into a plastic bag and set it to one side. The world beyond the curtained window was stained with a lovely apricot dawn. "If we don't get any haz-mat calls, we can make all of them this week."

"But you always get calls."

"Sometimes we get a quiet week."

"My luck won't hold."

She smiled absently, placing a bag of potato chips and a jar of sweet gherkins into a huge grocery sack along with the sandwiches. "I'm not Irish, either, so you can count on at least one haz-mat incident."

Linc perused the list with more than a little interest. Brie was efficient and organized. Each company had been checked at three-month intervals. He twisted his head to the left, watching her work. A blanket of contentment washed over him. What would it be like to wake up every morning with Brie? The idea was tantalizing. "On an average, how many haz-mat calls do you get a week?"

"Three."

Linc groaned.

"Now, that may include something as simple as checking out old chemicals in a high-school biology department to a full-scale incident. Saturday was considered a full-blown incident." She shrugged her shoulders and added three bright red apples to the sack.

"What are you doing? Preparing to feed an army?"

"No. Just two men who have the appetite of growing boys, is all," she answered blandly, setting the bag on the table. She went over to the coffeepot and filled her battered aluminum thermos.

"You make lunch every day?"

"Yes. Most of the time we're nowhere near a McDonald's or Wendy's. And if we get a call, no one feeds you during the hours you're working. You can't just shimmy out of your gas suit and drive down to the nearest fast-food joint and order a hamburger, then get back to the site."

Linc's eyes glimmered. "Pity. No wonder you're so skinny. You starve to death out there in the field. Jeff's built like a toothpick, too."

She laughed. "Don't worry, Linc, I'll make sure you're well fed."

"How did you know the way to my heart was through my stomach?"

"Oh, please," she said in an exasperated tone. "You're as obvious as a charging bull elephant, Linc."

He was rather pleased with the analogy. He watched her make another pot of coffee. "Thanks," he murmured.

Brie cocked one eyebrow. "I wouldn't be taking it as a compliment if I were you."

There was a knock at the back door and they both turned. Jeff waved and came in, dressed in his uniform. Before he was able to get out his greeting, the phone on the wall rang. Linc saw Brie's face close as she walked over to answer it. Jeff raised his hand in greeting and zeroed in on the grocery bag.

"Bad news," Jeff warned Linc in a conspiratorial tone, motioning toward Brie.

"Why?"

"The chief knows we meet over here at Brie's at seven sharp every morning. If something serious is up, he calls us here." Jeff grimaced. "It's gonna be a bad week if we're gettin' called by the chief this early."

Linc turned his attention to Brie, who was leaning against the wall, her features sober as she talked in a low voice. What was up? he wondered. Finally, she hung up the phone, her lips thinned.

"Jeff, that was the chief. You're to drive down to Reynoldsberg right now."

"What?" he crowed in disbelief.

Brie came to the table, pulling out three beef sandwiches and an apple. "Yeah," she answered in a clipped tone, anger in her voice. "Jim McPeak's partner, Bob Townley, just got slapped into the hospital with injuries from that train derailment near Englewood." She met Jeff's widening eyes. "You're heading south, Laughlin, so close your mouth and take this for your lunch. Where you're going, you're going to need it."

"But I haven't finished my training," he protested.

Brie tried to control her anger. The chief had already boxed her into a corner by forcing Tanner on her. Now he was taking her right hand away from her. "It doesn't matter, Jeff," she said patiently. "Come on, I'll walk you to your truck. There isn't time to waste right now. McPeak needs you." I need you, she thought angrily. Tanner knew nothing of procedures except as a fire fighter, which didn't mean much. Brie wanted to slam her fist into something just to relieve the frustration she felt. Saxon was taking advantage of her, and they both knew it. Why couldn't he have taken one of the other qualified people in Quadrant Two or Three?

Linc watched Brie leave, feeling her fury. He got up, picked up the grocery sack and headed out the door to the white whale. Minutes later, she appeared with Homely Homer in her cage, a jar of baby food and the thermos in the other hand.

Wisely, Linc said nothing as he opened the back door of the truck for Brie. She gently set the cage in a corner, holding it in place with a black rubber strap. She stepped out and he shut the doors and locked them. Until the pigeon was able to fly and hunt for its own food, Brie took the bird with her every day.

"Get in, I'll drive," he told her.

Brie glowered at him as if deciding whether to rip his head off or simply chew him out with a choice expletive.

"Come on," he coaxed. "The mood you're in, you'll get us killed." He saw Brie's eyes lighten and she lifted her chin, taking a deep breath.

"You're probably right," she muttered. "Okay, you drive."

Once on the road and heading toward their first stop, a chemical company outside Canton, Linc broke the brittle, icy silence. "For whatever it's worth, I'm sorry this happened, Brie. I know I'm not much use to you—yet. If I hit the manuals hard this week, maybe I'll be able to relieve you from some of that load you're having to carry all by yourself."

Brie's features softened, and she glanced at him. "Don't mind me, Linc. Every once in a while I need to sulk like a child and get it out of my system. Coffee?"

He grinned, giving her a tender look laced with care. "I think we both could use a shot."

She gave an unladylike snort, unscrewing the cap of the thermos with angry jerks. "A shot of something. Damn, I'm so mad I could spit nails!"

"Let's talk about it, then. No sense in bottling it up inside you." Maybe he'd get a bit more information.

Brie handed him his cup then poured coffee into it. "You don't deserve this kind of welcome into your new career slot!" She slid the thermos between their chairs, put both feet on the dash, scrunched down and glared straight ahead. "I'll tell you, sometimes, this job is the armpit of the universe. I hate getting screwed around like this by management. They should have taken a more seasoned veteran from one of those other quadrants to help Mc-Peak.''

"You don't think Jeff can handle it?''

"Yes, he can handle it. He may come off carefree, but Jeff is thorough and careful. Those two things will save your neck every time out.''

"Who's Bob Townley?'' Linc wanted to know.

"Him!'' Brie growled. "Bob's long on guts and short on common sense. Sometimes I could just throttle him. I'll lay you odds he got too close to one of those tank cars and breathed in that stuff. He's in the hospital with lung congestion because of it.''

"How serious?''

She gave a bitter laugh. "Don't worry. Bob hasn't bought it yet, and he's been in haz-mat for almost twenty years. He takes a hell of a lot of chances, but has always walked away.'' Her lips compressed. "This time he didn't.''

Linc divided his attention between the swelling morning rush hour of Canton traffic and Brie. "You might take Saxon's choice as a backhanded compliment to you,'' Linc offered, hoping to make her feel better.

Brie slid him a glare. "This better be good, Tanner. How?''

"You must be an ace at training people, or he'd never have taken Jeff over seasoned vets. That's a compliment to you.''

He was right, Brie decided. "Just pretend you don't know me for the next hour or two, okay, Tanner? When I get in one of these moods, I'm a brat to everyone around me. So just ignore me.''

He reached over, gently massaging her tense shoulder for a moment. "Lady, you're hard to ignore under any circumstances." Then he smiled. "Besides, I think you look provocative as hell when you pout."

She gave him an exasperated look. "Tanner, you really are a pervert!"

His laughter rolled through the van. Brie tried to hide her smile, but it didn't quite work. She'd never admit it, but Linc knew how to ease her anger. "You always this good at dealing with people?" she demanded tightly.

"Just people I like," he amended, trying very hard to remain innocent-looking.

Brie shook her head and drank her coffee. "Well, for better or worse, Tanner, you and I are stuck with one another."

"Don't make it sound as if we're married. I think I'm getting cold feet already."

She met his amused blue gaze, drowning in the warmth that he was lavishing upon her. And she hadn't forgotten when he reached out and slid his hand across her shoulder in an effort to soothe her. Hope sprang strongly in her heart as she looked at him. There was a vein of pure gold running through him, she realized. She lifted her cup toward him in toast. "I owe you one, Linc."

He nodded, his mouth quirking in a grin. "Okay, I'll remember that and collect soon."

A startling coil of heat sizzled through Brie at the inference in Linc's softly spoken words. She gave him a wry look but said nothing. "Well, the day's off to a fine start," she griped. "Let's just see how far downhill this baby is going to slide."

At nine o'clock Brie entered the office of Carter Fuel and Oil of Lisbon, Ohio, and was met by the owner, Frank Carter. Tall and lean, at thirty-five, he was a proud, handsome man. He scowled darkly from where he sat at his desk behind the counter.

"What the hell's up?" Carter demanded, standing. "You were here just three months ago."

Brie gave Carter a brisk smile meant to defuse his initial reaction. Many companies panicked when a haz-mat official walked in to inspect their premises. "Our quarterly inspection, Mr. Carter."

Frank moved to the counter that separated them. He looked at Tanner, and then focused his attention on Brie. "Look, this is ridiculous, Miss Williams."

Instinctively, Linc moved to Brie's elbow in defense of her. "Mr. Carter, I don't think you have anything to get upset about."

Carter glared at him. "I sell fuel oil, not hazardous chemicals. The fire marshal's office ought to be more interested in the chemical companies up the river from me than my small company." Out of frustration, he looked at Brie. "Don't you think this is ridiculous? Every three months you drop in here unannounced?"

Brie held on to her patience. "We realize fuel oil is low on the hazardous material list, but we'd like to check out the trucks, just to make sure they aren't leaking any oil, Mr. Carter. It won't take long."

Disgruntled, the owner turned to his office manager. "Earl, go with them. I've got too much work to do to play these silly games with the state."

Earl, who was bald and fifty, nodded and quickly got to his feet. "Yes, sir, Mr. Carter!" He gave Brie a smile and hustled his rotund form around the counter. "Come with me, Brie. I'll take you over to the garage where we keep the trucks."

They crossed the hard-packed dirt yard and out of earshot of Earl, Linc asked, "Isn't Carter a little rabid about us checking his trucks?"

Shrugging, Brie said, "No, because every company we

visit gets upset. They're afraid of the fines we might levy.''
She gestured at the fenced-in area that contained several
buildings and trucks. ''He's right. Fuel oil companies are
low on our list of concerns, but Carter's business is on our
way to two chemical plants on the Ohio River.''

Linc smiled. ''Luck of the draw, eh?''

''Yes. Carter's got a clean record, but it doesn't hurt to
keep fuel oil companies on their toes. Sometimes a truck
will have a leak, and they get lazy and won't fix it. Oil on
a road can create an auto accident.''

A huge German shepherd came trotting over, wagging
his tail in a friendly fashion at Brie. She leaned down,
murmuring words to the animal. Linc remained alert, looking around, mentally making notes that he'd later put into
his own notebook of evidence.

Just as Brie and Linc were ready to leave the office of
the second chemical company, at the close of the day,
Brie's beeper went off. She asked to use the phone, and
the secretary nodded. Giving Linc a frustrated look, Brie
muttered, ''Beepers going off usually mean a major haz-
mat incident.''

Linc nodded. ''Calling the FM?''

''Yes.''

Brie heard the line connect and the chief answer.

''Chief? It's Brie. What's up?''

Saxon's voice came across worried. ''Brie, is Linc Tanner with you?''

Confused, Brie said, ''Yes, he's here.'' The unspoken
why was left in the silence between them.

''Let me speak to him, please?''

She held out the phone to Linc. ''Chief Saxon wants to
talk to you,'' she said, sliding out of the booth.

Linc's scowl deepened, surprise flaring momentarily in

his eyes. "Me?" Saxon always talked to Brie whenever a haz-mat spill was reported. "What's going on?" he muttered, gripping the phone.

Linc's grip tightened on the phone. Something was up. His gut knotted instinctively, and he glanced at Brie, who stood beside him with her arms crossed, eyes reflecting suspicion as to why the call was for him.

"Linc?"

"Yes, sir."

"I want you to get over to Carol Holcomb's residence right away. I just got a teletype message from your office in D.C. via the Canton police that her house has been torn apart. It appears that it was broken into while she was gone."

Grimly, Linc listened. "I see. Burglary?"

"Not according to the Canton detectives. Nothing is missing. Carol Holcomb called in tears to report the break-in to the police department. The house is apparently a shambles. It appears as though three or four people were looking for something. Just thank God she and her daughter weren't there when they broke in."

Linc broke into a cold sweat, his eyes never leaving Brie's face. His instincts were screaming danger so loudly. "When did this happen, sir?"

"Carol Holcomb left for the grocery store at four o'clock this afternoon and returned an hour and a half later. The police were called, and after a preliminary investigation, they sent a report to your office, as they had been instructed earlier when the ATF made their initial contact with them. I was then informed via the FM as to who you were. Your boss, Mr. Cramer, wants you to get over there and investigate. Talk to Mrs. Holcomb and see if you can find anything out. Then contact a Detective Brad Gent at Canton police. He'll let you read their reports. When you're done, contact Cramer and me. I want to know what the hell is happening. I'm not so sure Mrs. Holcomb's residence being broken into is a fluke. I want Brie protected. Her house could be next. We just don't know if this is an isolated incident or not.''

Linc's jaw tightened. ''Yes, sir. I'll do what I can. Goodbye.'' He hung up the phone, staring at it for several seconds before turning to face Brie and her questions. She couldn't know who he was. Not yet...

''The chief wants us to get back to Canton,'' Linc said, putting his hand on her arm and leading her out of the office. Outside, he said, ''Carol Holcomb's house has just been broken into.'' The color drained from Brie's face. For a fleeting second, he wondered if Brie knew something about it. He opened the door for her. She stared numbly at him.

''What do you mean, 'broken into'? Are Carol and Susie all right?''

He nodded patiently, coaxing her into the seat. ''They're fine. Tighten up that seat belt,'' he warned her.

The hour it took to get to Canton was reduced to forty minutes. Her fists were tightly clenched in her lap as she wondered how Carol really was. This was all they needed six months after John's death. Her brow furrowed as she looked at Linc's blunt features. It was on the tip of her tongue to ask him why the chief had called and asked for him. Why discuss the break-in with Linc and not her? She was too upset to think clearly and pushed the questions aside for now.

Brie's brows drew down as they approached the street she lived on. ''Linc, what are you doing? I thought we were going over to Carol's house.''

''We will. First I want to check something out.''

Confused, Brie stared at him. He had been silent all the

way back. The way he had driven, like a professional race-car driver, he had to devote all his concentration to the task. Why was he going to *her* house? Brie became even more confused when he made the van move very slowly up the tree-shrouded drive. Impatient, she rubbed her brow.

Linc's eyes narrowed as the house came into view at the end of the curve. There were no cars in the driveway other than Brie's Toyota. Everything looked peaceful and quiet. He'd know in a few minutes if someone had broken into her house. Casting a glance out of the corner of his eye at Brie, he realized she was fuming. He stopped the van.

"What are you doing parking this far from my house, Linc? What's going on? You're acting odd."

He took her impatience in stride, never allowing his gaze to leave the house. All the windows looked closed. The front door didn't look jimmied or tampered with. Maybe if they were lucky, her house hadn't been touched. "I want you to stay here, Brie," he told her, opening his door.

"What? Linc—"

He snapped his head to the right, pinning her with his narrowed cobalt gaze. "Stay here," he ordered in a low tone. "I don't want you out of this car for any reason unless I say so. Understood?"

Brie blinked, stunned by the coldness emanating from him. Her lips parted in shock, and she nodded. "All right."

A twist of a smile touched his mouth. "Just trust me."

Trust him, Brie thought, sitting like a caged tiger in the idling van. Why was Linc acting so odd and distant? She watched as he approached the back door to her house. The way he walked, the way he carried himself was entirely different from what she'd seen. Brie sat there, feeling stunned, getting more and more upset by the minute. The way Linc slowly opened the screen door and carefully unlocked the back entrance made her take whatever he was doing seriously. Her heartbeat picked up as he slid like a shadow through that slit and disappeared inside.

She fidgeted. Linc came out five minutes later, some of the harshness gone from his unreadable face. As he got into the van she couldn't help snapping, "Look, I want to get over to Carol's. I don't know why you stopped here. Now if you're done, can we go?"

Linc shot her a look and said nothing, turning the van around. "We'll be there in a few minutes." Brie's home had been untouched.

Carol gave a cry when she saw Brie at the front door. Making her way through the litter of debris on the floor, Carol said, "Brie, thank God, you're here!" and threw her arms around Brie.

Brie returned the embrace and felt shock go through her as she surveyed the living room. She was barely aware of Linc coming in after her.

"My God, Carol," she stammered, releasing the blond woman, "what happened?"

Carol rubbed her reddened eyes, streaked with mascara, and made a helpless gesture. "You tell me. The police have been here for hours questioning me." She sniffed. "Come on in, although I don't know where you can sit."

Brie's heart contracted when she realized Carol was trying to make a joke of the situation. "This is awful," she said, seeing the strain in Carol's pale face. "What about Susie?"

"As soon as I saw this, I called her grandmother. She came over and picked Susie up. I just couldn't let Susie see how badly the house is torn up." And then Carol sobbed. "Oh, Brie, this is frightening! First John's death and now this...this evil thing. What have I done to deserve all this?"

Linc remained in the background, watching Brie closely as she comforted Carol Holcomb. His instincts had taken over, and he moved through each room, cataloging all that he saw. Whoever had done the dirty work knew what they were doing. There wasn't a drawer unopened and turned over to spill out its contents, a closet not empty of clothing, shoes or toys. Mattresses were yanked off beds, baring the box springs. Pillows had been slit open with a very sharp knife, the goose feathers sprinkled throughout the bedrooms. He stood in the master bedroom, surveying the professional search that had taken place. What were they looking for? Did Brie know about the break-in? Or Carol? He turned and went downstairs, his face grim.

Brie looked up from the couch where she sat with an arm around Carol's shoulder. A thread of relief flickered through her. Linc looked so capable that she automatically felt safer in his presence. He came and knelt in front of Carol.

"Look, how about if we take you out and get you a cup of coffee or something, Mrs. Holcomb? Let's get away from this place for a while. Afterward, we'll bring you back, you gather up whatever you need for the next couple of days in the way of clothes and I'll get this place back into order for you."

Carol's face sagged with relief and gratefulness. "I couldn't let you do that, Mr. Tanner—"

"Call me Linc. And I think right now, after all you've gone through, you don't need to try to get this house straightened up by yourself."

Brie's grip on Carol's shoulder became firmer. "He's right, Carol. We'll call the chief and request tomorrow off.

We can clean this up for you.'' She wanted to cry because of Linc's generosity.

Linc saw the sunlight in Brie's wide eyes, and he managed a slight smile for her benefit. The house was a disaster area, and Brie looked so damn beautiful and untouched in it. A cold blade of terror crept up his spine. This could have happened to Brie's house. Or was Brie a part of this?

"Come on, let's get you that cup of coffee and we'll discuss what can be done to help you," he murmured, helping Carol stand.

Brie sat beside Linc in the restaurant booth, their legs brushing occasionally against each other. Linc had been right, the coffee was a good idea. Brie hadn't realized how upset she was until she felt her fingers tremble when she picked up the spoon to stir the cream and sugar. Linc saw it, but said nothing.

Carol gave them a grateful look. "I think I will take your offer of help. But I can't let you two do it by yourself."

Linc nodded. "Are you sure it won't be too upsetting?"

She shook her head. "Compared to John's death, nothing could ever be that upsetting," she murmured, "not even the house being ransacked."

"Carol," Linc began, "do you have any reason to suspect why someone might want to do this to you?"

"None. None at all. I just think it was a vicious gang of vandals. At least, that's what the police are saying."

They're lying through their teeth, Linc thought. He kept his voice low and coaxing. "Did John have any enemies?"

Carol gave him a weary look. "The police asked me the same thing. John was a good man. Just ask Brie. He loved her like the sister he never had. John didn't ever make enemies. He always made friends.''

"That's true," Brie volunteered, looking at Linc's harshly set features. "I was always the hard nose collecting the enemies. He wasn't.''

"What do you mean?"

Brie didn't like the edge in Linc's voice or his sudden interest in her statement. "Nothing, really," she muttered.

"No, what did you mean?"

Her nerves were frayed. "When I first started in hazmat, I was uncompromising with chemical companies who were breaking the law. Over the years, John taught me how to be less abrasive with the people we had to deal with, that's all.''

"Any names pop into your head who might have a reason to get even?" Linc held his breath.

Brie shrugged. "A few, like Bach Industries. Like I said, John smoothed the situations over and got the same things accomplished as I did, only with less abrasion. The ones that were guilty were heavily fined by the state.''

Linc turned his attention to Carol, who was looking extremely fatigued. He looked at his watch. It was nearly eight o'clock. "How about if we get you some overnight clothes and you can drive to your mother's house? Brie and I can start on the cleanup tonight, and you can join us tomorrow morning.''

Carol reached out, touching Linc's hand. "I think it's a great idea. Frankly, I'm so washed out by all this that I'm ready for some sleep.''

Brie's face softened. "Come on," she said, scooting out of the booth and rising, "let's get going then.''

Chapter Six

It was almost one in the morning when Brie staggered into the cleaned-up living room and flopped down on the couch. The house was quiet except for Linc working upstairs. He had asked her to put down the names of those companies who bore a grudge against the haz-mat office. Brie wrote for a short while, then gazed around, exhaustion pulling at her. She buried her hands in her face and took a long, deep breath.

That was the way Linc discovered her when he walked silently to the entrance of the room. Brie looked broken, her shoulders hunched, face buried in her hands, elbows resting on her knees. Did she know something she was hiding, and was it eating at her? He had claimed the opportunity to go through each room in the Holcomb house, looking at everything closely. Thus far, he had found nothing that indicated John Holcomb had something to hide. What about Brie? Did she know something John knew, and was it their secret? Grimly, he walked up to her and knelt in front of her.

"Hey," he called softly, pulling Brie's hands from her face, "let's go home. You're whipped."

Brie offered him a weary smile, strengthened by his attention and unexpected tenderness. He had been so hard, cold and efficient since returning to the Holcomb house, saying little, as if he were in a totally different world as he sifted through the debris. "You're right. I am."

"Come on, let's lock this place up and call it a night."

Brie pushed away from the couch. "I hope we have a quiet night."

"So do I," Linc said. If an emergency arose, their day off could disappear.

"I don't know about you, but I'm going to grab a shower when we get home," Linc said.

"Fine. I'll feed Homer, then go to bed."

Linc managed a slight smile. "Sounds good." Right now, his focus was elsewhere. He was staring at the sheet of paper Brie had written on. Later, he would take that list to the Canton police, use their computer facilities and tie into the ATF terminal.

It was nearly two o'clock when they arrived at Brie's home. She was the last in the door and shut it behind her.

"I told you to keep that door locked, Brie. Anybody could just walk in here."

Stung, she felt her cheeks flush with anger. Linc placed his canvas bag on the floor in the kitchen and walked over to her. He hadn't meant to rip her head off as soon as he got in the door. He settled his hands on her shoulders. "I'm sorry. I didn't mean to yell at you."

Brie resisted, holding his stormy gaze. "Why are you upset, Linc? I don't understand why you're so jumpy. Ever since Carol's house was vandalized—"

"It wasn't vandalized," he ground out, releasing her. It hurt that she resisted his apology, but what else could he expect? How would he react if she had walked in the door and jumped on him? He pushed his fingers through his hair, walking around the kitchen like a caged animal.

Brie crossed her arms, watching him. "What are you talking about?"

Linc halted at a chair and glanced at the table. A sharp ache centered in his chest. There was no way Brie was going to become a casualty in this case. He said, "First, John's suspicious death. Now John's house is torn apart. Why? What was he hiding?"

"Linc, **John** was hiding nothing!" Brie's voice grew strained as she stared at his hard, implacable features. "I don't know why you keep digging at me with that angle. He had nothing to hide! He was always aboveboard."

"All right," Linc continued in the same tone. "What about Jameson Chemical, Cordeman Transport or Bach Industries?"

She blinked. "Those are names from the list I gave you. They've all been fined by John and me. What about them?"

"Yeah, that's what I want to know from you. What about them, Brie? Remember me asking you if anyone had made any vague threats to you or John?"

Her temper was fraying. "Yes, I remember," she said, pronouncing each word emphatically, matching his grim posture.

"I asked you if any of them had reason to get even with you. A vendetta. And you said no." His knuckles whitened against the back of the chair he was resting them on.

Brie glared at him and turned away. "I gave you the list. What else did you want?" she snapped.

Linc's nostrils flared, and his eyes turned thundercloud

black. "According to your notes on these companies, Jameson has had to pay 1.5 million dollars in fines you leveled against them. Cordeman said 1.2 million, Bach 1.8 million. That is reason enough right there to want to wipe you and John off the face of this earth!" he said, walking toward her and gripping her shoulders.

A soft gasp escaped her, and she tried to twist free of Linc's capturing grasp. His sudden explosion of anger and action stunned her. "Let me go!"

"I'm not hurting you. Now stand still."

Anger warred with hurt in her as she stared at him. Suddenly, the man was a stranger to her. She felt the contained violence in him and thought it was aimed at her. He pinned her savagely with his eyes.

"Tell me about these three companies. In detail. Now." He released her and stepped away, waiting.

Brie rubbed her arm. Linc hadn't hurt her physically, but it felt like it. "You've got a problem, Linc," she shot back, her voice shaking with anger. "Earlier tonight you were sneaking around like some damn cop, and now you're giving me the third degree. Don't you think I had enough of that when I was recovering in the hospital? Don't you think I told those detectives at that time about those three companies you just mentioned?" Her eyes narrowed. "Just who the hell are you?"

Linc wanted to shake Brie, to tell her the truth. To tell her just how much danger he felt she was in. But he couldn't. Not yet. Not until he was satisfied she was completely innocent. She had to be hiding something! She was doing it for John because of their special relationship. His voice came out low and guarded. "I'm going to drop over to the police department and do a little snooping around. The fines levied by the attorney general's office against those companies are public record. Anyone can get the info if they're a little persistent. I want to see if I can dig up any information the detectives might have overlooked.''

Brie had backed against the counter, standing up to Linc. ''That still doesn't explain *your* behavior. Tonight when we came back to the house, you acted as if someone was in here just waiting for us. And then you went around checking every window and door latch. You never did that before when you were here.''

''Yes, I did. Only you didn't see me do it, Brie.''

Her eyes lost their anger. ''Why are you trying to frighten me?'' The words came out soft and strained. ''Don't you think I've suffered enough? I don't need you jumpy and nervous, too.''

Linc closed his eyes and settled his hands on her shoulders. ''Brie, I'm not doing this to hurt you.'' He bit back so much of what he wanted to say. Instead, he continued on in a low tone. ''More than anything, I want you safe. I think, in some ways, you want to forget that John was probably murdered. From the drawing you did for me of the wires from the explosion that killed John and from their color, it's obvious they're the kind used by the military. That stuff is not sold on the open market.'' He raised his head, holding her wavering green gaze. ''I know, because I've handled them in the Marine Corps. They're highly reliable in any type of weather condition, and damn near foolproof. Whoever rigged that explosion either stole the wires outright or bought them on a black market.'' His fingers tightened on her flesh. ''Either way, Brie, it screams at me that the people who laid that trap for you were paid professionals who knew where to get the best equipment to do the job. There's no doubt in my mind that John was murdered.'' He dragged in a deep breath, watching his words strike Brie with force. ''With Holcomb's house being a target, I feel yours will be, too, if they didn't find what they were looking for." He grew desperate. "I can't—won't risk you being here alone when or if they come."

Brie sighed, all the tension draining from her body. "My God," she whispered unsteadily. And then, "Why didn't you tell me about those wires before this?"

Linc wanted to bring her into his arms, needing her womanly warmth, her softness, some reassurance against an unknown future for both of them. But he remained where he stood. "I didn't want to alarm you, Brie. I could be wrong." He inhaled the sweet scent of her hair. "You've gone through enough. You didn't need me yelling like Chicken Little that the sky was falling in."

She stood uncertainly, suspicion in her eyes along with exhaustion. "Isn't it?" she muffled.

He released a ragged breath. "Maybe. I don't know yet." He knew. Linc stilled his anger. Pulling Detective Gent aside, he tried to convince the policeman to release a squad car to keep a watch over Brie's house when they were gone during the day, but the detective had refused. They could only spare one, and that one was going to keep watch over Carol Holcomb's residence. Linc swallowed his frustration over the idiotic move of the police department. He drew Brie into his arms.

"I'm sorry," he said huskily against her velvet cheek. "I didn't mean to yell at you."

Brie nodded, accepting his explanation. She leaned heavily against him, needing his strength right now. "It's so unreal, Linc. It's like a nightmare that never ends...." Her voice died in tremulous silence.

He heard the terror leaking through her tone and held her as tightly as he dared. "I'm here," he told her. "And until we get this situation resolved one way or another,

I'm not letting you out of my sight, little cat. So don't worry, you can sleep at night.''

Brie melted beneath his blue eyes, which were stormy with turmoil. "Somehow, I get the feeling you're very good at being that watchdog you were talking about earlier.''

Linc nodded, feeling guilty over hiding the truth of who he really was. "You're right,'' he whispered thickly. "I'm very good at what I do. So don't let this break-in tear you apart. We'll be fine as long as we're together.''

The tenderness of his look dissolved her tension. "For once, I'm glad you're a chauvinist,'' she admitted, trying to smile after he released her. "I think I'm in need of some cavemanlike protection. I'm feeling terribly vulnerable and naked.'' She rubbed her arms slowly, frowning, thinking of the ramifications of Linc's assessment.

"Hey, now, stop that,'' he chided, placing his arm around her shoulder and giving her a squeeze. "We'll go about our normal duties. You concentrate on haz-mat, and I'll keep my eyes peeled.'' He could have kicked himself for having to disclose information to Brie. He had done it in hopes that she would reveal what she might know about John or what he was hiding. It hadn't worked, and in the end had only upset her more. Agitation and anxiety were clearly written in the depths of her jade eyes.

The phone was ringing. And ringing. And ringing. Linc rose off the couch in a stupor, stumbling toward the kitchen in the darkness. He crashed into Brie at the corner. Groggy, Linc stumbled, reaching out to stop her from falling. Myriad sensations rushed through him from the collision of her soft, rounded breasts against his naked chest, the warmth of her hand on his shoulder and the moist sweetness of her breath against his neck.

"You all right?" he mumbled, trying to orient himself to the present.

Breathless, Brie left his arms. "Y-yes...I'll get the phone." And she disappeared like a beautiful wraith. Linc stood dazed and touched his brow. What time was it? Three in the morning. He forced himself to the kitchen. He froze at the door, his sleep-ridden eyes widening as he drank in Brie with the phone in her hand.

The moonlight pierced the curtains at the kitchen window and back door, bathing her in a silver incandescence. The silky white nightgown clung to her body like a lover's caress, and his breath caught in his throat. Her hair, pleasantly mussed, softened her already lovely face. Her full lips looked so damned provocative. When she looked up and realized he was standing there staring at her, her eyes widened.

Linc saw something he would never have thought he would see in a woman her age—shyness. There was pleading in her eyes as she was caught and held in his hungry gaze. Turning, Linc stumbled into the darkness of the house in search of her robe. He found it at the bottom of the brass bed and brought it to her. Brie was seated at the table, hastily scribbling instructions, her voice low and still husky with sleep. Linc settled the silk robe around her shoulders and stepped back, realizing Brie's discomfort that he might have seen her twisted, red flesh a second time.

By now, the shock of running into her then seeing her clothed in that devastating nightgown was wearing off. Linc could see well enough in the moonlight and began to make them a pot of coffee. From the sounds of the phone call, he could tell it involved a haz-mat incident. The sandalwood scent of Brie lingered in the air, and he savored her scent. He leaned against the counter, allowing her honeylike voice to flow over him as she gave instructions to the caller. And when Linc realized she was staring at him, he cursed himself. Right now, all he wanted to do was walk those few steps, take her into his arms and press her length against him. He felt his body growing rigid and knew that evidence of his need would soon be visible. Concentrating on stopping this unexpected reaction, Linc pushed away from the counter and headed to the living room to dress in a clean uniform. The night was shot anyway.

Linc was sitting on the couch pulling on his socks when Brie appeared at the entrance to the living room. She had her robe on. Her arms were crossed against her breast and her face was sober. "We're going up to Cleveland. The bomb squad from their police department just called."

Linc rapidly put it together. Cleveland was where John was murdered. "What else?"

She shrugged tensely. "They got an anonymous caller telling them there were explosives in a warehouse out near the lake."

Explosives, his area of expertise. He shoved on his boots and walked over to her. Brie's face was shadowed with concern, and she was pale. "They find anything?" he asked quietly, coming to a halt inches from her.

Brie rubbed her forehead. She was achingly aware of how strong, confident and calm Linc was—and how devastatingly masculine. Her voice came out in an unexpected wobble. "Yes. A couple of bundles of TNT along with some jars with a crystal content." She raised her chin, meeting his eyes, needing his nearness. "Probably picric acid or something. Anyway, they can't identify the contents in the jar and they don't want to move it until they have confirmation from us on what it is and if it's safe to move. They can handle the dynamite easily. It's just the other stuff they're not sure about.''

He settled his hands on her shoulders. Brie was trembling. His fingers tightened slightly on her warm flesh. ''It's going to be all right,'' he told her quietly, holding her wavering gaze. Her lips parted, and Linc groaned to himself. Oh, God, just to lean down and touch her wine-red lips and take away the pain he saw so clearly in her haunted eyes.

Brie swayed toward him, and she heard a soft gasp escape him as she leaned her head on his chest. His heart was beating strongly against her ear, while her heartbeat was erratic. A quiver raced through her as she felt his hands loosen from her shoulders and his arms gently wrapped around her, drawing her close to his seemingly indestructible body. Just for a second, she cried to herself, let me forget! ''Linc...'' she said in a ragged whisper.

Linc brushed her hair with a kiss, inhaling her warm, feminine scent all over again. Hot, scalding fire uncoiled deep within him as he felt her arms slowly go around him and she pressed herself against his hard contours. With one hand, he stroked her silky hair. ''It's going to be all right, kitten,'' he whispered, his voice strained. ''I know what's going on inside that head of yours. I can see it in your eyes. This time, it's going to be different. No one's going to get hurt, I promise you.''

A shudder ran through her, and Brie clung to his dark, healing voice. ''I—I'm afraid,'' she said hoarsely. ''It's so much like the other call that got John killed.''

''Shh, I know that.'' Linc managed a strained smile and gently drew her inches away from him. He didn't want to, but if he didn't he knew he'd overstep the boundaries of trust he was building with her. But he wanted to kiss those trembling lips.

"Now listen to me," he said, his voice more authoritative. "My specialty is explosives. I know them like the back of my hand." He gave her a slight smile and brushed away a strand of hair that had fallen across her brow, tucking it gently behind her ear. "I also know the kinds of wires used on that stuff. If it's a setup, we'll know going in."

Her eyes rounded with terror. "But we didn't last time, Linc."

He gave her a small shake. "Neither you nor John was an expert in explosives, Brie." His face hardened. "I am. I spent sixteen months in Nam finding and detonating all kinds of explosives under the worst possible conditions. Believe me when I tell you nobody can fool me when it comes to a setup with explosives. Now go on, get dressed. I'll get the coffee in the thermos and have the van waiting for you by the time you're ready." Linc reluctantly released her, watching her closely. At first Brie swayed, then she seemed to draw on some reservoir of strength within her and stepped away. If she was a killer, this was the best act he'd ever seen put on for his benefit. It could be a trap to kill him, he realized. But one look into Brie's eyes and Linc nearly rejected the possibility. Her voice was low and tortured.

"I won't take long."

The drive would take two hours. At three-thirty in the morning, the interstates were free of all but a few cars. Red lights flashing, the white haz-mat van moved at a steady sixty-five miles per hour toward its goal on the lakefront of Cleveland. Linc glanced at Brie. She had been silent since they had gotten in the van.

"Tell me one more time about those wires leading from the drums that you and John saw."

Brie stared out into the darkness. "They were gray

wires, four of them leading to the center drum. They had red things on them.'' She rubbed her brow. ''I drew a picture of them for the investigating officers and one for you.''

''Draw them again for me now?''

Without a word, Brie took a pen from her pocket and the clipboard from the dash and painstakingly drew him the picture he requested. Her lips tightened as she bore down on the pen. ''I've always thought that, since John was murdered, I would be next.''

The admission came out so low that Linc barely heard it. He snapped his head toward her, his eyes narrowing. ''What makes you say that?''

Brie shrugged. ''Just a gut feeling, Linc. Nothing I can prove.''

Frustration curdled in his throat. ''Who do you think did that to John?''

She closed her eyes and tipped her head back. ''That's like asking me to find the needle in the haystack.''

''Look, you've got to be more specific with me, Brie. Who holds a grudge against you? You leveled fines against a lot of companies. Certainly there has to be a specific company. Who's really angry about being caught? Could they have put a contract out on you two? Have you received any threatening phone calls? Letters?''

''Slow down, Linc. I can answer only one question at a time.'' Again, his eyes had that look in them, and Brie wasn't sure if he was friend or foe. She hadn't even had time to ask him about his odd and unexplained behavior over the break-in at Carol's home, or the fact that the chief talked to him about it, and not her.

He grimaced. ''Sorry. It's just that I'm worried, that's all.'' He almost said I care so much for you, Brie. I'm not going to let anyone even get close to harming you. No matter how hard he tried to see her as a suspect, his heart kept insisting the opposite. He swallowed all that, concentrating on her halting answers.

"We never got threatening calls or letters. A few company officials hinted that we'd be sorry if we had the state attorney general go after them."

"Are there any other names beside the ones on the list you already gave me?"

She gave him a disgruntled look. "Now you sound like those damned investigators."

He ignored her sudden sarcasm, not understanding it. "Just think."

Brie placed the clipboard on her lap and rubbed her temples gently. "Linc, I was barely out of my coma and in so much pain I didn't know who I was, where I was or what happened, but those investigators were in there, hour after hour, grilling me the same way you're doing now. And what has it gotten us? Not a damn thing." Her eyes were bright with hurt. "John's dead, and the Cleveland police are no closer to who did it than months before."

Linc's mouth flattened into a single line. "They shouldn't have questioned you like that. With those kind of deep burns, you had to be almost out of your mind with pain." He glanced at her, his eyes turning tender. "I'm sorry they did that to you, Brie, for whatever it's worth." The bastards were unprofessional in the worst way. If he'd been in charge of the investigation, he'd have waited until she was at least stabilized.

Her heart ached with humiliation. What was happening to her? Brie had never spoken about her three months in the hospital to anyone, not even her parents. She gave Tanner a confused look. "How do you know so much about burns?"

His smile was cold, matching the glitter in his darkened

eyes. "Remember, I was in Nam." His voice was lowered. "My best friend, Captain Dick Martin, got third-degree burns over fifty percent of his body from a booby-trapped line of explosives. I was the first to reach him and I rode out with him in the med-evac helicopter." His tone grew hoarse. "My tour was up in two weeks. As soon as I made it to the Philippines, on the way home, I stopped by the burn unit at the Navy hospital there. Dick was like a brother to me. I decided to take my thirty days' leave and stick it out with him. I saw his agony, Brie. I heard his screams as they soaked him in that water, filled him full of morphine then peeled that burned flesh from him."

Brie shut her eyes and turned her head to one side, feeling nauseous. "Then you know…" she whispered rawly.

He reached over, sliding his fingers across hers, which were curled tightly into a fist. He massaged her hand until he felt her fingers loosening. Her flesh was damp and cool. "Yes, I know, kitten. That's what I wanted to tell you the morning you woke up screaming from that nightmare. I understand your shyness and not wanting anyone to see those scars." His voice deepened, and he gripped her hand firmly in his. "More importantly, I know what courage it takes to fight back from something like this, Brie. I saw the psychological damage it inflicted on Dick. They gave him support and therapy, but he was never the same. But you—" he swallowed hard against a sudden overwhelming torrent of emotion "—you're whole. You're functioning despite the burns. And the loss of John. Believe me when I tell you, lady, you are brave in a way I've seen few people be in my life."

Tears pricked her eyes, and for a moment, Brie thought she was going to cry. But the tears just stayed there, and so did that huge, clawing sensation in her chest. Without a word, she lifted Linc's hand and pressed her cheek against the back of it. "Thank you."

Silence returned to the van. Brie held his hand for a long time, his touch giving stability to the world falling apart around her. Linc understood in a way few ever would. At times, she could feel his gaze upon her, but it didn't bother her as it did before. There was so much she wanted to blurt out and share with him, but the time and place were wrong. They were going to Cleveland. To a warehouse very close to the location where John had lost his life. And this time, Linc was with her. A searing pain ripped through Brie. What if Linc was killed? That would mean the loss of yet another partner. Brie couldn't stand the avalanche of pain that followed. She bit down hard on her lower lip, afraid that she would cry out.

The garish lights provided by a fire engine washed over the area. Brie walked at Linc's side, careful to make her face devoid of any emotion as they made their way toward the huddled group of fire fighters, police and reporters. Linc's presence shored Brie up enough so that she could think and act coherently. He stood to her side and slightly behind her, saying little as she covered all the salient points with the officials.

Linc stared at the aging warehouse made of wood; its roof was sagging. The full moon rode high in a sky tinged from light gray to terrifying total blackness. Linc kept his ears on Brie's conversation with the police bomb squad while his gaze swept the area. Except for the red and white lights flashing against the warehouse, the place looked like a scene from someone's worst nightmare.

A plan was made. Linc would make a careful, thorough investigation with Brie at his side while the rest of the officials remained at a safe distance. With Brie's drawing of the wires from the previous explosion and powerful flashlights in hand, they began a painstaking inspection of the outer perimeter of the warehouse. From time to time, Linc would stop and show Brie certain items, teaching her his trade. He didn't tell her, but in his mind they were no longer in Ohio. Right now, they were out in the jungles of Nam looking for a hidden trip wire that could blow them all away.

Sweat glistened on Brie's tense features as they completed the inspection of the perimeter, satisfied no wires led outside from the warehouse. She looked up at Linc's hard, unreadable face.

"We have to go inside." It was a statement, not a question.

"Yes, but I want you to wait out here for me, Brie." She was still a suspect and could possibly put him in a situation where he could be killed.

Her eyes widened enormously. "No!" It was just like before—John sending her away while he moved closer to investigate. She wouldn't do it again!

Linc gave her a patient look. "You have to trust me, Brie. There's no sense two of us going in there. I've got your drawing. That's all I need."

Stubbornly, she shook her head. "I won't let you go alone. We're a team. I won't stay out here."

His mouth remained compressed. Using all his instincts and experience, he studied her ruthlessly. Brie didn't have the face or eyes of a killer. All his senses told him she was scared to death. If she came along, he'd have to be on guard toward her and toward the situation. A double-edged sword. Damn. The look in her eyes told him she wasn't going to be left behind. "All right, let's go. But stick close. If I tell you to hit the deck, do it."

"Fine," she answered faintly, taking a better grip on the flashlight.

He took her arm. "Let's go."

Brie's heart pounded without letup. Her chest was aching and her throat so tightly constricted that it hurt to breathe. She and Linc headed toward the area where the explosives had been located. The beam from the flashlight stabbed through the pitch blackness, and Brie slipped her hand through Linc's arm. There was no sound except for her harsh breathing and the scrape of their boots against the dusty, cracked concrete beneath them.

Linc froze. "There." He moved the light down slightly.

Brie swallowed hard. There were five sticks of dynamite on the floor between two stacks of crates. Next to the dynamite was a mason jar with a blue lid.

"Kneel down," he ordered quietly.

She knelt, keeping her trembling light focused on the explosives. Brie watched in fascination as Linc shone his beam at different angles. Finally, he slowly got to his feet. He turned, his face grim.

"Stay here," he growled.

The cold command rooted her to the spot. This was a different Linc Tanner than the one she knew. Brie watched as he moved like a cat, no sounds coming from his heavy boots as he approached the explosives. Her breath caught as he stood only a few feet from them, carefully searching for wires that might lead from them. Tears stung her eyes, and Brie wanted to call out for him to be more careful than he ever had in his whole life. Her limbs froze, and her stomach shrank into a fierce, white-hot knot.

Linc dropped to his belly, all his awareness focused on that lone jar. He was a foot away from it. Sweat ran down his tense face, and he narrowed his eyes as he studied the contents. The bomb squad was ten feet away when it had first discovered the explosives and had backed away. There was a tattered label on the side, and he gently slid forward, his breath lodged in his throat as he read the faded label: picric acid. Swallowing, he gauged the crystals with even more respect. One jolting movement and he'd have his face blown off. If one crystal fell and struck another, it would set off an explosion that would level one third of the warehouse. He didn't forget that Brie was only ten feet away. She would probably be killed, too. The thought made his mouth go bitter with bile. He got lightly to his feet, the front of his uniform filthy with dust.

Brie watched him walk back to her as if he were on eggs. He reached out, lifting her from her crouched position, his hand firm on her elbow. He didn't know who was more scared in that moment. Brie's eyes were wide with terror. The moment he touched her elbow, he saw some of the fear drain from her eyes, and he was thankful that he had such a profound effect on her.

"It's picric acid," he told her softly. "There are about four ounces of it."

"Crystallized?" she croaked.

"Yes. Enough to blow this warehouse to hell and back. Come on, let's get out of here. We'll leave through the opposite entrance. I don't even want to risk walking by that stuff."

Brie agreed, her fingers at the base of her aching throat. Her knees were suddenly wobbly, and it took all her remaining strength to walk under her own power. Once outside, the cool night air hit them. Linc shut off his light, and darkness engulfed them.

"Come here," he grated softly, taking her into his arms, realizing she couldn't possibly be acting. In that instant, Linc knew she was a victim, not a suspect. As he folded her into his arms, he realized that all that remained to be done was to prove that to the satisfaction of everyone else.

She came without question, and his arms went around her, drawing her against him. A ragged sigh broke from her lips as she nestled her head beneath his hard jaw. The silence cloaked them, and all she was aware of was his sweaty male scent, the roughness of the uniform beneath her cheek and the drumlike beat of his heart. Brie sensed that some sort of emotional bonding was taking place between them. Time wound slowly to a halt as he held her tightly, his cheek against her hair. Nothing else mattered in that minute. Finally, Linc released her. She could barely make out the features of his face as she looked up at him. He gave her a grim smile.

"Come on, we've got our work cut out for us."

They greeted the rising sun with bloodshot eyes. Brie watched as the bomb squad trailer, bearing the jar of volatile picric acid in a sand-filled metal case, slowly pulled away. Taking out the dynamite had been easy in comparison. Brie was grateful that the bomb squad removed the jar. She had lost count of how many times she had removed the liquid and crystallized form of acid. It took incredibly steady hands and no fear of dying. She had neither right now. She lifted her chin, meeting Linc's weary eyes, aware of the warmth that continued to throb between them.

"What do you say we go home and get some sleep?" she asked.

He pushed several strands of dark hair off his brow. "I'd say it sounds like one hell of an idea."

Brie nodded. "You want to drive? I'll go to the fire chief and sign the last of the forms."

"Yeah, I'll do it." Linc started to turn away, then hesitated. "What about Homely Homer? Shouldn't she be hungry by now?"

A softened look came to Brie's features. For someone who knew little about animals and professed a dislike for them, Linc was turning out to be suspiciously different. She would ask him about that change some time. "Yes, there's a jar of baby food next to the cage. Just put it in there for her. And don't get alarmed if she starts nuzzling you with her beak when you do it. She'll think you're her mother."

He snorted and turned. "First time I've been a mother in that sense of the word," he grumbled, walking away. There was more to digest. As Linc fed the pigeon, he assessed Brie's actions throughout the crisis. There were several times she could have endangered his life and hadn't. Grimacing, Linc realized that Brie was a victim, and he disliked the sham he had to continue to play with her. Linc would rather have had Brie be a suspect. That way, he could continue to fight his attraction to her. Now that she was a victim, all his overprotective feelings would emerge, throwing an entirely different light on his relationship with her.

"A mess," Linc growled, putting the bird back in the cage.

Brie handed Linc the last of the coffee from their thermos. The interstate highways were heavy with rush-hour traffic into Cleveland. Thankfully, they were leaving. She felt an inner glow as Linc gave her that heated look that always suspended her breath for an instant.

"When you finish your coffee, why don't you stretch out in the back and catch a few winks," he suggested.

Brie sipped the coffee. "No, I'll stay up here and help keep you awake."

His mouth quirked. "Anyone ever appreciate how the haz-mat people go beyond and above the call of duty?"

"No. It's an expected part of our job, Linc. I warned you about putting in long hours."

He nodded. "All I want is a shower. I smell."

"Far be it from me to say that."

"You're a saucy cat for this time of the morning."

Heat stole into Brie's cheeks as she met his smiling blue eyes. "Jeff accused me of having a sense of humor at the worst of times. I guess it's true."

Linc squinted against the rising sun. "I like your humor. In my business I've found the people who can keep it in the worst situations are the ones who are the most reliable. They won't buckle under the stress."

Brie agreed. "I think our brand of comedy is labeled black humor at best."

"To an outsider hearing us, I'm sure it is. What they don't realize is that it's a way to relieve the stress and pressure we're feeling."

"Speaking of stress, did you manage to feed Homely Homer?"

He smiled, and she noted how his teeth were white against his growth of beard.

"Yeah."

"You like her?"

He gave a slight shrug. "She's okay for a pigeon, I guess."

Brie was watching him closely. "I think you like animals a lot more than you want anyone to know."

"Just never was raised around them much as a kid," he mumbled evasively.

"What happened, Linc?" Brie asked in a softened tone. "You try and make me believe you're a big, pushy bully who hates women, children and animals. I know you don't hate women too much, or we wouldn't be working so well as a team. I haven't seen you around children, so I'll reserve my opinion on that. The other night when you met Homely Homer, I saw the look in your eyes.''

Linc shot her a disgruntled glare. Brie was too damn good at people watching. Much better than he gave her credit for. Agents had that knack of noticing the most minute of body language signals, not someone like Brie. "What look?" he growled, trying to bluff his way out of the situation.

Brie chortled delightedly, putting both feet on the dash and relaxing. "What look?" she mimicked. Her green eyes, although ringed with exhaustion, were filled with tenderness. "Despite all your growling, I think you wanted to pet and hold her."

"You have an unnerving habit of being insightful, Ms. Williams," he muttered.

"But I'll never use it against you, Linc."

"My experience has been different with women, Brie."

"Time will prove me on that point. You're stuck with me whether you like it or not."

Now she was teasing him, he was sure. "Am I complaining?"

Brie met his smile, drowning in the warmth she saw in his face. "So, tell me about the animals in your life, Linc Tanner. Why are you so afraid to reach out and share yourself with that little bird?"

He sobered abruptly, twisting beneath her laserlike insight. "You missed your calling," he muttered. "You should have been a shrink."

Her laughter was spontaneous and lilting. "Oh, please! Why should it bother you that someone besides you has the ability to see past walls and facades of another human being? Do you think I'll use that information against you, Linc? No, on second thought, don't answer that.''

"The more someone knows about you, the more vulnerable you become to them," he stated stubbornly. "You bare your soul to another person and you're practically telling them where your Achilles heel is located."

Brie had the good sense to remain sober beneath his assumption. "You're right."

"And I don't think either of us is the kind of individual who gives much of himself away to anyone."

She was quiet for a moment, digesting their conversation. Linc was right, as usual. Gently, Brie steered him back to the subject she wanted him to talk about. "Who took the joy of loving animals away from you as a child, Linc? I can tell you like Homely Homer or you wouldn't have remembered to feed her or offered to do it."

Linc rubbed his face. "A long time ago, when I was about eight years old and living in the Bronx, I found this little gray kitten under a cardboard box by a trash dumpster outside an Italian restaurant. He couldn't have been very old, because his eyes were barely open. The family I was living with at that time had six foster kids, including me." His voice turned grim. "The old lady was getting a hefty allotment check for keeping the six of us. She spent it on new clothes and a car while she fed us cheap junk food.

"The kitten was mewing, and I rummaged through the boxes around the bottom of the dumpster until I found him." He smiled softly. "He was the furriest little thing. I'd seen cats before in the neighborhood, but they always ran when you tried to go up and pet them. Not that I blamed them. A lot of the kids hated cats and would throw anything they could get their hands on at them. I guess he thought I was his mother or something because he kept crying and sucking my fingers when I held him. So I tucked him inside my shirt and went to the back door of the restaurant.

"There was a cook there by the name of Davis. He always knew I hung around. I got up my courage and pounded on that back door until someone answered it. Thank God, it was him. I showed him the kitten and he broke into this big, toothy smile and told me what I had to do. He came back about ten minutes later with some warm milk and a glass eyedropper. He showed me how to fill the eyedropper and feed the kitten. So, before school, I'd race over to the restaurant where I had a box by the back door, feed the kitten and barely make it to class on time. After school, I'd run back there and feed him again. And at night, I'd sneak out the window in our bedroom where we all slept, and feed him a third time."

Brie swallowed, her eyes luminous. "That was wonderful. And Davis...the man had a heart."

Linc nodded grimly, keeping his eyes on the road before them. "Yeah, things went pretty good for a while. The kitten grew fast. He had big yellow eyes and long gray fur. And it got so he'd hear me coming and meet me. I couldn't believe an animal would do that. He'd begged to be lifted and carried. And when I would pick him up, he'd lick my chin and purr like crazy. I really liked that."

Brie heard the pain in his voice. "Something happened to the kitten, didn't it, Linc?"

He nodded his head. "It seemed like everything I touched, no matter how much I loved it, was taken from me. At one foster home I was happy. The man and woman really loved me. And then she finally got pregnant and they reluctantly gave me back to the orphanage because they just didn't have the money to support two children. Then I landed in that viper's nest where the woman used us to obtain extra money." He shook his head, silence settling between them. Finally, Linc said, "The kitten was hit by a garbage truck. When I found him that night, I just sat huddled against the brick building in that alley holding him and cried my eyes out. After that, I swore no one would ever hurt me again. I wouldn't let any human or animal get close enough to me to make me cry. I just couldn't accept it anymore, and in my eight-year-old mind, it was the only acceptable solution to the situation."

"And that's when you joined one of those street gangs?"

He turned, aware of the compassion written so clearly in her face. "Yeah. I became a real hard nose. Started skipping school, getting in trouble with the cops, and finally I got dumped into juvenile court. The only good thing out of that was that the viper gave me back to the orphanage because she didn't want to have to keep coming down to the police station to pick me up."

Brie felt the ache widening in her breast for him. Their lives were so completely different from one another. "And yet, you've made something decent out of your life despite a bad start. I think that says something about your caliber as a human being, Linc."

"Don't put me on any pedestals, Brie. I still carry a lot of that inner toughness around with me on a daily basis. At age fourteen I met this parish priest who used to walk the worst alleys of the Bronx. He changed my life. He took me under his wing and straightened me out to a large degree. Father O'Reilly got me a scholarship to a local university and told me I had to have a degree in order to make it out in the world. So I scraped up the funds by working at a restaurant at night and going to college by day. I got a BS in chemistry."

"So your unimpressive grades weren't from the girls and partying? They were from working until odd hours of the morning, getting a few hours' sleep, studying, then going back to class.''

He grudgingly nodded. "If it hadn't been for Father O'Reilly's belief in me, I'd never have gotten through. At the time, I felt so proud of myself. I'd made it. I'd made something of myself. I was no longer a pawn someone could push around. I wouldn't be known as 'that orphan' or 'foster brat.' From then on, I was a graduate. I had respect, Brie." His brow furrowed. "I don't know if you can understand that. I was raised in Italian neighborhoods where respect was the thing. If you didn't have respect, you didn't have anything."

"You've come a long way."

"Now don't get moon-eyed over my life. There's no such thing as a happy childhood for any kid. I don't care if he was born with a silver spoon in his mouth or was a ghetto rat."

"I wasn't getting moon-eyed, to use your words," she defended swiftly.

"You're such a marshmallow. I should have known better than to tell you about myself."

A smile touched her lips, and she reached out, placing her hand on his broad shoulder. She enjoyed the strength she felt beneath her fingertips. "I'm glad you told me, and I promise I won't cry. Okay?"

"You're still a marshmallow, Williams. Through and through."

She allowed her hand to slip off his shoulder. "If you call being kind to animals and people being a marshmallow, then I guess I am."

"My definition of one goes further than that," he muttered. "You wear that heart of yours on your sleeve."

"Nothing wrong with that, Tanner."

He snorted and rubbed his watering eyes. "Like hell

there isn't. Every vulture in the world can spot a patsy like you a mile away and take advantage of the situation.'' Like he was doing, and it ate him. Brie didn't deserve to have her trust twisted like this, and manipulated.

Brie groaned. ''You're such a pessimist! Thus far, I'm still alive and in one piece at age twenty-nine. Now, I call that surviving.''

His grin was wry. ''I call that lucky.'' And then he wondered how many men had taken advantage of Brie's open, honest nature. Maybe she had learned to protect herself by remaining private. But beyond those walls of privacy, where he had already found himself, she was a sitting duck for an emotional bullet that could wound her gravely. At that moment, Linc didn't like himself very much. Brie was open to him, not even realizing he held the bullet that could destroy the trust she shared with him. A bitter taste coated his mouth, and he looked away, unable to meet her warm, vulnerable eyes.

Chapter Seven

Five days of working together, Linc thought, as he gathered several manuals from the rear of the white van. Another day on the road inspecting chemical companies was at an end. Brie took Homely Homer into the house. It's gone too fast, I want it to slow down. And then he laughed at himself. If he was honest with himself, he would admit how he liked living with Brie, even though they slept in different rooms.

His mind ranged over the clues he had picked up over the week. Brie had given him a more thorough list of companies who had threatened John or her in some vague way. Cramer was pulling the records on those companies to check the number of violations they had, if any. The company who had the most reason to kill would most likely be the one with the most fines. And Linc had continued to pry information from Brie, who was totally unsuspecting of his motives. She was taking his probing curiosity in stride, thinking all his questions were normal for someone who was breaking into the job.

In a week, they had stopped at fifteen different businesses that used or manufactured some form of chemicals that, under improper conditions, could create a hazardous material situation. Linc found these inspections enormously interesting. He cataloged every company representative's reactions to her request to go over files of transported chemicals to and from the business. And when he asked to accompany Brie to check where the contents were located she was delighted, having no idea that he was looking for totally different reasons. Brie had been pleased with his careful investigation of each of the businesses they dropped in on, commenting that he had the earmarks of a fanatic. He had only smiled and mentally logged in the nuances of each establishment. Every night, after Brie had gone to bed, he had taken out his notebook, written out thorough descriptions of the types of chemicals carried and the reactions of the reps. Cases were broken by dogged thoroughness, not luck, and Linc had the patience of Job when it came to collecting all the seeming loose ends to the puzzle. He was very good at putting evidence together after a certain number of leads had been investigated.

Linc followed Brie inside their home. He smiled at himself. He thought of her house as their home. Well? Wasn't it? Two people in a house, both fairly content with one another's presence, constituted a home. He scowled. How had Brie grown on him in five days' time? Linc found himself loath to leave her home and move into his new apartment. He would miss her bright morning humor, her coffee, her laughter, which was coming more and more easily each day they were together, her natural warmth and sensitivity, and yes, even Homely Homer. Linc grinned. Brie and that ugly duckling of a bird of hers. Even when he had been married to JoAnne, his home life was never as it had been in the past five days. The basic difference was that Brie actively sought a part in living life, and JoAnne had been content to let it pass by her. If Brie wasn't out dutifully weeding her garden, she was mowing the lawn, sneaking enough time to bake a cake, read one of her silly romantic novels and staunchly defend their value to him, cut some of those bright tulips and sweet-smelling hyacinths and place them in a vase near the couch, or so many other little, important things. He would miss her. A lot.

"Just think," Brie said, turning on the Tiffany lamp in the living room. "Your last night on that old, lumpy couch. I'll bet you're happy about that."

"I was getting kind of used to it," Linc protested, managing a smile. He sat down on the couch, unlacing his boots and taking them off. It was almost eleven, and he was tired. Brie looked fresh, despite the twelve hours they had put in that day. She took Homer's cage and carried the bird to the sewing room.

In five days, they had fallen into a routine in the evenings. Brie would shower first, stick her head around the corner and tell him the bathroom was free, then disappear into her bedroom. Tonight, he didn't want her to disappear so soon. He yearned to stretch their last hours together. Linc found himself hungry just to sit near Brie and talk with her. Those times were so rare between phone calls, haz-mat incidents and her heavy lecture schedule. They would stagger in late, wash, then fall asleep.

Linc brightened. Since he had been at the house, Brie had had no recurrence of her nightmares. He had deliberately not talked to her about them, saving it for a time when they wouldn't be pressured by external demands, when he could devote himself to helping her work through that trauma. He knew he could help Brie; it was simply a matter of patience and timing.

"I'm going to bed now, Linc. The bathroom's all yours."

Linc frowned and rose just as she disappeared. "Wait, Brie."

Brie reappeared, dressed in the appealing apricot robe that brought out the color of her complexion. Her hair was mussed, and Linc had the urge to tame those strands into place. He saw her eyes widening as he walked over to her. Even in his stocking feet, he towered over her. What was she feeling? Longing? He took a deep breath, thankful that there was no longer the fear he had seen in her eyes when they had first met. No, during this week trust had jelled between them.

"Yes?" She stood uncertainly before him, hands clasped in front of her. Her mouth went dry as she saw the naked hunger in Linc's cobalt eyes.

"What time are you waking up tomorrow?" He wanted to reach out and bury his fingers in her soft, velvet mane of hair.

"Six. Why? You don't have to get up." She smiled. "You get to sleep in as late as you want, for once."

That was the truth. Up at six, home around eleven every night. And no time for themselves. It was wearing on him already. "Wake me, okay?"

"Well, why?"

He reached up, lightly brushing her flaming red cheek. "Because I enjoy having coffee with you in the morning. Is that reason enough?" he asked huskily.

Brie's heart pounded in her breast, and she stepped away from Linc. "Okay. I'll see you in the morning then. Good night." She turned, walked down the darkened hallway and quietly shut her bedroom door.

Linc stared at the door for a long time. Give her time, he cautioned himself. Don't push her. She wasn't the type of woman who could be bulldozed into a—What? One-night stand? Linc even felt a twinge of guilt. Brie was worth more than that. How much more? Disgruntled, he picked up his pajama bottoms and headed for the bathroom, lost in his own thoughts. What did he want from Brie? She was supposed to be protected. He was a glorified guard dog.

Brie jerked up in bed, a scream ready to tear from her lips. Disoriented, she gasped for breath, trying to get control of the unleashed emotions threatening to overwhelm her. The room was dark, the light of the moon making her surroundings gray and forbidding. Shakily getting to her feet, she slipped the robe over her shoulders. Her mouth was dry and her throat constricted. She needed a drink of water. The clock on the bed stand read three o'clock. Deluged with harsh emotions over John's death and questioning her own fear, Brie went to the kitchen.

A sliver of moonlight sliced through the curtains as she picked up the glass she always had sitting near the sink. Her fingers trembled badly, and it slipped from her hand, shattering loudly in the porcelain basin. Brie stood frozen, hands over her pounding heart, staring at the jagged pieces of glass. That was how she felt—so many parts and pieces of herself torn and mangled beyond any hope of repair. A sob caught in her throat, and she took a step away from the sink.

"Brie?"

Linc's sleep-thickened voice sent a quiver through her. Brie turned jerkily, her gaze moving across his dark-haired chest to the powerful width of his shoulders and up to his concerned features. His eyes were dark and alert with a trace of fear in them. She swallowed.

"I—" Her voice was barely a raw whisper.

Linc moved forward. "What's wrong, Brie?" He saw her eyes turn luminous with tears. "Those dreams again?" he guessed.

Brie nodded, needing to be held badly. Twisting her head, she looked at the fragments in the sink. "I—I broke it," she cried, burying her face in her hands.

"Come here," he said roughly, his voice charged with emotion. He settled his hands on her shoulders. She was trembling badly, the gown damp beneath his fingers. A soft groan came from deep within him as he brought her into the safe harbor of his arms. Her hair was cool silk against his chest, her velvet cheek like a brand on his flesh over his pounding heart.

Brie tried to take a deep breath and closed her eyes tightly, burying herself deeply in Linc's arms. "I—I'm so afraid…out of control…"

He winced as he heard the anguish in her voice. Gently, he framed her face between his fingers, lifted her chin up so their eyes met. "Listen to me," he said thickly. "You need to let it go, Brie. Let all of what you're feeling go. Do you hear me?"

Brie's lips parted as she felt the heat of his hands against her cold flesh. "B-but if I do…I'll fly apart…I'll—"

"No," he whispered harshly, his fingers tightening. "Let those tears fall, kitten. Cry for what you've lost and for how much you hurt. Come on, I'll be here for you. You aren't going to lose control. Trust me, Brie. Trust me."

The ragged thickness of his voice tore away the last of the fears that had held her tortured emotions at bay. Tears formed and slowly rolled from the corners of her eyes.

Then came a low moan. Brie clutched at his hard, solid arms, clinging as if she were going to fall. She saw his face lose its hard lines and soften. The moment his thumbs brushed away the first of the tears, an explosion of pain and anger burst within her.

Linc braced himself. Brie's lips, now wet with tears, formed in a helpless cry, and he crushed her to him, burying his head against her hair. The sobs racked her body, the sounds torn from deep within her, and he felt every one of them. She had tried so hard for so long to be brave and in control when any other human would have capitulated to the terror and trauma long ago. Linc felt her knees giving way as she surrendered to her pain. In one motion, he gathered her up in his arms and carried her through the dark house to the couch where his blanket and sheets lay in twisted disarray.

He sat down with Brie on his lap, her head buried beneath his jaw, her fists on his chest. He held her and rocked her. His voice was raw as he urged her to get it all out. Her anguished cries slowly died down, and after a while she lay silent against him. An occasional spasm passed through her. She hiccuped, and Linc smiled. Brie was so soft and warm, her breasts were grazing his chest, her hip nestled against his. The sandalwood scent teased his nostrils, and he inhaled her feminine scent, which made him heady with desire for her.

His mouth rested on the damp strands of hair clinging to her wet cheek. Don't kiss her! a voice screamed in his head. He was taking advantage of Brie's lowered guard. Linc had urged her to trust him enough to allow him to help her and now... He groaned, feeling her fingers uncurl and flatten out over the mat of hair on his chest. His mouth moved down the curve of her cheek, and he tasted the salt of her tears. Linc pressed her urgently against him, savoring her velvet-smooth flesh beneath his questing mouth. His heart thundered heavily as he felt Brie move a mere fraction of an inch so that he could kiss her.

He didn't know why her action caught him off guard. Brie was a woman so different from his experience that it had never entered his mind that she might also be drawn just as powerfully to him. And yet, as his mouth barely brushed her trembling, wet lips, an incredible surge of joy went through him, stunning him with its intensity.

Her mouth was like a lush flower opening to his tender advances, he thought as he traced the curve of her lips. Her breath was broken and ragged, and he was vaguely aware of her fingers curving around his neck, drawing him closer, melding to him. His breath caught as he gloried in her shy response to his mouth. She tasted sweet, so very sweet. Her lips were yielding beneath his pressure, and achingly feminine. Sensations roared through Linc, and he fought for control. He wasn't sure who needed to be kissed more. What he did know was that they had kissed for different reasons—Brie, because she needed human contact and care in the aftermath of grief; he, because... Linc opened his eyes and stared down at Brie's pale features.

Gently, he caressed her lips one more time before pulling back. His heart was a drum beating heavily in his chest. Everywhere Brie touched him, he was on fire. His body was rigid, and he knew without a doubt that she had to be aware of his need of her. His fingers trembled as he stroked her hair. Words were useless as he sat with Brie in his arms in the quiet living room. Linc was aware of her breathing and her heartbeat slowing.

Brie closed her eyes, too devastated by the stormy release of her bottled-up emotions, needing, wanting Linc's touch. Each time he caressed her hair, he took away a little more of her pain. His wiry hair beneath her cheek tickled her nose, but she paid it no heed. The thudding beat of his steady heart promised her that there was constancy in her shattered universe. Her world centered on Linc, his arms providing her protection against the emptiness she felt in the wake of her tears. Brie took an unsteady breath, a tremor passing through her as she vividly remembered Linc's mouth moving searchingly across her lips. His tenderness opened the doors to her heart, flinging them open, and helpless, she drowned in his strength.

"Linc…" Her voice was wobbly.

His hand stilled on her hair. "Don't try to talk yet, Brie," he coaxed, pressing a kiss on her damp brow. "Just lie there and rest. We have time, kitten." Or did they? Guilt seared through him. He'd just committed a terrible error in judgment. His heart didn't think so, but his head did. Linc was getting involved. What would Brie do when she found out he'd lied to her? Abused her trust in him? Suddenly, Linc panicked.

Obediently, Brie closed her eyes, sinking into the throbbing silence, Linc's breath flowing across her brow and cheek. How long she lay there, Brie didn't know. Had she fallen asleep with Linc's chest as her pillow and his heart providing the balm she needed? The wonderful masculine scent of his body, the warmth of his flesh and the wiry mat of hair beneath her cheek and hand soothed her further. Was there anything more special than care and love shared between a man and a woman? Brie thought not, nuzzling her lips against his corded neck.

Linc changed position slightly so he could tip his head back. Had he dozed? He wasn't sure until he lifted his head and looked at the clock. Four o'clock. "Feeling better?" he asked Brie, his voice gravelly.

Brie nodded, not trusting her voice, her throat raw and dry from her wails of pure anguish. Linc's hand settled on her hair, and he gently raked his fingers through the silken mass. The sensation was utterly drugging to her.

"You slept for a while," he murmured. Linc should have been groggy, but he wasn't. His awareness was hotly centered on Brie and how good she felt in his arms.

"W-what time is it?"

"Around four."

She didn't want to stir from his arms. "I'm sorry..."

"I'm not. That's been a long time coming, kitten." His fingers brushed her cheek. "And I'm glad you shared it with me."

Brie was silent for a long time, staring into the darkness, focusing on the beat of Linc's heart. "You're a good man."

Linc managed a slight chuckle. "JoAnne would tell you differently."

She ran her hand across his collarbone, aware of the muscled strength that lay beneath her palm. "I'm not JoAnne."

"No, thank God, you're not." He gently moved her as he sat up, keeping her deep in his embrace. Looking down at her, Linc held his breath. She was gazing up at him, her eyes dark and luminous. Fragile. The word slammed home to him. He had to try to tread a fine line with her, keep his distance and continue to provide her the stability she needed. A faint smile touched his mouth as he reached down to brush some strands of hair away from her brow.

"You're good in a crisis, Linc."

"I've had a few myself." There was self-deprecation in his voice.

Brie closed her eyes again, allowing his voice to flow through her. "I've been wanting to cry for such a long time," she began tremulously. "And the tears just wouldn't come. I cried when I came out of that coma and

Chief Saxon told me John was dead." Her fingers tightened on his arm. "I couldn't even make the funeral. I cried for Carol and Susie, because I knew just how much they loved John."

Linc kissed her hair. "But you never cried for yourself, did you, Brie?"

She turned, burying her face on his neck and shoulder, her arm slipping around him. "It was awful," she muffled. "Awful."

He began to rock her as the tears came again. "You endured three months of pain in that burn unit all by yourself, didn't you?"

"Y-yes," Brie said, choking. "H-how could I let my parents or my brother see me screaming like that?" She shuddered in memory of those times when she had to soak in warm water and they had torn dead flesh from her healing wounds.

Linc tightened his embrace, burying his head against hers, eyes tightly shut. "Listen to me, kitten. You're a woman of tremendous strength and courage. I've seen that rare kind of combination in some men, but never a woman before. And with that steel will, you can hold a lot at bay that ordinary people would have been forced to release a long time ago. In some ways, you've carried an even greater load because of that." He inhaled the silky scent of her hair, fighting to keep himself on a tight rein. "There's nothing wrong with crying, Brie. And there's nothing wrong in letting others see you be human. Stop trying to be Super Woman. Just be yourself. That's enough."

Brie struggled to sit up. She remained sitting next to him, his arm draped in a relaxed manner around her waist. Sniffing, she wiped the last of the tears away, giving him a shy look. The tenderness she saw in Linc's features stag-

gered her. Was she looking at a different man? Then Brie
realized that he, too, hid behind walls, just as she had. How
many sides were there to Linc? A smile pulled at her lips,
and she reached out, trying to dry his chest of all her tears.
He caught her hand, pressing it where his heart lay.

"Don't erase what we shared," he told her in a low
voice, his eyes stormy.

Her fingers tingled wildly upon contact with his hard
flesh, and Brie was achingly aware of Linc as a supreme
male. The black hair on his chest intensified his rugged
looks; the planes in his face were etched sharply against
the shadows of the retreating night.

"We've shared nothing but my pain in the five days
since we met, Linc."

A gentle smile tugged at his mouth. "Am I complaining?"

His teasing was back, and Brie rallied beneath his ca-
joling. "No. But I can't help thinking what you must think
of me."

"I accept you, Brie. *All* of you. I kinda like the way
you are."

A tentative smile stretched across her lips. "You really
are a masochist."

He dislodged himself from her and rose. "Stay there,"
he told her in an authoritative tone. Brie gave him a questioning look as he disappeared into the kitchen. He returned a few minutes later, and she noted how his thin
cotton pajama bottoms hung from his hips, showing a dark
line of hair that disappeared beneath the loosely knotted
drawstring. Linc knelt in front of her, placing a shot glass
in her hand.

"Here, drink this," he said gruffly, one hand resting on
her silk-covered thigh.

Brie stared at it. "What is it?"

"Apricot brandy. Found it the other night when I was digging in the refrigerator for that last piece of lemon pie you made. Now, go on, drink it. All of it."

She tipped the small glass to her lips and gulped it down. A fiery sensation spread rapidly down her throat into her stomach; relaxation flew through her almost immediately afterward. Linc took the glass from her hands and placed it on the lamp table.

"Okay," he said, lifting her in his arms. "It's time for you to go to sleep."

Brie gasped softly as he picked her up and brought her against him. Automatically, her arms settled around his neck, her head resting on his capable shoulder. "I can walk," she protested.

"I know you can. I just like having an excuse to stay close to you."

She closed her eyes, trusting him completely. "You're good with people, Linc Tanner."

He carried her to the bed and gently laid her down. Brie looked so small and helpless in that huge brass bed. He forced himself to cover her, drawing the quilt up around her shoulders.

"Just with certain special people," he corrected quietly.

The brandy was having a powerful effect on Brie. She tried to keep her eyes open, but it was impossible. Reaching out, her slender hand hanging off the edge of the mattress, she murmured, "Thank you, Linc. I don't know what I'd have done without you..."

His eyes softened as he heard her exhausted words. How could she be anything but a victim in all this? Against his better judgment, Linc leaned over and brushed her parted lips with a kiss. "Good night, Sleeping Beauty. You're one hell of a woman in my book."

* * *

Linc glowered at the packed and unpacked boxes lying at his feet in the center of his apartment. His boss had sent them as part of the ruse Linc had to continue to play. It was Sunday night, and he still wasn't moved in! As he glared at the nondescript beige walls, the ivory drapes and ivory furniture, he thought how dull the room looked in comparison to Brie's living room. His mood had deteriorated since Saturday morning, when he woke up at eight to find Brie had made coffee, left him a note and had already gone. Throughout that day, while helping Jeff move his furniture from a third-floor attic apartment into a van, Linc wondered if Brie had left him asleep because she was too embarrassed to face him.

Hands resting on his knees, he sat in the middle of the carpet, damned unhappy. And he knew why. He missed Brie acutely. He'd never missed another woman in his life as he did her. Before, he had always been able to separate business from pleasure, work from play. This assignment was turning out all wrong, and it left him feeling nakedly vulnerable. Linc got to his knees and began to unpack the last box of books, which would go up on the bookshelves on the opposite wall. He itched to pick up the newly installed phone and give Brie a call to see if she was home yet. He didn't like the idea of her going anywhere without him! But how was he going to lie his way out of moving into an apartment just so he could stay in her home to guard her? She'd misinterpret his motives, and that could be just as disastrous. No matter what happened, Linc had to try to keep a certain distance from Brie.

It was almost nine o'clock when the doorbell chimed. Linc frowned, getting up and making his way through discarded packing boxes. Who could that be? He wasn't expecting anyone. He opened the door, and his heart began pounding. Brie stood there with a small cardboard box in her hands. Just seeing her smile melted his bad mood, and Linc grinned.

"I didn't expect you."

Brie tried to tame her thumping heart, remembering all too clearly Linc's tenderness and his kisses. She had been able to concentrate on little else. She was thankful there were no haz-mat calls, and she could do the workshop for the various fire departments with her eyes closed.

"By now I thought you might be ready for another home-cooked meal." She held the box toward him. "Supper. Are you hungry?"

Linc groaned, eagerly taking the small box. "You've got to be the world's best lifesaver. Yeah, I'm starved. Come on in. At least the kitchen is in decent shape," he muttered.

Brie tried to ignore her vivid awareness of Linc as she followed him. She put her hands in her pockets and looked around the rectangular room. Linc had put the box on the table.

"Nice," Brie approved. She pulled open a drawer by the sink and found silverware.

He snorted. "Compared to your house, it's nothing."

Brie felt a twinge of happiness when she saw Linc's face soften as he opened the foil-wrapped meal.

"I don't believe this. Stuffed pork chops, rice, gravy, peas and a salad."

With a laugh, Brie pulled out a chair for him. "Come on, sit down before you faint, Tanner. You'd think no one ever made a home-cooked meal for you the way you're behaving."

"Wait, there's one more. Is this dessert?"

Dessert is kissing you, Brie thought. "Yes. Why don't you save opening it for later? A surprise."

Unable to wait, Linc lifted out the plate and carefully

unwrapped the foil around it. "A cherry pie. I'll be damned." He looked at her as she sat down. "How'd you have time to make all this stuff?"

She enjoyed his pleasure over the food. No wonder women liked cooking for their men when they made a meal seem as if it were a treasure. It would be easy to cook for Linc on a daily basis because he was grateful for her efforts. "I got home at six tonight and got to thinking that you've probably been subsisting on Wendy's and McDonald's hamburgers."

Linc sat down, eager to eat. "Ask me where all the fast-food places are now and I can tell you," he muttered. He was about to dig in when he looked at her. "Have you eaten?"

She had come to expect that of Linc—the ability to share with another. "Yes." Brie looked down at her uniform. "As you can tell, I didn't even change. I got home and started cooking."

Between bites of the succulent stuffed pork chops, Linc asked, "How'd the class go?"

"Good, as usual. The guys really got into the tactics and strategy sessions on Sunday. They had a good time and learned something in the process.

"Brie, this is delicious."

She smiled, resting her chin on her clasped hands. Just for you, Linc. For all your kindness and understanding. Through her lashes, Brie wondered how she could have thought Linc was such a bastard. Of course, they had gotten off on the wrong foot, but things were changing now, rapidly.

"How come you let me sleep Saturday morning?"

Brie roused herself, addressing his question. "I was going to wake you, but you looked so tired, Linc." She gave him a slight smile, meeting and holding his probing blue gaze. "I didn't have the heart to wake you. I was groggy from being up that night. Why should I have made you as miserable as I felt?"

He spooned a portion of rice and gravy into his mouth and was silent for a moment. "Oh, I don't know. I think we're pretty good being miserable together."

She smiled softly, meeting and drowning in his tender gaze. "Yes, yes we are. I still haven't thanked you for holding me…helping me through all that, Linc."

He had finished the dinner and got up to set the plate on the counter. Then he sat down. "You'd have done the same for me," he told her.

"Yes."

He folded his arms on the table, holding her wavering gaze. "How are you feeling since it happened?" Linc had worried about the deception he was playing on her. It wasn't time yet to tell her the truth because he felt she was still under too much strain. And besides, the more Brie trusted him, the more she was readily volunteering things about herself. All the scraps of evidence would eventually yield an answer.

Brie looked at the ceiling. "Fragile. As if I've had a baby-bottle brush wipe me clean inside." She lowered her head and pointed at her tear-filled eyes. "I also cry at the drop of a hat now."

Linc saw a tear drift down, leaned over and brushed it away with his thumb. "That's a good sign," he murmured.

"Is it?"

"Yeah. It means you can begin to heal now. Holding all that stuff inside was stopping you from healing, Brie. Until you get rid of the poisons you're holding, you remain raw."

She sniffed, took a Kleenex from her pocket and dabbed at her eyes.

Linc saw the frail quality in Brie's face and heard it in her voice. The cleansing had left her more vulnerable than she was comfortable with. As much as he wanted to reach out and take her into his arms or kiss her, he knew he didn't dare. Right now she needed a good friend to talk things out with. *Friends.* He laughed at himself. Another first. He'd never tried to establish a friendship with a woman before. Now it was happening.

Brie closed her eyes, resting her brow against her clasped hands. "I feel so awkward, Linc. You're almost a stranger. My parents, my brother and Carol have all reached out to try to help me." She lifted her lashes, staring blindly at the kitchen wall. "And I was afraid. Embarrassed. You should see the stack of letters I have to answer, the phone calls I have to make. I've avoided so much in the past three months."

Linc forced himself to reach for the cherry pie and begin eating it. Guilt jabbed him sharply. He'd already read those letters. How would Brie feel if she knew that? Linc didn't want to look too closely at the answer. His stomach knotted in fear. "Part of healing is getting back into contact with the world, you know. Why don't you go home and if you're up to it, give your mom and dad a call? Maybe pen a few letters. Sort of get back into the swing of living again." The last thing he wanted was for Brie to leave so soon after she had arrived.

"I know you're right. But I feel so...breakable right now, Linc. I feel as if any moment I'll just burst into tears. Thank God, I didn't do it in front of today's class. If I start crying on the phone with my mom..."

Linc gave her a steady look. "It's normal, Brie. Take my word for it."

She gave him a tender smile. "The voice of experience speaking?"

He nodded, not tasting the cherry pie. "You don't need another sad story tonight. Why don't you get your nice-looking rear out of here and go talk to some of those people who love and care about you so much?"

He lay in his own bed, with its nondescript wooden head and footboard. Nothing so individualistic as brass, he thought, like Brie's bed. Hands behind his head, Linc stared at the ceiling. There was no fan gently whirling to move the air as there had been at Brie's home. He scowled. Dammit, he missed her. And her house. Was he missing married life? Linc snorted with disgust. He'd never shared with JoAnne what he had with Brie in the past five days.

Brie was bringing out surprising and unknown facets of him. Why hadn't JoAnne? The difference between the two women was stark. Brie was assertive, JoAnne utterly passive. Brie took life by the throat, JoAnne allowed it to flow by her. Brie was highly emotional, making him feel as if he were on a roller-coaster ride. JoAnne was like a steady beacon, favoring peace above everything. She would rarely respond with a raised voice. Come to think of it, JoAnne never once lost her temper. If he and Brie were married, she would never stand still for his long absences. He wouldn't, either. He'd want to come back to Brie more than once every three or four months.

Linc rolled onto his side and stared at the white curtains covering the window. A streetlight cast unnatural brightness into the bedroom. He missed the moonlight falling through the pale green sheers of Brie's living room, giving everything a softened, almost magical quality. His mind revolved to JoAnne. In all fairness to her, she wasn't at fault. He'd simply married the wrong type of woman. He needed someone of Brie's volatility, openness and assertiveness. She made him come alive. She *was* life, he admitted. She felt deep and hard. And so did he, he was discovering, because Brie was bringing out all those stored emotions from him.

All right, little cat, we have time, he thought. Time. He was getting a lot of pleasure out of waiting for her and he'd never felt that before. He liked the idea of getting to know her before taking her to bed and making love to her....

Linc rolled on his back, hands behind his head again, the sheets in a twisted tangle around his naked body. No. I'm going to make love *with* you, little cat. He wanted to give her as much as he knew she was going to give him in return. Linc shut his eyes, dwelling on that last pleasant thought. Yes, Brie was a giver. And he, by nature, was a taker. Or was he? What was this driving need to give back to her, then? He'd never wanted to do that with another woman.

When this investigation was completed, what was he going to say to Brie? How could he defend his deceiving her to get her trust?

With a groan, Linc rolled on his belly, shoving the pillow off the bed with one dark-haired arm. Go to sleep, pal, he ordered himself. You've got another tough week in front of you. Then he thought of how he'd be spending that week with Brie. He could tolerate anything as long as she was with him. Anything.

Chapter Eight

Linc had just stopped the white whale in front of Brie's home when their beepers went off. A week had passed since Brie had appeared on Linc's doorstep with a home-cooked meal, and they had just had a long day on the road. Brie groaned as she stepped out of the van to go inside the house and make a phone call to the FM's office.

She came out scowling. "There's a report of a Bach Industries tanker dumping chemicals at the edge of a farmer's field up in Ashtabula. If we hurry, we might catch him," she told Linc breathlessly.

It was another haz-mat incident. Feeling grim, Linc nodded. They changed clothes and grabbed food in case they were stranded on a long call. Brie checked on Homely Homer in the back of the van; the bird had to take another ride with them. Then they were pulling out of the driveway. Linc drove as Brie pulled out a map of northeast Ohio and spread it across her lap.

"What's the name of the farmer who made the call?" Linc questioned. There hadn't been time to discuss the call before.

Brie traced the quickest route to the reported area. "David Reynolds. He owns a farm up in Ashtabula County, close to Lake Erie." She pulled the folded paper from her breast pocket where she had written the farm's address as well as directions on how to get to it. "He said he saw a big tanker truck with Bach on the side of it stop near a roadside ditch and start pumping something out. When he went to investigate, he said the driver warned him away with a sawed-off shotgun."

"Wonderful," Linc muttered darkly.

"This isn't the first time that's happened with Bach," she said softly.

Linc remembered Bach had the best reason to kill John and Brie. The largest fine in the United States had been levied against the company a year ago, and John was killed three months after the fining. He felt fear and didn't want Brie out on this dangerous assignment. "Does Reynolds know what was being pumped out?"

"No."

"Did he see any placards on the truck that might give us a number so we can trace it through one of our manuals?"

"No."

"Great. This is stacking up to be quite some call."

Brie's mouth thinned. "Yes, it is."

Linc swore softly. "We'll be getting back at midnight at the earliest."

She nodded. "And that involves only driving time, not handling the incident itself," she reminded him. Brie reached over, placing her fingers on his shoulder, reveling in his powerful build. "Welcome back to the real world, Tanner."

He shot her a look. "I've been working on this job for only three weeks and I've got a gut full of this being called out twenty-four hours a day, seven days a week. I'm burned out already."

She gave him an understanding smile, tiredness shadowing her eyes. "Try three years of it. Or, like John, five years."

Linc shook his head, wanting this case broken open and solved. This job was killing. How had Brie managed to stay on top of the mental strain, the hours, and yet remain alert and capable of handling incident after incident without making an error? It was phenomenal. She was phenomenal. All the more reason to protect and keep her safe, he thought.

By the time they reached the area, it was dark. It was a moonless night, and the country highways had no streetlights to help them find the small roads given in the directions. Using a flashlight, Brie found wooden signs with peeling paint. Linc was holding on to his anger and frustration as he took the haz-mat truck slowly down the road that would lead to the Reynolds farm. The road was heavily rutted and potholed, and he had to put the truck in low gear.

They went seven miles into the countryside before Brie pointed to a farm sitting high on a hill. "This has to be it. Hold on, let me go out and look at the mailbox and see if Reynolds's name is on it."

Linc waited, always alert, his gaze perusing the dark countryside. There was no sign of a tanker, and relief sizzled through him. Brie climbed in.

"Success! David Reynolds. Okay, let's go up there and talk with him.

Dogs barked and bayed as they slowly drew to a halt in front of the old stone farmhouse. Brie quickly got out, anxious to talk with Reynolds and get something done about the situation. A porch light came on, and a man in his seventies went out to meet her.

Brie smiled and held out her hand. "Mr. Reynolds? I'm Brie Williams from the hazardous material unit."

The man's silver hair glinted in the yellow light above them. His pinched and weathered face drew into a smile of relief.

"Glad you're here." He produced three Polaroid shots. "The Bach tanker's gone, but I got these pictures of him dumping, miss."

Excitedly, Brie showed Linc the photos. Reynolds had wisely moved far enough away not to get shot at, but close enough to show the tanker dumping the chemicals into the roadside ditch.

"These are wonderful, Mr. Reynolds. I'd like to file a report on what you saw."

"Surely, come right in."

Maybe this was the break they needed, Linc thought as they walked into the home filled with antique furniture. He hoped so. By midnight, they should be home, getting some badly needed sleep. But his night was just beginning. As soon as Brie filed the report, he'd take a copy over to the Canton police and send it to the ATF and Cramer. Bach Industries was going to be scrutinized by every law-enforcement agency computer, and their board members run through an FBI check. Nothing was going to be over-looked after the Holcomb break-in.

It was midnight when they arrived at Brie's home. Linc frowned. Something looked wrong. The screen door was ajar. He knew Brie had closed it before she came back to the van. He shut off the engine, the hair on his neck rising.

"Stay here," he warned her quietly.

Brie frowned, half asleep.

"What...?"

"Your back door is open."

Immediately Brie sat up. She became aware of Linc's on-guard stance. "Oh, no..." Memories of the break-in at Carol's house returned to her. "It had to be the wind that pulled the door open," she stammered.

Linc got out, telling her with a look to stay in the van. "I hope you're right." He approached the door with extreme caution. As he pulled the screen open, he saw crowbar marks on the door. With a gentle push, the door swung wide into the darkness of the kitchen.

Linc heard no sounds, only the hollow ring of emptiness as he stepped into the kitchen and switched on the light. What met his eyes sickened him. The entire kitchen was in shambles, nothing neglected, everything torn out, opened and spilled on the floor, table and counter. The pit of his stomach knotted as he cautiously went through the rest of the house.

Whoever had done this was gone. He stepped over the clutter, frantically trying to find the words to tell Brie. He knew how much love she had put into this home. His heart was pounding with pain—her pain. As he stepped toward the van, he saw her wide, questioning eyes, as if she already had guessed what had happened.

"Linc, what is it?"

"Your house," he croaked, opening the door for her, gripping her by the arm, "has been broken into."

He measured his words slowly. "Whatever it is they're looking for wasn't found at Holcomb's house, Brie. They think you have it."

Brie's fingers rested on her aching throat. Her house. Her beautiful house, which was a magical, healing place, had been broken into. She shut her eyes tightly, fighting back the tears that wanted to come. She had spent three years lovingly painting, wallpapering and adding just the right appointments that would reflect her private self.

"Did you hear me?"

Linc's voice grated over her nerves, and she realized she had been holding her breath. "Y-yes, I heard you. Linc, do you think they tore up my house as badly as Carol's"

He heard the anguish in her soft voice and kept his firm grip on her arm as he led her to the back door. "Yes." He was lying. Brie's house was in worse shape than Holcomb's. Whoever was looking for something tore Brie's place apart and went over it with a fine-tooth comb. He felt her icy fingers clutch at his hand and he felt her terror. "Just hang in there. We'll get to the bottom of this."

Brie stood numbly in the living room. She heard Linc call the police, and minutes later, she watched several uniformed and plainclothes detectives wandering in and out of the rooms. She saw a man with powder and a brush at the front door. He's looking for fingerprints, she thought. Linc went to her, and his hand encircled her shoulder. Brie leaned against him, needing his silent strength.

Linc was watching her closely. He felt a tremble go through Brie. He was nauseated by the destruction. There wasn't one dish left in the cupboards; all of the dishes lay shattered on the kitchen floor. The paper that lined the cupboards had been torn away, exposing the wood. Linc recognized Detective Gent, who stood at the entrance to the kitchen.

"Come on," he coaxed Brie hoarsely. "Detective Gent wants to talk with us, Brie."

Brie stood in what was once her wonderful, junglelike living room. The trees had been turned upside down, the catch pans torn off the bottom, as if someone was looking for something small enough to wedge between the pan and pot. Each of her expensively framed photos of African wildlife had been torn off the walls, slit and torn out. The back on the television had been removed, the cushions on the rattan couch ripped open. Nothing was left untouched in the raping of her house. As Brie stood in Linc's arms, she felt stunned and in shock. Carol's house had not been as brutally mutilated as hers.

It was almost three in the morning when the detectives finished questioning her. Brie was dazed, unable to think any longer. She had sat on the floor with Linc beside her, answering Gent's long list of questions in a monotone. Finally, the police said they would come back tomorrow. Silence swelled around Brie as all the men left in their black and white cruisers. Woodenly, she had gone to her bedroom and stood beside her bed, staring at the goose-down mattresses torn open and the feathers scattered everywhere. With trembling fingers, Brie touched the cool brass of the footboard.

Linc found Brie standing there, head bowed, her hand pressed against her closed eyes. ''Let's go,'' he urged huskily, taking her into his arms.

''Go? Where?''

He winced at the vacant expression in her eyes and her voice full of defeat. Linc studied her intently, feeling her despair. His arms tightened protectively around her.

''Home,'' he said thickly. ''With me.''

Brie's heart somersaulted. Only this time, it was with warmth, not dread. She studied his dark gaze that said so much and rested her head against his chest, allowing the beat of his heart to smooth the ragged edges of her composure.

''Yes, I'll go home with you...''

Fighting to contain a caldron of untapped feelings, Linc could only nod. He gave her a brief squeeze, looking over at Detective Gent.

"We'll be in touch," Linc promised grimly.

Gent nodded. "You bet."

"I'll call your office tomorrow morning."

"Fine, Mr. Tanner. Until then."

Centering all his attention on Brie, Linc led her through the clutter in the rooms and to the kitchen door. There was an awful darkness in her jade eyes that frightened him. All Linc wanted to do was take her to bed with him, hold her and drive away all the pain.

As they slowly walked to the van, Linc decided that somehow, Brie was at the center of the case, even if she was the victim. And even after what had taken place at her house, she honestly still didn't seem to know why. Taking a last look at her as she climbed into the van, Linc silently promised her that he would put an end to this case—soon.

In silence they drove to his apartment. Linc led her inside. "Listen, you take the bedroom," he told Brie. He opened the door and gestured toward the dark interior. "I'll sleep on the couch."

Despite her bone-deep exhaustion, Brie resisted. "Linc, you'll be more comfortable in your own bed—"

Leaning down, he pressed a kiss to her sable hair. "Don't fight me, little cat. Get a good hot bath, change into your gown and sleep."

It was a gruffly spoken order. And it sounded heavenly to Brie. A bare hint of a smile tugged at the corners of her mouth. "Okay. I'll see you in the morning."

"Fine." As soon as she was in bed, Linc was going to the Canton police to get in touch with Cramer.

Eyes burning with fatigue, Linc entered his apartment. It was nearly five o'clock. The time at the police station, much of it spent on a computer terminal connected to the ATF office in D.C., had turned up little.

Linc took a quick shower and put on his pajama bottoms. He opened the door that led to his bedroom to check on Brie. He saw her sleeping, the covers having slipped from her waist and bunched around her legs. Smiling tenderly, Linc padded softly to the bed. His eyes adjusted to the semidarkness, and he could see that Brie's face was clear of all tension. Her lips were slightly parted, and alluring.

Dragging in a deep breath, Linc carefully pulled the sheet and blanket up to Brie's waist, tucking her in. She stirred but didn't awaken. He stood there for long, torturous moments. Linc didn't want to leave. The urge to lie next to Brie and hold her throughout the long night was overwhelming. The couch in the living room was waiting for him. He should go....

Brie stirred, stretching. She felt someone nearby. When she dragged open her eyes, she realized Linc was standing by the bed, his features harsh and lined with worry.

"Linc?"

"Shh, go back to sleep, little cat. You're exhausted."

A slight smile tugged at her mouth as Linc ran his hand across the crown of her hair. "I'm feeling better."

Swallowing hard, Linc nodded. "Good." His voice sounded strangled. Brie's sounded like velvet. The ache in him grew. How he wanted just to hold her close to him. Her eyes were clouded with sleep, and he knew she wasn't really that awake at all. He ran his fingers through her silky hair. A soft sigh came from her.

"My mom used to do that," she whispered, closing her eyes again.

"Yeah?" He never wanted to stop, his trembling fingers

lightly brushing the curve of her cheek. Brie was so soft, so womanly that a keen hunger swept through him.

Brie nodded, snuggling into the pillow. "When I was scared, she'd come and hold me. Then she'd make me feel better," she murmured, her words barely audible.

His throat constricted. "Are you scared?" His voice was barely above a whisper.

Raising her lashes and meeting Linc's gaze, she nodded. "Y-yes…"

"Do—do you want me to hold you?"

She captured Linc's hand and held it against her cheek. "Will you?"

Taking a shaky breath, Linc nodded. "As long as you want."

"All night?"

He managed to smile. "All night," he promised huskily, removing his hand from hers. Linc moved to the other side of the bed. His heart was pounding heavily in his chest. As he slid into bed, he realized that Brie had already sunk back into sleep. He moved to take her into his arms, knowing she probably wouldn't recall their conversation in the morning. It didn't matter. All he was going to do was hold her, give her that feeling of safety so she could continue to heal herself.

"Come here," he murmured softly. A groan escaped him when she turned over and blindly sought his arms. He felt the warm sleekness of her silk nightgown. Brie rested her head against his shoulder, hands pressed to his chest. Her scent entered his flared nostrils, and Linc's heated blood rushed with throbbing urgency throughout him. He had to strangle the urge to wake Brie and make slow, delicious love with her.…

Memories of her house being broken into flooded Brie's awakening mind, and she burrowed more deeply into

Linc's arms. His naked chest was warm and firm beneath her cheek. As she lay there, listening to his heartbeat, her arm wrapped around his torso, she admitted how much he'd come to mean to her on a strictly personal level. Was it love?

With a sigh, she closed her eyes, feeling Linc's arms coming around her as he awakened. She had nearly married once, but the emotions she'd felt then were not as strong and vibrant as what she felt toward Linc. His heartbeat quickened, and she knew he was fully awake.

Wanting to erase the terrible events that were stalking her, Brie pressed herself against his entire body, wanting to lose herself in Linc.

Linc levered himself upward on one elbow, gazing down at Brie in the early morning light. Her eyes were lustrous with invitation, lips parted, begging him to kiss her. He'd waited so long for her silent invitation to love her. He'd done right, and it felt good, knowing that she wanted him at last. He threaded his fingers through her silky hair, and she responded with a sigh. Her fingers moved across his shoulder and back.

"I've waited a long time for this," he told her, pressing his lips to her hair, inhaling her feminine scent. Linc ignored what his mind was screaming at him, that Brie didn't know he was an agent, that he had come to her in deception and cloaked with lies. Shoving that reality aside, he trailed kisses from her temple, across her cheek and to her awaiting lips, feeling her unfettered response.

"So have I," she said, sighing, raising her lashes, drowning in his cobalt eyes, which burned with hunger.

Linc nodded. "That night I held you on the couch and caressed you, I had wanted to carry you to the bed. I wanted to do a hell of a lot more than just hold you after

you cried." His voice lowered to a gritty growl. "I wanted
to make love to you, Brie. I wanted to erase all that hurt
that was left in you from your storm of tears. I wanted to
be there in the morning and have you wake up in my arms,
knowing that I was there for more than just a one-night
stand." He shook his head, mystified at the depth of his
feelings for her. "I didn't even want to leave you from
that moment on."

Brie stared at his rugged face and the grim set of his
mouth. With a thrill, she realized Linc was revealing another part of himself to her, and elation soared through
her. This was the Linc she had always known existed beyond those walls he had set around himself. "So you felt
the best way to help me was to create distance between
us, of a sort?"

His gaze rested on her serene features. "I want to love
you," he said thickly, his body going hard with need of
her. He saw and felt Brie arch against him.

"Linc," she said huskily, "I don't want that distance
between us any longer."

With a groan, he brought her to him.

Brie closed her eyes, opening her arms to receive him.
The instant his mouth molded firmly over hers, a small
moan of pleasure escaped from her. Her arms followed the
curve of his shoulders. The white-hot shock of need uncurled heatedly in her as she felt him shift so that she was
lying beneath him. His breath was moist and ragged
against her cheek.

"Open your mouth," he rasped, "I want to taste you,
Brie. All of you…"

Another bolt of pleasure unwound through her as his
tongue gently explored her mouth. An ache, so intense and
startling, made her gasp as his hand trailed a path of fire
around her breast. She felt her nipples growing hard, throb-

bing, begging to be touched by Linc. Her breathing became uneven, and she hungrily returned his fierce kiss. Brie ran her fingertips over his back, reveling in the movement of his muscles.

She was totally unprepared when Linc tore his mouth from her lips, captured one of her nipples beneath the gown and sucked it gently. A cry of need tore from her, and she arched toward him, filled with the ecstasy of pleasure. Another cry tore from her as Linc gave the other nipple equal attention, easing the ache there. His trembling fingers pushed the straps of her gown aside, and Brie froze. Her eyes flew open and she lay staring up at Linc, feeling a mixture of shame and shyness. He leaned down, kissing her lips, and she knew it was a kiss meant to give support, not ignite passion. He was breathing harshly as he rested his hand upon her injured shoulder.

"I'll be gentle," he told her.

His hand had begun to push the fabric away to expose the angry red flesh that Brie was so ashamed of. She tensed, her eyes going wide with pleading. He leaned down, kissing her lashes, nose, cheek and finally her mouth.

"Listen to me." Linc breathed thickly against her ear, holding her close. "It makes no difference to me about your burns. They aren't the whole of you. It's only skin, not your heart, that's been wounded." He brushed a kiss on her cheek, sensing she was beginning to relax and accept his touch. "It's what I see and feel from your heart that I want you to share with me. Your warm, giving, loving heart." He shuddered when she pressed herself to him. "I ache for you. I want you so bad that I would tear this world apart to be with you." He gently pulled down the strap. "What you have is in you. In your heart, Brie. Give that to me. Let me drown myself inside you..."

Tears clung like shimmering diamonds to her lashes. Then she opened her eyes, wrapped her arms around his neck and met his burning gaze. "Yes," she whispered unsteadily. "I'm not afraid anymore."

He smiled tenderly. He leaned down to place moist kisses in the valley between her breasts as he released them from the captive material. She was so beautiful, he thought, after he'd undressed her. He quivered as she lay before him on the dark wine-colored blanket, her body a creamy white with graceful curves. Pleasure sang through him when she sat up and with trembling fingers of her own helped him shed his pajamas. He liked her participation, finding it provocative. And when she came to him, settling on her knees between his legs, pressing her lips to his, his surprise melted into a caldron of fire.

He ran his hands down her torso, rested them on her hips and drew her to him. His body throbbed with heat and growing fire. A small moan of pleasure broke from her parted lips as he suckled her nipples, hands cupping their curved roundness. She was magic. She was a dream. And so much a woman. Dazed by her ability to take and to give in return, Linc brought her down upon him. He knew that because of Brie's burns, he shouldn't lie on her and have the sheet and blankets rub against her tender, recovering flesh.

Brie's heart thrashed wildly in her breast; her body screamed to be freed of the torture of needing Linc. Hot flames were burning inside her, and Brie was barely aware when he lay back, taking her with him. He lifted her easily, as if she were a feather. The instant she settled against his hips and the hardness of his body pressed against her soft, womanly core, a sweet quiver rippled through her. It was so exquisite, so shattering that Brie could only grip his arms. And when he arched against her, a sob tore from her lips and she felt need as never before. Fire spread through her belly down to where she needed to join with him. As if he had sensed her need, Brie felt herself lifted, and in the next second, she welcomed him into her.

Sensations overwhelmed her as he moved against her in the way only a man can with his woman. Liquid heat built rapidly through her, and Brie tensed. A shattering explosion roared through her, robbing her of breath, stealing her senses and hurling her to the edge of an unnamed universe. She rested her head on Linc's shoulder and called his name over and over again. His hands gently caressed her back and hips and he called thickly to her, moving, bringing her into fiery rhythm with himself once again. This time, she was aware of his power, his maleness and strength as never before. His hands tightened against her hips and he thrust deep and hard into her. Brie felt their universes collide, then fly apart in an eruption of golden light as they shared the ultimate with one another, the gift of themselves.

Linc lay there long afterward, breathing raggedly, his heart thudding savagely in his chest. Brie lay against him, her head on his shoulder. He could only feel. Thought was nonexistent, banished into exile. He ran his hands lightly down her body, which was slick and hot. Her heart was skittering, and he smiled. She was boneless, her giving, spent body molding and curving to the harder planes of his own. His hand settled on her velvet brown hair and he ran the strands between his fingers.

"You're like a feline," he said in a gritty voice, "purring and rubbing against me."

Brie couldn't open her eyes, wrapped in euphoria. "I've never thought of myself as a cat," she admitted, her voice wispy.

Linc opened his eyes. "You're the first woman I've met who reminded me of a cat. There's something about you…'' He groped for words that refused to come because he was still held in the glowing, throbbing spell of what they'd just shared. He cupped her face, staring into her half-closed eyes fringed with dark lashes. Her lips were slightly swollen, and he immediately felt regret, not wanting to have hurt Brie. But she had come to him with her fire to match and mate with his, and it had torn away all his best intentions.

"Any regrets?" he asked her.

Brie closed her eyes and gave a small shake of her head. "No." She opened them and stared at him. "And you?"

Linc warmed to her. No other woman had ever asked him that. Or perhaps, cared enough to ask. For her, physical union went far beyond physical needs. But he had always known that. For Brie, the union was a nonverbal commitment of herself to him, and he was suddenly moved by what had occurred between them. He managed a slight smile, thinking how beautiful she looked after their loving, hating himself for having to keep a lie between them. "No. No regrets," he told her softly. He saw the smoldering gold flame in her eyes suddenly die, and his hands tightened on her jaw. "What is it?"

Brie placed her lips against his palm, aware of the roughened texture of his flesh, then rested her head in the crook of his shoulder. "I'm scared, Linc," she admitted.

His hand came to rest on her uninjured shoulder. "About what?"

"Us. Me, rather." She took a breath and rushed on, her words coming out in a torrent. "I know your kind. And I accept that. But it's the first time I've accepted it. I'm used to a one-to-one relationship where more counts than just the bedroom scene. I want…no, need that depth of sharing with a man." She swallowed hard. "And I know from the way you've talked in the past that a woman is pleasure.

That's all. I knew all that before we made love with one another, and I accepted that about you. I'm not going to play a game with you and try to get you to change.''

She had courage, Linc thought. And she was clear-headed. She was right—women were to be enjoyed in bed. But he had enjoyed Brie in and *out* of bed. ''In the past three weeks you've taught me something, little cat—what it's like to be a friend to a woman.''

There was disbelief in her voice. ''I have?''

He smiled and kissed her hair. ''I've changed my mind about women because of you.'' He sighed. ''And it's got to be due to you. I like you as my friend, too. I like all the things we do together.'' Then he added as she raised her head, hope in her lovely green eyes, ''In and *out* of bed.''

Tears scalded her eyes as she held Linc's tender gaze. ''You mean that?'' she asked. His answering smile caressed her.

He wiped the tears from her cheeks. ''Yes, I mean that. You're different, Brie. And it's hard to put into words what I'm talking about. You aren't like other women. You're unique, one of a kind.''

Brie leaned over and kissed his roughened cheek, then nuzzled her lips near his ear. ''No, I'm not so unique, Linc,'' she whispered. ''All I did was refuse to allow you to put me into that mold. And you had no choice because we worked together. There are many other women out there like me. Circumstances just haven't been there for you to see or discover that.''

He buried his face in the curve of her neck, tasting her sweetness and the saltiness of her skin. ''There may be, but I'm interested only in you, woman. Now, come here...'' He gently rolled her onto her back, levering himself beside her. Just the sound of her voice and the brush of her fingertips on his skin sent his body into rigid awakening once again. He wasn't sure who was more surprised by it—him or Brie. But if she was surprised, it didn't show in her welcoming green eyes. He leaned down and cherished her full lips, and he knew—she loved him. Brie was incapable of hiding her real feelings, and Linc felt a powerful current of fear and joy jag through him. His new awareness made the kiss he gave her that much sweeter. Brie deserved happiness. She deserved to laugh. He had seen life dancing in her eyes. She was like the sun, touching and coaxing life from the earth.

And what was he bringing her from himself? Lies, deceit and distrust. His heart felt as if it was ripping in two. How could he tell her? When? What would happen to this fragile joy they now shared? Linc didn't want it destroyed. But how could he make Brie believe him? That his feelings for her were genuine? That he never meant to hurt her? Oh, God, he was going to, and he'd never felt as miserable.

Chapter Nine

"So what now?" Brie asked quietly over breakfast with Linc.

"I called the FM when I was at the police department, and McPeak and Laughlin will fill in for our quadrant while we push this investigation on who's after you."

"Linc, if they want to kill me, why haven't they done it yet?"

"They may have tried with that second explosive device up in Cleveland we answered."

Brie nodded. "It might have been. But they're tearing up our homes, not firing shots at us. Or me."

Linc agreed with her. "Whoever it is is looking for something, Brie. Some tangible piece of evidence that was either in your possession or John's." He shook his head and scowled. "Believe me, I've been through all your paperwork and John's, and I can't find anything that would incriminate any company except for Bach. I just can't figure it out. When John died, did Carol give you anything of his?''

Brie thought for a moment. ''I was in the hospital when she called up one day. Carol was in tears, I remember that much.''

''What else?'' Linc asked, hoping against hope that she could provide a clue or lead.

''I was on painkillers at the time, Linc. I think…I think she was going to throw out all his haz-mat books and manuals. I told her I'd take them, because John had some old ones that were out of print that had valuable information in them.''

''Did you pick them up when you got out of the hospital?''

She shook her head. ''Carol had a key to my house, and she said she'd take the boxes over there. When I got home, there were three boxes in the living room near my bookcase.''

''What were in those boxes?''

''Books and manuals.'' Brie looked at him. ''I can show them to you if the person who broke into the house didn't take them. What will you do with them?''

''Well, whatever they're looking for is probably small and could be tucked away. It means sifting page by page through all of John's books.''

Sudden excitement coursed through Brie, and she sat up. ''Linc, I'll know if any of his books are missing!''

''How?''

She clapped her hands. ''I have a Rolodex that has every title and author of the books I own. That was one of the things I did right after I got out of the hospital. The books that belonged to John, I made a notation on each card. We can find out right away if all his books are there. And if they aren't, we'll know within a couple of hours, and that would give us a lead!''

Linc resisted her enthusiasm. ''It's a lead,'' he admitted gravely. He reached out, caressing her hair. ''The house is a mess, Brie. Are you up to going over there?''

She gave him a tender smile, sliding her arms around his shoulders. ''I'm ready to tackle it.''

He ran his thumb across her flushed cheek. ''From now on, I want you to be extra careful. Just stick close to me. If I tell you to hit the deck, do it without question. Okay?''

Brie swallowed hard, seeing the military part of Linc surfacing. ''Yes, I'll always listen to you.''

He grinned, trying to relieve some of the strain he saw appearing at the corners of her mouth. ''You mean you'll stop being bossy at haz-mat spills?'' he taunted.

Brie managed a smile, loving him for his ability to ease the pressure from her. ''That will never happen, Tanner.''

With a groan, Linc got to his feet, pulling her along with him. ''I was afraid of that.''

As Brie walked through her home, she felt the strong urge to start cleaning immediately, but she knew how important it was to find the Rolodex. So instead she merely waded through the overturned furniture in the living room.

Linc spotted the Rolodex on the carpet next to the cherrywood desk. He gestured for her to come and sit next to him. ''Take a look at this and give me the titles of John's books and I'll make a list of them.'' Everywhere Linc looked, books were scattered like leaves off an autumn tree. There were hundreds of books to search through. It was going to take a long time to find them all—if they were still in the house.

Several minutes later, with thirty-five books stacked in

piles, Brie called off the last title. She looked at the miniature towers that surrounded them.

"They're all here, Linc." Triumph was in her voice.

He took five books from the first stack. "That's a good sign, little cat. Now comes the hard part—going through them page by page, looking for a clue."

She joined him on the couch they had righted. "If there is one," she groused.

Linc nodded, opening the first book. "Right. But judging from the break-ins, there's probably something in one of these books that might point a finger. It's the only link I can think of between you and Carol and John."

Almost three hours later, Brie got up. "Nothing," she groaned, rubbing her neck, which she had held in the same angle for so long. The sun had changed position, leaving a muted light in the living room that she loved so much. "Come on, let's take a break and I'll pour us some coffee." At his apartment, she had wisely filled both their thermoses with coffee and brought them along with some cups.

Reluctantly, Linc followed her into the kitchen, taking the book he was thumbing through with him.

"John was one for highlighting things in yellow and making notes in the margins, wasn't he?" Linc made himself comfortable at the table.

"Yes, he was very thorough," she answered, filling the cups and sitting down opposite him.

Linc thanked her for the coffee and settled back with the book, slowly turning page after page. John's handwriting was clear and precise compared to his own hen scratchings. He read every margin note and highlighted sentence trying to figure out if they had any significance to the case.

He sat up, frowning. "Come here, look at this," Linc said, placing the book on the table.

Brie stood and leaned over Linc's shoulder, looking at where he held his finger. In the margin John had written, "PCB in #2. See Earl."

"What do you make of it?" Linc asked. "This is a chapter on polychlorinated biphenyl—PCB."

She rested one hand on Linc's shoulder, studying the cryptic note. "PCB in number two could mean a lot of things. Number two tank or tanker?"

"Earl? Who's that?"

Brie searched her memory. "Linc, I don't know when John might have made that note. He was forever making notations. Earl might have been one of his teachers in college, for all I know."

Excitement surged through Linc, and his mind began to work. "Number two could be a fuel oil grade, too. Couldn't it? You know, the oil people use to heat their homes."

"Yes, it could." Her brow wrinkled. "But PCB in fuel grade oil is illegal because PCBs are known to cause cancer."

Linc got even more excited and snapped his fingers. "Wait a minute! A certain level of PCB is found in the oil of older transformers. It could refer to an electric company, one of the companies you gave a hefty fine to— Ohio Utility."

"By law and EPA regulations, that oil is to be drained from the transformers and trucked to disposal sites."

Linc nodded, putting his finger on the name Earl and tapping it. "I'm going over to the police department." He'd call Washington and get their computers to check on all the company representatives that John and Brie had checked in the past five years to see if an Earl showed up.

"Okay, go ahead," Brie said. "I'm staying here to clean up."

After working six hours nonstop, Brie sat at the kitchen table. Slowly, her home was taking on a familiarity once again. Her mind returned to Linc and his keen interest in her problem. Every time she thought of him, her body felt like a simmering caldron of fire. Brie tried not to think of the obvious, that she was possibly falling in love with Linc. There was nothing not to like about him, she decided, feeling serene for the first time in nearly six months. He was honest, hardworking and loyal, attributes she applauded.

Linc came back four hours later. He entered the room, a look of triumph on his face.

"We may have struck pay dirt," he said, sitting down next to her on the couch. "Earl Hansen, the representative from Carter Fuel and Oil, was coughed out by the computer."

"Oh, Linc, he couldn't possibly be a suspect!"

"Everyone is at this point, Brie."

Brie shook her head, not wanting to believe it. "Linc, he's a dear, sweet man." She grimaced, seeing the implacable set of Linc's jaw. "He used to bring me wildflowers from around the corner of the office," she muttered defensively. "How can a man who is that thoughtful and sensitive be contaminating fuel oil?"

He reached over, capturing her hand. "Believe me, little cat, people will do anything with enough reason," he murmured. Linc saw the genuine distress in Brie's eyes and felt badly.

"What are we going to do?"

He held her cool, damp hand in his, trying to soothe

her. "I think I'll pay a visit to Carter Fuel under cover of darkness, take a few samples from their underground tanks and get the oil analyzed. If they are mixing PCB with good fuel oil, it isn't going to be in their office records, you can count on that."

"And if the PCB shows up?"

"Go to the authorities and have them arrest Earl and Frank Carter."

Tears gathered in Brie's eyes. "Earl is innocent! He just isn't the kind of man who would do something like that, Linc."

His mouth tightened. "Don't forget, John was murdered, and someone tried to kill you, too," he told her quietly. His words had a chilling effect on Brie. He hated shattering her illusions about people.

"All right, then I'm going with you."

"What?"

Brie got up. "I said I'm going with you."

"No way. This could get dangerous, Brie. How do we know Carter doesn't have a security guard who patrols that place at night?"

"Carter has a huge German shepherd that's loose within that fenced area." She gave him a slight smile of triumph. "And I just happen to know the dog, Captain, very well. If I'm along, I doubt if he'll bark or attack you when we go over the fence to get those samples."

Linc chafed, he didn't want Brie along. But a dog was harder to fool than a sentry, and dogs barked, alerting everyone.

"Besides, Linc, if Carter does have PCB in the fuel oil, how do we know it's in the underground tanks? Why couldn't it be in any one of the five trucks in his garage?"

She was right. That would mean taking several samples and spending a lot of time collecting them. The possibility of getting caught was doubled because of the time factor. If Brie did come along, that time could be cut in half. "Okay, you're coming along," he said gruffly, standing. "First let me contact the police." In reality he'd contact Cramer at ATF, apprising him of everything, in case something went wrong. That he had to put Brie in a potential line of fire agitated Linc. It would be so much simpler if he could walk in with a search warrant. If he did, Carter would get suspicious, legally stall for time, then remove any evidence before they could get their samples. And then where would they be? Dammit!

Brie crouched next to Linc, her heart hammering away in her throat. She checked the time on her watch: three o'clock. Linc had made her get into her dark blue uniform and wear a long-sleeved black sweater beneath it to cover her arms. Then he had produced a tin of black substance and she had had to smear it all over her face until only the whites of her eyes showed. She wore a thin black knit cap over her hair. Linc had on a different outfit: a body-molding black nylon suit. He looked frightening, Brie thought. This was the military part of Linc Tanner with which she was now dealing. Every piece of equipment he carried on his person had a use, including the 350 magnum in the black shoulder holster. A shiver crawled up her spine. When she questioned his expertise, he muttered something about learning it in Vietnam. She believed him.

"There goes the cruiser," Linc whispered, nodding to a Litton police car that crawled by the facility, which sat at the edge of town. "He won't be back for another hour. Okay, go get Captain."

Brie gave him a frightened look, felt his hand gripping hers and rose. They had been sitting for a while near the brush along the creek behind the fuel oil company. They had made sure no one was inside the compound and that the police cruisers passed by at regular intervals. She was amazed at what Linc knew about this sort of activity and was a little in awe of him as a result.

She stumbled going up the sandy incline. Quickly recovering, Brie walked with a confidence she didn't feel toward the fence. Captain was on his feet, his hackles rising, his huge yellow eyes becoming wolflike slits.

"Captain!" Brie called softly, whistling to him. "Come on, boy! It's Brie, remember?" What if the German shepherd didn't recognize her? He had always followed her around when she visited before. Brie crouched down by the wire fence, calling the dog. Sweat popped out on her upper lip and her mouth went dry when Captain began an ominous growl. He approached her in long, graceful strides. It was a moonlit night, and Brie could see the feral glitter in the animal's eyes. She shoved her hand through the wire and held it out to him, wondering if he was going to bite her. A choked sound came out of her throat as Captain opened his mouth, revealing his white fangs.

"Captain!" she called more firmly.

The German shepherd halted a foot from her.

"What's the matter with you? You know who I am. Brie, remember?" She worked her hand farther through the fence, the flesh pinched by the wire. "Now come here! Come on!"

Captain hesitated then gave a friendly wag of his tail. Relief surged through Brie as she felt Captain's welcoming tongue on her fingers. She slowly got up on wobbly knees, the dog whining and remaining where he was. In a moment, Linc was at her side.

"Grab his collar and keep him occupied." Linc put down a small satchel, then pulled out a hypodermic needle filled with a clear liquid.

Brie's eyes widened as she saw him sink the needle into Captain's hindquarter. Moments later, the dog slowly sank to the ground. Brie uttered a cry.

"You didn't kill him, did you?"

Linc threw the satchel over the fence. Gripping her by the waist, he said, "No, he'll be unconscious for about an hour if I've guessed the dose correctly. Okay, up you go. Remember, swing one leg clear."

The six-foot-high fence was no problem with Linc's help. Brie jumped to the dusty ground and watched as Linc took the fence like a black panther. He gently picked up the dog and placed him in the shadows, making sure he was in a comfortable position.

Brie's mouth was dry, like the ground they treaded lightly upon. Her heart was hammering without pause. Each sound, no matter how far away, made her freeze. They reached the garage, and began to take samples from each of the five trucks. Linc, collecting from the underground tanks, was out in the open, visible to anyone. Would they be discovered?

Her hands trembled and she spilled some of the oil from the last truck over her gloved hand. She placed the cork in the plastic test tube and quickly made her way out of the garage, quietly closing the door behind her. A hand closed around her mouth, and Brie struggled, a scream strangling in her throat.

"Quiet!" Linc hissed into her ear, dragging her against the building.

Her breast rose and fell sharply. Linc slowly loosened his hand, and Brie gulped in several breaths of air. Then she froze. She heard it too. Men's voices, two of them. She twisted to look up at Linc's hard, sweaty face. What should they do? The sounds of the chain-link fence padlock being opened and the gate swinging wide grated on her exposed nerves. Linc pulled her behind him, signaling her to stay silent.

Brie had never felt so helpless. Or in so much real danger. Haz-mat incidents were nothing compared to this. She saw Linc slowly unsnap his holster, draw out the lethal-looking magnum and hold it ready. They were crouched at the far corner of the building with the fence and stream directly behind them. Brie saw two policemen enter the area, their flashlights moving through the darkness. They had mistimed the cruiser. She shrank against Linc as the officers walked up to the office door, tested it, then went back to their cruiser after locking the gate.

Linc turned, looking at Brie. Despite the blackness on her face, he could see the strain in her wide eyes. Without a word, he slipped his arm around her shoulders, drawing her close, needing her warmth. He helped her stand, realizing she was shaky. So was he. He always trembled after the danger was past. Keeping his hand on her elbow, he guided Brie to the fence and helped her over. As they were walking down to the bank, they heard Captain groan and flail around. Brie halted, watching the dog to make sure he would be all right. Linc waited patiently. He knew how much she cared for animals, and as Captain groggily got to his feet, shaking himself unsteadily, Brie looked at Linc, gratefulness evident in her eyes. He smiled and placed his hand on the small of her back. He led her toward the stream and to the van parked in a grove of cottonwoods.

"What's next?" Brie asked tiredly as Linc swung the van into the driveway of his apartment building.

He glanced at her. "A shower and bed for you. I'll take these over to the Canton police and have them analyzed by their lab."

Bed and sleep. Both sounded wonderful. Brie realized

she felt more than exhausted. She didn't want to believe that Earl Hansen would do something as horrible as mixing PCB in people's fuel oil. "It has to be Bach Industries, Linc, not Carter Fuel."

"I hope you're right," he murmured. "Come on, I'm going to grab a shower, change, then leave."

Linc quietly unlocked the door and slipped inside. The sun had been up since six-thirty, and he'd greeted it with bloodshot eyes at the police station. It was almost eight o'clock before he'd returned home to Brie. While he dealt with the details of this investigation in the past hours, he had thought of her—and their fragile relationship built upon lies and deceit. Linc had already seen the tears in Brie's luminous eyes, her belief in mankind eroded.

Linc stood in the bedroom doorway, drinking in Brie's sleeping form like a man dying of thirst. Only he was aching to take her into his arms where she belonged. He walked to the bed and gently sat on the mattress. When he pushed back several strands of hair from her brow, she stirred, and a tender smile pulled at his mouth. You respond so beautifully to just the slightest touch, he told her silently. Linc leaned over to place a warm kiss on her parted lips.

Brie awoke in his arms, and with his name on her lips, she pulled him down upon her. She welcomed his kisses down the length of her neck and over her collarbone. Nestling his face against the soft firmness of her breast, inhaling her feminine scent, he groaned.

"This is the way it should be," he said.

With a sigh, Brie murmured, "Always."

Linc rose up on one arm, keeping a hand resting on her hip, drowning in her slumberous green eyes. "Are you awake enough to talk?"

Brie nodded, feeling the sweet ache of wanting Linc. "Yes. What time is it?"

"A little after eight," he murmured, running his fingers through her hair.

"Did you find out anything?"

"Plenty. One tanker you took a small sample from has a level of more than fifty thousand parts per million of PCBs. That's extremely high levels, not to mention illegal."

Brie struggled to sit up, the covers falling away to reveal her white silk nightgown. Disappointment clouded her features. "Now what?"

"Well, we illegally obtained those samples, so we can't use them as evidence. So now we have to get a search warrant. Of course, Carter will fight that."

Brie pushed her hand through her hair, trying to wake up. "Linc, what if we go talk with Earl? My gut says he's just not a criminal. Maybe if we can get a confession from him or something..." Her voice trailed off.

"It's worth a try," Linc admitted slowly. "If we could get Hansen to turn in evidence to us, he might be able to plea bargain his way out of this mess. I don't know. I'm not the attorney general."

Hope sprang to her eyes. "You mean, if he testifies that Carter is doing this, Earl might not have to go to jail?"

Linc nodded. "Whoa. As I said, I'm not an attorney. I can't promise him or you anything, Brie."

She slipped out of bed and put on her floor-length robe, her eyes alight with excitement. "Let me get dressed, then let's drive down to see him."

Exhaustion was lapping at Linc. The bed felt so good to him right now. All he wanted to do was crash for a few hours. "Okay, little cat. Get dressed, and we'll go have a chat with your friend." He scowled. "But you realize that

Earl could have been the one who tried to have you killed?"

Brie halted at the bedroom door, the possibility sinking in. "Y-yes, I realize that, Linc." Her fingers curled around the doorknob. "I just don't want to believe he would do such a thing."

Linc lay down, arms crossed on his chest after Brie had disappeared into the bathroom. She had every faith in the world in that untarnished heart of hers. How he hoped for her sake that Earl was innocent. But wasn't that one of the many facets of Brie he loved? Her view of people, that they weren't all bad or had ulterior motives.

But would she be able to feel that way about him after the case was solved? After she knew who he really was, and how he'd lied to her? Throwing an arm over his eyes, he sighed loudly. In the past week, he'd fallen in love with her. Once he'd made up his mind she was the victim and not the killer, all the held-back feelings in his heart rampaged through him.

Linc knew their love hadn't stood the test of time in order to become stable enough to ride out problems. His lies were more than a problem, though, and he knew it. *God, let her be understanding with me. Please. I need her, want her.*

Dragging his arm off his eyes, he stared numbly at the white ceiling. He didn't know he was going to fall in love with Brie. And neither did she. Love was the wild card, and when she knew the truth, there was every possibility of it being destroyed. No! He'd just found her. If Carter Fuel and Oil turned out to be a red herring and the investigation had to continue, when could he tell her? And how? Linc decided that there was no good time to inform Brie he was an agent. When he did, all could be lost. No, it was best to keep his cover until the case was solved.

Maybe, by that time, their love for one another would have grown enough to take the traumatic shock in stride instead of getting destroyed. He certainly hoped so.

"Mrs. Hansen?" Brie called, knocking at the screen door of the small, single-level dwelling. She cast a glance at Linc, who stood there stoically. She knocked again. It was ten-thirty on Saturday.

Flora Hansen walked to the door, her thin body covered in a cotton shift that had been washed and worn many times over, the colors faded from the material. Her hazel eyes held a look of confusion as she stood looking through the screen at them. "Yes?"

"Hi, I'm Brie Williams, Mrs. Hansen. And this is Linc Tanner. We're with the Hazardous Material Bureau of the fire marshall's office. Is Earl home?"

Flora frowned. Although she was probably in her early fifties, she looked nearly ten years older. Her hair was almost white, in need of a combing and some care.

"Well, yes, Earl just got home. May I see some identification, please?"

"Of course," Brie murmured, pulling out her badge and holding it up to the screen. Brie had decided that they should come to see Earl in civilian clothes so they wouldn't scare him any more than necessary. She wore a silky, short-sleeved orange blouse and a white cotton skirt with sandals.

"Flora?" It was Earl's voice floating through the house.

Flora turned. "There's some people here to see you."

Brie watched Earl's face turn ashen as he approached the door.

"Brie? What are you doing here?" he asked in amazement.

Linc stepped forward, his hand moving to the handle of

the screen door. "Mr. Hansen, we need to talk with you privately for a few minutes. Would you like to come out here on the porch?"

Flora knew when she was being politely asked to leave and did so, but only after settling her paper-thin fingers on her husband's pudgy arm. Earl's eyes rounded, but he did as Linc suggested. Linc motioned to the porch swing, taking an old chair that was in need of sanding and a new coat of paint.

"Sure. What's the problem, Brie?" Earl asked, sitting down, clasping his hands between his legs.

Brie swallowed, her heart aching for Earl. The man was so frightened, his darting brown gaze moved back and forth between her and Linc. She deliberately kept her voice soft and opened her hands in a gesture of peace.

"Earl, we need your help."

Earl flinched visibly, color draining from his florid features. "About what?"

"About the PCB we found in truck number three, Earl."

He reared back, as if struck. He turned to Linc and waited and watched. He licked his lips then mopped his brow with a handkerchief. "PCB?" he whispered, his voice cracking.

Brie was dying inside. "You know about them, Earl, and so do we. Please don't try to play games with us. I don't want to see you go to jail."

Linc's voice broke the brittle tension surrounding them. "If you turn over state's evidence, it might mean that you'll be granted immunity, Mr. Hansen. Tell us what we want to know and maybe you can stay out of prison."

For a moment, Brie thought Earl was going to faint. The man bowed his head then looked toward the screen door to make sure his wife wasn't standing there. He twisted the handkerchief between his short, thick fingers, as if waging war within himself. "My wife has cancer, Brie."

"Oh, no. Oh, Earl, I'm sorry. I didn't know." Automatically, she placed her hand on his shoulder.

Linc quickly added up the weight of Hansen's admission. "How would you like to be in prison and your wife alone here? By herself." It was a cruel question, but it had the effect on Earl that Linc had hoped for.

Hansen snapped up his head, his eyes filled with tears. "Okay, okay...yes, there is PCB in the grade-two fuel oil. But it was Carter who did it!" He got up, hand pressed against his glistening brow, terror in his eyes. "Carter said if I didn't go along with it, he'd fire me. And where would I be? My wife needs continuous chemotherapy. I don't have enough medical insurance. He said if I didn't keep a second set of books, he'd let me go. Do you understand? I can't let my wife get worse because I don't have the money to pay the doctor bills. Carter promised me that if I went along with this, he'd see that I had enough to help Flora." He turned away, burying his head in his hands, sobbing.

Brie was up in an instant, tears glittering in her eyes, her hand coming to rest on Earl's rounded shoulder. "Oh, Earl," she whispered, "why didn't you come to us? Do you know what PCBs are? What they'll do to people?"

Linc got up and led Hansen back to the porch swing. Brie sat down with him. Linc took the chair, and he waited for Hansen to compose himself. The man raised his head, his reddened eyes filled with anguish.

"I don't know what they are," he admitted miserably. "Carter said it was nothing to worry about. He said he was just doing some friends a favor by taking the oil off their hands instead of having to transport it to a chemical dump where it would cost a lot of money to dispose of."

Brie clenched her hands in her lap. "Earl, PCBs, if inhaled for a long enough time, can cause cancer. By law, any oil with PCBs in it has to be disposed of and the EPA notified. It's illegal to do what Carter's been doing."

Hansen stared at her. "My God, no…" Then his face turned an angry plum color, his voice wobbling. "Carter's been putting PCBs in the fuel oil people have been burning for the last three winters."

A gasp escaped Brie, and she met Linc's stormy gaze.

"That bastard!" Hansen cried hoarsely, getting to his feet. "Carter lied to me!"

If Linc hadn't caught and held him, Hansen would have gone after Carter. Brie watched the two men struggle briefly on the porch, Linc's superior strength and height quickly subduing Earl. Linc forced him to sit down.

"Tell us what you know, Hansen."

Brie sat there for the next half hour, listening to the horror story. Carter had made a contract with a New Jersey firm to haul the PCB-laden fuel oil to Litton where it would be mixed with clean fuel oil. He had been selling the contaminated mixture for three years.

Linc's face became grimmer. "Earl, do you know if Carter hired some professionals to murder John and Brie?"

Earl tried to wipe his eyes of his tears. He glanced at Brie. "Yes, he did. Honest to God, Brie, I didn't know about it until later. If I had known before, I swear, I would have warned you."

Brie forced back all her emotions. Even though she hadn't been killed, she hadn't completely escaped Carter's greedy, inhumane deed.

Linc leaned forward. "Where were these hired professionals from, Earl?"

"Some guys from New Jersey," he said bleakly. "Or maybe it was New York. I don't remember."

"Why did he want John and Brie killed?"

"John came in seven months ago to check the books like he always did. I had been working on the second set of books, the one that kept track of the PCB oil being trucked in. At the time, I didn't realize the mistake I'd made. John had asked for a copy of those two pages with the information on them, and one of the secretaries ran the copies for him. I had been on a phone call and just told her to give him copies. He thanked me and left." Earl took a deep breath. "When I realized what I'd done, I lived in terror of Carter finding out. I knew John was onto something when Brie came back two days later. Normally, I keep the second set of books in the safe, and even the secretaries didn't know what was going on." He glanced at Brie. "When Carter saw you come in two days afterward, he got suspicious. He was upset. He wanted to know why you had visited us again so soon. He thought you suspected something.

"Carter started threatening me with losing my job and letting Flora die. I finally broke down and told him that John had two pages from the wrong set of books." Earl closed his eyes, taking a deep breath. "He flew into a rage, then he picked up the phone. He ordered me out of his office and I left. When he came back out, he was calm. He said not to worry, that everything would be taken care of and we'd get those copies back." Wringing his hands, he stared at his feet, his voice raw. "And when I saw in the papers a couple days later that John had died in an explosion and you were in the Cleveland burn unit in critical condition, Brie, I died inside. I knew then that Carter had called someone."

"He put out a contract on them," Linc growled through clenched teeth. He got up, moving his shoulders to relieve the tension in them. He turned to Brie, and his heart contracted. Brie looked devastated. He wanted to protect her from all this, from Earl's complicity, but he could not. "Okay, Hansen, I want you to come with us. The Canton police will want your affidavit. You'd better get yourself a lawyer while you're at it. I'll do everything in my power to see that you get immunity, but I can't promise anything. Do you understand?"

Earl held Brie's luminous gaze. "I never meant to harm anyone, Brie. You've got to believe that."

"I—I believe you, Earl. And I'm sorry for Flora. For you."

He shook his head. "What a mess." He slowly got to his feet, as if in a daze. "Give me a few minutes, will you? I've got to think of something to tell Flora. I can't just tell her the truth and then walk away for a couple of hours."

Linc nodded. "Take as long as you need," he said softly.

Brie stood after Earl went into the house. She went to Linc and pressed her cheek against his chest, needing his love, his embrace. "So many things are falling into place, Linc," she said in a strained tone.

He kissed her temple. "They are," he agreed. "Why did you go back to Carter's two days after John was there?"

"I was sick the day Earl gave John those copies. The only reason I came back was because John had left his clipboard with our list of contact companies on it. And I remember Carter giving me a funny look when I came in. Normally, he's civil and cool. That day, he looked like a rabid dog who wanted to bite someone."

Linc took a deep breath, rocking her gently in his arms. "That also explains why John's house was ransacked. Carter obviously had someone hired to look for those copies."

"John never showed them to me, Linc. I was never aware of them. It was three days after he got those copies that the explosion occurred and he died."

"Maybe he wanted to do more investigation before he told you about it, Brie. I don't know. We'll never know. But John did put those notes in that one book, so he must have suspected something."

"I'm sure he did," she said tiredly. "John was never one to jump to conclusions, Linc. He was very careful about compiling evidence against any company we were investigating. The reason he probably put those notes in the book is that he was doing further study on PCBs. I'm sure he was suspicious, but waiting to gather more information before he said anything to me." She managed a painful laugh. "John also knew how much I liked Earl."

"Maybe, in his own way, John was trying to protect you, little cat."

Brie shut her eyes tightly, tears squeezing out. "Knowing John, he probably was."

"Like me, he had a soft spot in his heart for you," Linc murmured, kissing her damp cheek. "Just hang on, this is almost over. We've got most of the case solved. Now it's just a matter of getting Earl's statement and having the cops pick up Carter." Dread filled him. The case was solved, and now he had to tell her the awful truth. With a ragged sigh, Linc held her tightly, afraid to let go.

The phone was ringing when Brie and Linc entered his kitchen. They had just come from her house where Brie had fed Homely Homer. Wearily, he picked up the receiver, expecting it to be another haz-mat call. Instead, it was Carol, asking for Brie.

"Is everything all right?" Brie asked, concerned. It was

nearly midnight and totally unlike Carol to call at that time.

"Everything's fine, Brie. I'm sorry to call you at Linc's so late, but something just struck me. Remember when you asked me the other day about those boxes of things I brought over to your house?"

Brie rubbed her brow, groggy with exhaustion. "Yes. The three boxes of books that belonged to John?"

Carol's voice became excited. "There were four boxes, Brie, not three. I was in such a stupor when I brought them over to your house. I remember putting three in your living room and the other smaller one down in your basement. It has a red diagonal slash on the top. It didn't contain books, just pamphlets, brochures and photocopied stuff. I didn't think you'd want that in your bookcase, so I took the liberty of putting it in the basement."

"My basement?" Brie shot a look at Linc's weary features. He had been up for almost forty-eight hours. "Thanks for telling me that. I'll go check to see if it's there, Carol. Good night."

Brie hung up the phone. "Come on, we're going to the basement. If we're lucky, we might find those two photocopied pages," Brie said breathlessly.

Chapter Ten

"My basement looks like a rat's nest," Brie apologized, descending into the damp cellar. A lone yellow bulb flickered as she stood at the bottom of the stairs. Linc joined her, staring at the wooden crates and cardboard boxes piled helter-skelter. He frowned, moving with his flashlight toward the far wall.

"Many of the older homes around here don't have real basements. The people just dug out the dirt. Mine is one of those." Brie looked around. "I wonder if the men who broke in got down here and looked through this stuff?"

"It looks like it," Linc muttered.

"Let's see if we can find that box."

Linc handed her the flashlight. Exhaustion was making him almost dizzy. "You hold the light, and I'll lift some of this stuff out of the way," he muttered. To his surprise, the box had been on the bottom of a pile. They took it upstairs, setting it on newspapers on the table.

Brie opened the box. "It doesn't look disturbed, Linc. Maybe they missed it in their hurry."

"Could be." He scooped out half the contents and handed them to Brie. "Let's sit down and go through it, then. For once, maybe lady luck's on our side."

She glanced at him. "I don't know why you're putting so much importance on finding those copies. Earl said there's a second set of books."

"Yes, but what if Carter destroys those books and records before the police can get to him? We won't have any proof then."

Glumly, Brie agreed with his faultless logic. For an hour, the only sound around them was the movement of papers and opening up of manuals and brochures. Brie got up at one o'clock and made some fortifying coffee. Her eyes softened as she looked at Linc. A day-old beard darkened his face, making his cheeks look hollow. The shadows beneath his eyes told her of his weariness, and all she wanted to do in that moment was take him into her arms and hold him.

"Brie?"

She turned, coffee in hand. "Yes?"

Linc slowly removed two neatly folded papers from between the pages of a manual. "Come here. I think we might have found it."

Her heart leaped as she walked over to Linc. He opened up the papers, which were damp and moldy smelling. "It's them," she confirmed hoarsely, taking a closer look.

There was satisfaction in Linc's voice. "Now we've got that bastard right where we want him." He traced his finger across the page. "Look, the name and address of the New Jersey outfit." His eyes glittered. "John didn't die for nothing, Brie. With this kind of information, we're going to crack this nut all the way up to the kingpins. I promise you.''

Brie's eyes widened in surprise when she saw Chief Saxon at the Canton Police Department. She and Linc had brought Earl Hansen in for a statement. Brie decided to talk with Saxon while Linc went upstairs with Hansen.

"What are you doing here?" she asked.

Saxon smiled. "I got the call from ATF that Linc and you had busted the case." He gripped Brie's arm. "Congratulations—"

"ATF?" Brie interrupted, frowning.

Saxon's brows rose. "Didn't Linc tell you yet?"

"Tell me what?" Her heart started a heavy, warning beat in her chest.

"That Linc Tanner is an ATF agent who went undercover, posing as a haz-mat technician to find out who murdered John." Saxon smiled sadly. "I'm sorry we couldn't tell you at the beginning of all this, Brie, because ATF thought you were a suspect. Until ATF was satisfied you didn't set up John, Tanner had to treat you like a possible enemy. You understand, of course?"

Brie closed her eyes, sagging against the wall, leaning against it for support. Linc Tanner was an agent. An undercover agent! He'd lied to her! She tried to breathe, but it was impossible. Pain, like a knife, sliced through her.

"Oh, God," she whispered hoarsely. Then her eyes filled with tears. "No."

"I'm sorry, Brie. I thought Tanner had already told you at this late date. Stupid of him not to." Saxon came over, placing a hand on her shoulder. "Are you all right?"

She choked down sobs, her anger over Linc's deceit rising. She loved Linc unequivocally, honestly. His love, if it could be called that, was nothing more than cover. Lies and deceit, that was all he'd given her.

"Brie?"

Brie brushed the tears from her eyes and shoved away from the wall. Breathing hard, she turned on Saxon. Her words came out in hurt, punctuated snatches. "You knew. You knew all along. And you thought I killed John! How could you?"

"Well—"

"You thought I was capable of killing John!" She was almost screaming.

"I didn't, but Tanner couldn't be sure," he sputtered. "Look, I didn't mean to upset you like this, Brie. You've had a rough six months, and I haven't helped—"

With trembling hands, Brie jerked open her purse. "No, Chief, you've just helped me make a decision I've been straddling the fence over since John was killed." She jerked out her badge case. Shakily, she pulled the silver badge out and gave it to Saxon. "I quit."

Stunned, Saxon looked at the badge he held in the palm of his hand. "But—"

"No," Brie began in a low voice, struggling to shut the purse because her hands shook so badly. "This has been a long time in coming. Too many hours, too little help from the main office. John did it for five years. I did it for three. I can't take it any more, and I'm not ashamed to admit it. There are other priorities in my life I want to pursue."

Saxon shook his white-haired head. "Please, Brie, think this over. I know you're disappointed that our office planted an ATF agent with you, but it was necessary."

Her nostrils flared with anger. "It was unnecessary to think I was a suspect!" She brushed past him. "I'm going home to get my place and myself in order. And tell Tanner I don't ever want to see him again! Do you understand?''

"Yes."

Whirling toward the doors, Brie almost collided with a police officer. She muttered an apology and headed into the sunlight. She hailed a taxi. Damn Linc Tanner! He'd used her emotions to get her trust, then her heart. All along, he was just waiting for her to spill whatever she knew.

Linc was always asking questions, always super alert. Why hadn't she seen it? Recognized it? He'd abused her love just to find out if she was a suspect or a victim! Clenching a handkerchief in her fist, Brie bowed her head, a small sob finally escaping.

Linc watched Saxon make his way toward him where he stood with Detective Gent and Hansen. The chief looked strained.

"Chief?" The man's features were positively gray.

"Linc, may I see you privately for a moment?"

Detective Gent gestured to Hansen to take a seat next to his desk. "You're done for now, Linc. If I need anything else, I'll give you a call at your apartment."

"Fine." Linc managed a slight smile at the sweating Hansen. "Earl, just cooperate, and I believe things will go a lot easier on you."

"Of—of course."

Linc followed the chief out the door. "Where's Brie?" he asked, looking around.

"Gone," Saxon said flatly. And then he muttered, "I thought she knew you were an ATF agent, Linc, and she didn't." He opened his palm, showing him her badge. "Brie's quit the department." And then, more quietly, he added, "She's upset and said she didn't want to see you again, either. I'm sorry, Linc. I really blew it."

Linc sucked in a sharp breath, pinning Saxon with a glare. "You what? You told her?"

"I'm sorry. I blundered."

Linc clenched his fists. His worst nightmare had just come true.

"She's mad and hurt, Linc."

His anger turned to frustration, then anguish. Dammit, he loved her! "No kidding," he snarled, heading for the stairs.

"Wait! Where are you going?"

Tanner jerked a look up at the chief. "Where do you think? Over to her house to try to explain things."

"But she said she didn't want to see you."

Wiping sweat off his brow, Tanner shrugged. "Tough. I love her, and there's no way I'm walking away from her or this situation."

Brie stood just inside her living room, looking around. Her home had been in a shambles, and now her life was. Tears dribbled down her cheeks, and she sniffed, wiping them away. She walked around. Linc had held her on that couch while she cried out her heart, trusting him, learning to reach out once again and express her feelings. They had shared their first kiss on that couch....

With a little cry, Brie turned away. She had trusted Linc, had given him her life, and all along he'd suspected her of being a killer. His tenderness, his kisses were all an elaborate sham to get her to spill whatever she knew.

Brie stumbled into her bedroom, the only room in the house that had been completely returned to its original state after the break-in. She sat on the mattress. When had she fallen in love with Linc? It didn't matter; her heart was aching so much that it felt as if her entire chest was being shattered.

She heard the back door being opened and then closed. Trying to blot the tears from her eyes and wondering who it was, Brie reached for a handkerchief.

"Brie?" Tanner stood tensely in the bedroom door, his face filled with anguish.

"You!" she cried, leaping to her feet. "Get the hell out of here!"

He winced at the anger in her voice. "No way," he growled, moving toward her. Before she could escape, Linc grabbed her by the arm, forcing her toward him.

Brie struggled to get loose. "Let me go! Let me go, you liar!"

Tanner saw the pain in her huge green eyes. He didn't want to hurt her, he'd hurt her enough. "Settle down," he said softly. "Listen to me, Brie. Just take one minute and listen to me. I can explain everything."

Fury goaded her into trying to throw off his hold on her arms, but it was impossible. "Explain what?" Brie cried hoarsely. "You *lied* to me, Linc. I was a suspect! You thought I was the killer all along! Everything you did... your kisses...your tenderness, was a sham, a lie!"

He gave her a little shake. "No, Brie, I love you. That was never a lie—"

"No!" she wailed, throwing off his hold. She staggered backward, caught her balance then moved around the bed, keeping distance between them. "Everything you did was an act, Tanner. Everything! How do you think I feel?" She struck her chest. "I loved you! I fell in love with you. I don't know how or when it happened, but it did. And what I feel—felt was real. I didn't lie. You did!"

He stood there, every breath fiery agony. Brie loved him. "I love you, too, Brie. That was never a lie." Holding out his hand, Linc pleaded, "Please, you've got to believe me. Falling in love with you wasn't something I planned on. Yes, you were a suspect. But put yourself in my shoes. Wouldn't you have done the same thing if you were a stranger coming in on a case like this? I had to get enough evidence one way or another to make a decision about you."

Brie glared at him. "I'm sorry," she said, "but I can't put myself in your shoes."

"Please, Brie, hear me out," Linc begged softly. "Maybe I wasn't honest with you on a lot of things, and believe me, I feel badly about it, but my feelings for you were never a lie. They're real." Linc touched his heart. "You have to believe me, Brie. I love you. Can't we hold on to that one fact, that truth, then sort through the rest of this stuff together?"

Brie suddenly felt dizzy. She closed her eyes, touching her damp brow. "I don't know where truth and lies begin and end with you," she whispered raggedly.

"Come on," he coaxed. "Sit down on the bed. Let me explain, little cat. Please...for both our sakes, hear me out."

Trying to assess Linc through the wall of pain she felt over his betrayal, Brie finally moved. Tensely, she sat on the edge of the bed.

"Good," Linc said in a trembling voice, going to sit on his side of the bed. Where to begin? How to convince Brie? Never had Linc wanted anyone more. Never had he felt the fear of loss as sharply as now. Linc hadn't prayed in years, but he did now, remembering prayers Father O'Reilly had taught him. Wrestling with words, phrases, trying to get them into some kind of coherent order, the minutes passed, the silence brittle between them.

"When I first came on this case," Linc began in a low

voice, "I was burned out. I tried to get out of it, but my boss in D.C. promised me a long-overdue desk job if I took it." He held Brie's gaze, loving her more than he ever thought he could love anyone. "I'd almost been killed on that last case, and coming on to this one, I was very jumpy. And I did treat you as a suspect.

"But, as I got to know you and saw you in all kinds of different circumstances, I began to feel differently, Brie." Linc grimaced, unable to hold her gaze. "The first night I went through your desk, reading some letters from your family and friends."

Brie gasped. "You what?"

Wincing, Linc nodded. "Yeah, I feel pretty bad about it, Brie. I'm sorry." Forcing himself to look at her, he saw the sparks of anger in her jade-colored eyes. "It was the first evidence I had that you hadn't set up John. Then, after that, I waited to see if you really were genuinely affected by John's death, or if it was just a cover and you were playing a part with me."

"I never once playacted," Brie whispered. "Every emotion, every feeling you saw in me was real, Linc. And that's more than I can say for you."

Hanging his head, he nodded. "Yeah…I know." Closing his eyes, feeling as if Brie was slipping away from him, he went on. "Somewhere along the line, I started falling in love with you, the woman, not the haz-mat tech. Sure, I respected your knowledge and what you did, but the more I was around you, the more you affected me on some unknown inner level of myself." Lifting his head, Linc held her gaze, seeing very little anger left in her eyes. Groaning to himself, he remembered the luster in them after he'd made beautiful love with her. The ache in his chest widened.

"Little things you did, like fixing me homemade meals

and desserts…and Homely Homer…'' Linc cleared his throat, watching her face lose all its tension, replaced with tenderness. "You made a house a home, Brie. I never realized it until I was living with you those first five days. I never had that feeling with JoAnne. It's you, how you are, the way you see the world, that made me realize a lot of things.'' He absently picked at a loose thread on the quilt thrown across the bed. "I found myself telling you about me, something I'd never done. It actually felt good to talk to you about my growing-up years. JoAnne never knew about them. I was…ashamed of where I'd come from.''

Brie bowed her head. "Oh, Linc…''

"No, let me finish. Please. That night you broke the glass in the kitchen and I held you on the couch…kissed you…'' Linc took in a broken breath. "At that point, I knew you had been the victim, and weren't the killer. All I had to do was prove it to the FM and ATF.''

She lifted her chin, staring at him, tears in her eyes. "Then why didn't you tell me?''

Linc held her wavering gaze, aching to reach across the bed and pull her into his arms. "Because you were so fragile. I didn't want to upset you any more than you already were because you were trying to recover. It was a lousy judgment call on my part, Brie.'' He ran his fingers through his hair. "Remember. This is Linc Tanner, the tough kid from the Bronx who had shielded himself from any kind of emotional involvement. To tell you the truth, I didn't know how to deal with you. I'd fallen in love with you, Brie, and I was limited by my inexperience. I didn't know what to do or how to do it.''

"I failed you. I can't tell you how many sleepless nights I spent because I was lying to you. I was afraid to tell you, because I knew you liked me a lot, and I loved you.'' He shook his head. "I didn't know you loved me...not until just now..."

Linc's torn admission was dissolving her anger and answering her questions. His features were drawn in agony, his eyes reflecting his panic and fear of having lost her. "Then your childhood was real, it wasn't a lie."

He cleared his throat, unable to hold her compassionate gaze. "At no time did I lie to you about my past or about my marriage to JoAnne. Brie, I just didn't tell you who I was, that was all. How we got along, our feelings, my thoughts and what I shared with you, were real. Please believe me." His voice cracked.

Brie turned away, staring numbly at the flowered wallpaper, the silence weighing heavy in the room. Linc had no reason to lie now that he'd told her he was an ATF agent. He was here, trying to salvage what was left of their relationship, which had been shattered by his lie. Turning, she studied him in the silence.

Linc forced out, "You're like that kitten I found, Brie. You bring out all the good things I've been hiding from myself."

Brie sat, finally understanding Linc and what she meant to him.

Linc forced himself to move, to get to his feet. He'd done what he could to try to convince Brie of his love for her. "I'll get going now, Brie. I've made a mess of your life. I'm sorry, I didn't mean to hurt you. I only meant to protect you, and in one way I did. In the other way, I screwed it up."

Linc made his way out of the room and down the hall. Misery suffocated him. Well, what did he expect? For Brie to forgive him? Slowing down, he gave the living room a longing look. Brie always had living trees and plants in there, symbolizing life. She was life, he thought. Brie had given him life by simply being herself. She had brought the gift of knowing he wasn't the cold robot JoAnne had always accused him of being. Brie had brought out his softer, more vulnerable side, and he liked himself and what he was becoming.

"Linc?"

He halted, hearing Brie's strained voice. He turned and saw her in the hall, her face pale. He braced himself, knowing he deserved whatever she was going to tell him. He had lied to her. He had been deceitful. "What is it?" His voice was hoarse.

Brie made a gesture toward the living room. "I need some help getting this house cleaned up. Do you think you could hang around a few days and help me before you leave?"

He saw the hope burning in Brie's green eyes. His mouth dropped open and he snapped it shut, not believing his ears. "Stay? Here?" There was disbelief in his voice.

Managing a strained smile, Brie nodded. "Yes."

Risking everything, Linc said, "If I stay those few days, I'm not leaving, Brie. Do you understand that?"

She took in a ragged breath. "I don't want it any other way."

Linc closed his eyes, feeling dizzy with elation. Brie had believed him! He loved her, and now he was going to get a chance to prove it. Opening his eyes, he managed a sour grin. "Sure?"

"Very sure," Brie answered, opening her arms to him.

Chapter Eleven

The lap, lap, lap of water against the boat nearly lulled Brie to sleep. She heard Linc casting out again with his rod and reel, the nylon singing through the air. The combination of sun, the sweet smell of the lake and the incessant breeze tempted her to give in to the fingers of sleep. She lay on the bottom of a fourteen-foot wooden boat, which was anchored near the edge of a huge island of lily pads. Good bass fishing, Linc had told her earlier in a conspiratorial tone. And she had laughed, throwing her arms around him. Where had the weeks gone?

After finding John's evidence, which had put Carter behind bars, it seemed as if her life had speeded up. Earl Hansen was granted immunity because he was going to testify for the prosecution. The ATF was following up on the New Jersey end of the investigation, which had already ballooned into scandalous proportions. And Linc had protected her from the press when the story finally broke. He had remained at her side when both state and government law-enforcement officials had questioned her for days on end.

A soft sigh escaped Brie. She had drawn even closer to Linc, if that was possible. Throughout the investigation, they had turned to one another for support and love. Suddenly, she felt the entire boat jerk, and her eyes flew open.

"I got one!" Linc crowed triumphantly, the rod bending as he played the fish who had taken the bait.

Brie sat up, sleepily rubbing her eyes. Life with Linc had been a miracle. The house was back in order; so were their lives. Days had melted into weeks, and then into six months. Homely Homer had grown up and spread her wings. She was free and happy.

Shortly after the trial in which Carter was sentenced to prison, Linc had presented her with two airline tickets to Calgary, Canada, and a brochure on mountain cabins two hundred miles from the Canadian city. He humbled himself to ask and not to tell her that she was going with him for two weeks to escape. And she loved him for his thoughtfulness and said yes.

Watching Linc, she noted how his face reflected excitement as he reeled in his catch. For two days now, since their arrival, he had been trying to get a huge widemouthed bass that was so much a part of the blue lake's fame. No stranger to fishing, Brie had counseled Linc on what type of equipment he should use. Being a city boy, he felt he knew better. Instead of using a plastic frog and jiggling it in the water, he had decided on a night crawler dropped to the bottom of the lake.

"This is a big one, Brie. Look at it pull. This is going to be the biggest bass that's ever been—"

Suddenly, Brie broke into laughter. What surfaced wasn't a bass, but a turtle. Linc scowled as he stared down at the dark green amphibian floating peacefully beside the boat.

"I'll be," Linc muttered. Then a grin cracked his mouth and he turned to see Brie holding her stomach because she was laughing so hard. It was so good to see her relaxed and happy again. It was worth hooking a turtle instead of a bass.

Brie slid an arm around his neck and rested her head against his. "You're one of a kind, Tanner. You really are. I told you if you used worms and fished off the bottom that you'd get garbage."

He pressed a kiss to her jaw. "You never said anything about turtles. Now help me get that hook out of that poor critter's mouth so we can let him go about his business."

"City boy," she teased, expertly sliding the hook free with pliers and giving the turtle a pat on its broad-shelled back. She sat up and handed Linc the hook minus the worm.

He set the rod and reel aside and pulled Brie into his lap. "I'm done fishing for today. I'm glad you didn't pick up that camera and catch me with my 'bass.'"

Brie pressed her mouth against his clean shaven cheek, inhaling his male scent. "You're going to have to bribe me to keep quiet about this, Tanner. This is one fish story that's too good *not* to be told."

His blue eyes darkened. "Why you little—"

Brie wriggled out of his arms and sat in the bottom of the boat where she had spread a sleeping bag for comfort. She watched Linc's expression as he came after her. The dangerous glint in his cobalt eyes sent her pulse skyrocketing and her body crying for his touch. She wasn't disappointed as Linc took her into his arms, pressing her against him, and began a slow assault of kisses.

"You know," he said, "you are getting out of hand."

Brie sighed as his tongue traced her mouth. "You're reverting back to your chauvinistic cave-man tactics again," she reminded him huskily, staring up at him through half-closed eyes.

Linc nipped her lips, then relished her feminine softness. "I know. You just bring it out in me, Ms. Williams. Mmmm, you taste good, like a salty and sweet marshmallow." He saw the look of pleasure in her eyes.

Brie caressed his cheek. "I love you."

"How much?" he wanted to know, kissing her fingers.

"With all my heart."

"How about for the rest of your life?"

Her arms tightened around his neck. "Linc…"

"Do you love me enough to spend the rest of your life trying to change me and my chauvinistic ways?"

"Oh, Linc, I never thought you'd want to…"

He heard the wobble in Brie's voice and knew he had surprised her. "Open the tackle box," he said after a moment.

"What?"

He gave her an amused look. "Open the tackle box."

It sat near her, and she flipped the latch, slowly opening the lid.

"Now what?" Brie asked, not quite sure what he was up to.

"The third plastic box. The one with the big hooks. Take it out and open it up."

Her hands trembled slightly as she picked up the case and slid the cover off. A gasp escaped her. There, amid hooks of shiny brass, was an engagement ring. Only it wasn't the usual diamond ring. Brie stared at it in awe. The ring was gold, but the oval stone was the most beautiful color of forest green she had ever seen.

"Let's see if it fits," Linc murmured next to her ear. "The stone is a green tourmaline from Brazil."

Brie watched with widened eyes as he slowly slipped the ring on her fourth finger.

"Perfect. Well, what do you think?" She heard the satisfaction in his voice.

"I—it's lovely, Linc. So lovely…"

"Want to wear it for a while and see how it feels?" he asked, his lips against her cheek.

She managed a choked sound. "Wear it for a while and see how it feels?"

He shrugged, holding her captive in his arms. "A modern woman like yourself might have to get used to wearing something that might make her feel like she was losing her freedom or whatever."

Brie didn't know whether to cry for joy or laugh at his taunting. "Linc Tanner, how can you tease me at a time like this!" The sunlight made her ring sparkle, as if it had a thousand emeralds.

"Actually, my joking is to cover up my terror at your saying no."

She turned, seeing doubt in Linc's eyes. "I love the ring," she said in a low, trembling tone, "but even more important, I love you. And I will for the rest of my life."

Linc gave a ragged sigh, as if a huge load had been lifted from him. "Good," he said roughly, taking her into his arms. "Because I didn't know what I was going to do if you said no."

She gave a soft laugh, feeling deliciously giddy with joy. "You wouldn't have given up that easily, if I know you."

He grinned and kissed her hair. "You got that right, little cat. I'd have pursued you—"

"And badgered me."

"Hey, that's unfair!"

"And browbeat me."

"How can you say those kinds of things? I'm a nice guy."

She gave him a playful jab in the ribs. "You conceited male animal." Suddenly, she frowned. "Why on earth did you put an engagement ring in a tackle box?"

His grin widened. "I thought I'd hook you on marriage. I know I'm not the biggest fish in the pond, the wealthiest or even the most successful. I guess I'm sort of like that turtle—not what you might have expected."

Brie closed her eyes. "You were unexpected," she began quietly. "As far as success or wealth, that doesn't matter to me, Linc. I love you for yourself."

He nodded, at a loss for words—for once.

Brie opened her eyes, her fingers wrapping around his solid arms. "Linc?"

"Yes?"

"I'm not going back to haz-mat work."

He sat very still. "All right. I understand. We all have our limits, Brie. Don't feel ashamed."

"I don't. I'm twenty-nine, Linc. Professionally, I'm pleased with what I've done and accomplished. I've suddenly discovered I want to settle down and make home-cooked meals every day. I want children."

"At least two." Linc turned Brie to face him, and he thought how young and beautiful she looked. "And since the desk job Cramer promised me has come through, it'll be no more undercover work for me. I'll be punching the clock in Canton, Ohio, from nine to five every day and have weekends off. How does that sound?"

Relief shone in her eyes. "Wonderful. That means you won't be risking your life anymore, either."

"Neither of us will. Believe me, it's a big load off my

mind, little cat. You were good at your job, but I'd have lived in absolute hell wondering day in and day out if you were safe.''

Tears blurred Brie's vision. "We'll just risk our lives with one another.''

He smiled. "You're all the challenge and excitement I'll ever need.''

* * * * *

Dear Reader,

Paladin's Woman is a prequel to my popular series
THE PROTECTORS, with Nick Romero acting as a
bodyguard to the heroine, Addy McConnell, whose life
is threatened by an unknown assailant. Nick appeared as
a secondary character in my very first Intimate Moments
novel, *This Side of Heaven,* and I knew immediately that
he was hero material and simply had to have his own
story. There was something irresistible about Nick, a
Latin lover bad boy, who had earned his scars as a navy
SEAL and later as a DEA agent. Most women couldn't
resist Nick, but Addy wasn't like most women. Her
ex-husband had emotionally wounded her, and only a
man like Nick could rebuild her self-confidence. Under
Nick's protection she learned how a real man treats his
woman, and looking at herself through his eyes, she
saw herself as beautiful for the first time in her life.

Sam Dundee and his Dundee Private Security agency
play a part in this story, as does Elizabeth Mallory, the
heroine of another prequel to THE PROTECTORS,
The Outcast. If you're a fan of my ongoing Intimate
Moments miniseries, you will enjoy taking a look
back at Sam and the heroes who were forerunners
of the Atlanta bodyguards you know and seem to love
as much as I do. And if this is the first time you've read
a Beverly Barton book, I hope you will find this special
love story to be one you will long remember.

All my best,

Beverly Barton

PALADIN'S WOMAN
Beverly Barton

Special thanks to several good friends:
Gail Froelich, my Huntsville tour guide;
Edna Waits, for all the research material;
Willie Wood, for being a good listener and
giving great advice; and Linda Howington,
for reasons too numerous to list, but especially
for giving me a great title.

Prologue

Hoisting the beer bottle toward the woman sitting on the edge of the bed, he saluted her, his mouth widening into a smirk. "Tonight's the night."

"Are you sure?" Leaning down, she picked up the black silk robe from the floor. "If everything doesn't work perfectly and your man botches things, her daddy will call in a bodyguard like that." She snapped her fingers, her sharp mauve nails clicking together.

Reaching out, he circled her neck, caressing her naked flesh. "Don't you have any confidence in me?"

"Of course." She glared at him, a mixture of desire and fear in her eyes. "I just don't want anything to go wrong. We've worked very hard and been planning for a long time. There's so much at stake."

Gliding his hand downward, he cupped her breast, flicking his nail across the tight nipple. "Millions and millions."

She sighed when his caress roughened. "If anything goes wrong—"

He laughed. "Nothing will."

"Kidnapping is a federal offense. We could both wind up in prison. I just wish there were some other way. I hate the thought of—"

"Don't think about anything except all that beautiful money Rusty McConnell's going to lose to keep his precious Addy safe." He shoved her down on the bed, straddling her hips.

"You won't hurt Addy. You promise?"

"She won't be hurt. My guy said he'd use chloroform, then keep her bound and blindfolded until Big Daddy gives us what we want." He touched his lips to hers, whispering into her mouth. "You know I wouldn't lie to you."

All the while he took his pleasure with one woman, he thought of another. Addy McConnell. Sweet, sweet Addy. He had no intention of harming her—not until he'd taken what he wanted from her—not until her father had followed instructions and the authorities were off on a wild-goose chase. He really didn't want to kill Addy, but he didn't have any choice. Once his plan went into action and he'd accomplished everything he set out to do, Addy would have to die.

Chapter 1

Who was he? Addy McConnell wondered. He didn't belong here. She was certain of that. Despite the fact that he wore a black tuxedo similar to the ones worn by most of the men in the room, he didn't blend into the crowd. For one thing, he was taller than the average man, at least six foot three, and his big, muscular body appeared constrained by the confines of his well-fitting clothes. His black hair, though cut conservatively short, was slicked back away from his dark face, and a band of thick waves curled about his neck. His cheekbones were broad and high, his chin square with a slight cleft. A pair of deep-set brown eyes surveyed the gathering of Huntsville's social elite.

And a small diamond stud glittered in his left ear.

No, Addy thought, whoever he is, neither she nor her father had invited him to the party. That meant he was either a friend of Dina's, or he had crashed the engagement celebration of the year.

She'd been watching him for at least ten minutes, but the man hadn't glanced her way. He appeared to be either distracted or bored. Perhaps both.

Addy hadn't missed the way most of the women in the room kept looking at him. Several had made advances. When he'd smiled and spoken to those women, they'd practically melted at his feet. A charmer. A Latin lover. A very dangerous man. All those expressions flashed through Addy's mind.

When a waiter offered him a drink, he declined. Using the black cane he held in his right hand, he limped away from the young brunette who'd been trying, in vain, to attract his attention.

Addy wondered what had caused his limp. He leaned heavily on the gold-tipped cane. Bracing himself against the wall near the French doors, he closed his eyes. She noticed a sudden tremor in his hand that clutched the walking stick, and knew he was in pain. Some irrational emotion stirred within her. She wanted to ease his pain.

With a disgusted grunt, Addy looked away, scanning the room for sight of a familiar face, anyone who would take her mind off the mysterious dark stranger. She really didn't know what was wrong with her. Men, as a general rule, didn't interest her much. Her ex-husband had cured her of any desire she'd ever had to experience the joys of a sexual relationship. So, why did this man, this dangerous-looking interloper, fascinate her so much?

"He's gorgeous, isn't he?" Janice Dixon said. "Can you imagine what he looks like without his clothes?"

Addy tried not to laugh at her cousin's comment. Petite and bosomy, Janice Ann Dixon issued an invitation to the male sex without even trying. But being a highly sensual creature, Janice took every advantage of what Mother Nature had given her.

"I'm sure he'd be willing to oblige, if you asked him," Addy said.

"You think he's easy, huh?"

"No." Addy suspected that despite the fact the handsome stranger emitted an easy charm, a dark and perhaps even troubled soul existed beneath his captivatingly smooth exterior. "But he most definitely is a man, and I've yet to see a man you couldn't seduce."

Janice snorted, the sound mingled with laughter. "I don't know if I should be flattered or offended."

"Be flattered."

"You seem unduly interested in our mysterious *señor*." Janice glanced across the room, then nudged Addy in the side. "He's going out onto the patio. Why don't we follow him?"

"Go right ahead." Addy had never chased a man, never followed one, never pursued one in any way, shape, form or fashion, and she certainly had no intention of starting now. Thirty-five was definitely too old to change the habits of a lifetime.

Long-legged and elegant in her purple silk jumpsuit, Ginger Kimbrew slipped her arm around Addy's shoulder. "Every woman in the room is in heat, and I see that includes both of you."

"Go away, Ginger," Janice said. "If three women follow him outside, it'll be a bit obvious, don't you think?"

"I don't have to follow him. We've already been introduced." Smiling, Ginger eyed Addy. "You have no idea who he is, do you?"

"No," Addy said. "Should I?" She turned to face her father's private secretary.

"I take it that dear step-mommy-to-be hasn't introduced you."

Addy was well aware of the animosity between her fa-

ther's fiancée Dina Lunden and his most valued employee
of ten years. Dina resented any attractive woman in
Rusty's life, and Ginger, who had hoped her position as
mistress would one day be elevated to wife, hated the
woman who'd finally trapped the man she wanted. "Dina
invited him?" Addy asked.

"She most certainly did." Ginger's smile widened, her
lavender-shadowed eyelids almost closing.

"How do you know?" Janice turned her head quickly,
looking up at the taller woman.

"I asked him," Ginger said, grinning, her wide red
mouth exposing a set of perfect white teeth. "I introduced
myself and asked if he'd crashed the party or if he had an
invitation."

"You did what?" Addy stared at Ginger, amazed anew
at the woman's lack of manners. But then, Addy admitted
that many of the new breed of Southern women didn't
worry overly much about manners. Her grandmother,
mother and aunt would have been appalled.

"He's Dina's brother-in-law." Ginger seemed delighted
to be the one with so much information on the most interesting man at Dina Lunden and D.B. "Rusty" Mc-
Connell's engagement celebration. "Well, actually, ex-
brother-in-law is more accurate. He's Dina's first
husband's brother."

"Dina seems to stay on friendly terms with all her former husbands' relatives," Janice said. "Just look how
close she and her stepson are."

"Brett Windsor is very attractive," Ginger said. "If you
like the Ivy League type. He's Dina's third husband's son,
right?"

"That's right." Addy glanced toward the French doors,
wondering what Dina's former brother-in-law was doing
out on the patio. Had one of the female guests proposi-

tioned him? Was he meeting her outside? A shiver of unexplainable excitement rippled through her. A vision of herself standing on the patio appeared in her mind. The dark stranger held her in his arms, his wide, full-lipped mouth moving downward.

"I knew he was a Latin lover boy," Janice said, again elbowing Addy in the side. "Hey, didn't you hear what Ginger said?"

"What?" Half dazed by the vividness of her daydream, Addy stared at her cousin in confusion.

"His name is Nick Romero. Oh, God, don't you just love the sound of it?" Janice was practically writhing.

"I think the proper term is Hispanic." Ginger looked at Addy, seeking her agreement. "Anyway, you're right about one thing, the term 'Latin lover' does come to mind the minute you see him."

Addy wondered how much of Ginger and Janice's conversation she'd missed while indulging in a fantasy about the man they were discussing. It was quite apparent that the man had a mesmerizing effect on women, and she absolutely refused to allow any man, not even this one, to arouse any long-dead dreams of passion. No, she'd happily settle for the nice, warm feelings she shared with her friend Jim Hester. Though neither wealthy nor sophisticated, Jim was a dear man, and he possessed something that Addy desperately wanted, had wanted for as long as she could remember, had mourned the fact, after two miscarriages, that she might never have one of her own. Jim Hester had a child.

Addy didn't want or expect passion. As a Plain Jane, she'd long ago learned that despite the fact she had no problem attracting men, it was always her father's millions that attracted them and not her beauty or charm. Dina's stepson, Brett Windsor, definitely saw dollar signs whenever he was around her, so she didn't encourage him.

"I think you and I should give Addy a shot at Nick Romero," Janice said, and laughed when she saw the stricken look on her cousin's face.

"You're right. After all, a man like that just might find Addy's sweetness and innocence a real turn-on." Ginger stopped a waiter, retrieved a canapé from a silver dish, then popped it into her mouth.

"I'm hardly innocent," Addy said. "I'm a thirty-five-year-old divorcée, not an eighteen-year-old virgin."

"Regardless of that fact, you could write everything you know about sex on the head of a straight pin." Janice stopped a waiter for a fresh glass of champagne.

"Would you look at that?" Ginger nodded toward the French doors where a stunningly beautiful Dina Lunden was slipping outside.

Addy watched. Dina's black satin gown shimmered, every inch adhering to her slender body in a way that accentuated her round hips, her small waist and her voluptuous bosom. Even at forty-six, the woman reeked of sex appeal and looked at least ten years younger. It didn't hurt that she was classically beautiful, with a kittenish type of sexuality. The kind that had made Marilyn Monroe a legend.

"Looks like step-mommy-to-be has beaten us all to the punch," Ginger said. "I wonder what she wants to talk to Nick about in private?"

"Are you implying that there's something going on between Dina and her former brother-in-law?" Addy asked.

"There's one way to find out," Ginger said.

"We could all three go outside for a breath of fresh air," Janice said.

"No." Addy held up a restraining hand. "You two stay

here and enjoy the party…and make sure Daddy doesn't come outside.''

Nick Romero leaned his hip against the brick patio wall. Damn, his leg ached. He'd been standing too long. Ever since an Uzi had ripped his leg open nearly seven months ago, he'd had to learn to live with pain. Indeed, the pain had been his friend. As long as he could feel the pain, he was alive. While he'd passed in and out of consciousness, he'd kept reminding himself that as long as he could feel, he wasn't dead. And so he had embraced the agony, he'd clung to it. He'd been damned and determined that no maniac's sneak attack was going to kill him. After all, he'd lived through Vietnam, through almost ten years as a Navy SEAL and nearly a dozen years as one of the DEA's top agents. He hadn't overcome poverty and prejudice and the constant threat of death to let some psycho from his best friend's past destroy him. No, Nick Romero was made of stronger stuff.

He smelled her perfume before he saw her. Heavy, spicy, erotic. Even when Dina Lunden had been Dina Romero, his brother Miguel's wife, she'd bathed herself in cologne. Back then, it had been the cheap stuff, the kind you bought in dime stores for a dollar, the kind that Dina could afford on her waitress's salary and her husband's meager wages from farming. But once Miguel had gone to work in the oil fields, Dina started buying her perfume at the drugstore.

Funny, what a guy thought about when he smelled a woman's perfume. Of course, Dina wasn't just any woman. She was special. Despite the fact that what he'd once felt for her was long dead, she would always be special. A man never forgets his first love, especially if she was his brother's widow.

"Nicky." Her voice had that same soft, little-girl coo it had so many years ago. "I saw you come outside and thought now might be a good time for us to talk. Privately."

She was still a damned good-looking woman. Still sexy as hell. The one blonde he'd never been able to forget. "Talk away. I'm listening."

She moved forward, stopping hesitantly. She reached out, her long, slender fingers draping themselves around his forearm. "I've missed you, Nicky. It's been a long time."

"Not so long, Dina." She had such a hypnotic smile. A smile that promised so much and gave so little. Nick knew how deceptive everything about this woman could be. "I came to your last engagement party and your last wedding." He noticed that her smile scarcely altered, but the light in her eyes dimmed ever so slightly. "It couldn't have been more than three years ago."

"Almost five." She squeezed Nick's arm, her sculptured pink nails biting into the fabric of his tuxedo. "You haven't missed one of my weddings, have you, Nicky? Except…"

"Except the one that you didn't invite me to."

"I thought you'd forgiven me for marrying Briley Fuller so soon after Miguel died."

Nick tilted her chin with his index finger, looking directly into her big blue eyes. Like her lips, those eyes promised so much. False promises. "I've forgiven you for everything. It's myself that I've never been able to forgive."

"Silly boy, you didn't do anything wrong." She nudged her body closer, pressing her full breasts against his chest.

"I lusted after my brother's wife, and when he wasn't three months cold in the ground, I screwed her." Even, now, after all these years, he could still taste the bile as it rose to his throat, still hear the condemnation on his grandmother's tongue when she found Dina in Nick's bed. He'd thought he was in love. He'd been seventeen. And he'd been a fool.

"Miguel was dead. I was lonely." She ran the tips of her long nails across his jaw. "And we wanted each other."

Taking her by the shoulder, Nick pushed her away from him. "I was seventeen. I wanted a woman, and at that time you were my ideal. Blond, big-boobed and knowledgeable."

She laughed, the sound like a high-pitched bell. Clear and sharp and feminine. "I'm so glad we've stayed friends, despite the fact you wouldn't even speak to me after I married Briley. He was a mistake, but...he was so rich."

"You seem to like your men that way," Nick said, glancing over Dina's shoulder toward the French doors. They had just opened, and a tall, slender redhead was looking straight at him.

Nick's gut tightened. There was something familiar about the woman, her titian hair, her towering height, her strong features. She certainly wasn't classically beautiful, but she possessed an earthy appeal that not even her plain dress and subdued hairstyle disguised.

"You mean that I like rich men?" Dina asked.

"Yeah, rich mistakes. How many will this make? Five?"

The redhead walked out onto the patio, closing the doors behind her. She stood less than twenty feet away. And she was still staring at him. He felt an odd sensation in the pit of his stomach. Amazed at his reaction, Nick admitted to himself that the tall, skinny redhead turned him on. He couldn't remember the last time he'd been so fascinated by a woman.

He shook his head. *Damn, who would have believed it?* She certainly wasn't his type.

"Rusty will be my sixth husband. You never count Miguel."

"Do you know a tall, slim redheaded woman wearing a gray silk dress?" Nick asked.

"Why?" Dina's voice trembled slightly.

"She's standing just a few feet away watching us."

Dina swirled around, her most dazzling smile in place. "Addy, darling, do come over and meet my Nicky."

He surveyed *darling* Addy from the top of her curly red hair to the tips of her gray leather heels. Thick, unruly flame-red hair. Plain but expensive two-inch heels. A neat little gray silk dress covered her model-thin body. It didn't cling or drape; it simply covered. Despite the fact that this woman obviously didn't dress to attract men, Nick found her very attractive. Even though he truly liked women, all women, he usually preferred sexy blondes with round curves.

Darling Addy stared at him intently, as if she were trying to gauge the extent of his personal relationship with Dina. She seemed interested in him, but not enthralled the way so many women usually were. He didn't know exactly what it was about him that piqued female interest, but he wasn't about to deny himself the pleasures of being considered a Romeo.

"Oh, Nicky, do say hello to Addy McConnell, Rusty's daughter." Dina glanced nervously back and forth from Addy to Nick. "Addy, this is my brother-in-law, Nick Romero. He's flown in from Florida just for my engagement party."

Smiling, Nick held out his hand. "Ms. McConnell."

She stared at his hand for several minutes, then offered hers. "Mr. Romero."

When he didn't immediately release her hand, she tugged gently. He held fast, pulling her closer. When she was only inches away, he gazed into her eyes, almond-shaped green eyes—cat eyes—framed by thick reddish-brown lashes. "On closer inspection, I see a definite resemblance to your father. Same hair, without the gray. Same eyes, only brighter. And you're much prettier than Rusty. Your mother must have been quite a beautiful woman."

"She was, but I don't look anything like her. I'm pure McConnell. Through and through. Just ask Daddy." Addy jerked her hand out of Nick's. "We're pleased that you could fly in and share this special night with Dina. Will you be staying here at the house?"

"No," Dina said, her lips puckered in a seductive pout. "I told him there was more than enough room, but he booked into a hotel. Wasn't that naughty of him?"

"You should have stayed here." Addy nodded toward the house. "This place is almost as big as a hotel and there's no one living here right now except Daddy, Dina and Brett."

"Brett Windsor's living here?" Nick asked.

"Brett's considering some local investments. He'll be getting his own place soon." Dina patted Addy on the arm affectionately. "Brett thinks the world of Addy, but she won't give him the least little bit of encouragement."

"Is that right?" Nick tried to keep the sarcastic tone out of his voice. He'd just bet that Brett thought the world of Addy. He thought the world of Rusty McConnell's millions was more like it. Brett Windsor had inherited half of his father's estate and Dina had inherited the other half. That had been fourteen years and two husbands ago. Nick doubted if either one of them had a dime of Ashley Windsor's six-million-dollar legacy.

Dina glanced toward the French doors where the man in question stood. "There's Brett now. I should go and assure him that Nicky isn't a rival, shouldn't I, Addy?"

"By all means." Addy waved at Brett, who flashed her a brilliant smile and waved back at her. "I'll entertain Mr. Romero."

"What?" Dina laughed, fluttering her eyelashes. "Nicky, you behave yourself with Addy. After all, she's my Rusty's only child and he adores her."

"I promise to be on my best behavior." Nick glanced at Addy, wondering what she thought of her father's fiancée.

"I'll hold you to that." Giving Nick a flirtatious smile and Addy an affectionate pat on the arm, Dina sauntered toward her third husband's son.

"Your brother was one of Dina's husbands?" Addy asked.

"Her first husband." Nick realized that this woman didn't like Dina, and her curious green eyes said that she wasn't sure she liked him either.

"Then you've known her for a long time?"

"Since I was fifteen, and I'll be forty-four soon."

"She seems very fond of you."

"She is." Nick noticed the surprised expression on Addy's face. Had she been expecting a denial? "But then, Dina is very fond of a lot of men."

"And, if my father is any indication, a lot of men are fond of Dina."

Nick reached out and took Addy's hand, slipping her arm through his. She didn't resist. Grasping his cane in his other hand, he walked them toward the French doors. "Will Dina be your first stepmother?"

"If Daddy marries her, she will be."

"You don't like Dina?"

"Dina and I have an understanding," Addy said, hesitating before entering the house again. "We tolerate each other. In front of Daddy, we're always cordial."

"If it's any comfort to you, Ms. McConnell, Dina probably won't be a part of your life for more than a few years. As you already know, her track record in the marriage department isn't very good."

"Daddy's crazy in love with Dina, despite her—er—track record."

They stepped inside the house, into the throng of celebrants, into the midst of bright lights and loud music and the hum of hundreds of voices. People filled the downstairs of Rusty McConnell's three-story mansion.

When Addy took several steps away from him, Nick reached out, detaining her by grasping her slender wrist. "If I could dance, I'd ask you for the next one." He almost laughed when he saw the look of surprise on her face.

"Why would you do that?" she asked, a genuinely puzzled look in her eyes.

"Because I'd like to hold you in my arms." Nick knew what women liked to hear, and he'd always had a knack for saying the right thing, for pushing the right buttons. He was adept at using words to achieve his goal, and he usually meant most of what he said. He never blatantly lied to a woman or made promises he didn't keep.

"You're wasting your time flirting with me, Mr. Romero. I'm immune to charming men."

The moment she spoke, he realized that he had indeed meant what he'd said to her. He did want to hold her in his arms. For some odd reason he felt that Addy McConnell needed someone to hold her, to care about her, to protect her. Stupid notion. Why would the heir to a multimillion-dollar aerospace firm need a crippled ex-DEA agent to take care of her? "Some charming man broke your heart?"

"Some charming bastard married me for my daddy's money."

Her smile was as deadly cold as any Nick had ever seen. This woman truly was immune to charm. Did she hate men? he wondered. All men? Or just the charming ones?

"His loss, I'd say."

"Yes, it was," Addy agreed, then walked away from Nick.

He didn't follow, but he watched her. She was tall. At least five ten or eleven in her two-inch heels. Rusty McConnell was Nick's height. Six three.

Addy was slender, but not too skinny. Her shoulders were broad, her waist tiny and her hips well-rounded. She paused by the side of a voluptuous creature in a red sequined dress, whose frosted blond head barely reached Addy's shoulder. Apparently the woman was a close friend. She and Addy were laughing.

Nick noticed how very different the two women were. The blonde was his type—bold and sexy and bosomy. So why did she pale beside Addy? Nick couldn't understand what it was about this redhead that made the blood run hot in his veins. The blood in her veins was probably mixed with ice water. And she didn't have any breasts, at least not enough to fill out the front of her plain little silk dress. She was small but no doubt firm. He guessed that her nipples were a pale coral to match the peachy tint of her creamy gold complexion. He wanted to see those small breasts, those tight little nipples.

Her hair intrigued him, that thick mass of fiery red curls. Nick felt certain that beneath the rather drab exterior a colorful woman existed. The very thought of discovering what treasures lay buried under that plain gray dress suddenly aroused him unbearably.

He noticed Addy turn abruptly toward the center of the room where Dina was tugging on the tail of Rusty McConnell's tuxedo jacket. When Addy took a step away from her friend, Nick moved forward, following her. Suddenly she broke into a run. Nick couldn't keep up, his gait hampered by his limp. People moved back, making room for Addy's mad dash through the crowd.

"Get out of here, Carlton, or I'll throw you out myself!" Rusty bellowed, his deep voice loud over the band music that continued playing.

With Addy on one side and Dina on the other, the two women tried to hold Rusty away from a younger man who had stopped on the dance floor and still held his partner in his arms. The woman was quite young. No more than twenty-five. And very, very pregnant.

Nick moved closer, stepping up beside Brett Windsor who stood directly behind Addy. Windsor was a pretty boy. Tall, blond and muscular.

"Daddy, don't do this. Remember your blood pressure." Addy clung to her father's huge arm.

"Listen to her, Rusty darling." Dina clung just as tenaciously to his other arm.

"He wasn't invited," Rusty said. "How the hell did you get in here, Carlton?"

The other man, a good-looking guy in his mid-thirties smiled at Rusty. Nick thought the smile said a lot. It was actually a smirk.

"Lori and I received an invitation. I presented it at the door." The dark-haired young man gave his companion a gentle hug. "I thought perhaps you'd finally decided to let bygones be bygones."

"I didn't issue that invitation and neither did Addy. Do

you honestly think that after what you put her through she'd want to see you and...and your pregnant wife?" Rusty yanked free of his women, came up to the other man, towering over him by a good four inches, and punched Mr. Carlton in the chest with the tip of his meaty index finger.

Addy stepped forward, slipping her arm through her father's. "Daddy, don't do this." She turned to the couple. "Gerald, you and Lori shouldn't have come here. You're not welcome, and whether or not you received an invitation, you weren't invited. Please go."

"I told you we shouldn't have come," Mrs. Carlton said, turning her brown, puppy-dog eyes to her husband beseechingly.

"I guess the McConnells hold a grudge for life," Gerald Carlton said, looking directly at Addy. "You certainly haven't changed, Adeline. Still as plain and understated as ever, and still letting Daddy fight all your battles. Too bad you didn't inherit his strength—and his sexual appetite."

Nick knew Rusty McConnell was going to deck the younger man. Hell, *he* wanted to hit the sonofabitch and he didn't even know him.

Addy gasped, then grabbed her father. "No, don't. It's what he wants."

Nick stepped forward. He slipped his cane between Gerald Carlton and Rusty McConnell. Both men stared down at the black cane, then up at the man who had dared to interfere.

"Rusty, despite the fact that you're Addy's father and would love to take care of this matter, don't you think it's my place?" Nick turned his cane, positioning the tip in the center of Gerald's chest.

Rusty glared at Nick, obviously dumbfounded by his action. "Why...what—?"

"What do you think you're doing?" Addy whispered, her voice a hiss.

"I'm doing what you've been trying to do," Nick said, low and soft, for her ears only. "I'm trying to stop your father from killing this man."

"Who are you?" Gerald Carlton asked.

"I'm the man who's asking you to step outside," Nick said.

Gerald Carlton studied Nick, taking in every aspect of his appearance. His gaze stopped on Nick's cane, the tip lying against his own chest. "You're not some sort of bodyguard for Rusty. He'd never hire a cripple to protect him, so just who are you?"

"Now see here, Romero—" Rusty said, his voice a snarling growl.

"You're right. I don't work for Rusty." Nick slipped his arm around Addy's waist, pulling her close to him. "This is personal."

Addy's mouth opened in a silent gasp, but Nick had to give her credit. She didn't say a word. She didn't panic. Instead, to his delight, she swayed slightly toward him, resting her body against his.

Gerald laughed, a rather boyish, unmanly laugh. "You can't mean to imply that you and Addy...that—"

"Let's just say that I'm a man who appreciates all the special qualities in Addy that you were apparently too blind to see, let alone appreciate." Nick removed his cane from Gerald's chest, then used it to indicate the foyer. "You have two choices. You and your wife can leave now, or...your wife can take you home after you and I have a little discussion outside."

Gerald laughed again, but the laughter did not reach his eyes. He glanced around the room. Except for the band playing on, the room was deadly quiet. People were gaping, mouths open, eyes wide, waiting. Gerald looked at Nick. Nick smiled. A part of him hoped this clean-cut, sissified Anglo would step outside with him. Nothing would please him more than to show Mr. Carlton that he was one cripple who could easily beat the hell out of him.

"Gerald, let's leave now," his wife pleaded.

"If you're really bedding her," Gerald said, a self-satisfied grin on his face, "then I hope Rusty is paying you enough to make it worth your while."

Rusty lunged for Gerald, but Nick stood firmly in the way. He loosened his hold on Addy, shoving her gently away. Only two people heard the deadly warning Nick uttered, the words vulgar and succinct. Rusty and Gerald stood dead still. Gerald's face turned ashen. He grabbed his wife by the arm and made a hasty exit. Stopping at the double doors leading into the foyer, he gave Nick a nasty look, fear and hatred in his hazel eyes.

Rusty McConnell, big and broad and in superb physical condition for a man well past his prime, slapped Nick on the back, then placed his arm around his shoulder. "Did you mean what you said to him? Would you do it?"

"In a hot minute," Nick said, then glanced over at Addy, who looked rather lost, her face pale, her eyes overly bright as if she might burst into tears at any moment. "I take it that Gerald Carlton is the bastard who married you for your daddy's money?"

"How very astute of you, Mr. Romero." Addy stepped away from the woman in the red sequined dress who appeared to be trying to comfort her.

"Call me Nick." He smiled. She didn't. "After what just happened, everyone is going to assume that we're already on a first-name basis."

"So you should be," Rusty said, giving Nick another strong pat on the back. "I could have handled that pipsqueak Carlton without any help, but I have to admit I like the way you stood up for Addy. You're the kind of man she needs.''

''Daddy!''

''Rusty, what a thing to say.'' Dina reached for Rusty's big hand, squeezing it tightly. ''Nick and Addy just met, and I hardly think they're a suitable match.''

The crowd began moving about and talking again, several people taking advantage of the dance music, others seeking hors d'oeuvres and champagne. Brett Windsor stepped forward, placing a comforting arm around Addy's waist. Nick had the irrational urge to coldcock Mr. Ivy League. Windsor hadn't kept Addy's father from killing her ex-husband. Windsor hadn't defended Addy when Carlton bad-mouthed her in front of everyone. Windsor hadn't been willing to take the other man outside and teach him some manners.

If anyone should be taking Addy McConnell in his arms, it shouldn't be Brett Windsor. He, Nick Romero, should be the man. But before he could make his way to Addy, to claim her attention, she walked away with Windsor. Rusty still had his big arm draped around Nick's shoulder and Dina had slipped between the two of them, taking each by the arm.

Nick watched while Windsor led Addy out onto the dance floor, took her in his arms and waltzed away with her.

Addy accepted her wrap and purse from the maid, whom she didn't know. Someone new Dina had hired, no doubt. Since becoming engaged to Rusty, Dina had moved into the mansion and hired several new servants, claiming there wasn't enough staff to adequately care for such a large estate. Of course, Rusty was agreeing to anything Dina wanted these days. No fool like an old fool in love, Addy thought, hating herself for considering her father foolish. But he was. He didn't seem to care about Dina's past, about all her former wealthy husbands.

Stepping outside onto the large veranda, Addy decided the night was too warm to warrant her shawl. She looked around for Alton, her father's chauffeur. She didn't see anyone, not even one of the parking attendants. Maybe they were taking a break. After all, it was barely eleven and most people wouldn't even begin leaving until after midnight. But she'd had just about all of Rusty and Dina's engagement party she could take. The thought of celebrating her father's upcoming nuptials to a woman who'd been married five times and unashamedly used sex to get what she wanted from men didn't sit well with Addy.

What was it with men and sex? she wondered. No matter what their age, they all seemed to have their brains in their pants. Even her father. It really hadn't bothered her so much when she found out that he'd been having an affair with his secretary, Ginger, for nearly eight years or that there had obviously been numerous women during the years since her mother's death. Maybe even before…after Madeline Dela-court McConnell had shut herself in her room…after the delicately beautiful Mrs. McConnell had lost all sense of reality and retreated into a fantasy world of her own. A world that didn't include kidnappers who had murdered her nine-year-old son.

Shaking her head, Addy walked down the steps leading to the circular drive. She wished she had driven her own car here tonight, but her father had insisted on sending Alton. Her father was overprotective where his only child was concerned. He had been ever since Donnie's kidnapping and death when she was six. He didn't like her driv-

ing from downtown Huntsville at night alone, even though
the trip took less than twenty minutes.

Alton and the others were probably in the kitchen drinking coffee. Or they could be in the garage, where Alton
would be showing them Rusty's antique car collection. She
decided to wait a few minutes. After all, she wasn't in any
hurry to go home, just in a rush to escape the party.

The party alone would have been bad enough, but three
unexpected guests had turned the evening into a real nightmare. Addy suspected that Ginger had mailed Mr. and
Mrs. Gerald Carlton an invitation to tonight's shindig. The
woman would have done anything to ruin Dina's big night.
Ginger probably hadn't even thought of how Gerald's
presence would affect other people—namely Addy Mc-
Connell. And she hadn't cared how Addy would feel seeing Lori, carrying Gerald's third child. She had tried twice
to give Gerald a child. She'd failed miserably both times.

Addy gazed up at the dark sky, at the softly glowing
June moon and questioned the powers-that-be as she'd
done so many times in the past. Perhaps she'd wanted too
much, had dared to ask for more than was her due. After
all, she'd been born with a silver spoon in her mouth. Her
father was a multimillionaire by the time he was thirty-
five. Her mother had been one of the loveliest and wealthiest young debutantes in the state of Alabama. Never once
had she wanted for anything money could buy. But, oh,
how she had longed for the things in life that were beyond
price.

She had longed for a normal mother, one who wasn't
under a nurse's care. She had longed to be just one of the
kids, not "that rich girl," not Rusty McConnell's only
child. She had longed for love and passion. She'd gotten
an unfaithful husband who'd married her for her father's

money. And she'd longed for a child. She'd lost two babies before her fifth month of pregnancy.

Engrossed in thought, Addy strolled farther and farther down the circular drive, past limo after limo, past several Mercedes, BMWs, Jaguars and Porsches.

Nick Romero had been the other unexpected guest, a man she couldn't even begin to understand. There was something about him that intrigued Addy, and something that frightened her. Suddenly she realized that the very thing that intrigued her was the same thing that frightened her: Nick's sensuality. When he looked at her, it was as if…as if he wanted her. She knew that couldn't be right. Tall, flat-chested, redheaded Addy McConnell wasn't the type of woman who evoked passion in men, and most certainly not a man like Nick Romero—big and dark and devastatingly attractive, a man who made women swoon.

Addy felt a steely arm slip around her waist, then saw the rag in the man's hand as it came toward her face. Dear God, someone had grabbed her from behind…someone was going to hurt her. When she opened her mouth to scream, the hand came down over her face, covering her mouth and nose with the rag, the smelly rag. Acting purely on instinct, Addy struggled, trying to free herself. She kicked backward with her heels, hoping to make contact with the man's legs. He held her tighter. She rammed her foot into his ankle and struck him in the stomach with her elbow. Groaning, he loosened his hold on her.

"Be still, bitch," he said, his voice sharp.

When he tried to cover her face with the rag again, she bit down on his hand. He snatched his hand away, cursing loudly. Addy took her chance, whirling around. For a split second, she saw his face in the moonlight. He was a stranger. He grabbed for her. She turned and ran. He ran after her.

He reached out, knocking her down on the pavement, then falling to his knees to straddle her hips. The force of his attack knocked the breath from her lungs. He jerked her up off the driveway.

"They wanted things done up all nice and neat. Said to use the chloroform. Said not to hurt you." He jammed a gun in her ribs. "But they didn't bother telling me that you were such a feisty bitch! So no more Mr. Nice Guy. Understand?"

Addy nodded. What was she going to do? She had to get away. This man could rape her, torture her, kill her. But who *was* he? Someone had sent this maniac after her. But who and why? Dear God, was this an attempted kidnapping? If Rusty McConnell lost his one remaining child to a kidnapper, he wouldn't be able to live through the tragedy a second time. All Addy could think about was her father.

Her high-pitched, ear-splitting scream shattered the nocturnal solitude.

Chapter 2

Nick didn't know why he'd followed Addy McConnell outside. He wanted to see her again? Yeah. He wanted to talk with her? Yeah. He wanted to get to know her better? Yeah. He wanted to drag her into the back seat of one of those big, shiny limos parked in the driveway and find out if she was as frigid as her ex-husband had implied? Damn, yes. Some gut-level instinct told him that Addy was as fiery as her hair, as hot and wild as the look he'd seen in her bright green eyes. But she would be that way only with him...only for him.

He heard the scream. A bloodcurdling scream of pure fear. And then he saw them. The tall redheaded woman and the muscular youth who held her. She wasn't struggling, she was just standing there in his arms, screaming. Nick moved forward cautiously, knowing he mustn't surprise Addy's attacker. He cursed his bad leg for slowing him down. Time was of the essence. He wouldn't have been the only one who'd heard her screams. Soon the lawn would be swarming with curious guests. No telling what the assailant would do if confronted by a mob of onlookers. He could panic and kill Addy.

Nick saw the gun held to Addy's ribs. The metal housing sparkled like shiny glass when the moonlight struck it from the right angle.

Nick eased off the veranda and out onto the drive, his steps faltering slightly as he leaned heavily on his cane. He could make out only the shadows of Addy and the man holding her captive. He crept along behind the parked cars, edging his way closer and closer to the woman he desperately wanted to save.

Nick saw several uniformed chauffeurs coming around the house, followed by five parking attendants in white coats. Damn! He hastened his lame gait, cursing the pain in his calf. He had to get to Addy.

The mansion's double front doors swung open. At least two dozen people ran outside, Rusty McConnell leading the pack. Double damn!

Nick crouched down behind the driver's side of a white Rolls, peering over the hood. If he reached out he could touch the hem of Addy's dress.

"Damn you, bitch," the man with the gun shouted. "See what you've done. See what you've done!"

He jerked Addy away from the passenger side of the Rolls, twisting her arm behind her back and pointing the revolver directly at her head. Addy had stopped screaming. Her face, only lightly covered with translucent makeup, was almost as gray as her dress. The fear reflected on her peachy flesh made the smattering of tiny freckles across her nose visible even in the moonlight.

Nick knew he had few options. Capturing the assailant wasn't his top priority. Saving Addy was. That meant disarming her attacker before he had the chance to use his gun.

"Good God, it's Addy!" Rusty McConnell bellowed like a wounded bull, his voice carrying loudly in the stillness.

Nick could hear the rumble of voices, the tantalizing moan of a saxophone from inside the house, the labored breathing of the sweating man who began walking backward, practically dragging Addy with him. Nick slipped around the side of the Rolls, keeping his head low, groaning silently as excruciating pain radiated from his calf up into his bent knee. Coordinating his movements perfectly to keep pace with Addy and her kidnapper, Nick reached the rear of the car the moment they did.

He had one chance and one chance only. If he failed... If the man panicked...

Nick made his move. The man, young and scared, his dark eyes riveted to Nick, swung Addy around hard, using her as a shield. His long, sandy ponytail flipped over his shoulder. He tightened his hold on Addy. For one split second, he raised the gun a fraction of an inch, the barrel shining brightly just above Addy's head, the man's white hand clearly visible against Addy's flame red hair.

Using his trained warrior instincts, Nick raised his black walking stick with split-second precision. The gold tip touched the assailant's hand. He reacted quickly, shoving the gun against Nick's cane. Nick pressed the concealed lever. A sharp stiletto sprang from the tip of the cane and pierced the attacker's hand, slicing through flesh and muscle. Blood gushed from the wound. The man yowled in pain, dropping the gun. The metal rattled as it hit the driveway. Using his good leg, Nick extended his foot and kicked the revolver under the Rolls. The young would-be kidnapper, having lost his gun and inadvertently released

Addy, glared at Nick, who swiftly and adeptly pulled the knife out of the man's hand and, with a quick press of a lever, returned the knife to its secret bed within his black lacquer stick.

When the young man made a move toward Addy, Nick used the gold-tipped staff to ward him off. Twirling the cane around, Nick slapped him across the face, bloodying his nose.

Nick heard the sound of voices coming closer, the loud pounding of running feet. Panting, the assailant glared over Nick's shoulder, then back at Nick. Easing away slowly, the man turned and broke into a full run. Nick made no attempt to follow. He leaned over to help a badly shaken Addy McConnell to her feet. Her tightly coiled topknot had come loose. Thick, heavy tendrils of bright red hair fell down her back, over her ears, and wispy curls framed her face. The sleeve of her unflattering gray dress was ripped, one of her two-inch heels was missing and there was a run in her panty hose that stretched from her ankle all the way up and beyond the hem of her dress. Her silver and black beaded purse rested at her feet where it had fallen from her shoulder.

The delicate fragrance of her expensive perfume mingled with the heady odor of her female perspiration. Nick could smell her heat…and he liked her uniquely sweet scent.

Leaning on his cane, Nick pulled Addy up against his body, hugging her close. Her breathing was labored, her eyes wild with fear, her full lips parted in the prelude to a sigh or a moan or a cry. Nick wasn't sure which. God, he wanted to kiss her. He wanted to hold her so close, so tight, that she would become a part of him. He wanted to run his hands all over her, from neck to knees, to make sure she was unharmed, to reassure her by his touch that she was alive.

The voices and running feet came closer. Within seconds a crowd would surround them. He looked at Addy. She looked at him.

"Oh, Nick…" Her voice was pleadingly soft, issuing both thanks and invitation in the way she uttered his name.

She leaned into him, resting against him. She put both of her arms around his waist, clinging to him. He'd never felt so much a man. Not in all his life. Was this what it felt like, he wondered, to protect your woman?

"You're all right, Addy." Nick lowered his head, his breath mingling with hers. "He didn't hurt you, did he?"

"No—not really—just…just scared me." She raised her lips to his.

Just as Nick's mouth covered hers, he felt the hardy slap of Rusty McConnell's big hand on his back. "What the hell was going on? Who was that man?"

Addy turned her face toward her father, but she remained in Nick's arms, her hands clutching at his back. "He…he was trying to rob me," she lied. "Nick showed up just in time. I…don't know what I would have done."

"The police have been called." Rusty stared at his daughter, doubt and fear raging in his dark green eyes. "Some of the men are trying to catch your attacker. I'd let the dogs loose if we didn't have guests wandering around out here."

Nick could feel the quick, hard beat of Addy's heart where her chest rested against his side. Her breasts were crushed into him. They weren't as small as he'd thought, but they were just as firm.

There was more to this attack than a man trying to steal a woman's purse. If that was all the man had been after, he'd have taken it and run. No, the man, whoever he was, had wanted Addy, had been trying to take her with him. That meant he was either a rapist or a kidnapper. If he'd been a murderer, he could have shot her before Nick saw them. Addy was lying to her father, and Nick didn't understand why. Who was she trying to protect? Surely not her attacker.

"Did you get a good look at his face?" Rusty asked. "Could you identify him?"

Addy nodded. Trembling, she clung to Nick.

"I'll get rid of everybody as quickly as I can," Rusty said. "You aren't going back to your house tonight. You can stay in your old room. I'll have Mrs. Hargett get it ready for you."

"The police will probably want to question everyone," Nick said. "Just in case anybody saw something. But I think Addy and I are the only ones who can identify her attacker. There's no need for them to grill her. I got as good a look at him as she did."

"I'll get Dina," Rusty suggested. "She can stay with you, Addy. A girl needs another woman at a time like this."

"No, Daddy. Really. I'll—I'll be all right." Addy twisted the back of Nick's tuxedo jacket in her hand, wadding it into a wrinkled knot. "If I can just go inside…get away from all these people staring at me. Something to drink. Brandy, maybe. Or a shot of whiskey. And—and—" she looked at Nick. "And Nick—Mr. Romero could go with me."

"Huh?" Rusty's gaze moved from his daughter's face to her arms that were clinging to Nick. "Take her inside, Romero. And stay with her. I'll take care of everything else. You take care of my daughter."

Nick heard both the entreaty and the warning in big Rusty McConnell's voice. The man knew he would protect

Addy with his life. He also knew that Nick wanted her, and wanted her badly. A man could always tell when another man was proprietary about a woman. Nick had seen that look in many a man's eye. He'd never thought another man would ever see it in his. He hadn't felt possessive about a woman in twenty-five years. Not since he'd been seventeen and in love with his brother's wife.

"Well, they weren't a whole hell of a lot of help, were they?" Rusty McConnell stomped across the cream and gold Persian rug in his living room. Running a big hand through his thick, cinnamon-streaked white hair, he chomped down on his half-smoked Havana cigar.

"Now, darling." Dina draped her small, delicate arm around her fiancé's thick waist. "I think the officers did a thorough job. My goodness, they questioned every guest and gave all of us the third degree. It's two-thirty, and we're exhausted. Why don't we go to bed and—"

Unconsciously, Rusty jerked away from Dina's possessive hold, turning to Addy. "You're not going home. Do you understand? Mrs. Hargett's already got your room ready."

"I'll stay here tonight, Daddy, but in the morning, I'm going home." Addy refused to allow some maniac's attack to turn her father into the fanatically overprotective parent he'd been years ago. From the time she was six and her older brother had been killed by his kidnappers, Addy had lived in a gilded cage, a poor little rich girl unable to flee the golden chains that kept her *safe*. Not until her marriage to Gerald had ended had she found the strength and courage to escape Rusty's loving captivity.

Rusty's gaze swung around, focusing on his niece. "That boyfriend of yours is outside waiting. Why don't you go on home, Janice. And, if Addy isn't up to coming in to work Monday, you handle things.''

"Now, Daddy, don't go making any decisions for me.'' Addy gave Janice a knowing nod and tried to smile. "Go on home with Ron. I'm fine.''

"I'll see you Monday,'' Janice said, giving Addy a quick hug. Walking out, she paused. "Uncle Rusty, you know that M.A.C.'s day-care center can't function without Addy.''

Rusty didn't acknowledge his niece's parting comment. Turning all his attention on Brett Windsor, he resisted Dina's attempts to put her arm around him. "What the hell are you still doing here? Go on up to your room, Windsor. I need to talk to Addy and Nick. Alone.''

Addy bit her tongue to keep from chastising her father for his rudeness. A worldly wise man, a self-made millionaire, D.B. McConnell could be charming if the occasion called for it, but otherwise he didn't bother with the formalities of courtesy. Good manners were something that, even in her declining years of mental illness, Madeline Delacourt McConnell had instilled in her daughter, and Addy abhorred the lack of them in anyone, even in her own dearly loved father.

She reached out, placing her hand on Brett's arm. "I'll see you in the morning at breakfast.''

His smile only enhanced his already handsome face. His dark blue eyes changed from brooding to pleasant. Addy returned his smile, thinking how attractive Brett Windsor was, with his sandy blond hair, his tall, muscular body, his quick wit and attentive manner. Too bad his interest in her was only monetary. As much as she liked Brett, there was no doubt in her mind that his sole interest in her was her daddy's money. Of course, he had no idea that she knew what was behind his phony smiles and attentive manner.

"Why don't you escort your stepmother upstairs?" Rusty said. "This hasn't been the best of nights for her."

"But, Rusty, darling, I should be here with you," Dina protested. "A wife should always be at her husband's side, sharing the good and the bad, giving him her support and love."

Addy wanted to say "poppycock." Dina protested being asked to leave because she didn't want Rusty making any decisions without her. After all, she wasn't his wife, yet, and she didn't want anything to postpone or prevent their upcoming nuptials. Without moving, Addy saw Nick in her peripheral vision. He was staring at Dina, a quirky little smile on his face. He knows her, Addy thought, and can see straight through her the way I can.

"You're exhausted," Rusty said. "There's nothing you can do for Addy or for me, tonight. I'm sorry our engagement party ended on such a sour note." He pulled Dina into his arms, her small body lost in his enormous bear hug. "I just want to go over things again with Addy and Nick."

"All right, Rusty, whatever you want." Reluctantly, Dina accepted Brett's arm and the two left the room.

The moment the door closed, Rusty turned to his daughter. "Now, little girl, I want you to tell me what you didn't tell the police."

"I don't know what you're talking about. I told the police everything." Addy crossed her arms over her chest and plopped down into the cream brocade Queen Anne chair by the fireplace.

"Don't play the innocent with me. I know damn well what happened tonight! Somebody tried to kidnap you." Rusty hovered over Addy, glowering at her, daring her to deny the truth.

She'd been afraid this would happen. Her father was too

smart, but it had been worth a try, to protect him from worry and to protect herself from his reaction. "The man was trying to rob me, Daddy."

With an exasperated grunt, Rusty turned to Nick. "Do you think he was trying to rob her?"

"No, sir." Nick glanced at Addy, who glared up at him, a slight tremor moving her head, as if she wanted to give him a negative warning but realized her father was watching her. "The man was either a rapist or a kidnapper. My guess is that your daughter can tell us which."

How was she going to fight both of these men? Addy wondered. Obviously, Nick was on her father's side. She glanced back and forth from the big dark Hispanic to the big fair Scot, both men of equal height and similar physiques, although Rusty's body had broadened and softened slightly with age. *Birds of a feather*. Two strong, overbearing, macho men.

She realized Nick and Rusty were staring at her. "All right. He was trying to kidnap me, but he didn't. I'm fine. Nick foiled his rather clumsy attempt."

"Why the hell didn't you tell the police?" Rusty bent over, placing his meaty hands on the armrests of Addy's chair. Lowering his head, he narrowed his green eyes and frowned. "You didn't want me to know. Is that it, little girl?"

Shoving on her father's burly chest, she pushed him away, then stood up. "Daddy..."

Rusty turned from her, walking across the room to the long windows that faced the veranda of his white-columned mansion. "I'll call the police in the morning and tell them. We'll have to take the proper precautions."

"Daddy...don't." No, she couldn't bear it. Never again. She was free and she intended to stay free. "If you want to hire someone to follow me around, keep watch on my house, that's fine. Even put on some extra guards at work, that's okay, too. But—I will not move back here and I will not be kept under lock and key.''

''We'll discuss this in the morning after we've all had some rest.'' Rusty nodded toward Nick. ''Alton's brought Nick's things over from his hotel and Mrs. Hargett has put him in the room beside you.''

''What?'' Addy exclaimed, her gaze riveted to Nick's smiling face. Just what was going on here? She felt as if these two had telepathically decided what was best for her.

''I'd prefer him in the room with you, but I didn't think you'd ever agree to that.'' Rusty's grin was pure masculine superiority.

''Why on earth would you put Nick—Mr. Romero next to me? I'm sure you've already called in an army of guards to surround this place.''

''We'll have more than enough security by tomorrow,'' Rusty said. ''But regardless of that, Nick's the kind of man I want close to you if there's any trouble.''

''How do you know what kind of man Mr. Romero is?'' Addy asked.

''Are you forgetting he saved you from a kidnapper tonight, little girl?''

''For heaven's sake, stop calling me that! I'm thirty-five years old.''

Completely ignoring Addy's demand, Rusty surveyed Nick from head to toe. ''I ran a check on Nick. Just a preliminary check, when Dina said she'd invited her brother-in-law to come for the party and to stay a few days. Did the same thing with Brett Windsor. No big deal.''

''But why, Daddy? That's an invasion of privacy.''

''Brett Windsor has shown an interest in you. I wanted to see just how much money he did or didn't have. I wouldn't want you to have to go through the same kind of mess you did with Gerald.''

"Give me some credit, Daddy. You didn't have to run a check on Brett. I've known all along that it's your money he wants and not me.''

"So we're both smarter than we used to be, but it's better to be safe than sorry.''

"Some of us are smarter," Addy mumbled under her breath.

"Insulting Dina in front of her brother-in-law?" Rusty laughed.

"I'm going to bed," Addy said, heading for the door. "And in the morning, I'm going home."

"Nick, you go on with her, see her tucked in all safe and sound." Rusty commanded, but a trace of chuckling humor softened his words.

Addy stopped dead in her tracks. Without turning to face either man, she said, "What did you find out about Mr. Romero that makes you think he's so trustworthy?"

"He fought in Nam. Spent ten years in the SEALS. Went in when he was eighteen. He was a DEA agent for nearly a dozen years.'' Rusty paused, as if waiting for his daughter to comment. When she didn't, he continued. "He came from nothing and made something of himself, just like I did. I think Nick and I are a lot alike. Besides, he's one of Sam Dundee's best friends, and Dundee said that, despite Nick's bad leg, he's one of the toughest, meanest sonofabitches he's ever known. The kind of man you'd want on your side in a fight.''

Addy knew she'd made a mistake in asking. Obviously, Nick Romero possessed all the requirements her father considered important in a man. Close friendship with Sam Dundee, whose private security agency her father had used on more than one occasion, was a definite plus in his favor.

What more could Rusty McConnell ask for? "With such glowing credentials, I think you should just adopt him—then Dina would have someone around to amuse her when you're too busy."

Rusty's big body shook with laughter. "Dina has Brett for that. Besides, I was thinking I wouldn't mind having a man like Nick for a son-in-law."

Nick's gut twisted. His heartbeat accelerated. What the hell kind of game was McConnell playing? When he saw the stricken look on Addy's face, he wondered if she hated the idea of marriage or just the idea of being married to him. "Don't worry, Addy, I'm not the marrying kind." He gave Rusty a hard stare. "Maybe you'd better just adopt me."

"You take care of our Addy." Rusty walked over and draped one arm around Addy's shoulder, then reached out and placed his other arm around Nick. "If you hear the least little peep out of her during the night, you rush right on in. You—" he turned to Addy "—behave yourself and cooperate."

Rusty walked them to the double doors leading out into the foyer. Stepping away from them, he laid Addy's hand on Nick's arm.

"Why don't you just play along with your father?" Nick whispered. "It'll make it easier for both of us."

"It's obvious that you don't know Rusty McConnell, Mr. Romero. He doesn't respect easy compliance, especially not in his daughter. He expects me to fight back."

"Have you always?"

"No, I haven't." Addy allowed Nick to lead her up the winding staircase. "Daddy has always loved me. Adored me, really. But when I divorced Gerald and moved out of this house, Daddy learned to respect me and accept what I wanted.''

''And you're afraid this kidnap scare will somehow turn back the clock to the way things used to be?''

''I won't let that happen.''

Nick didn't doubt her. There was more to Addy McConnell than met the eye. Was that why he felt so attracted to her? He couldn't figure it out. She was far from his type. Hell, she wasn't much to look at. Too flat-chested, too plain, too tall and too hostile toward men. He liked women who liked men. Soft, fluttery females. Sultry, sexy ladies who enjoyed flirtation and seduction. Experienced women who knew the rules and played the game to perfection.

Addy McConnell didn't fit the description. But there was something about her, something lonely and vulnerable, and something filled with raging hunger. She hid it well, but Addy was a woman in need. And Nick wanted to be the man to fill that need.

Addy opened her eyes. Dawn light filtered through the sheer panels that covered her bedroom windows. She'd forgotten to draw the yellow drapes last night. An early morning hush enveloped the room. Stillness. Quiet. Then she heard the woman's voice coming from the room next to hers, the room her father had assigned to Nick Romero.

Addy scooted to the edge of the bed, slipping into her blue house slippers. Feeling around at the foot of her rumpled bed, she found the blue robe that matched the lace-trimmed cotton gown she wore. When she'd moved out of her father's mansion nearly seven years ago, she'd left everything behind. She wanted nothing that reminded her of the three years she'd spent with Gerald or the two heartbreaking miscarriages she'd suffered. But her father had kept not only her room unchanged, he'd kept every one of her possessions, including her clothes.

Walking softly, Addy made her way to the door, cracking it slightly open. When she heard Nick's door opening, she closed her own, leaving just enough space so she could peep into the hallway. Dina slipped out of Nick's room. He stopped in the open doorway. She stood close, her body grazing his. Dina wore a sheer black silk negligee. Addy gasped at the sight of Dina's near nakedness. My God, had the woman no shame?

Dina ran her long nails down Nick's cheek, then across his lips. Addy sucked in her breath.

"We're in agreement, then," Dina said, breathlessly. "You won't say a word to Rusty about—about what happened, will you? He might not understand."

"It's none of my business." Nick looked down at the small blond woman who had once tempted him beyond reason. Strange how age and experience change a man. "But Rusty McConnell is nobody's fool. My guess is that he already knows exactly what you're all about and he wants you anyway. Why not be totally honest with him and see what happens?"

"Silly boy. You know better than that. You men are all such fools when it comes to women. You get so possessive and can't bear to think that we might be as experienced as you are. We're supposed to be thankful to all the women who taught you how to be studs in bed, but you're jealous of the men who taught us how to be pleasing."

"Hell, Dina. Rusty knows you've been married five times, doesn't he?"

"Yes, but—"

"Go back to bed before Rusty wakes up and finds you gone. It would be easier to explain everything about your past to him than it would to explain what you've been doing in my bedroom at five-thirty in the morning."

She ran her fingers down his throat, across his bare chest to the undone snap of his tuxedo trousers. "All we've done is talk."

Nick grabbed her hand, shoving it away. "And that's all we're going to do, now or ever. I'm not a sex-hungry seventeen-year-old."

Addy didn't want to listen. She wanted to close the door and forget what she'd seen and heard. But she couldn't. She owed it to her father to find out what was going on between Dina and Nick, didn't she? Of course she did. *Liar,* her conscience screamed at her. *You're jealous.* How could this have happened? she wondered. How could she have allowed herself to become interested in a man like Nick Romero?

It was because he'd rescued her that she'd started thinking of him as a knight in shining armor. During the few hours of restless sleep she'd had, she'd dreamed of Nick. Black eyes. Bronze skin. Big and broad and strong. She didn't want to think of him as her champion, as her own personal paladin, but she did. He had defended her from her ex-husband's insults and then saved her from an attacker. Nick Romero, no matter what else he was, was quite a man.

Dina reached out, allowing her hand to hover over Nick's bare chest. "If you're entertaining any fanciful notions about Addy, I'd advise you to forget them. Rusty keeps a close watch on his little girl's love life and he wouldn't approve of you."

"Now that's where you're wrong," Nick said. "Rusty McConnell wholeheartedly approves of me. Just earlier this morning, after you and Brett went upstairs, he told Addy that he wouldn't mind having me for a son-in-law."

"What?" Dina's voice screeched loudly.

"Quieten down before you wake Addy." Nick glanced at Addy's partially open door and smiled.

"You're leaving in a few days. Going—going to El Paso to visit your grandmother."

"I might stay around a while longer."

"Are you doing this to make me jealous?" Dina asked.

"Go back to Rusty's bed, Dina, and leave me alone."

"You can't ever forgive me, can you?"

"Leave, Dina. Now."

Swirling the floor-length robe as she turned, Dina marched down the hall, her chin tilted high. Addy watched until her father's fiancée turned the corner leading to the west wing of the house. She started to close the door. Nick Romero stuck his foot inside the narrow crack. Addy tried to shove the door closed. Ramming his shoulder into the door, he pushed it open.

"Up awfully early aren't you, Addy?"

"Something woke me."

"Something or someone?"

She glared at him, the corners of his mouth curving upward in a self-satisfied smile. He knew she'd seen Dina leaving his room in her see-through nightie and he didn't know whether or not she'd tell her father.

"I think we should have a little talk," Nick said, his body pressing against hers. "In private."

He was warm, his thickly muscled bronze chest like a hot pad where it touched her. Even through her gown she could feel his heat. The tremors began in her stomach, radiating upward and outward until every nerve in her body tingled. The reaction was totally unexpected. Being near a man had never shaken her so badly.

When he grasped her elbow, maneuvering her backward into her room, she made no protest. But when he shut the door, she stepped away from him, wary of his intentions. She didn't know this man, this brother-in-law of Dina's, this former DEA agent. How did she know he was trustworthy, despite her father's approval? Rusty had liked Gerald in the beginning, had been impressed with his knowledge of aeronautics and the day-to-day running of a company like M.A.C.

"Stop looking at me as if you're afraid." Nick took a tentative step toward her, then stopped suddenly when he realized she was genuinely scared. "I don't ravish unwilling women if that's what's worrying you."

"I want you to leave."

"Not until I explain what Dina was doing in my bedroom."

"I don't care what she was doing, or what you were doing or if the two of you were doing something together."

"Adamant about it, aren't you?" Nick grinned at her, taking in the way Addy McConnell looked first thing in the morning. With her long red hair hanging freely halfway down her back and her tall, slender body encased in a cute little blue cotton nightgown and matching robe, she looked about twelve years old. Her face, scrubbed clean of the light makeup she'd worn earlier, radiated with a healthy glow. Her skin was golden tinted, with only a smattering of freckles here and there. A few on her nose. A few more on her throat and arms. He wondered how many there were on the rest of her body.

"Daddy knows that Dina isn't as pure as the driven snow…"

"But my guess is that Rusty wouldn't be pleased to find out that his fiancée, the woman he's bedding, was in my room trying to seduce me." Nick watched Addy closely.

"Was that what she was doing, seducing you?" Addy

maintained a calm control over her voice, praying that the quivering she felt inside wouldn't manifest itself in her words.

"It's an old game between Dina and me. Has been for years. She *tries* to seduce me. I reject her. She likes to think she's tormenting me, that I have to call forth all my strength in order to resist her." Not since that once, twenty-five years ago, when he'd succumbed to his brother's widow, had Nick ever given in to that specific temptation again. After he'd gone against his better judgment and made love to Dina, she'd told him she was going to marry another man. An older man. A more powerful man. A richer man. And he'd spent the rest of his life feeling guilty for bedding Miguel's widow, feeling as if he'd betrayed his brother. Oh, he'd been hot for her then, so hot he'd thought he'd die. But that fire had burned itself out a long time ago and he and Dina had somehow come through it as friends. Friends of a sort, that is.

"My father is very possessive. He wouldn't want to share her."

"He doesn't have anything to worry about where I'm concerned, but he might want to do a nightly bed check in Windsor's room." Nick didn't know it for a fact, but he was reasonably sure that Dina and her stepson had been lovers for years, between her marriages and perhaps even during them. He'd bet his last dime that Rusty McConnell wasn't aware of that little fact.

"What a hateful thing to imply!" Addy said. "You're probably trying to place blame on Brett to save your own hide. After all, I didn't see Dina coming out of Brett's room, did I?"

"Jealous?" Nick moved toward her, slowly, deliberately, like an animal stalking his prey.

"Of you and Dina?" Addy laughed, the sound blatantly phony. "Don't be ridiculous."

Nick reached out, slipping his hand beneath her hair, circling her neck. She gulped in huge swallows of air. Her eyes widened in a mixture of shock and excitement. He pulled her closer. In her bare feet, she stood five inches shorter than he did. The perfect height for him.

"You don't like me very much, do you, Addy?" He touched the tip of his nose to hers, and smiled when he heard her indrawn breath.

"I...I don't know you." Decently clothed in her gown and robe, Addy felt naked, bare to his gaze and touch. Vulnerable. Nick Romero made her feel vulnerable.

"I remind you of your daddy, don't I?" His breath mingled with hers as he lowered his head just a fraction. "All the qualities you dislike in Rusty, you see in me."

"He was right, wasn't he? The two of you are a lot alike."

"Probably." Nick watched her intently, amazed by his own desire for this tall, flat-chested redhead. "It's obvious that you love your father, why is it that you don't like him?"

"I—I do like him. It's just that—that he's so damned macho and controlling. So overprotective because he loves me. He thinks because I'm his daughter, he should be able to protect me from everything and everyone. He—he smothers me, sometimes."

"A man tends to be that way with the people he loves. His woman, his children, his family." Nick tightened his hold on Addy's neck, forcing her head upward toward his until only inches separated them. He touched her bottom lip with the tip of his finger.

She knew he was going to kiss her. What she didn't

know was whether or not she wanted him to. "Why—why are you doing this?"

"Damned if I know," he said, then took her mouth.

His kiss was gentle and seductive, a practiced perfection. Addy trembled, her own lips responding, surrendering to a power she'd never known, an enticement she was unable to resist. She sighed, longing for more. Placing his hand on her hip, he stroked her through her cotton gown as he deepened the kiss.

Addy eased her hands upward, twining them around his neck. The minute his tongue entered her mouth, he felt himself spiraling out of control. It had been a long time since he'd gotten aroused so quickly, so thoroughly. If he didn't stop things immediately, he'd be flinging her down on her bed and ripping off that little-girl gown she wore. He'd be finding out how many freckles she had on her body and exactly where they were located.

He broke away from her, releasing her, gently pulling her arms from around his neck. "You're wearing a disguise, Addy McConnell. You wrap yourself up in your Plain-Jane clothes and pretend you're an iceberg, that you dislike sex."

"It—it isn't a disguise." Her words came out choppy, on quick, heated little breaths. Nick had kissed her more thoroughly than she'd ever been kissed in her life, and she was still reeling from the aftereffects. "I am a Plain Jane who dislikes chest-beating Neanderthal men. And I am an iceberg. Just ask my ex-husband."

Nick walked away from her, then turned when he reached the door. "Why should I ask that bastard anything, when I got all the proof I needed, first hand, that you're hot as a firecracker?"

"I am not!"

Nick grinned. "That was a compliment, Red. I like my women hot."

"I am not one of your women."

Nick opened the door, paused briefly, then looked back at Addy. "But you will be." Before she could reply, he walked out and closed the door behind him.

She stood, speechless, her mouth agape, her gaze focused on the door. A riot of emotions exploded inside her. Desire. Anger. Passion. Outrage. She wanted to hit something, preferably Nick Romero. "Of all the overconfident, strutting peacocks! He's insufferable! If he thinks for one minute that—that…" Addy couldn't finish her sentence. Visions of Nick Romero's big body filled her mind. Nick, pressing down onto her, into her, his dark eyes devouring her as he took her. Addy shook her head, trying to erase her erotic thoughts.

In a few hours, after she'd pacified her father by having breakfast with him, she would go home. She had no intention of being around Nick Romero one minute longer than she had to. After today, she'd never have to see him again.

Chapter 3

Addy had delayed going downstairs for breakfast as long as she possibly could. Her father had already sent Mrs. Hargett upstairs twice, the last time relaying a command that she join the others at once.

Glancing out the windows onto the front lawn of her father's estate, located about ten miles outside of Huntsville, Addy thought again how much the rich green lawns and towering old trees reminded her of her mother's ancestral estate where they'd lived until Madeline's death. Wanting to escape all the agonizing memories of his son's kidnapping and subsequent murder and his wife's suicide four years later, Rusty McConnell had taken Addy away, moved her into a sparkling new mansion, pure and untainted by any reminders of a past too painful to remember. She had missed Elm Hill, the vast acres of rolling pastures and thickly wooded forests. Even now, she dreamed of someday returning and living out the rest of her life in the house where five generations of Delacourts had been born and raised. Someday…when she had laid all her fears to rest.

Her mother and Janice's mother had been the last of the line, both women now dead, leaving only the two cousins as heirs to family pride and genteel breeding. And Elm Hill had stood vacant for twenty-five years, Janice having neither the desire nor the money to renovate the old place and Addy, with more than enough money, but not enough courage to fight the demons from her childhood.

Instead, she'd bought a house in Huntsville's historic district, Twickenham.

A sharp, loud knock at her bedroom door snapped Addy out of her rambling thoughts. "Yes?"

The door opened. Mrs. Hargett stood outside in the hallway. "I'm terribly sorry to keep bothering you like this, but—"

"Is he threatening to come and drag me downstairs kicking and screaming?" Addy laughed, remembering how many times during her difficult adolescent years her father had issued similar warnings. Having a daughter with her mother's old-fashioned breeding but none of her delicate blond beauty had often confused Rusty McConnell. But not nearly as much as the mixture of personality traits she had inherited from Madeline and himself. Cool, calm and ever the lady. Rusty liked that. What he didn't like was her stubbornness, which was one of his own most prominent qualities.

"Yes, ma'am. That's what he said." Mrs. Hargett, small and skinny, with round black eyes that were the only bright spot in her pale colorless face, smiled, crinkling the feathery wrinkles that lined her eyes and mouth. "He ordered me to give you that message, but then he told me to wait. He looked over at that Mr. Romero, you know, Mrs. Lunden's brother-in-law."

Agitating circles formed in the pit of Addy's stomach. "You don't have to tell me. He said to let me know that if I didn't come down, posthaste, he'd send Ni—Mr. Romero up to fetch me."

"Mr. McConnell can be outrageous sometimes, can't he?" Mrs. Hargett shook her head, not disturbing one curl of her neatly permed short gray hair that was coated with a hair spray with the sealing powers of a good lacquer.

"There'll be no need for a return message." Addy picked up her purse from the nightstand. "I might as well get this over with."

Together, she and Mrs. Hargett descended the staircase, but once in the foyer the housekeeper turned toward the kitchen while Addy squared her broad shoulders and marched into the dining room.

Rusty McConnell disliked antique furniture. Elm Hill had been filled with five generations of acquisition. Every stick of furniture in this mansion was expensive and new. Rusty sat at the head of the dark oak dining table, a traditional-style buffet at his back, an enormous matching china cabinet at the opposite end of the room, directly behind Dina, who turned and glared at Addy, a look of resentment in her cool blue eyes. Addy wondered what had prompted that look. Something was going on. More than she'd bargained for, she feared.

"About time you got down here." Rusty flicked the ashes from the tip of his cigar into a small brass tray. "We've all finished with breakfast."

"I'm not hungry." Addy, her steps quick and unfaltering, sailed past Dina, not even acknowledging her presence. She stopped briefly to touch Brett on the back. He turned his bright smile on her. "Good morning."

"Why the hell did you put on that dirty, ripped dress you were wearing last night?" Rusty asked, scooting his chair backward, preparing to stand. "You've got a closet full of clothes in your room."

Standing by her father's chair, Addy placed a restraining hand on his shoulder. "Don't get up, Daddy." She bent down, kissing him on the cheek. "You really should have given those clothes to Goodwill or the Salvation Army years ago."

Rusty grunted, then gave his daughter a quick kiss on her forehead. "Sit down. We've got a lot to discuss."

"Make it quick." Addy didn't sit down. Picking up a cup filled with hot, black coffee, she brought it to her lips. "I'm going home, so don't try to stop me."

"I knew you wouldn't want to stay here," Rusty said. "So I've made arrangements to keep you safe in your own home."

Addy sipped the strong, eye-opening coffee. Suspiciously glaring at her father, she tried to figure out why he was being so agreeable. She'd been sure she'd have a battle royal on her hands this morning, certain he'd insist she move back into the mansion and be kept under lock and key twenty-four hours a day. "What's the catch?"

"I've hired protection for you." Rusty ran the tip of his big, meaty finger around his empty cup. Smiling, he glanced up at Addy, a mischievous twinkle in his green eyes.

"What did you do, call Sam Dundee this morning and have him fly in some of his men?" Addy hated the thought of someone following her every move, but it was an acceptable alternative to moving back to her father's house.

"I talked to Sam. He's arranging some extra security, but he suggested a private bodyguard for you, someone he thinks is the best my money could buy." Sticking his cigar back in his mouth, Rusty inhaled deeply, then released a cloud of smoke.

Addy felt the tension in the room, an underlying tremor of emotions coming from the others sitting around the table. She glanced over at Brett, handsome, syrupy sweet Brett, who simply smiled at her. But there was something in his eyes, an odd look that Addy didn't understand. Turning her attention to Dina, she again noted the resentment the other woman couldn't disguise.

Taking a deep breath, she finally looked at Nick Romero, whose tight jeans and cotton knit shirt took nothing away from his aura of sophistication. The tiny diamond stud glistened against his bronze earlobe. Addy tried not to remember the way he'd kissed her, the way he'd made her feel. She didn't want to have any more romantic fantasies about him being her personal champion, her paladin. But the minute she looked at him, her control slipped. A tingling warmth spread through her. She fought it, annoyed. Nick stared at her, his face blank.

"What do you mean, a private bodyguard?" She didn't like the sound of it.

"Sit down, little girl." Rusty reached into his pants pocket and pulled out a rumpled sheet of paper. "Take a look at this."

Addy picked up the paper, scanning the typewritten words. *Addy McConnell will not be harmed if you follow our instructions. We will contact you soon with our demands. Do not involve the authorities. Your daughter's life depends on your cooperation.*

Pulling out a chair, Addy sat down beside Brett Windsor. He casually laid his arm across the back of her chair. "It came in the morning mail," he said. "Rusty's been horribly upset since he read it."

"These kidnappers were so sure of themselves that they mailed this yesterday." Rusty grabbed the letter out of

Addy's trembling fingers. "Nick has already talked to the police and the FBI as well as Sam Dundee."

Jerking around, Addy glared at Nick, whose face was still as unreadable to her as hieroglyphics. "You've put Nick in charge?"

"Considering his background and connections, he volunteered." Rusty cleared his throat, and Addy knew he was trying not to reveal how overwrought he was, how deeply disturbed he was by the memories of that long-ago kidnapping that had ended so tragically. Addy would give anything to prevent the pain she knew he was feeling. Rusty McConnell was a good man. He didn't deserve such torment.

"The letter and envelope it came in will be thoroughly tested, but my guess is that it will be clean, the stationery the kind you can buy anywhere." Nick tapped the edge of the table with his index finger. "The type is computer printer. Most likely from a computer available to a vast number of people."

Addy watched Nick's finger as he continued tapping lightly on the table. She hated herself for remembering the way that finger had caressed her lips. "I suppose I should thank you, once again, for all your help, Mr. Romero. Too bad you're leaving in a couple of days. Going to El Paso to visit your grandmother, aren't you?"

Addy glanced at Dina, whose perfectly made-up face paled slightly, the lush pink blusher on her cheeks seeming overly bright. Her father's fiancée now knew that she'd overheard part of her early morning conversation with Nick.

"Maria is going to be so upset by your change in plans," Dina said, clasping her hands in front of her, cushioning them against her breasts. She looked pleadingly at

Rusty. "She's eighty-five, you know, and hasn't seen Nick in over a year."

"Why have you changed your plans?" Addy's heart sank. She didn't want this man here, disrupting her life, especially not now when she was going to have to fight her father to maintain her hard-won independence. She wasn't sure she had the strength to fight two domineering men.

"Your father has asked me to stay on, to help out." Nick leaned back in his chair, glancing first at Addy while he talked, then turning to Rusty. "You might as well go ahead and tell her. She's not going to like it."

"Addy—"

"Tell me what? About the extra security Sam Dundee has arranged, and about these private bodyguards?" Addy hated the way her father hesitated, realizing that he dreaded what he had to say. "More security here at the house? At the company?"

"Some, yes, but mostly for you," Rusty said.

"At the M.A.C. day-care center, right? And bodyguards to watch my house and follow me wherever I go?" She did hate the thought of losing her privacy and a good deal of her freedom, but she wasn't stupid. She knew when her father did something out of overprotectiveness and when it really was for her own good. "I don't like it, but I realize that it's necessary until the authorities discover whoever's behind this kidnap scheme."

"You're being very sensible about this," Dina said. "Rusty was so sure you'd rebel."

Addy thought that her future stepmother sounded disappointed that she wasn't fighting her father. "As long as Daddy understands that I'm not going to leave my home or give up my job, then he can hire a dozen bodyguards for all I care."

"He hasn't hired a dozen bodyguards for you," Brett said, his dazzling smile still in place. "Just one."

"I don't understand." Addy turned to her father. "One man can't stay awake twenty-four hours a day."

"He won't need to if he's sleeping at the foot of your bed." Brett glanced across the table, giving Nick a hard look.

"What?" Shoving her chair backward, Addy jumped to her feet.

Rusty slammed his big fist down on the table, the jar bouncing the china, crystal and silverware, creating sharp tinkling sounds. Creamed coffee sloshed out of Brett's cup. The centerpiece vase of roses teetered, but didn't topple over.

"Sam Dundee is sending some men for around-the-clock surveillance, at your house and at work, but I want someone right by your side, twenty-four hours a day, keeping you safe. Somebody with experience as a fighter, a warrior. A man who can kill to protect you if it comes to that."

"You've asked Sam Dundee to send a man to stay with me twenty-four hours a day?" Hot, spitting indignation filled her. She could not accept this decree. "No, absolutely not! I'm willing to agree to almost anything else, but not a live-in caretaker."

"I'm sorry, Addy, but I can't give you a choice in the matter." Rusty stood up and reached out for his daughter, then dropped his arms when she moved away from him.

"What if…if I agree to move back here?" Did her father have any idea what that offer had cost her? She was willing to take a step back into her sheltered past, if only he'd be reasonable.

"Wherever you stay and whatever you do, Nick is going to be with you. Do you understand that from now until the kidnapper is caught, Nick Romero is going to be your shadow?'' Rusty tried again to touch his daughter. Again she retreated.

"Nick Romero?'' Addy exclaimed.

"Sam Dundee agreed that he was the best man for the job,'' Rusty said. "I thought so myself, but had a few doubts because of Nick's....er...well, his bum leg. But Sam assured me that he doesn't have a man as capable as Nick. Sam said Nick Romero was the best.''

"I tried to convince your father that Nick wasn't fully recovered, that his being crippled would prevent him from being able to do the best job of protecting you.'' Dina clutched the white linen napkin in her small hands, twisting it around and around, her sharp pink nails biting into the material.

"His being crippled certainly didn't prevent him from rescuing me last night,'' Addy said, then realized, too late, that she'd just defended the last man on earth she wanted protecting her.

"Romero always has been the physical type,'' Brett said, surveying Nick's big body with a touch of superiority and a great deal of disdain. "Brawn over brains, so to speak.''

"A Navy SEAL and a top DEA agent has to have plenty of smarts,'' Rusty said, eyeing Brett with contempt. "And he's the only man I know, besides myself, that I'd trust to take care of my little girl.''

Addy didn't like the look her father gave Nick. It said they shared some special secret. Why did her father trust Nick so completely, especially with her life?

Dina voiced Addy's thoughts. "You certainly took an instant liking to Nick, didn't you?''

"Sure did,'' Rusty said.

"Of course, I've known Nick almost all my life and I

trust him, but—well…Addy's life will be quite safe with him, but I'm not sure about her virtue.'' Dina's smile radiated a frosty warning.

Addy glared at the older woman. Brett appeared shocked. Nick smiled. Rusty bellowed with laughter.

"Addy can protect her own virtue if she wants to," Rusty said, still chuckling. "I'm well aware of your brother-in-law's reputation with the ladies. I've got one myself. Nothing wrong with a man liking women!"

"Are you saying that you don't mind if Addy has to fight Nick off every night?" Dina ran her gaze over Addy's slender body encased in the simple gray dress, spotted with dirt and ripped on one sleeve. "Even though Addy's hardly his type, sooner or later, she's bound to appeal to him if the two of them are together constantly."

"Addy's not his type, huh?" Rusty reached out, pulling his daughter close to his side. She didn't resist. "Likes 'em shorter and fuller and sexier, huh?"

"I think Addy is lovely," Brett said. "She has a real cameo beauty, and such elegance."

"Thank you, Brett." Addy jabbed her father in the ribs with her elbow.

"If the time comes when Addy starts looking good to Nick, then I think she'll know how to handle him," Rusty said. "Addy not only looks like me, she's smart like me. She'll know exactly what to do with a man like Nick."

There was a conspiracy afoot. Addy was certain. Her father and Nick Romero knew something that no one else in this room knew. Something about her and Nick.

"I'm totally opposed to Nick getting involved in all this." Dina dropped her twisted napkin on the table. "He isn't physically sound. His last operation was only six weeks ago."

"I know how fond you are of Nick," Rusty said. "But

he's quite fit. Sam Dundee told me himself that he'd offered Nick a job with him as soon as he'd finished his visit to El Paso.''

"Well, Addy, what are we going to do with these men?'' Dina asked, but she didn't look at the younger woman.

"You can do whatever you want,'' Addy said. "I'm going home.''

"Not without Nick,'' Rusty said, giving her a tight hug.

Addy pulled out of her father's embrace, turned to Nick and smiled. "We can go in your car. Mine's at home since Daddy sent the limo for me last night.''

Nick stood, retrieving his cane from its resting place against the side of the table. Walking toward Addy, he offered her his arm. She glanced from his smiling face to his big arm, then looked over at Dina, who was watching them intently, a frown marring her perfect features. Addy slipped her arm through Nick's. "I wouldn't dream of making you sleep at the foot of my bed,'' Addy said, loud enough for everyone in the room to hear.

"I could take that as an invitation to share your bed.''

"It is an invitation—for you to sleep in my guest bedroom.''

"That won't do,'' Nick said. "I'll be too far away.''

"It's the room next to mine.''

"I should be in the room with you.''

Addy realized that three pairs of eyes watched them and three sets of ears listened to every word they said. When they reached the door leading into the foyer, she paused, glancing around the room. Her father seemed a little too pleased with himself. Brett was still smiling, but that odd look hadn't left his eyes. Dina was positively seething with jealousy. Addy wondered if her father was too blind to see it.

"We'll work something out," Addy said, then lowered her voice to a whisper as she and Nick stepped out into the foyer. "You are not staying in my room. I—I'm not going to fight Daddy about this. He's scared. Anything could happen with his high blood pressure and bad heart. I may have to endure your presence twenty-four hours a day, but I will not have you invading my bedroom."

"I never enter a lady's bedroom uninvited."

"Good. That settles it, then."

"Does it?" Nick asked, his smile widening at the look of surprise on Addy's face.

Huntsville traffic, especially on a Saturday morning, was maddening, but no better or worse than in any bustling city its size. Nick maneuvered his '68 silver Jag out of slow moving lanes and into more rapid ones, deftly avoiding the areas under construction as much as possible. The drive from the McConnell estate to the Twickenham district took almost twenty minutes. During the entire drive, Addy had been subdued. He'd wondered if she was pouting, but decided she wasn't the type. She was too direct. More likely, she was thinking about what had happened last night, how close she'd come to being a victim, and how drastically her life would change during the following days, maybe even weeks or months. There was no way to tell how quickly the authorities would nab the would-be kidnapper, or even if they would ever discover his or her identity. Money, if that were the true motive for the kidnapping, was a powerful inducement. There was the constant danger that he or she would try again.

"Turn here," Addy said pointing. "It's the second house. White with black shutters."

He parked the car in the small narrow driveway, killed the motor and glanced at Addy's home. Where her father's house was a replica of antebellum splendor, sporting huge white columns and a wraparound veranda, this house was authentic. Nick didn't know much about styles, but he could tell the house was old. Built long before the turn of the century would be his guess. Glistening snowy white in the noonday summertime sunshine, the house boasted a fresh coat of paint as did the glossy black shutters. Someone had spent a fortune restoring this place. That someone was probably Addy McConnell.

Opening the car door, Addy stepped out onto the sidewalk, stretching her long, slender frame that had been cramped in the confines of the small sports car. Nick watched the way she moved, all fluid and graceful. Her arms arched above her head, hiking up her skirt. He got a good view of her legs—small ankles, well-shaped calves, and long, trim thighs. Nick felt a tightening in his gut, and cursed himself for being a fool. Kidding Addy about seducing her was one thing, but actually doing it would be quite another matter. Kidding her was fun; the thought of making love to her actually scared him.

"Are you getting out or are you going to sit there staring at me all day?" she asked.

"I'll get my bag." He grabbed the battered brown leather suitcase he'd used for countless years and followed her up the steps leading to the small front portico supported by double columns on each side. "How long have you lived here?"

"For five years." She unlocked the front door. "Before that I shared an apartment with Janice. Before Ron came along."

"Ron's the boyfriend, right? The sulky-looking guy who picked her up last night?" Nick stepped over the threshold and felt as if he'd been transported back in time. The pale yellow walls added warmth to the wide foyer. A dramatic staircase, built against the left wall, curved upward.

"I didn't know you'd met Ron." Addy soaked in the beauty of her home, glancing around, proud of each familiar piece of furniture, each picture on the wall, every detail over which she'd fretted. "He's all right, I guess. Janice loves him and says they're getting married eventually. He's got a big chip on his shoulder when it comes to people with money. I think he's the type that would like to be rich, but doesn't want to work for it."

"Is Janice rich?" Nick ran the toe of his shoe over the blue and cream wool rug that covered the wide plank floor.

"It's a nineteenth-century Chinese rug." Addy pointed to Nick's feet. "And, no, Janice isn't rich. Her father squandered most of her mother's inheritance. All she has left is half interest in our grandparents' home, Elm Hill."

"Is everything in this room old?" Nick asked.

"Almost every item is antique," Addy said. "From the Federal period piano built around 1815," she pointed to the small musical instrument placed directly beneath the staircase, "to the Chippendale cherry side chairs, to that original Jan Weenix still life on the wall."

"Mmm… Is Elm Hill worth anything?"

"Yes, Elm Hill is definitely worth something. Why do you ask?"

"If Janice isn't rich, why doesn't she sell her half of the estate?"

"Our grandparents' will prohibits Janice from selling her half to anyone but me."

"Has Janice asked you to buy it?" Nick wondered about Janice's boyfriend. Rusty had told him that Ron Glover was a low-life creep who'd spent most of his teen years in and out of juvenile court. He'd been arrested numerous times as an adult, but had never been convicted.

"No. Why?"

"Just curious."

"Curious about Ron Glover, wondering if he's money-hungry enough to plot my kidnapping?" Addy placed her foot on the bottom step of the staircase.

Gripping his walking stick with one hand, Nick tightened his hold on his suitcase with the other. "Is he?"

Addy continued up the stairs, Nick following. "I don't know about Ron. It's possible. He's not a very nice man, but then neither is my ex-husband."

"Gerald Carlton? You think he might be behind the kidnap plot? Why? Rusty said his second wife's father is quite wealthy, that he made Gerald a vice-president in his company."

Addy opened the door to the first bedroom. "Gerald's *wife* is wealthy, not Gerald. Believe me, he's far more money-hungry than Ron Glover and far smarter."

Nick walked into the guest bedroom, a medium-sized square room. The upper walls were pale cream, the bottom wainscoted surface had been painted a light olive green. The bed, with tall, thin posters, stood in the middle of the room, an embroidered chenille spread covering it. To the left of the bed a wooden cupboard filled with knickknacks fitted neatly into the corner and a huge bedside table rested on a large area rug to the right. A stack of books lay atop the old chest nestled at the foot of the bed.

"Reminds me of a bed and breakfast I stayed in once a few years back." He set down his leather suitcase. "You really hate your ex-husband, don't you?"

"I did hate him for a long, long time. Now—now, I'm not sure. I don't wish him dead, but—but I hate seeing him so happy with his wealthy wife and fat, healthy babies."

"So we have two suspects," Nick said, sitting down on

the bed, testing it by bouncing lightly up and down. "New mattress?"

"What do you mean we have two suspects?"

"Well, not counting the fact that the kidnapper may be some stranger, some unknown criminal out to get rich quick, we have an ex-husband who obviously hates you and your father as much as you hate him…and we have your cousin's boyfriend, who'd like to get rich without earning his money the old-fashioned way."

"I see." Addy's face paled. "My room is right next door. I'm going to take a bath and change clothes. Why don't you look around and check the place out for yourself?"

"What sort of locks do you have on the doors? Dead bolt? And what about the windows? Is there a security system?"

"I don't know about the doors and windows, but, yes, there is a security system. It isn't on right now. I often forget to turn it on. I forgot last night. Daddy's always fussing at me."

"What about some lunch?" Nick suggested.

"Are you cooking?" she asked, then walked outside into the hallway.

"How about if we order pizza?"

"No anchovies," Addy said, "and lots and lots of black olives."

Nick inspected the room, wondering if the entire house looked like this. Picking up his suitcase, he lifted it onto the bed, then looked around for a closet. There wasn't one. Instead he found a large, mahogany armoire, empty except for several ladies' straw hats lying across the single top shelf.

Within a few minutes, he heard water running. Addy was taking a bath. His mind quickly spanned the short distance between Addy's bath and her naked body. He wished he wasn't so damned curious about what she looked like without her clothes. Probably skinny, he thought, then remembered the glimpse of her shapely thigh. Hell, he'd been a fool to agree to Rusty's request. He had no business playing bodyguard to Dina's future stepdaughter. He should have insisted Sam Dundee send in one of his best men from Atlanta.

Nick hated admitting that he didn't want another man guarding Addy McConnell night and day for God knew how long. She was a needy woman, ripe for the picking and he couldn't bear to think of her giving herself to some other guy, some guy who would break her heart. He, on the other hand, had the willpower to stay with her and protect her without seducing her, despite what he'd led her to believe.

And…he didn't trust anyone else to keep her safe. That was the bottom line. Addy was in danger, and there was something about her that brought out all the possessive, protective instincts deep inside him. The only way anyone was going to hurt Addy was over his dead body.

Addy and Nick sat in shield-back chairs with cane bottoms. The crusty remains of a large sausage pizza, with extra black olives, covered the grease-stained box lying in the middle of an oak trestle table. Nick took a deep swallow from his beer, sprawling his long legs outward, resting his heels against a braided throw rug.

"You know, Addy, you're taking this awfully well. A lot better than I expected. You've been playing the part of the perfect hostess ever since we got here."

"I don't want you in my house." She picked up a canned cola. "I don't want anyone acting as my live-in bodyguard. But my seventy-year-old father has high blood pressure, a bad heart, and he refuses to stop smoking those awful cigars. Things are going to be difficult enough without my acting childish. I plan to cooperate with you as much as I can.''

''You're being too nice to me.'' Nick glanced around the huge, oak-paneled kitchen. The floors boasted their original wide planks, and a chest-high brick fireplace covered a third of one wall. ''Are we playing some sort of game?''

''You're the one who seems to enjoy playing games.'' Addy sipped her cola, then frowned at him. ''My father wants you here. So be it. Despite the fact that I will not allow anyone, not even Daddy, to keep me locked up for my own safety, I know I'm in danger and I want protection, for my sake and for Daddy's. If anything happened to me—''

''Rusty told me about your brother.''

''They—they shot him in the head. Daddy gave them a million dollars, and they killed Donnie anyway. He was only nine. I was six.''

''And after that, Rusty kept you in a gilded cage?''

She nodded. He noticed the shimmering moisture glazing her eyes. She looked down at her lap, avoiding his scrutiny.

''You're right,'' Nick said, staring directly at her. ''I do like to play games, especially with women. And I can't promise that I won't play games with you, from time to time. You jump to the bait so quickly. I can get you riled up in no time and I admit I enjoy kidding you.''

''You annoy me by making sexual suggestions.'' Addy jumped up, pouring what was left of her cola down the sink drain. ''If you keep doing that, we're going to be fighting all the time. Is that what you want?''

''A little harmless flirtation is good for you, didn't you

know that?'' Nick picked up the pizza carton. Looking around for a garbage can, he saw none. ''Where's the trash?''

''In the pantry.'' She pointed him in the right direction. ''Save your flirtation for Dina and other women who enjoy it.''

''You might enjoy it, if you'd give me half a chance. Most women think I'm irresistible.'' Nick tried not to laugh when he saw the anger in her eyes. Somewhere along the way, Addy McConnell had forgotten how to have a good time, how to joke and laugh and be carefree. Maybe, during their stay together, he could teach her a thing or two about enjoying life. When the image of her lying upstairs in his bed, her curly red hair spread out and covering her naked breasts, flashed through Nick's mind, he groaned.

''I'm not into one-night stands or brief, meaningless affairs.'' Addy clutched the edge of the sink.

''I said I liked flirting with women. I didn't say I bedded every woman I found attractive.'' In recent years, Nick's tastes had become very discriminating and he'd sought more than sex from his relationships. Maybe he was getting old, but the idea of finding *the right woman* appealed to him more and more. Of course, she'd be curvaceous and blond. She'd have a sense of humor, enough to laugh at his jokes, anyway. Naturally, she'd be dynamite in bed and no more interested in marriage than he was.

''Since Dina pointed out that I'm not your type, why waste your time with me? Is it that important for all women to fall swooning at your feet?''

Nick laughed, picturing Addy swooning at his feet. He liked the idea, and wondered if there was any possibility that she—

The insistent ring of the telephone interrupted Nick mid-thought. Addy reached for the wall phone.

"Hello? Yes, he's here." She handed the red telephone to Nick.

"Nick Romero. When?... Where?... Yes, the wound would be in his right hand. A stiletto blade... Powerfully built. Young, maybe early twenties. Long brown hair... Okay. We'll be there shortly."

Addy gazed at Nick, wide-eyed. "What was that all about?"

"The police think they've found your would-be kidnapper."

"What? Has he told them who hired him?" On trembly legs, Addy walked over to Nick, grabbing him by the arm.

"He couldn't tell them anything. He's dead. Been dead since early this morning." Nick put his arm around Addy to steady her. She swayed into him slightly, then righted herself immediately, pulling out of his comforting embrace.

"What do they want us to do?" she asked. "Identify him?"

"Yes." He hated seeing that pale, haunted look on her face. "I can't leave you alone here, so I'll have to take you with me. But I can identify the body. There's no need for you to see him."

"Whoever hired him, killed him."

"It looks that way."

"He—or she—will try again."

"Probably." Nick wanted to pull her back in his arms and comfort her. He wanted to promise her that he'd take care of her, not let anyone hurt her. But Addy was afraid of him, scared of him as a man. And as much as he hated to admit it, maybe she had a right to be. He couldn't ever remember feeling so possessive and protective. Hell, maybe his taste in women was changing. Could it be that after all these years of chasing some bosomy blond dream, the woman destined to change his life was a skinny red-head?

Chapter 4

The room was cool. Nick was hot. He'd sprawled his big body out on the soft cream sheet, kicking the covers to the foot of the bed. Normally he slept in the raw, but considering the possibility that he might have to rush to Addy McConnell's defense at a moment's notice he'd left on his briefs.

He wasn't sure of the time, but figured it was close to midnight. After a quick supper of cold ham sandwiches and potato salad, he and Addy had sat in her small den adjacent to the kitchen and listened to one of her favorite tapes, the musical score from *Phantom of the Opera*. Having been raised in Texas, Nick preferred the elemental sounds of country, but over the years he'd learned to appreciate various types of music. He found that Addy's tastes were more select. She preferred classical and semi-classical above all else. She was a patron of the arts, having season tickets to the symphony.

More than one luscious blonde from Nick's past had

exposed him to the social world of the ultrarich. He fit in just as well with multimillionaires as he had with his Navy SEAL comrades and his fellow DEA agents. If Nick Romero was anything, he was adaptable. He had discovered early in life that the people who succeeded were those who found a way to use the system to their advantage. Even a half-breed Mexican kid with an illiterate dirt farmer for a father and a whore for a mother could rise above his humble beginnings if he had the guts and determination to change, to learn and grow, to assimilate every new experience, In other words, to adapt.

Listening to Addy move around in her room, Nick figured she was as restless as he, and was probably having a difficult time getting to sleep. Going to the police station had been far more upsetting for Addy than she'd been willing to admit. Nick was accustomed to crime, was used to being exposed to the seamier side of life where murder was a common occurrence. But Addy was not. When he'd tried to discuss the attempted kidnapping with her, she'd shied away from the subject and had downright refused to talk about the untimely death of her assailant, who had died from a fall off a steep embankment on Monsano Mountain.

Addy was scared, but was trying hard not to show it. Nick wanted to assure her that it was all right to be afraid, that it was not only normal but smart. Bravery and fear were constant companions, as inseparable as life and death. Fear could save your life, whereas fearlessness often proved fatal.

He heard the door to Addy's bedroom open, then the click-click tapping of her shoes. Suddenly, all sound ceased. He sat up in his bed, listening. The stairs creaked. Someone was walking up or down.

Easing open his own bedroom door, Nick surveyed the

darkened hallway. Moonlight spread out over the wooden floor like creamy yellow-white butter across dark toast. Still hearing the sporadic creaking, Nick eased carefully down the hall until he reached the landing. Addy, her satin high-heel slippers dangling from her fingers, tiptoed down the stairs. Nick sucked in his breath at the sight of her retreating back. Her tall slender body, visible in the soft moonlight, was draped in a pale lavender confection of gossamer silk and lace.

What the hell was she doing? She looked like a woman running away, trying to escape from someone or something. He'd like to go back to bed, go to sleep and forget that Addy, upset, uncertain and scared, was wandering around downstairs. But he couldn't. She was his responsibility.

He returned to his room, slipped into a pair of jeans and made his way quietly down the stairs, the faint tapping of his cane echoing in the stillness. From the foyer, he could see light under the kitchen door. He hated to intrude on her, to interrupt her privacy, but dammit, he wouldn't be doing his job if he didn't check on her.

Easing open the door, he stopped dead still when he saw her standing in profile, slowly pouring herself a glass of chilled white wine. Her red hair, deep and rich and gloriously bright like the rusty, red clay earth of Alabama, hung in curly disarray down her back and across her shoulders. The silky peignoir set she wore swept the floor. The robe, a sheer concoction edged with heavy lace at the hem and across the bottom of each long sleeve, had fallen open to reveal an empire style gown of the same diaphanous lavender material. The bodice, cut low and revealing the slight swell of Addy's breasts, was covered with matching lace.

Dear God, had he ever actually thought this woman, this

smoldering female temptation, was plain? If Addy Mc-
Connell chose to dress circumspectly in public, she re-
vealed her true sensuous self in her sleepwear. Nick's
whole body tightened with anticipation. He didn't think
he'd ever seen anything as desirable as the vision before
him, one he found difficult to believe was real.

"Addy?" Even to his own ears his voice sounded rough
and hard.

She jumped, startled by his invasion. With her green
eyes glaring and her pink mouth opening to a perfect oval,
she stared at him. He noticed that her hand, holding the
wineglass, trembled ever so slightly.

"Sorry if I frightened you." He walked through the
doorway and into the kitchen. "I heard you come downstairs and wanted to make sure you were all right."

"I'm fine." She set the glass on the counter. "I'm sorry
if I disturbed your sleep."

"I wasn't asleep." He eyed the wine bottle. "I'm your
bodyguard, remember? I don't sleep unless you do." He
nodded toward the sauvignon blanc. "Pour me a glass, too,
if you think it'll help us both get a good night's rest."

She looked at him with pleading eyes. "Couldn't you
leave me alone? I'm not used to having someone else
around, watching me, monitoring my every move."

"It can't be helped, so we'd both better try to make the
best of it." Moving slowly, Nick stopped just short of
touching her. His gaze traveled over her, from fiery hair
to bare feet. "What did you do with your shoes?"

"I tossed them in the chair." She nodded toward her
slippers. "There." Addy wished he would stop looking at
her. He made her nervous staring at her as if he could see
straight through her gown. But then, maybe he could. She
wasn't accustomed to men seeing her in her underwear or
her sleepwear, so she indulged herself in her passion for

sexy, frilly and very feminine attire that she alone would see. But Nick could see her. All of her, here in the kitchen light.

She could feel a delicious warmth spreading through her, casting a delicate pink hue to her naturally golden complexion. This man had a strange effect on her, creating a desire in her to experiment with the danger she knew he offered. Nick Romero would be an exciting, demanding lover. Something she'd never known. But she was a failure at intimacy, unable to respond properly, incapable of achieving fulfillment. She didn't dare risk the utter humiliation she'd feel if she disappointed Nick. She'd been devastated by Gerald's frustration over her inadequacies, and Gerald was certainly no match for a man like Nick, a man whose every look, word and move reeked of sensuality.

Nick caressed the neck of the wine bottle absentmindedly, wishing it was Addy's soft throat. Retrieving a glass from the row of crystal goblets inside the open cupboard, he poured the clear golden liquid.

Addy watched the way his big hand moved over the wine bottle and the crystal glass. She could almost feel his touch on her. Instantly her nipples hardened.

Taking a sip of the chilled dry wine, Nick looked up at Addy, his dark eyes conveying a message of desire. She tried to look away from him, but his gaze held her spellbound. When he glanced down at her breasts, she sucked in a deep breath, willing herself not to sway toward him.

"Why don't we take our wine into the den," he said. "We'll be more comfortable in there, and we can talk."

For a split second she thought he was going to touch her. She was half afraid he would and half afraid he wouldn't. "I...I don't want to talk. I just want to be left alone."

"But I can't leave you alone. You know that. It's my

job to guard you against danger twenty-four hours a day."
He could see that she was on the verge of angry tears. He
suspected that she was as upset over her reaction to him
as she was over the turmoil in her life. She was a woman
who seemed to pride herself on her independence and self-
control, and here he was undermining both. As long as the
threat of a kidnapping hung over her head, Addy would
require his presence as a bodyguard. And, as long as the
two of them were together, sparks were going to fly and
both of them were at the mercy of their own baser instincts. He didn't doubt for a minute that Addy wanted
him as much as he wanted her. He could see it in her eyes,
feel it in her body's response to him.

"Nick, please...don't—"

"Don't what, Red? I haven't done anything."

Did he honestly think he had done nothing? Addy wondered. Surely a man as experienced as Nick Romero knew
only too well what effect he was having on her. Circumstances might have forced her to accept his presence in her
home. Her life could be in danger, and she knew her father's health and peace of mind were at risk. If only the
man her father had chosen as her bodyguard was anyone
else on earth beside this devastatingly handsome man with
the power to awaken her long dormant sexual longings.

"Come on, Red, let's have a midnight powwow. We'll
swap old war stories." He placed his hand on the small
of her back, opening his palm to cover a wide expanse of
her silk-clad body. She tensed immediately. "Relax." He
gave her a slight nudge. "This has been a hell of a day
for you. You don't really want to be alone. You want to
talk and yell and scream and maybe even cry."

"You think you're so damned smart, don't you?" Addy
walked away from him, removing herself from his warm,

caressing hand. "For your information, Mr. Romero, I seldom cry. I used up a lifetime supply of tears years ago."

He followed her into the den, not replying to her comment. Somewhere behind the security wall she'd built around herself, Addy's deepest emotions still existed, waiting to be released. Nick wanted to be the man to penetrate that wall, to tear it down—brick by brick if necessary. He wanted to be the man to bring those buried feelings back to life.

Entering the dark den, Addy turned on a small brass table lamp decorated with china roses and covered with a parchment shade. A warm, mellow glow filled the room, revealing pale eggshell walls and an orderly clutter of antiques, from a painted Pennsylvania German chest to a Queen Anne curly maple chair.

Addy sat down on the old sofa which was covered with a paisley throw and held a variety of crewel, cross-stitch and needlepoint pillows. She clutched the crystal goblet in her unsteady hand, her eyes focusing on the liquid shifting back and forth. Bringing the glass to her lips, she sipped the wine slowly, trying to ignore Nick Romero when he entered her cosy, private hideaway. She'd been forced to share several hours with him before bedtime, all the while wishing she were alone. She'd been able to handle both Nick and her own emotions earlier, but now she felt vulnerable, less able to protect herself.

Nick walked across the wooden floor, barely noticing the throw rugs he stepped on as he made his way toward Addy. She sat on the small sofa. There was room for him, but he could tell by her stiffly arched back, her tilted chin and her cool manner that she would prefer he didn't join her. He sat down in a sturdy flowered wingback chair to the left of the sofa, a large round end table separating them.

He watched her. He'd seen people who tried to keep

everything bottled up inside. Sooner or later they exploded like a time bomb. Addy needed to release some of her pent-up emotions.

"Do you think Gerald Carlton could be behind the kidnapping attempt?" Nick asked, pleased when Addy glared at him with fiery green eyes. "Is he capable of murder?"

Taking another sip of her wine, Addy closed her eyes, knowing that images of her life with her former husband would flash through her mind. How many times, she wondered, had Gerald made her feel worthless as a woman? How many nights had she waited for him to come home from some other woman's bed? How many times had he accused her of being unattractive and frigid? But was he capable of murder?

"Gerald is capable of almost anything if there's enough money in it for him." She set her wineglass down on the end table and turned to Nick. "Could he kill for money? I don't know. Possibly. Probably."

"He really did a number on you, didn't he, Red?"

"I would prefer not to talk about my marriage."

"You prefer letting all that pain fester inside you like an infected wound? That's a mistake."

"What would you have me do? Pour out my heart and soul to you so that you can comfort me? Is your male ego so enormous that you think you have to prove to me how wrong my ex-husband was about me? Is that what this is all about? You want to prove that you're man enough to make the ugly, frigid, little rich girl enjoy sex for the first time in her life?"

Nick hadn't expected such a vehement reaction. Obviously, he'd struck a nerve, a sexual nerve. He took a generous sip from his own wineglass, then set it beside Addy's on the table. "Did you love Carlton when you married him?" Nick wasn't sure why he wanted her answer to be negative. What difference did it make if Addy had loved her ex-husband? It was apparent she despised the man now.

"What?" Dammit! How could she have allowed herself to lose control the way she had? She hadn't meant to blurt out such personal information, but Nick had angered her. Somehow this man she'd known for a little over twenty-four hours had a way of provoking her strongest emotions. Her first impression of him had been right. He was a dangerous man.

"Did you love Carlton?"

"I think so. It was no grand passion or anything like that. I was twenty-five and I'd lived a fairly sheltered life. Men weren't exactly beating a path to my door. Gerald was charming and attentive and—and Daddy liked him."

"But you weren't in love with him?"

"I have no idea what being in love means." Addy jumped up, her hands knotted into fists as they rested against her hips. "I don't want to talk to you about Gerald or about love or sex. Daddy's paying you to be my bodyguard, not my psychiatrist, so just leave me alone."

Nick stood up, reached down, picked up her wineglass and handed it to her. "I'd say you've been left alone for too long."

Hesitating briefly, she took the glass, making sure their hands didn't touch. "I like being alone. It's preferable to spending time with insufferably macho men who think a Plain Jane like me should be grateful they've shown an interest."

Nick laughed aloud at her words. Plain Jane indeed. Was it possible, really possible, that Addy had no idea how incredibly lovely she looked right this minute? Had her ex-husband totally destroyed her confidence in her sexual attractiveness? Damn, what Nick would give for five minutes alone with Gerald Carlton!

Stepping away from Nick, Addy downed the remainder of her wine, then set the glass on a nearby chest. Nick set his glass beside hers, then with a swift move that alarmed Addy, he stepped behind her, grasping one shoulder.

"What are you doing?" Her voice was breathless. His big hand clutched her silk-covered shoulder as he gave her a gentle nudge forward. "Nick, stop it!"

"I want to show you something," he said, giving her another shove. "Move, woman."

She balked, refusing to budge another inch. "Stop shoving me around and stop giving me orders. What's gotten into you?"

"I want you to walk out into the foyer."

"Why?"

"I told you. I want to show you something."

"This is my house. What could you possibly show me that I haven't seen a hundred times?" she asked, trying to pull away from him. He held her shoulder firmly.

"You have two choices," Nick said. "Either you march your little fanny out into the foyer or I'll carry you."

"You wouldn't dare." She eyed his cane.

"Try me."

She didn't bother to turn around and face Nick. She didn't have to see the look on his face to know he was serious. She could hear the determination in his voice. She knew that if he had to carry her, he would, even if walking unaided by his cane might be painful for him.

"Oh, all right." The day had been almost more than she could bear. Accepting Nick as a live-in bodyguard despite her desire to remain free. Finding out that the man who'd attempted to kidnap her last night had met a deadly fate at the hands of some unknown person or persons still intent on harming her. Realizing that, for the first time in her life, she was sexually attracted to a man. Strongly, irrationally attracted to a man she had begun to think of as her personal champion.

She simply wasn't up to any more emotional upheaval. She didn't have the strength to fight Nick. Not right now.

With his hand firmly planted on her shoulder, Nick guided her out into the foyer. Momentarily releasing her, he flipped the switch that turned on the chandelier. Light, glittering off the cut crystal, flooded the entrance hall.

Nick led her to the enormous gilt-framed mirror that hung on a side wall. He set his cane aside. Confusion filled Addy's mind and heart when Nick, standing behind her, his big, dark hands draping her shoulders like bronze claws, positioned her directly in front of the rectangular looking glass.

She tried to avert her eyes, as if afraid of what her reflection would reveal. When she gazed down at her feet, Nick released one shoulder, taking her chin in his hand and tilting her face upward. She closed her eyes. Whatever he was trying to do, she wanted no part of it. She wasn't going to let him make her see something she didn't want to see.

With his lips close to her ear, he whispered, "Open your eyes, Addy, and tell me what you see."

He ran his hand down her neck, caressing her throat. Then he reached out and encircled her waist with his arm, pulling her back against him. She felt his hard arousal against her buttocks. Inadvertently she cried out.

"Open your eyes."

"No." The word escaped from her throat on a tormented breath.

"If you're afraid to take a good look at yourself and tell

me what you see, then just listen and I'll tell you what I see.''

"Please, Nick—don't.''

He splayed his hand across her stomach. She jerked, an instinctive reaction that could have been fear or passion. Nick knew enough about women to understand that Addy was afraid. More of herself than of him.

"I see a woman, Addy. A woman. Not a girl and not even a lady, though I know that you are a lady in every sense of the word.''

She squirmed against him, trying to pull away, wishing she could escape before he said any more. "I hate you.''

"No, you don't.'' His voice was deep and dark and incredibly sensuous. "You hate yourself, don't you, Addy? I'm making you feel like a woman and that frightens you.''

"Why are you doing this to me?'' She struggled against him. He held her tightly.

"God, Red, stop that! You've already got me so hot I'm about to lose it.''

She stopped moving and stood perfectly still. His words seeped into her consciousness. Her body stiffened with denial, not wanting to admit that she was every bit as aroused as he was.

He ran his fingers through her hair, lifting it and watching the titian strands fall back to her shoulders as he released them. "You have beautiful hair. It's like fiery silk. Thick, wavy flames.''

When he pulled her closer and closer against him, she didn't resist. He was weaving a spell with his words, words that she warned herself didn't mean a thing. Nick was a practiced lover, a Latin Romeo with the ability to charm any woman. She couldn't let him charm her. She didn't dare.

"Your skin,'' he said, caressing her neck, pushing aside

her silk robe to fondle her shoulder. "Your skin is soft and smooth. All of your little freckles intrigue me. I'd like to kiss every one of them, and someday—someday soon—I will."

Addy drew in deep breaths trying to calm her raging senses. *Don't listen to him,* she told herself. *He doesn't mean what he's saying.*

He moved his hand downward, over her breasts, barely grazing her tight nipples. She closed her mouth, biting off a cry of excitement. Both of his hands spanned her waist. "Your body is sleek and slender and infinitely fascinating. When I first saw you, I thought you were flat-chested. I was wrong." He covered her small breasts with his hands, lifting their delicate weight, brushing her nipples with his thumbs. "They're high and firm and fill my hands. And I love the way your nipples hardened at my touch. You're a very responsive woman, Addy. Did you know that?"

She was beyond speaking, so she nodded. He buried his face against her neck, his mouth opening, his tongue lavishing seductive moisture on her heated flesh.

She leaned backward against him, unable to stop herself from succumbing to the enchantment of his words and the lure of his big hard body. Releasing her breasts, he slid his hands farther down her slender frame, stopping to grasp her hips, then gently kneading her buttocks. "Full and firm and tight." His hands skimmed the sides of her thighs. "Legs like a thoroughbred. Long and trim. Do you have any idea how much I want those long legs of yours wrapped around me?"

She groaned when he eased both hands across the front of her legs, delving between them, easing the silky fabric of her gown up against the hot moistness she could not hide.

"Open your eyes, Addy, and take a look at a beautiful, sensuous woman…a woman I want desperately."

She opened her eyes, took one look at herself in the mirror and squeezed her eyes shut. "No, no…no."

"You dress yourself in plain, unattractive clothes trying to disguise the beautiful woman you are, but you sleep in frothy negligees. I'll bet all your lingerie is utterly sexy and feminine, isn't it?"

She didn't respond. His hands still rested between her thighs. He lifted up, pressing his fingers against her. Thrashing her head from side to side, she moaned.

"I want to make love to you. To you, Addy. I don't give a damn about Rusty's millions and I don't care what your ex-husband says. With me…with us…sex would be different. Open your eyes, Red. Take a look at us and tell me that you know what I'm saying is true."

Addy opened her eyes slowly, forcing herself to look in the mirror. God, was that her? The woman she saw staring back at her *was* beautiful. She was filled with a beauty born of passion, her face flushed with desire, her body taut with longing. And Nick stood behind her, his big body hard against her, his maleness pounding demandingly. He moved his hands over her as she watched.

"What do you see, Addy? Tell me."

"It's not me," she said, her voice hoarse with mounting desire. "You've turned me into someone I don't know."

"It is you, Addy. The real you. The real woman who wants and needs. You're on fire. You're on fire for me."

"Nick?"

He turned her around, taking her in his arms. The image of the wanton woman in the mirror burned brightly in Addy's mind. Nick Romero was a sorcerer, a wizard, a magician. He possessed the power to drive her wild with desire, to make her look and act like a beautiful, desirable woman.

He was her defender…her champion…her paladin. And she longed to be his woman.

He nibbled at her lips, teasing them apart. She sighed, opening for his possession. He took her with a force that shook them both. He deepened the kiss. She clung to him, running her hands over his bare shoulders and back, pressing herself against him, hot and ready and desperate.

It was the most difficult thing he'd ever done, and he knew he would probably hate himself in the morning. But he couldn't take advantage of Addy. He realized that all he had to do was lead her to the nearest bed, and she'd let him make love to her all night. But tomorrow, she'd hate him and hate herself. He didn't want Addy McConnell's hate.

Releasing her mouth, he ran his hands up and down her arms. "We've got to stop, Red, or we won't be able to."

"Nick, I…please—"

He caressed her cheek with the tip of his finger. "I wanted you to see what a beautiful woman you are. Don't ever doubt that you're desirable. I want you, but I can't take you now when you're so vulnerable." The sad, puzzled look in her eyes told him that she was hurting, and it was his fault. Dammit all, the last thing on earth he wanted to do was cause this woman any more pain than she'd already suffered. "Do you understand what I'm saying and why?"

She stepped away from him, deliberately avoiding any eye contact with the mirror. "You're good, Nick Romero, damned good. A Latin lover and a Southern gentleman all rolled into one. A deadly combination. No wonder women can't resist you."

"Addy—"

She held up a hand to warn him off, then backed away slowly. "From now on, don't try to teach me anything else about myself, okay? Just do your job as my bodyguard and keep me safe. I—I'm not ready for a man as lethal as you…and I'm not sure I ever will be."

He watched her walk up the stairs. Her shoulders were erect, her head held high. He had no idea what was going on inside her, but he knew one thing for sure. Addy McConnell would never forget how beautiful and desirable she'd looked tonight. Unfortunately, neither would he.

Chapter 5

Nick wondered if Addy felt as if she were inside an armed camp. M.A.C. already had its own security force, but Rusty McConnell had ordered some highly trained professionals from Sam Dundee. The four men and two women who'd flown in from Atlanta the day before were on the job that morning when Nick and Addy arrived at the M.A.C. day-care center. Giving credit to Sam Dundee's superb training, Nick admitted that the six extra workers were as unobtrusive as possible, seeming to fit in as if they were long-time employees. But Addy McConnell could do little more than breathe without constant surveillance. Nick felt a little redundant and had told Rusty so when the two had shared an eight o'clock cup of coffee in the executives' office building. Rusty's long-time secretary Ginger Kimbrew had served them. The luscious brunette hadn't tried to hide her interest in Nick, and any other time he might have accepted her unspoken invitation, but, right now, the only woman who interested Nick was in an adjacent building trying her best to avoid any direct contact with him. Besides, Nick figured that Rusty and Ginger shared more than a business relationship, one that she wasn't quite ready to dissolve despite Rusty's engagement.

After fending off Ginger's blatant advances, Nick convinced Rusty that the hours Addy spent at M.A.C. would be the best time for him to play detective, using D.B. McConnell's money and power and his own government contacts.

Nick had decided that he'd make spot-checks on Addy during the day. His brain told him that it was part of his job. His male libido told him that he wanted to be near the desirable woman he'd held in his arms Saturday night. His heart refused to take part in the discussion.

A florist delivery boy accidentally bumped into Nick when they both reached out at the same time to open the door leading to the M.A.C. day-care center.

"Sorry, sir," the youth said.

Nick held the door open for him. "No problem. Go ahead. It looks like you've got your hands full." The overpowering sweet aroma of roses filled Nick's nostrils as he gazed down at the huge floral arrangement the boy held.

"Yeah, some guy must have it bad, huh? Two dozen red roses on a Monday morning."

The room they entered was a beehive of activity. Children of various ages, sizes, sexes and races were engaged in supervised play and work, while one select group of what Nick judged to be three-year-olds were lining up for mid-morning break. Janice Dixon handed out individual apple juice cartons while her helper gave each child a napkin and straw.

Nick saw Addy. Even though she only vaguely resembled the sexy woman from Saturday night, his body recognized the sensual beauty that lay behind the mask of baggy navy cotton slacks and oversized green T-shirt. He'd bet his silver Jag that underneath those nondescript casual clothes, Addy wore some skimpy pieces of lace and silk. Nick imagined her wearing emerald green bikini panties and matching bra, both the color of her incredible eyes.

Suddenly Nick noticed that Addy was deep in conversation with a slender dark-haired man in a three-piece business suit. Nick didn't like the way the man looked at Addy, as if he had some type of claim on her. And he hated the way Addy smiled and then laughed at something the guy said. She'd never smiled at him that way, and he realized that he wanted to hear her laugh—with him, and not another man.

While Nick stood back watching and brooding, the delivery boy approached Addy. "I'm looking for Addy McConnell."

"I'm Addy McConnell."

The boy handed Addy the huge green vase of red roses. "These are for you, ma'am."

Addy accepted the floral gift. Nick noted the surprised look on her face. Obviously it wasn't her birthday or any other special occasion. She turned toward her office, motioning for her companion to follow. Nick took several tentative steps forward, stopping just outside her open office door.

She set the flowers on her desk, then removed the attached card. Her smile widened. Her green eyes brightened. Nick wanted to know who'd sent the flowers that gave Addy such pleasure.

He marched into her office. "Morning." He looked directly at Addy, then shifted his gaze first to the flowers and then to the man standing beside her. "Just checking in. If you have a few minutes, we need to talk."

"All right. Come on in, Nick, and have a seat." Addy

sensed Nick's displeasure, but couldn't quite figure out what was bothering him. Did he feel as awkward about Saturday night as she did? Neither of them had spoken about the incident in front of the mirror. All day yesterday they had walked on eggshells around each other. ''I'd like you to meet Jim Hester, a friend of mine who just happens to be one of M.A.C.'s top engineers. Jim, this is Nick Romero, the man Daddy's hired as my personal body-guard.''

What was it with her? Nick wondered. Did she have a thing for engineers, or just engineers who worked for her father? And who was this guy, really, in whom Addy had confided about the attempted kidnapping? ''Hester.'' Nodding to the other man, Nick held out his hand.

Jim Hester shook hands with a firm, forceful grip that surprised Nick. The guy looked like a typical desk jockey with his pale complexion, thinning brown hair and slender build. ''I'm certainly glad to know that Addy's in such good hands, Mr. Romero. She's a special lady and we wouldn't want anything to happen to her. Tiffany and I are both very fond of her.''

''Tiffany?'' Nick asked

''My daughter. She's one of the three-year-olds taking a juice break right now. So, if you two will excuse me, I'll go join her while y'all talk business.'' Jim headed for the door, then stopped and turned around. ''You never did say who sent the roses.''

Nick didn't realize that he was holding his breath until Addy read the name on the card. ''Brett Windsor.''

''What the hell is Windsor doing sending you flowers?'' Nick's outburst seemed to have startled Jim and angered Addy, both of them turning to stare at him.

''Brett Windsor? I thought you'd convinced him months ago that you weren't interested,'' Jim said, smiling.

"I did, but Brett occasionally still sends me flowers." Addy glared at Nick. "Gentlemen do that sort of thing, you know. They treat you with respect and consideration. Things that Latin lovers obviously bypass on their way to seducing women into their beds."

Jim Hester cleared his throat. Addy's face flushed. Nick badly wanted to hit something.

"I'll stop back in and say goodbye before I return to work. If you two will excuse me, I'll see if Janice has an extra apple juice." Jim made his way out the door as quickly as possible.

Nick slammed closed the door to Addy's office. "So little Plain-Jane McConnell has two men in her life, huh?"

"It's not what you think." She didn't know why she was trying to explain to Nick about her relationships with Jim and Brett. Neither man loved her or desired her physically. One was only a friend and the other—

"Brett Windsor is good-looking and charming." Nick flung his arm out in a gesture of disgust as he pointed toward the roses. "He knows all the right things to say and do to impress a lady, but you know as well as I do that he's far more interested in Rusty's millions than he is in you."

"You don't think that I'm attractive enough to interest a man like Brett?" She threw out the challenge, daring Nick to reply. Smiling she leaned over and smelled the roses.

"Whether or not Windsor finds you attractive has nothing to do with this. The man is a user. He's been living off Dina for years." Propping his cane against the desk, Nick reached out, grabbing Addy by the shoulders. "Don't you realize that Brett Windsor is just as capable of a kidnapping scheme as your ex-husband? Encouraging him, for whatever reason, is a mistake."

"I have done nothing but discourage Brett. I'm not a total fool. Besides, I think you're overreacting because you're jealous of Brett's relationship with Dina."

"Dammit, Red, you say such stupid things! Dina is nothing more to me than a friend. I found out at an early age that she's poison to any man who cares about her." Nick pulled Addy close, so close that her breasts crushed into his chest. "Windsor is on my list of suspects. Stay away from him."

Addy twisted and turned in Nick's arm, trying to free herself. She hated the way he made her feel—all hot and damp and eager. "You're only my bodyguard. That doesn't give you the right to interfere in my personal life. The next thing I know you'll be telling me that Jim is on your list of suspects so I shouldn't see him anymore."

"Jim Hester isn't a suspect. Not yet." Nick lowered his head until his eyes met Addy's and his lips hovered over hers. "What's this Jim got that interests you so? He looks like a pretty ordinary guy. Is he divorced or widowed?"

Addy swallowed. She was hot. Nick was too close. She couldn't think. "Widowed. Why?"

"I just wondered…because of his daughter. She doesn't have a mother, then, does she?"

"No." Addy slipped her hands between her body and Nick's, giving him a shove. He held fast.

"I take it that you're very fond of Tiffany Hester."

"Stop questioning me like this. I don't like it." She struggled against him. "And I don't like your manhandling me whenever the notion strikes you. I may be your responsibility, but I'm not your personal property."

"That's a matter of opinion." Nick had never felt so possessive, so proprietary about a woman. He hated the thought that Addy might actually be interested in Brett Windsor or Jim Hester. Neither man was right for her. If either of them had been able to stir Addy's passions, she wouldn't turn into a smoldering flame every time he touched her. He, Nick Romero, was the right man to teach Addy what a sensuous woman she really was. No other man could do it. No other man would be allowed to even try. Hell, he was the only man who was ever going to touch her.

"When you interrupted Jim and me you said that you needed to talk to me, so say whatever you came here to say and leave. This place is crawling with security. I don't need you here and I certainly don't want you."

Nick glared at her, his black eyes boring into her. "How upset is Ginger Kimbrew that Rusty is marrying Dina?" Releasing Addy, Nick picked up his cane and stepped away, turning his back toward the wide expanse of windows that covered the back wall of Addy's femininely decorated office.

Addy sat down behind her white desk. "Ginger was Daddy's mistress for a number of years. She probably had high hopes of becoming the second Mrs. D.B. McConnell."

"How do the two of you get along?" Nick glanced around the room, taking note, for the first time, of the dainty lavender-flowered wallpaper, the matching gingham checked curtains at the windows and cushions on all the chairs. Ferns and green plants in various sizes filled every available space where sunlight could touch them.

"Ginger and I have never been close, but we've always been friendly. Why do you ask?"

Nick saw the realization dawn in Addy's eyes. "A woman scorned is capable of almost anything, right? What I'm wondering is if Ginger wants revenge against Rusty enough to plot the kidnapping of his only child."

"Oh, Lord, I'd never considered Ginger."

"Consider her. It won't pay to overlook any possible suspect and every conceivable motive."

"You don't think the motive is money?"

"I don't know. Hate and revenge are often as powerful as greed." Nick turned to her, wishing that he could give her the answers to all the questions he saw in her eyes. "Just don't trust anyone. Except your father and me."

"I hate living like this. I despise having to suddenly distrust people I know and like. But most of all I hate having you in charge of my life." Swinging around in her swivel rocker, Addy stared up at Nick. "Get out of here and leave me alone. Okay?"

He hated the pleading sound in her voice, knowing how difficult it had been for her to gain her independence and what a struggle it was for her to keep Rusty from controlling her life. "I'll check back in around lunchtime. Maybe we could go out for a bite."

"I'm sorry, but I'm having lunch with the children today."

"Then I'll join you and the romper room crowd. It's been years since I've eaten peanut butter and jelly sandwiches."

Addy's eyes widened. She hadn't expected him to invite himself to join her. "Fine. Be here at noon."

"You've got a date." Nick smiled all the way out of the office, not once turning around to see the expression on Addy's face.

Damned obstinate man. Overbearing. Bossy. Of all the men in the world, why was Nick Romero the one who'd come to her defense and rescued her from a kidnapping attempt? And why did her father like and trust him so much that he'd handed her over into Nick's safekeeping? And why, dear Lord, was he the first man since her divorce who made her think about risking her pride, her heart and her body?

Five minutes later, Addy looked up from her desk to find Jim Hester standing in the open doorway. She'd been so lost in her thoughts that she didn't know how long he'd been watching her.

"Come on in, Jim."

Closing the door behind him, Jim took a seat across from her desk. "Mr. Romero is a very interesting man."

"I imagine most people find him interesting." Addy wasn't quite sure where this conversation was going.

"Women in particular, I guess," Jim said.

"I understand he has a reputation. Why are you so interested in Nick?"

"Because you're so interested."

"I am not…I—Is it that obvious?" Addy couldn't deny her feelings, not to Jim. He was too good a friend, too dear and kind a man.

"I had hoped that someday you and I—Well, Tiffany and I are both terribly fond of you and—"

"There's nothing going on between Nick and me. Daddy's hired him as my bodyguard until this kidnapping threat is over. I'm not Nick's type. He isn't interested in a permanent relationship and I can't handle a temporary affair."

"Then you'd better watch out, Addy. That man wants you. And I'd say he's used to getting what he wants. I'd hate to see you get hurt." Jim stood, then walked over to Addy's side, placing his arm around her shoulders. "I admit that I'd rather not be on the receiving end of Nick Romero's wrath, but if you want to try to use me as a buffer, I'll take my chances."

Addy laughed, thankful that Jim understood her so well.

If only she'd fallen in love with him instead of the idea of being a mother to his child. "Thanks. I—I don't think you'll be in any danger. I doubt if Nick would actually fight over me." Then she remembered Friday night when he'd come to her defense against Gerald at her father's engagement party.

"Don't sell yourself short, Addy. The way that man was acting today, I'd say he'd do more than fight for you. I think he'd kill for you."

"That's what Daddy's hired him to do, if it's necessary. But that's his job. It isn't personal."

"Don't kid yourself. It's definitely personal with Mr. Romero."

Janice Dixon rushed into Addy's office. "Sorry to interrupt, but Brittany McKinney has thrown up all over the bathroom and won't let anyone touch her. She's crying for her mother."

"Go take care of Brittany," Jim said. "I'll see you tomorrow when I stop by for juice with Tiffany."

"Call Brittany's mother," Addy said. "She works in the secretarial pool. I'll walk Jim out and go see if I can calm Brittany down until her mother gets here."

"Looks a bit out of place, doesn't he?" Janice whispered to Addy while the two women watched Nick Romero, who was sitting between a couple of three-year-old girls.

Addy's gaze moved over the big man whose very size dwarfed the small stool on which he sat. He had removed his jacket before sitting down to share vegetable soup and grilled cheese sandwiches with the children.

"He doesn't seem too uncomfortable, but then he has the awed attention of two females." Addy laughed, amazed that Nick could charm even preschoolers. His easy camaraderie with the children had surprised her, considering his background. She couldn't help but wonder if he'd ever thought of becoming a father. For one unguarded moment the thought of giving Nick a little girl of his own flashed through Addy's mind.

"He's looking this way," Janice said. "What's going on between you two?"

Addy fixed her gaze on Nick, then smiled and waved at him from her position at the table opposite his. "He's teaching me how to play games."

"What?" Janice choked on her iced tea.

Raising her voice, Addy called out, "Are you enjoying your lunch, Mr. Romero?"

"The food's not bad," he said. "And the company is— entertaining." He looked around the table where children of various sizes and sexes were munching on their sandwiches, slurping their soup and loudly sipping their milk.

"If you'd care to stay for nap time, I'll let you read them a story." Addy couldn't help noticing how totally at ease Nick seemed, crouched there in the middle of so many toddlers. Many men, especially hard-edged military types, would have been nervous, even wary, around small children.

A little brown-eyed girl sitting beside Nick looked at him and smiled. When he smiled back, she held up her unopened milk carton.

"I can't get it open," she said, handing the milk to Nick.

He took the carton, pulled apart the spout and returned the open container. "Here you go."

Just as the little girl's fingers tightened around the carton, the boy sitting next to her lost his balance on his stool and fell over on her. The milk sloshed out of the open container and splattered across Nick Romero's pale blue shirt.

Stunned, Addy watched the milk soak into Nick's clothing. She jumped up, rushing over to where the little girl sat crying.

"It's all right," Nick tried to assure the child. "It's just milk. It'll wash out."

"I didn't mean to do it," the child wailed when Addy crouched down beside her. "It was Barry's fault!"

"Stop crying, honey. Mr. Romero isn't angry." Addy motioned for one of her assistants, a heavyset, matronly lady, to take charge of the children at the table.

As soon as the assistant had lined up the three-year-olds and ushered them into another room for nap time, Addy turned to Nick. "You'd better come into my office and get out of that wet shirt. Lucky for you we have a washer and dryer, so we can clean you up in a few minutes."

"I take it by your calm manner that accidents like this are a daily occurrence." Nick grinned when she gave him a you've-got-to-be-kidding look.

"Accidents like this are an hourly occurrence, sometimes more often than that. We're dealing with preschoolers here."

Nick followed Addy into her small, cheerful office. She closed the door and turned to him. "Take off your shirt." She held out her hand.

He looked at her outstretched hand, then up into her sparkling green eyes. "Just what I like, a forceful woman."

Letting her hand drop to her side, Addy willed herself not to blush. "Nick…"

He began unbuttoning his shirt, very slowly. Addy steeled herself against her body's reaction. She refused to look away shyly. Nick would know for sure that the sight of his naked chest excited her.

"I'm afraid I don't have anything large enough for you to put on while we're washing and drying your shirt. I could send someone over to Daddy's office for one of his shirts." Addy tried to concentrate on Nick's face, focusing her attention on the glittering diamond stud in his ear. But when he pushed his shirt apart and tugged it out from beneath his belted slacks, her gaze traveled downward to the wide expanse of darkly tanned, thickly muscled chest.

"I'll be fine. It's warm in here." Removing his shirt, he handed it to her.

She grabbed the shirt quickly, but couldn't keep herself from staring at his chest. He was magnificent. Big. Manly. A thick matting of black hair covered his chest from nipple to nipple, a thin dark line trailing down to his navel and beyond. Addy didn't think she'd ever seen anything quite so sexy.

"Sit down. I'll put this in to wash and be right back." She opened the door, grateful for the excuse to escape.

"Addy?"

She stopped, but didn't turn around. "Yes?"

"I don't suppose you've got a cup of coffee in this place, do you?" He sat down on the lavender gingham cushion padding her chair.

"I—I'll bring you some."

"Thanks."

Leaning back in the wooden swivel desk chair, Nick slipped his hands into his pants pockets. He hadn't been blind to Addy's reaction when he'd removed his shirt. He liked the idea that just looking at him had turned her on. Sex was always better when both parties were equally aroused, and despite what Addy thought of herself Nick had no doubts that she would be one of the hottest women he'd ever bedded.

"What do you mean you don't have it?" a loud masculine voice demanded.

Nick sat up straight, listening. He glanced at the slightly ajar door that led to the small hallway separating Addy's office from the main playroom. He eased himself out of the chair. Leaving his cane against the wall, Nick clung to the side of the desk as he made his way closer to the door.

"I mean I don't have it!" Janice Dixon hissed. "How could I ask Addy for another loan right now when she and Uncle Rusty are half out of their minds worrying about the kidnapping? It would look rather strange, don't you think?"

"Maybe you're right, but we've got to figure out something. I've got to have that two thousand soon or I could wind up as dead as Addy's kidnapper."

"Ron, I'm scared. What if the police question you, and they just might, considering your background?"

Nick hobbled away from the desk, grabbing a chair near the door to steady himself. Peeking through the narrow opening, he saw the back of Janice Dixon's ripe little body. Ron Glover, tall and dark, faced her.

"They've got nothing on me, sugar. I was nowhere near Addy McConnell Friday night until long after the kidnapping, and nobody can trace me to the guy who fell off Monsano Mountain." Ron reached out, circling Janice's neck with his hand, pulling her closer. "See what you can do about getting me the money."

"Shhh! Don't talk so loud. Nick Romero is in Addy's office." Placing her fingertips over Ron's mouth, Janice nodded.

"What? Why the hell didn't you tell me?" Ron's voice lowered to a whisper. "That guy's bad news, Jannie!"

"He can't hurt you, Ron."

"That's right, sugar. No two-bit, crippled, ex-DEA agent is a match for me." He lowered his head, taking Janice's eager mouth.

Just as Ron kissed Janice, Addy rounded the corner, a mug of steaming black coffee in her hand. The minute Nick saw her, he hobbled back across her office and sat down behind her desk.

"Hello, Addy," Ron said. "Hope you don't mind me stopping by to see my girl."

"Janice's personal life is her own business," Addy said, then walked past the couple, pushed open the door and went into her office.

Addy set the coffee mug down on her desk in front of Nick. "There's sweetener and creamer inside the top drawer on the left."

"I take it black, remember?"

"I didn't remember. Why should I?"

"No reason." He smiled. "Thanks anyway."

Sitting down in the maple Boston rocker a few feet from her desk, near the corner by the windows, Addy began rocking back and forth. "As soon as your shirt is ready, you can leave and get back to *playing detective.*"

"I've been *playing detective* right here in your office."

"Oh? How's that?"

"By eavesdropping." He picked up the mug she'd set before him.

"On Ron and Janice, no doubt."

"They were having a very interesting conversation about money." Nick put the mug to his lips, sipping the dark rich coffee.

"It's no secret that Janice supports Ron, and I know that several loans I've given her have been for him." Addy stopped rocking. "I've tried to make her see what a sleazeball he is, but she refuses to listen to reason. She's crazy about him.''

"Yeah, well, *love* can make people do strange things.''

"Are you an expert on love?''

"Hardly, but I've been around enough to know that people who think they're in love can do some pretty stupid things. Take your cousin Janice. If she's that hung up on Glover, she might be persuaded to do anything he asks of her.''

"Like helping him plot my kidnapping. Is that what you're saying?''

"Like I told you earlier today, Red, don't trust anyone except your father and me.'' Nick hated throwing suspicion on Addy's cousin. It was obvious the two women were genuinely found of each other. But if Ron Glover did have Janice completely under his control, she could be dangerous to Addy.

"I can't believe—'' The jarring ring of the telephone cut off the rest of Addy's comment.

Nick glanced at the white phone sitting atop the desk. "Want me to answer it?''

Addy jumped up, quickly making her way to the phone. "Hello, M.A.C. Day Care. Addy McConnell speaking. May I help you?''

A muffled masculine voice said, "If you know what's good for you, you'll tell your daddy to follow my instructions.''

The color drained from Addy's cheeks and her eyes widened. "What did you say? Who is this?''

"What's wrong?'' Nick asked.

"Unless I get what I want, accidents could start happening,'' the voice said.

"Accidents? What sort of accidents?'' Addy's fingers tightened around the receiver.

Standing, Nick retrieved his cane and walked around the desk to stand beside Addy. "Give me the phone."

"It would be terrible if something happened to you. You can't be protected from everything. What if a bomb were planted at the day care? Not only would you get blown into a zillion pieces, but so would all those little kiddies. Tell your daddy that I'll be in touch soon." The sinister voice on the phone snickered several times before hanging up.

Addy trembled, her heartbeat accelerating. When she tried to replace the receiver, her hand shook so badly she almost dropped the telephone. Nick grabbed her by the shoulder, turning her to face him. He could tell by the glazed look in her eyes and the deadly pallor of her normally golden complexion that the caller's message had frightened her badly.

"Come on, Red, tell me what that was all about."

She stared at him, and for one split second she wanted to scream. "It—it was a man." Addy looked into Nick's black eyes, eyes filled with genuine concern. "His voice was muffled...like he was talking through cloth or something."

Nick tightened his hold on her shoulder. "What did he say?"

"He warned me that, if Daddy doesn't follow his instructions, he'll get to me somehow, even if— Oh, Nick, he said that something could happen here at the day-care center...that a bomb could explode, that—" Addy choked back tears and blinked several times in an effort not to cry, but the thought of anything happening to her precious children played havoc with her emotions.

"My God!" Nick pulled her into his arms, stroking her back with one hand. Resting his cane against the desk, he cradled her head with the palm of his other hand. "If this was no idle threat, then we're dealing with a madman."

Addy snuggled against Nick, knowing she was safe. The warm masculinity of his hairy chest sent a current of desire spiraling through her. She laid her head on his naked shoulder. She couldn't explain her reaction to this man. He was practically a stranger, a man who made no secret of the fact that he was a ladies' man, and yet she trusted him. Held within the comforting security of his strong arms, she realized that Nick Romero would indeed protect her at all costs.

He *was* her paladin.

"Oh, Nick." She swallowed the tears, refusing to give in to the overwhelming urge to cry. "The voice said that he'd be in touch with Daddy and give him his instructions!"

"Whatever's going on here is more complicated than any of us thought." He grabbed Addy's chin in one big hand and tilted it upward, forcing her to face him directly. "I swear that we'll catch this man, whoever he is."

Tears caught in her throat making it impossible for her to reply immediately. She simply stared at Nick, trying to convey what she felt in the expression on her face. Her eyes, moist with unshed tears, softened with tenderness, and she forced a weak smile.

"Trust me to take care of you, Red." Nothing had ever been so important to him. He wanted her trust. He wanted to make her feel safe and protected.

"I trust you, Nick. With my life if not with my heart." She reached up, placing her hand on his cheek.

He covered her hand with his own, brought it to his lips and kissed her palm. "I don't want to break your heart, Addy, but I'm beginning to think that you just might break mine."

She clung to him unashamedly, absorbing his strength, his raw masculine power. "Oh, Nick, what are we going to do?"

It hurt him deeply to see her like this, so vulnerable and unsure. With a possessiveness he knew only with this woman, he lowered his lips to hers. "I won't let anyone hurt you. No matter what I have to do, I'll protect you." He covered her mouth with his, sealing his promise with a kiss that claimed ownership.

Chapter 6

Addy slipped the navy blue dress over her head. Zipping it quickly, she turned to face her image in the cheval mirror. She looked…presentable. Not strikingly beautiful, not sexy and desirable, but neat and well-groomed. So what difference does it make? she asked herself. Over the past seven years since her divorce, she'd learned to appreciate her ordinary appearance—her plain face and thin body. But in the five days since she'd known Nick Romero, he had undermined her contentment, making her long for the kind of beauty men appreciated.

Sitting down on the edge of her pencil-post bed, Addy picked up her sedate navy pumps off the Oriental carpet and slid her feet into them. She stretched one of her long legs out in front of her, scrutinizing the shape and length. Her legs weren't bad; they just might be her best feature. *Dammit! Stop doing this to yourself.* She hadn't felt so insecure about her looks since she'd been married to Gerald, who'd taken every available opportunity to remind her of how inadequate she was. But Nick had never once implied that he found her less than attractive. Indeed, his every word, his every action, had suggested the opposite.

Last Saturday night, when they'd known each other for only twenty-four hours, Nick had held her in front of the foyer mirror and practically made love to her, forcing her to face herself, to see herself as an aroused and sensuous woman. She had tried all week to erase that memory from her mind, but she couldn't forget how she'd felt or the way she'd looked. She had been beautiful in those moments of passion. Nick's praise and adoration had made her beautiful.

But Nick Romero was a temporary fixture in her life, a man who, once the kidnapping threat ended, would leave her life as quickly as he had entered it. No matter how he made her feel, she couldn't risk letting him break her heart. He'd made it perfectly clear that he wasn't averse to having an affair with her, and she'd made it equally clear that she wasn't interested. She could handle friendships with men; however, a sexual relationship was taboo unless the man in question could prove his love for her. Only a man who loved her would be patient and understanding, helping her overcome her deficiencies as a woman. Only a man who truly loved her wouldn't give a damn about her daddy's millions.

Addy glanced at the colorful flowered scarf lying on her dressing table. She'd bought the scarf in a moment of weakness, thinking it would brighten up some of her drab outfits. But she'd never worn it. It was too flashy.

Picking up her delicate gold watch out of her small jewelry case, Addy focused on the row of violets sitting atop the pine chest of drawers. She smiled, remembering how for the past three days the florist delivery boy had brought her a large container of violets, each with a small lavender and white ribbon. No card had been included, but she knew who'd sent them. Each day she'd brought the violets home with her, and Nick hadn't said a word. But she knew they were from him. Laughing, Addy fingered the velvety softness of one tiny leaf. No wonder Nick was so popular with the ladies. He was a romantic. Most men sent red roses. Roses were pretty standard, but only a man who really understood women would take the time to choose a flower that matched a woman's personality. She supposed Nick saw her as a shrinking violet. Or was there another meaning behind the flower he'd chosen for her?

She heard the rap of Nick's cane as he walked down the hallway from his bedroom to hers. Without giving any more thought to the matter, Addy grabbed the large, colorful scarf and draped it across her right shoulder.

Nick stopped in the open doorway, surveying Addy from head to toe. Damn, he wished her outer garments were half as sexy as her lingerie. At least the scarf added a touch of color to the plain navy dress. He wondered what had prompted her to act so impulsively. In the five days he'd known her, not once had Addy worn anything stylish, colorful or alluring—except her lingerie. He hadn't seen her sleeping attire every night, but on the nights that he had, she'd worn frothy concoctions that took his breath away.

"It's almost seven-thirty." He stepped just inside her open doorway. "Time to leave."

Smiling, Addy turned to face Nick. "Try to be cordial to Jim if you see him today, and at least be civil to Ron when he picks up Janice."

"I'm having a more complete check done on Glover. From what my contacts have already found out, he's more than capable of plotting your kidnapping, and he's just the type to use threats."

"Do you think he's capable of murder? After all, the person behind my kidnapping has already killed once." Addy walked over to Nick and the two stepped outside into the hallway. "If I thought Janice was in danger—I mean, if Ron is really—"

Nick put his arm around Addy's waist, giving her a reassuring hug. He couldn't tell her that there was a possibility that Janice, so enamored of a hood like Glover, was actually his accomplice. Of course, both Ron and Janice could also be completely innocent. "I don't think Janice is in any danger, whether or not Glover is the kidnapper. He'd have no reason to harm her."

Together they descended the stairs, Addy slowing her stride to accommodate Nick's limp. His big hand stayed on her waist, warm and reassuring. She liked it when Nick touched her, even casually, and he'd touched her often in the last few days, despite her coolness toward him. There had been no more kisses, and Addy knew she should be grateful. Nick's kisses were lethal.

He escorted her outside to his Jag, opening the door and helping her into the seat. Before starting the car, he turned to her. "You look lovely."

Swallowing hard, Addy stared directly at Nick, wishing her heart would stop beating so rapidly. "It's the shawl. It adds color to—"

"It's not the damned shawl." Nick revved the motor, his big hands clutching the steering wheel. "It's you, Addy. You're lovely."

"Tha—thank you." Nick wasn't the first man who'd given her compliments, and, unfortunately, he wasn't the first one she'd believed. Did she dare trust Nick Romero? Did she dare listen to her heart?

"You've got three men chasing you." Nick backed the

silver sports car out of the driveway. "How the hell can you consider yourself unattractive and undesirable?"

Addy sat up straight, looking away from Nick's lean, hard face. Glancing out the window at the stately old homes and towering green trees as they drove past Jefferson Street, she remained silent, unsure how to answer Nick's question.

Nick chose the route leading through downtown. He didn't like Addy's silence any more than he liked the way she'd turned all moody and distant the last few days. He'd done everything he could to reassure her, but the waiting— the endless waiting—for word from the threatening phone caller had played havoc with her nerves. It hadn't helped any that Rusty McConnell had been growling like a papa lion, frightened for the safety of his only cub. Nick knew that Addy worried more about her father than she did about herself.

But Nick worried about Addy. In less than a week's time, she had become important to him. Far too important.

Within ten minutes they turned into Research Park. Grassy green fields and majestic, tall trees lined the streets of the park, each street named after a space shuttle—Columbia, Discovery, Endeavor. Nick pulled the Jag into Addy's private space in the M.A.C. day-care center parking lot.

When she clasped the door handle, Nick reached across the console, taking her hand. "He's bound to contact Rusty soon. Then we'll know what we're dealing with and how to handle the situation."

Looking down at Nick's big hand grasping hers, she sighed. "I hope you're right. I don't know how much longer Daddy's going to be able to endure the waiting."

Nick squeezed her hand. "Your father's tough, Red. He can stand a lot more than you think he can."

"It's not fair for him to have to go through this again—living in fear of losing a child to a kidnapper."

"That's not going to happen. I won't let it."

Turning her head slightly, Addy glanced at Nick. A shiver of something akin to excitement raced through her. How had she allowed herself to become so dependent on this man? And why did his protectiveness make her feel safe and yet vulnerable all at the same time?

Nick met Addy in the hallway leading to her father's office. Rusty had summoned them both on an *urgent matter*. Addy's face was flushed, her eyes overly bright. Nick could see the way her hands nervously clutched her leather purse. Only someone who knew her well, someone who'd spent endless hours with her, could tell that Addy was upset. Although their acquaintance was less than a week old, Nick had come to know Addy in a way he'd never known another woman. Except Dina. The truth of the matter was that he'd never spent as much time with another woman. Day and night. Sharing meals with her, sleeping in the room next to hers, listening to her talk and laugh and argue, and catching glimpses of her elegantly slender body covered by nothing more than her sexy lingerie.

Addy McConnell, taken in small doses, could be dismissed as nothing more than a skinny redhead. Nick understood why so many men had overlooked the real value that lay hidden behind her Plain-Jane facade, and had taken an interest in Addy solely because of Rusty's money. But Nick had learned, to his own detriment, that Addy McConnell, taken in large doses, could prove fatal to a confirmed bachelor who'd always prided himself on being a love 'em and leave 'em ladies' man.

He couldn't remember ever wanting a woman so badly—not even when he'd been seventeen and thought he'd die from wanting his brother's wife. At forty-three, he'd known his share of women, and could easily have his pick of dozens of beauties. So, why didn't the idea of bedding some bosomy blonde appeal to him?

"Ginger wouldn't tell me anything," Addy said, her long legs slowing their pace to keep step with Nick's slower, halting gait. "Did she tell you why Daddy wanted to see us?"

"No. She just said to get to Rusty's office pronto, that it was urgent." Reaching out, Nick pulled one of Addy's trembling hands away from the purse she clutched at her waist. "Whatever it is, we'll take care of it. Rusty, you and me. The three of us together."

Addy halted her steps, stopping to stare at Nick. "You mean that, don't you? You actually think I'm capable of being part of the solution."

Nick paused, then squeezed her hand. "You're a smart lady, and from what I've seen, you're pretty tough. You're the one whose life is in danger, so it stands to reason that you'll want to cooperate with the two men who'd die trying to protect you."

"Nick...I—" She'd never known a man like Nick Romero. He overwhelmed her by almost everything he said and did. And he constantly surprised her. Did he, she wondered, realize how possessive he sounded, how much like a man in love? Dear Lord, she couldn't allow herself to indulge in that particular fantasy.

"Come on, Addy, your father's waiting." He tugged on her hand. She gave him a half-hearted smile and started walking again.

The receptionist stood up when they walked past, watching them enter Ginger's office. She wasn't at her desk, but stood in the open doorway to Rusty's office.

"He's on the phone with the police." Ushering them

inside, Ginger closed the door. "Can I get either of you something to drink?"

"No, thanks," Nick said.

Addy simply nodded.

Rusty slammed down the telephone, the crashing sound reverberating around the room. He turned his dark green gaze on Nick. "From now on, I want you so close to her that she can't breathe without you hearing her." He glared at Addy. "And if it takes handcuffing you to him, then I'll see to it. Understand me, little girl?"

Addy rushed to her father, putting her arms around him. He crushed her in his arms, almost pressing the breath out of her. She knew that something terrible had happened. Rusty's ruddy face was flushed crimson, his thick lips drawn in a fine line of pain, and his big, meaty hands shook with the force of his rage.

"What is it, Daddy? What's happened? Has *he* called?"

With one big arm still draped around Addy, Rusty leaned down, picked up a sheet of paper off his desk and handed it to Nick. Nick took the paper, reading it silently, then looked at Rusty holding his only child protectively in his arms. Dammit, he wouldn't want to be in Rusty's shoes. But, in a way, he was. Addy wasn't his beloved child, but she was going to be his woman and her safety was as important to him as it was to her father.

"What's this?" Addy asked, reaching out for the paper Nick held in his hand.

Nick released the paper, allowing her to take it. Rusty kept his supportive arm around her. She scanned the letter, similar to the one her father had received almost a week ago, the morning after the failed kidnapping attempt.

"Oh my God!" The letter fell from Addy's fingers and floated to the carpeted floor. "Now we know what the kidnapper wants."

"If M.A.C. doesn't withdraw its bids on the NASP contract, then Addy's life is in danger," Rusty said. "That contract is worth millions. Hundreds of jobs that are threatened because of the economy can be saved."

"The kidnapper isn't some madman who wants a ransom, is he?" Addy's mind rioted with a dozen different thoughts, finally calming to focus on one possibility. "Gerald! It's Gerald, isn't it? If M.A.C. doesn't bid on the NASP contract, then New Age Aerospace has a good chance of becoming a NASP contractor, and not only would that add greatly to Gerald's standing with his father-in-law, but it would be the perfect revenge on us, wouldn't it?" Looking up at her father, she knew that he'd come to the same conclusion.

"New Age Aerospace isn't our only competitor," Rusty said. "We can't rule out someone at one of the other companies."

"Rusty's right," Nick said. "Just because Gerald Carlton has a personal reason to want to see M.A.C. lose the contract doesn't mean he's the only suspect."

"You can't agree to this." Addy pulled away from her father. "We have to make a bid on the NASP contract. There's too much money and too many jobs at stake to buckle under to this threat."

"Baby girl, we're talking about your life." Tears clouded Rusty's vision as he took his daughter's slender hands into his enormous grasp. "Nothing is more important to me than you."

"Oh, Daddy, I know that." Addy wanted to comfort her father, but she was incapable of easing his fears. "There's no way anyone can get to me with all the protection I have." She focused her attention on the big, dark man whose very presence in the room made her feel safe. "My God, how do you think anyone could get through Nick?"

"We have to consider all our options," Nick said, his heart thumping at a deafening roar. Addy trusted him! Really trusted him. "First, tell me about this NASP contract."

"NASP is the National Aero-Space Plane, the X-30. It's one of the boldest concepts that the Air Force and NASA have ever conceived," Ginger Kimbrew said, making her presence known for the first time since Addy and Nick had entered Rusty's office.

Nick turned to Ginger, understanding how intricately involved she was in every aspect of the McConnell Aerospace Company. "I'll contact Sam and have him check out all the competition, all the possible contractors who'll be bidding."

"The five prime contractors that comprise the NASP National Program Office are based near Air Force Plant No. 42 in Palmdale, California." Rusty helped Addy into his huge leather chair, then sat on the edge of his desk. "There's no need to run a check on those guys. Their part in NASP is a done deal. But the big boys are ready to let Huntsville in on the deal, and M.A.C. wants to be part of the team."

"This is a visionary aircraft," Ginger explained. "It would enable the U.S. to have routine access to space from a runway. Access embodied in the X-30."

"Propulsion is NASP's biggest worry. That's where M.A.C. comes in. Our engineers are primed and ready for this project." Rusty's excitement danced in his eyes, vibrated in his deep, strong voice.

"You understand why Daddy can't give in to this threat, don't you?" Addy asked Nick.

"There's one possibility that we're all overlooking," Nick bent over and picked up the threatening letter, then laid it on Rusty's desk. "What if the NASP contract isn't

the real motive? What if someone is using it as a red herring?''

''What are you saying?'' Addy scooted to the edge of
her father's chair.

''It never pays to jump to conclusions.'' Tapping his
finger on the letter, Nick glanced from Addy to Rusty.
''This letter would have us believe that the person behind
Addy's kidnap attempt doesn't want several million in ransom money, but does want Rusty to lose millions on an
important government contract. Reputable competitors
don't deal this way. They have families of their own.''

''Carlton is too hot-headed and bent on revenge to consider anything but getting what he wants.'' Rusty struck
his desk with his closed fist. ''So help me, if he's behind
this, I'll—''

''Rusty, calm down.'' Ginger rushed forward, reaching
out pleadingly. ''This isn't doing your blood pressure or
heart any good.''

''She's right, Daddy. If Gerald is behind this, he'd like
nothing better than to see you drop dead from a heart attack.''

The outer office door swung open. Dina Lunden and
Brett Windsor swept into Rusty's private domain, the hag-
gard receptionist following them, screeching that they
couldn't interrupt Mr. McConnell, who'd given strict instructions not to be disturbed.

''What's this about you dropping dead from a heart attack?'' Dina asked, making her way directly to Rusty. Dina
eyed Ginger, who had her hand on her boss's arm. Releasing Rusty, Ginger stepped aside.

''Nothing for you to worry about, honey.'' Rusty jerked
Dina up against him. She buried her face in his chest.

''But I do worry about you, darling. Especially now that
Addy's in such danger.'' Purring like a kitten, Dina rubbed

her head against Rusty as she slipped her arm around his waist. "Has something else happened?"

"Is there some reason you and Windsor came by today?" Nick asked, barely giving Dina a glance as he concentrated all his attention on Brett Windsor.

"I'm meeting Rusty for lunch. It's almost noon." Dina took a quick look at her diamond-studded wristwatch. She ran her hand up Rusty's chest, caressing him. "What's wrong, darling? Tell me."

"We received another threatening letter," Rusty said.

Nick groaned. Why couldn't Rusty keep his mouth shut? He was a smart man, but damned stupid when it came to Dina. He shouldn't trust her so completely, and he sure as hell shouldn't trust Windsor. "The police have already been informed, and we're calling in the FBI."

"The FBI?" Dina's big blue eyes darted a startled expression from Rusty to Nick.

"I'll fill you in on all the details at lunch," Rusty said, stroking Dina's back. "Ginger, you take Dina and Brett here on into your office and get them some coffee or tea or something until Nick and I finish making a few phone calls."

"Oh, Rusty," Dina whined.

"Now, now, honey, go on."

"Are we going to be awfully late for lunch? Our reservations are for twelve-thirty." Dina pulled away from Rusty, a pouty look on her beautiful face.

"Ginger, call and have our reservations changed to one o'clock." Rusty glanced over at Brett. "Entertain your stepmother until I'm free."

"Of course." Brett came forward, taking Dina's arm and leading her toward the door.

Addy watched the way Nick stared at Dina, as if he found her disgustingly fascinating. A hot surge of jealousy ripped through Addy. Dina looked so feminine in her chic little summer suit. The beige silk draped and caressed her body as if it loved to be next to such voluptuousness. Suddenly, Addy felt like a frump in her navy dress, despite the colorful scarf draped across her shoulder.

Watching Dina and Brett make their exit, Nick thought what a perfect pair they made. Except for the twelve-year difference in their ages, they suited each other to a tee. Both were blond and beautiful, flawless in appearance but sickeningly self-centered and selfish. It was a pity they'd gone through old man Windsor's fortune so quickly. The only thing lacking in their relationship was money, which both of them seemed to value above anything else.

Brett halted just as he ushered Dina into Ginger's office. He turned, flashing his brilliant, toothy smile at Addy. "Why don't we join Dina and Rusty for lunch? Ginger could make the reservations for four."

"I...I don't know." Addy didn't want to go to lunch with her father and Dina. She wanted to go back to the day-care center and share a meal with Nick, who always showed up just in time for lunch each day. She glanced at Nick, wishing he would say something that could prevent their having to join the others.

Nick didn't say or do anything. He didn't even look at her.

"She'll go. It'll be good for her to get out." Rusty glanced at Nick. "Make the reservations for five, and have a couple of Dundee's boys tag along behind us."

"I need to take care of some things at the center before we go to lunch," Addy said. "Give me a buzz when y'all are ready to go."

Addy walked through Ginger's office. Her father's secretary was on the phone changing Rusty's lunch reservations, and Brett was pouring himself a cup of coffee from the machine on a nearby table. Dina reached out, grasping Addy by the wrist as she passed her.

"We need to talk."

"About what?" Addy asked, glancing down at Dina's long, sharp nails. She jerked her wrist free.

Dina looked over at Ginger, then at Brett. "Why don't we go on into the receptionist's office? I'll send her on an errand and we can have a little privacy."

Addy didn't want to talk to Dina about anything, and she certainly had no desire to be alone with her. She didn't like Dina. And she didn't trust her.

"I'm in a hurry, Dina. If Nick and I are going out to lunch with you and Brett and Daddy, I have to get back to the center and handle some problems there."

When Addy walked away, out into the reception area, Dina followed. "I need to talk to you about Nick."

Addy slowed but didn't stop. Dina Lunden was the last person on earth with whom she wanted to discuss Nick. "I don't have time."

"Ms. Harkin, go find me some aspirin. I feel a terrible headache coming on," Dina told the receptionist.

"I have some aspirin in my desk." Ms. Harkin opened the center desk drawer and reached inside.

"Don't be obtuse, Ms. Harkin. Find somewhere to go for a few minutes and leave Ms. McConnell and me alone."

"I—I don't know if I should, Mrs. Lunden. I mean…" The young woman floundered in an attempted explanation.

"It's all right, Joyce," Addy said. "Go ahead and take an early lunch."

The moment Joyce Harkin left, Dina turned to Addy. "I want you to ask Rusty to replace Nick with another bodyguard."

"What?"

"You may feel extremely flattered by Nick's attentions, but I can assure you that, in the long run, he'll only wind up hurting you." Dina's cool gaze traveled over Addy's slender body with the scrutiny of a trained spy seeking to discover any hidden detail. "You can't possibly believe that *you* could capture and hold a man like Nick Romero."

Addy felt the sting of Dina's words as if they'd been a physical slap. She didn't need the other woman to remind her of how totally inadequate she was. "My relationship with Nick is none of your business."

"But of course it is. After all, I'm practically your stepmother." Dina moved to Addy's side, a false show of concern on her face. "I love you because you're Rusty's child, and I like you, too. You're such a nice person, Addy. Really too nice for a bad boy like Nick."

"If you're so concerned about Nick acting as my bodyguard, why haven't you said something to Daddy yourself?"

"I have, but he simply won't listen to me." Dina sighed dramatically. "Men are such stubborn creatures, aren't they? Your father has this mistaken notion that Nick would make the perfect husband for you."

Addy couldn't stop the bubble of laughter in her throat from erupting. "I can't picture Nick as anyone's husband."

"Certainly not. Nick's too much of a free spirit." Dina seemed to relax, placing her hand on Addy's arm. "I should have known you would be sensible about this. After all, you're too smart to allow yourself to be used again."

"Yes, I am," Addy agreed. "But Nick isn't the sort of man who'd use me. I've learned that much about him. He's nothing like Gerald, and I honestly believe money doesn't mean anything to him."

"Nick isn't interested in Rusty's money the way your

former husband was, that's true enough.'' Dina tugged on Addy's arm. ''Why don't we sit down and I'll tell you some things you need to know about Nick so you'll understand my concern.''

Addy stared at Dina, trying to figure out what the woman's real motive was. Could she actually be concerned, or was she jealous? ''I don't need to sit down. Just tell me what you think I need to know.''

''Very well.'' Dina's words escaped in an aggravated huff. ''Nick sees you as a challenge, I'm quite certain of that. Women usually succumb to his good looks and charm quite readily, but since you haven't, he'll use whatever means necessary to seduce you. His rather substantial male ego is involved. Women don't say no to Nick.''

''What makes you think he hasn't already seduced me?'' Addy didn't like the smug look on Dina's face.

''He hasn't. I'd know if you and Nick were lovers. I've known Nick since he was fifteen. The two of us have no secrets.''

Pulling away from Dina, Addy said, ''Nick told me that you and he play a game where you try to seduce him and he resists.'' Addy watched for any change of expression on Dina's face or in her eyes. She saw only the slight flickering of Dina's long, dark eyelashes. ''Are you sure the real reason you want Nick replaced as my bodyguard is because you're worried about me?''

''What other reason could there be?''

''Perhaps you're afraid that I might mean more to Nick than a conquest, that his feelings run deep enough to consider making a commitment to me.''

The reaction Addy had been waiting for appeared on Dina's face. Her rosy cheeks flushed brightly and her blue eyes burned with indigo fire. She tightened her hold on Addy's arm, her nails biting into soft flesh. ''Don't be an idiot. You aren't Nick's type. I'm Nick's type. Ever since we became lovers when he was seventeen, he's looked for me in every woman he meets. I have no doubt that when he's making love to those other blondes, he pretends he's making love to me.''

Salty, burning bile rose in Addy's throat. She had suspected that Nick and Dina had once been lovers, but hearing the woman admit it was almost more than Addy could bear. She tried to keep her reaction from showing, from being so blatantly obvious. Nothing would appease Dina's spiteful jealousy more than seeing Addy upset by her scandalous admission that Nick had bedded his brother's wife. Addy had never dreamed Nick would have betrayed his own brother. Maybe she didn't know him as well as she thought she did.

''I couldn't care less about you and Nick,'' Addy lied. ''But I think Daddy might care.'' Addy was pleased to note Dina's shocked expression.

Dina's face paled noticeably. ''I'd rather Rusty didn't know, but if telling him is the only way to get Nick out of your life and end Rusty's obsession with the idea of marrying you off to Nick, then perhaps you should tell him.''

Brett Windsor opened the door connecting the reception area to Ginger Kimbrew's office. ''Addy, I'm glad you're still here.'' Brett glanced from Addy to Dina, then back to Addy. ''Is there something wrong?''

''No,'' both women replied simultaneously.

''Well, Ginger has changed the reservations. All she had to do was mention Rusty McConnell's name. Amazing what wealth and power can do, isn't it?'' Brett stepped between the two women, giving Dina a questioning glare before turning to Addy. ''Has Dina said something to upset you?''

"I'm afraid Addy wasn't prepared to hear the truth about Nick. It seems she's quite smitten with him. Such a shame to see a dear, sweet girl like Addy making a fool of herself over a man—"

"I think you've said enough, Dina." Brett put his arm around Addy's quivering shoulders. "Addy has better sense than to fall for Nick Romero's rather obvious charms. Despite his smooth exterior, your brother-in-law is still as rough and uncivilized as he was when he was in the SEALS."

"I'd rather not discuss Nick with either of you." Addy started to pull away from Brett, but hesitated when she saw Nick standing in the open doorway, his dark eyes glowering at her. She leaned into Brett's embrace, slipping her arm around his waist. "Why—why don't you come over for dinner some night soon?" The minute the words escaped her mouth, Addy regretted them. How could she act so childishly, trying to use Brett to make Nick jealous?

Brett's smile dazzled Addy with its perfection. "I suppose Nick will have to be there, won't he?"

"You've got that right, Windsor, but you and Addy can just pretend I'm not there." Nick glanced back into Ginger's office where her shapely behind was bent over her desk. "I could ask Ginger if she'd like to make it a foursome."

"Good idea." Brett leaned down, planting a sweetly romantic kiss on Addy's lips.

Shocked, Addy had no intention of responding until she heard Nick's feral growl from across the room. In her peripheral vision, she saw Nick take a tentative step in her direction. Without thinking of the consequences, she responded to Brett's kiss with a passion born of her own anger and jealousy. Damn Nick for making her care about him when he was probably still in love with Dina.

Nick stopped dead still, then walking as fast as he could hampered by his bad leg, he fled past Addy and Brett and a cattily smiling Dina as if the hounds of hell were on his heels.

Addy pulled away from Brett, staring at Nick's wide back as he exited the reception area. She swallowed hard, wondering why she suddenly felt afraid of the man in whom her father had entrusted her life.

Despite the cool flow of air from the overhead fan, Nick's body glistened with sweat. He'd been punishing himself with a series of sit-ups he had hoped would exhaust him enough to sleep. He'd been seething with anger all day, ever since he'd walked in on the sickeningly sweet sight of Addy returning Brett Windsor's caress.

Clutching his fists at his sides, Nick beat the mattress, wishing it was Windsor's pretty-boy face. What the hell did Addy mean responding to Windsor with such passion? She didn't love the guy, and by her own admission, she didn't trust him. Just what had been going on?

He suspected that Dina had something to do with it. That mocking smile on her face had given her away. He knew Dina and all her little tricks. She had done or said something to Addy that made her angry with him, had made her want to get back at him. And by God, she had, in the worst possible way. He hated these feelings of jealousy. The last time he'd been jealous, he'd thought he was in love with Miguel's wife. He'd been a fool! Damned if he would ever let another woman make a fool of him.

The last thing he should be worrying about right now were his possessive feelings for Addy. Not when she was in real danger, when her very life could be at risk. He should be concentrating on keeping Addy safe, not succumbing to the powers of the green-eyed monster. Somewhere out there was a man or a woman primed and ready to kidnap Addy if Rusty McConnell allowed M.A.C.'s bid on the NASP project to stand. Nick knew that all his energy should be focused on making sure that didn't happen, regardless of what decision Rusty made about the contract bid.

He and Rusty had discussed the situation with Ned Johnson, the FBI agent assigned to the case. The federal government didn't like any type of threats being made that involved one of their pet projects—and the NASP project was a number one priority for both NASA and the Air Force.

Sam Dundee had assured Nick that he would run a check on all of M.A.C.'s competitors and have a complete report faxed to him by Monday morning at the latest. Nick knew he could count on Sam. They didn't make men any smarter, tougher or more trustworthy. Sam was one of the best friends Nick had ever had. They'd shared more than danger during their days with the DEA. They'd shared their pasts, their problems and occasionally their women.

Somewhere in the back of Nick's mind a damned pesty little suspicion wouldn't go away. What if the NASP bid had nothing to do with the kidnap attempt? What if there actually was another motive? Did he dare risk Addy's life by not paying attention to his gut instincts? Often, in the SEALS and as a DEA agent, the only thing that had saved him was his instincts.

He had pretty well ruled out Ginger Kimbrew as a suspect. The woman was too much in love with Rusty McConnell to be a threat. If the NASP bid turned out to be the real motive, Gerald Carlton headed the list, but if there was another motive—money, for instance—then Ron Glover jumped to the number one spot, followed closely by Brett Windsor. And there was always the off chance

that Janice Dixon could be helping her boyfriend or...
Nick hated himself for suspecting Dina. She was spoiled,
self-centered and money-hungry, but he honestly didn't
think she was capable of kidnapping or murder.

A loud tapping on his bedroom door drew Nick from
his thoughts. Rising up on his elbows, he stared at the
closed door. He made no response. The tapping began
again, then he heard Addy's whispered voice.

"Nick? Nick, may I come in?"

He flipped the switch on the bedside lamp, positioned
himself against the headboard and wiped the sweat off his
face with the palm of his hand. "Yeah, come on in."

The door opened slowly, Addy peering in before she
stepped inside and took several steps toward Nick. Seeing
him lying in bed, wearing nothing but a pair of nylon
shorts, she halted, staring at him with questioning eyes.
"I—I want to know what's wrong."

"Why do you think something's wrong?" Damn, did
she have any idea how she looked, standing there in the
dim light, her titian hair tumbling down her back and onto
her shoulders? She was wearing gold satin pajamas that
hung loosely on her slender frame, but they didn't disguise
the elegant line of her body or the pouting tips of her
nipples. Just the sight of her aroused him.

"You haven't spoken two words to me since before
lunch today." With slow, deliberate steps she made her
way to the side of the bed.

Nick didn't move a muscle. At least not intentionally.
One part of his body had a mind of its own. "I thought it
best if I kept my mouth shut. Once something is said, you
can't take it back."

"You're angry with me, aren't you?" She held her
hands, twined together, in front of her. She didn't look

directly at Nick, but down at the chenille spread folded back at the foot of the bed.

"You're too smart to try to use Windsor to make me jealous, so why did you?" He reached out, grabbing her wrist, tugging her down onto the bed beside him.

She gasped, but didn't struggle. "What makes you think that's what I was doing?"

He released her, then waited to see if she'd get up. She didn't. She sat, ramrod straight on the edge of the bed, close to but not touching him. "You don't care anything about Windsor, and you know he's only interested in Rusty's money, so what other reason could there be?"

"I am not going to become just one more of your women." Her voice trembled with emotion.

Nick ran his hand up her back, savoring the feel of her rich satin pajama top beneath his fingertips. He knew Addy's flesh would be twice as soft and smooth. She jerked, but didn't pull away. "What did Dina say to you?"

"What makes you think Dina—"

Wrapping his arm around her waist, he jerked her up the bed and to his side. She faced him then, glaring at him with both expectation and challenge in her glittering green eyes. "Let's stop playing twenty questions, Red. What did Dina say that made you so upset with me that you used Brett Windsor to hurt me?"

"My kissing Brett hurt you?" There was genuine awe in her voice, as if she were dumbfounded that she held that much power over Nick's feelings.

He grabbed her chin in his big hand, squeezing tightly but not painfully. "You know damned well that it ate me alive seeing you kiss him that way."

"Dina told me that—that you and she had been lovers."

Nick didn't respond. His hand on Addy's back stilled. He took a deep breath. "Yeah. A long time ago, when I was just a green kid whose raging hormones ruled his body.'' He felt her quiver.

"You—you slept with your brother's wife?"

"I slept with my brother's widow. Once."

Addy released the breath she'd been holding, then reached out to cover Nick's hand that held her chin so firmly. "Did you love her?"

"Look, Addy, what happened between Dina and me was so long ago that it has no bearing on the here and now. On the two of us." He didn't think Addy would understand if he admitted the truth. How could he explain to her that there was more than one kind of love, and that what he'd felt for Dina had been the absolutely worst kind—the most destructive kind?

"She thinks you compare every woman to her, that she's still the woman you want."

Nick flung off Addy's hand and released her chin. He jumped up off the bed, knocking Addy over in the process. She gazed up at him. "If I wanted Dina, I could have had her a thousand times over." The truth of his words rang in his ears like a dozen clanking bells. There hadn't been a time in the past twenty-odd years that he couldn't have bedded Dina. Between husbands or even during her marriages. She had no conception of the word "fidelity," and in other women, it didn't matter. But in the woman he loved, it was of paramount importance. He'd spent his entire life seeking a replacement for Dina, when in his heart he'd known she was his for the taking. He didn't want her. And he sure as hell didn't love her.

Pushing herself up with her elbows, Addy sat in the middle of Nick's bed. "I want to trust you completely...in every way, but—but I'm not prepared to take that kind of risk unless I can be sure of you."

"Sure of me how?" He glared at her, his big bronze body towering over her.

Addy had never wanted to touch a man the way she wanted to touch Nick. He was so utterly masculine that the very sight of him took her breath away. "If you want me, you're going to have to earn the right to make love to me."

"I'm going to what?"

"I want to be sure that I'm important to you, that you really care about me, that your desire for me is real."

Nick grabbed her hand, shoved it against his arousal and held it there. "That's real, Addy, as real as it gets."

She felt the throbbing evidence of his desire, and the shocking realization that she had evoked such a strong response in him tempted her almost beyond reason. Almost, but not quite. "Gerald could get hard, and he could ram himself into me, but he didn't care anything about me. I didn't mean anything to him but a way to get Daddy's money. When I give myself to a man again I don't want to have any doubts that I'm all he wants, all he cares about, above and beyond anyone or anything else."

Nick dropped his hand. Addy's hand slid down the front of Nick's shorts, her fingers caressing him. He groaned. "How the hell do I prove something like that to you?"

Addy walked toward the open door. "I don't know, but I'm sure you'll find a way."

With that said, she left. Nick stood, watching her as she disappeared into the hallway. Damned stubborn woman. She was asking too much of him. There was no way he could prove himself to her, was there? She was asking for the kind of love that didn't exist—not in his world.

Hell, he'd never had to prove himself to a woman. If she thought that he'd ever come to her begging, then she'd better think again.

Nick fell into the bed, his hot, aroused body pulsating painfully with a need that he knew only one woman on earth could appease. And that woman had just told him that if he ever wanted to find release between her long silky legs, he'd have to earn the right to make love to her.

Chapter 7

Hot June sunshine played hide-and-seek with gray, mid-morning rain clouds, creating a hazy, overcast daylight. Standing at her kitchen window, Addy watched the warm breeze floating through the trees and shrubs in her backyard, swaying the tops of the red azaleas and teasing the clematis vine clinging to the wooden fence. Everything looked the same as it had for the past few years since she'd purchased the house in Twickenham, since she had begun a new life, totally on her own. She had grown to love the sameness, the routine pattern of peacefulness, and, above all else, she had learned to appreciate her independence.

But things were not the same. An unknown person's threats had changed her life, throwing her cherished order into chaos, reverting her father back into the overprotective parent he'd once been, and utterly destroying her hard-won privacy and independence.

Addy placed the last lunch plate into the dishwasher, then wiped her hands and laid the towel on the counter.

Glancing out onto the rock patio behind her house, Addy saw Nick Romero, his broad back facing her, as he sat drinking a tall glass of iced tea. As much as the menacing kidnapper, Nick had altered the course of Addy's life, his very presence a disturbing force she found difficult to handle.

More than anything she wanted to believe that his interest in her was genuine, that he truly desired her as a woman and not as the heir to a fortune. If she allowed her romantic nature to override her common sense, she would give herself to Nick, heart and soul. Already, she fantasized about him, seeing him as her knight in shining armor, the man who would cherish her and protect her...forever. But Addy had learned to control the romantic girl within, giving her realistic self the upper hand. Trusting her life to Nick was easier than trusting her own heart.

The portable phone sitting outside on the patio table rang, jarring Addy out of her thoughts. Opening the door, she stepped outside just as Nick answered.

"Hold a minute, I'll get her," he said, then shoved the chair back and stood.

Before he could turn around, Addy walked over to him. "Is that for me?"

Nick gave her a long, hard look, then handed her the telephone. "It's Jim Hester."

Addy returned Nick's scrutiny as she accepted the phone. "Hello, Jim." Addy walked around the patio, savoring the feel of the warm sun and the pleasant breeze.

"I just wanted to check on you before I leave for Washington," Jim said. "I need to know that you're all right."

"I'm fine. Honestly."

"Addy?"

She could tell by the unusual edge to his voice that

something was bothering him. "What is it, Jim? What's wrong?"

"Well, I—I thought you should hear it from me."

"What?" She had never known Jim Hester to be so mysterious.

"I'm taking Tiffany with me on this trip, and…I'm taking Carol Stilwell with me."

Addy could hear Jim's deep breathing, could feel the utter stillness. "You're taking your sister-in-law?"

"Yes, well—"

"It's all right, Jim." Addy walked farther away from Nick, knowing he was listening to her every word. "If you're trying to tell me that you and Carol are—are involved, I understand."

"I just didn't want you to think that I'd been leading you on and fooling around with Carol at the same time." Jim's voice sounded strained, pleading. "I guess I've always known that nothing would ever come of our friendship. And since Romero showed up… Well—I need someone, Addy, and so does Tiffany."

"Of course you do, and believe me, I understand. Good luck, Jim. I—I hope everything works out for you and Carol."

They said their goodbyes. Addy punched the off button. Nick came up behind her, leaning over to take the phone out of her hand.

"You didn't want Jim Hester, despite the fact that he's a nice guy. You wanted to be a mother to his daughter."

She would have preferred not to discuss that situation with Nick, even though it was obvious that he'd overheard every word of her conversation and had jumped to the correct conclusion. As foolish as the notion seemed, Addy couldn't help feeling like she'd been dumped. "I thought you didn't like Jim."

"I changed my mind about Hester. I wanted to dislike him, but I couldn't. He's all right, Addy, but he's not the man for you." Nick tossed the phone into a cushioned lounge chair.

Addy fiddled with the drawstring on her yellow walking shorts. "Let me get this straight. You've warned me off Brett Windsor because he's only interested in my money and you think Jim was the wrong man for me because all I wanted from that relationship was to be a mother to Tiffany."

"That about sums it up."

"I'm surprised you aren't telling me that you're the right man for me. Now would be the perfect time, wouldn't it?" Addy couldn't bring herself to face Nick. Somehow she knew he was smiling, that self-assured, macho smile.

"I am the right man for you, and we both know it."

"You're wrong, all wrong." She turned, forcing herself to look at him, determined to remain in control. "What you want is another conquest. You want—"

"I want you." Nick focused all his attention on Addy, his dark eyes reaching out, pulling her to him, mesmerizing her by their look of heated desire. "I don't want another woman, and I couldn't care less about Rusty's millions. All I want is you. Your body, your mind, your heart. Everything that makes you Addy."

When Nick reached out and took her hand, she jerked away from his touch as if he'd hurt her. "Don't do this to me. I can't handle it."

She ran from him, her bare feet racing over the warm flagstones. Nick didn't follow her immediately. Running his fingers through his thick black hair, he cursed himself for a fool. He couldn't seem to get it right with Addy. With other women he'd always been the smooth Romeo, who knew exactly what to say and do. With Addy it was different. She was different. The woman was driving him crazy. She wanted him to prove himself to her, and he had no earthly idea how to go about doing it.

He gave her five minutes alone—four minutes more than he wanted to give her. He found her in the den, staring out the window. She'd wrapped her arms around herself. Her shoulders drooped in defeat.

"Addy?"

Her body stiffened, but she didn't turn around or reply. He walked over to her. More than anything he wanted to pull her into his arms. He didn't dare. At this precise moment she'd fight him like a wildcat. Addy was a woman who needed persuasion, and he was damned and determined that he was going to be the man to persuade her.

"Come on and sit down," Nick said, his big hand hovering over her shoulder. It was all he could do to keep from touching her. "Why don't we just sit and talk for a while?"

"I don't want to talk to you." Addy kept her back to him. "I want you to leave me alone."

"Were you this stubborn as a little girl? If you were, Rusty must have had his hands full raising you."

Some of the tension drained from her body. It wasn't a visible thing, yet Nick sensed it. He lowered his right hand to her shoulder, making sure his touch was light and non-threatening.

Addy felt the warmth of his touch through her blouse. His hand was big and hard and strong, yet his grip on her shoulder was unbearably tender. Hating herself for enjoying the feel of his hand on her body, she refused to look at him. She didn't trust herself to remain in control if his eyes were still filled with desire.

"I'll never lie to you." Nick balanced his cane against the wall, then placed his left hand on her other shoulder, turning her around toward him. "I'm not looking for love and marriage and I'm not making you any forever-after promises."

Addy glanced down at the Sarouk rug beneath her bare feet. Her vision focused on the intricate gold, rust and blue pattern. "What—what can you give me, Nick, in return for my blind faith in you?"

He reached out, slipping his fist beneath Addy's chin. "I can give you passion and fulfillment. I can make you glad that you're a woman."

She was tempted, so very tempted. But men said whatever they thought necessary to get what they wanted. They sought out your weaknesses and used them against you. Men did that sort of thing. Gerald had.

He tilted her chin upward, forcing her to face him. Her eyes widened with a mixture of anger and embarrassment. Every word he said was true, but how could he make her believe him? "Addy?"

"I'm not going to sleep with you, so you might as well give up on me. I—I don't like sex, and I refuse to become one more in a long line of women who've shared your bed."

Releasing her chin, Nick stepped away from her, but didn't break eye contact. "You didn't like sex with Gerald. That doesn't mean you won't like sex with me."

"You are, without a doubt, the most egotistical man I've ever known. I'm no good at sex, and not even a Latin stud like you can change what's lacking in me. I'd disappoint you, Nick, so why don't you stop pursuing me and put us both out of our misery?"

"The only thing that's going to put us out of our misery is making love. I've just got to figure out a way to prove myself to you." Walking over to the stereo unit hidden inside the huge oak cupboard, Nick checked through

Addy's tape and disk collection. "Don't you have any-thing except classical and semi-classical stuff?" He held up a tape. "Well, what have we here? It's not exactly Ricky Van Shelton, but it's not Beethoven either."

Addy couldn't stop looking at him, puzzled by the sud-den change in his conversation from something extremely personal to something totally insignificant. What was he trying to do, throw her off guard?

Nick inserted the tape in the player, then leaning heavily on his cane, walked over and sat down on the sofa, tossing several pillows onto a nearby round table. Suddenly the sound of soft, romantic music permeated the room. The mixed voices of men and women sang "Close to You." Nick patted the sofa. "Come sit down and we'll talk."

Addy gave him a wary stare. "I don't trust you."

"Yes, you do. It's yourself you don't trust."

Addy moved toward Nick, slowly, cautiously, intent on proving him wrong. A show of bravado was called for here. She wasn't a silly young woman eager to believe a man's sweet lies. She was a woman who'd gone through her trial of fire, and she could handle anything, including the likes of Nick Romero.

Addy sat down, making sure she was as far from Nick as she could possibly get while sharing the same small sofa with him. "I don't want to talk about sex."

"Fine. Let's talk about Addy McConnell when she was a little girl." Nick scooted several inches toward her, then propped his big feet on a tiny needlepoint footstool. "What did you do for fun?"

"I—I took riding lessons, swimming lessons, tennis les-sons, piano lessons—"

"Whoa, Red! I asked what you did for fun. Lessons aren't fun."

"I enjoyed my lessons, even if there were never any

other children around...only my bodyguards.'' Addy
shifted nervously when Nick draped his arm across the
back of the sofa.

An entirely instrumental rendition of the "Gone with
the Wind" theme filled the room. Addy sighed. Nick
smiled.

"You really were a poor little rich girl, weren't you?
An overprotected, pampered Southern belle in a golden
cage. Didn't you ever spend any time with other kids?"

"No. Only when Janice was allowed to visit and when
Daddy gave me my yearly birthday party.'' Addy remembered those precious visits with Janice, who had become
her dearest friend—her only friend. And the parties had
been like dreams fulfilled when the children of M.A.C.
employees were brought out to the mansion to celebrate
her birthday.

"What about school?" Nick inched closer to Addy. She
didn't seem to notice.

"I had private tutors. Public school was never considered, and Daddy thought private schools weren't safe."

"Are you saying that you never did anything just for
fun? Spontaneous things? Crazy things?"

"Everything I did had to be supervised, otherwise it was
unsafe. I—I did have privacy in my room. I learned to
escape into books. They became my friends.'' It had been
in those books that she had become a part of the fantasies,
the romantic legends, the tales of knights and their ladies.
As a child she had first read of Charlemagne and his twelve
paladins—the *douze pairs* who were his bodyguards and
companions.

When Nick eased his arm around her shoulders, she
started to pull away, but realized that she didn't want to
leave the warm comfort of his embrace.

"There was a world of difference in our childhoods.

Nobody ever watched over me. The only person who even cared where I was or what I was doing was my grandmother. My father was a field hand who was either working or boozing it up. He finally drank himself to death.'' Nick tightened his hold on Addy when she snuggled against him, bending her knees as she lifted her feet onto the sofa.

"What about your mother?" Addy asked.

"My mother." Nick grunted. How could he possibly explain a woman like Kitty Romero to Addy? "My mother liked men. All men. While my father drank, she whored around. She left us, my brother Miguel and me, when I was ten."

"Oh, Nick, I know how difficult it is to lose a mother."

"Red, losing my mother was a godsend. She was nothing but white trash. My grandmother was the only mother we ever really knew. Kitty did us a big favor by leaving."

Addy could hear the pain in Nick's voice, the anger he tried so hard to deny. When she laid her head on his shoulder, she felt him stiffen and then relax. "My mother committed suicide when I was ten. She—she had a nervous breakdown after Donnie…when Donnie was murdered."

"I didn't intend for us to talk about gloomy subjects." He loved the feel of her so close to him, her head resting against him, her whole body snuggling to him with such trust.

"Then maybe we shouldn't talk about our childhoods."

"Mine wasn't all bad," he said, reaching down to take her hand in his, holding it palm up. "Miguel and I were close, and we had a lot of fun together. He was five years older, but he never tied to brush me off so he could run with the older guys. He took me everywhere with him." Suddenly, Nick's whole body tightened, his face rigid. "Damn!"

"What's wrong?" She gazed up into his face and almost cried at the sorrow she saw in his dark eyes.

"I can't seem to steer clear of gloom and doom." When she stared at him questioningly, he said, "Miguel was killed in an oil rig accident when I was seventeen. God, I thought I'd die when we lost him!"

"He—Miguel was married to Dina."

"Yeah." Nick squeezed her hand, then released it and withdrew his arm from around her shoulders. He looked at her, sensing the waves of sympathy flowing from her, washing over him. He grabbed her face in his big hands, cradling her gently. "Tell me about your birthday parties, Red. I never had a birthday party in my whole life."

Instantly Addy realized that he didn't want to talk about Miguel and Dina and his relationship with them. Addy smiled at Nick. "Oh, my birthday parties were grand affairs. We had them at Elm Hill before Mama died, and then at Daddy's new house afterward. All of M.A.C.'s employees' children came. It was always a catered affair with a huge cake, ice sculptures that held the ice cream and thousands of helium balloons released into the air. And entertainment. A pony ride, a clown, and a band when I got older." Tears gathered in her eyes. She willed them away. She didn't cry. Not ever. Not anymore. "I always loved my birthdays. It was the only time I never felt— confined."

"I got invited to a birthday party once. One of the kids at school. I don't think I ever envied another kid so much in all my life." Nick ran his hands down Addy's neck, across her shoulders, and down her arms. He stopped at her waist. "It was no big production like your parties. Just cake and ice cream. A few drooping balloons. But what I remember were the presents. All that bright wrapping paper and ribbons and all those gifts." He pulled Addy toward him. She went willingly. "I was lucky if I got one present at Christmas, and never on my birthday. Grandma would always remember. When I was little she'd give me a dime to go to the store for ice cream. We were so damned poor."

"My father grew up poor, too." Addy could not resist the hunger in Nick's eyes. "You and Daddy really do have a great deal in common, don't you?"

"Yeah, in more ways than you'd ever imagine." Nick lowered his head, his lips brushing hers. "We both care a hell of a lot about you."

Being kissed by Nick Romero was very much like being burned by a painless fire, a fire that consumed and left you hot but unharmed. His lips were warm and damp and demanding. He nibbled, he teased, then parried before thrusting. She groaned into his open mouth, accepting the invasion of his tongue, feeling herself slowly but surely unraveling from within. Spiraling tension built low in her stomach, the pressure mounting as it invaded the very core of her. Her nipples tightened. Her small breasts suddenly felt very heavy.

She clung to him, not wanting these strange but wonderful new feelings to end. Nick wasn't just her bodyguard. He wasn't just some Latin lover out to score. He was a man who'd known his share of pain. A man whose childhood still tormented him as Addy's did her. Poverty and neglect had soiled the pure happiness of his boyhood. Enviable wealth and constant protection had taken the joy from her girlhood.

Nick deepened the kisses, devouring Addy with his passion. He gave his hands free rein, allowing them to roam over Addy's body at will. She was willowy thin and so delicately made that he could easily break her in two with his hands. He covered one breast with his palm, savoring the feel of her jutting nipple against his rough flesh. He wanted this woman—wanted her in a way he didn't understand. She was more than a body, more than the means of physical release. He wanted to absorb her, to bring her to him and make her his.

Nick lifted Addy onto his lap. She felt the hard, pressing throb of his arousal against her bottom. Her mind screamed that it was time to run. Her love-starved body silenced her mind by squirming against Nick while she thrust her tongue out to meet his.

He knew if he didn't stop now, it would be too late. Addy was responding to him, wild and hot and wanting. But she wasn't ready for him. He hadn't proven himself to her. When he took her, he wanted her to know what she was doing, to be sure of him and of herself. He wanted her to accept the fact that they were destined to become lovers, but he didn't dare risk letting her think there could ever be more to their mating. Addy had to come to him fully prepared to accept a short-term relationship.

He slowed the kiss, soothing her body with gently caressing strokes. Releasing her mouth, he leaned his forehead against hers. "I love the taste of you, Addy, and the feel of you. You've gotten me so excited I'm hurting."

"Nick?" She spoke in a hushed whimper, her arms still draped around him, her body still seeking closer contact with his.

He patted her face, tenderly, softly. "It's going to happen for us, but only when you're ready."

Pulling away, Addy stared at him. Her eyes were wide and round, her mouth open on a sigh. "You—you really do want me, don't you?"

"More than I've ever wanted another woman."

She slipped off his lap, then stood. Gazing down at him, she reached out with trembling fingers, then jerked her hand back before looking directly into his desire-filled eyes. "I want to believe you…I want to—"

"And you will, when I've proven myself to you."

"Nick?"

"When there are no more doubts in your mind or your heart, then you'll come to me and I'll give you more pleasure than you could ever imagine." He saw the startled look cross her face, the sweet, pink flush that stained her cheeks. "Don't worry about what happened in the past. You aren't frigid or inadequate in any way. When you decide the time is right, I'll show you just how good at sex you can be."

Addy couldn't breathe. Her lungs refused to function, so heavy was the weight of emotions pressing down on her. Nick's words set off an explosion of sensations inside her, frightening her into action. Turning from him she fled, running out into the hall.

Nick sat on the sofa, his body aching with unfulfilled desire. With any other woman, he'd have taken her body, given her satisfaction and felt only mild affection for her the following day. Addy McConnell was different. He knew that once he'd experienced the ecstasy of being buried deep inside her hot, sweet depths, neither of them would ever be the same again.

Damn, how had this happened? How had he allowed himself to get so emotionally involved?

Addy stood in the foyer, gripping the staircase banister with her damp hands. She could hear her heart beating, drumming loudly in her ears. Her mind reeled from the sure knowledge that she had come close, very close to succumbing to Nick Romero's dangerous charm. Perspiration moistened her aroused body.

He—not she—had called a halt to the passion that had

consumed them both. He could have taken advantage of her, but he hadn't. That proved something, didn't it? Wasn't his consideration of her feelings a sign that she could trust him?

Slumping down on the bottom step, Addy propped her elbows on her knees and cradled her chin and cheeks in her hands. Dear Lord, how had her life gotten so far off course? How had she, in one week's time, gone from a sensible, independent woman in control of her own life to a romantic fool bound to an irresistible man, dependent upon him for protection and yearning for him to give her love?

The doorbell chimes echoed loudly in the foyer. Addy jerked, startled by the sound. Staring at the door, she hesitated momentarily, then made her way forward, peeking through the privacy viewer to see the mailman standing on her front porch. Without giving it another thought, she unlocked and opened the door.

"A package for you, Ms. McConnell." The tall, bearded mailman had been making the rounds in the Twickenham district ever since Addy had moved here five years ago. She didn't know his name, but recognized his friendly face.

"Thank you." She accepted the brown paper-wrapped box, then turned and stepped back into the foyer.

Nick grabbed the package out of her hands. "Why the hell did you open the front door? You should have called me!"

"It was the mailman, for heaven's sakes." Addy pulled on the package that Nick had slipped under his arm. "You don't think someone would send a bomb through the mail, do you?"

"It's been known to happen." He took the package into the den and set it down on the sofa. Addy followed closely behind him. "Get out of here. We have no idea what's inside and I don't want you anywhere around when I open this thing."

"We should call the police. Let them open it." She couldn't bear the thought of something happening to Nick. What if it were a bomb? What if he died keeping her safe?

"I won't take any chances, Red." He looked at her concerned face, that golden face with a smattering of freckles across her perky little nose. "I know what I'm doing. I'm highly trained, remember?"

Addy nodded, then walked out of the room, making her way down the hall and out onto the patio. Dingy clouds obscured the sun, casting a dreary glow over the gravel walkway leading to the wooden bench near the hedge that closed off the yard from the alley. The breeze picked up force, swirling minuscule particles of dirt and loose grass into the air.

Addy sat down on the backless bench, her nervous fingers idly picking at the profusion of flowers surrounding her. A dozen different questions whirled about in her mind, thoughts and images tormenting her with doubt, possibilities filling her with dread. She hadn't been expecting a package. She hadn't ordered anything, and the box was wrapped in plain brown paper and tied with string, childlike in its simplicity. Her name had been printed in bold black letters, the stick-on kind that could be purchased in any stationery shop.

Minutes ticked by, soundless except in her mind, where each second toned louder than a striking mantel clock. What would Nick find inside the mysterious package? Her feminine instincts told her that the contents weren't harmless, that they would, somehow, be connected to the man threatening her safety. Both she and her father were convinced that Gerald Carlton was the most likely suspect, but

Nick hadn't allowed their certainty to sway his judgment. He'd told them that the only way to keep Addy safe was to keep an open mind, to suspect everyone, whether or not their motives were obvious.

The sound of distant thunder announced the possibility of rain. Glancing toward the west, Addy saw a dark horizon. With a great deal of anxious turning and twisting, she managed to stay seated, though she longed to rush back inside to be with Nick, to share whatever fate befell him. She didn't want him facing danger alone.

The moments dragged by like hours. The rumbling thunder grew close. The wind whipped around Addy, tousling her loosely confined hair and blowing dust into her eyes. No matter what, even if it started to rain, she wasn't going to move from this spot until Nick came for her. If she stayed right here and waited, everything would be all right. She would be all right. And Nick would be all right.

Sharp, bright lightning streaked the sky. Addy closed her eyes and prayed. The first tiny droplets of rain fell, hitting her bare arms and legs, sprinkling the bench and the gravel walkway. Thunder boomed loudly. Opening her eyes, Addy stared at the back of her house. Nick stood in the doorway, the open box in one hand, his black cane in the other. She gasped, relief spreading through her like syrupy sweet jelly over hot biscuits.

Jumping up, she ran to him. The dark sky exploded with lightning, the clouds bursting with rain. Nick wrapped his arm around Addy, holding the box behind her back as he pulled her close.

"Oh, Nick, I've been so worried!" Burying her face against his shoulder, she clung to him, whispering his name over and over again.

"I'm fine, Red." He didn't want her to see the contents of the box, but he knew he couldn't protect her from them.

She would demand to see what lay inside and he had no right to refuse. She needed to know what type of lunatic they were dealing with and understand that they didn't dare narrow their list of suspects down to Gerald Carlton.

Nick pulled her with him into the kitchen, dropping the box on the countertop, then jerking Addy's trembling body against the solid strength of his own. He stroked her neck, her back, her hips, his big hand moving up and down slowly, caressingly. He threaded his fingers into her hair, pulling free the long titian strands from the thick bun.

She looked at him and knew that she loved him.

"Addy?" He had never seen an expression so serene on a woman's face. It was as if Addy had discovered some wondrous truth that erased all her pain and anger and fear.

"I was afraid…if there had been a bomb—"

"No bomb. Just pictures, and newspaper photos and articles." He circled her neck with his hand, soothing her damp flesh with the pad of his thumb. "You're not going to want to see those things, Red, so why don't you just let me tell you what they are."

She stared deeply into his dark eyes which were filled with tenderness and concern. "The package is from *him*, isn't it, the man who's determined to keep M.A.C. from bidding on the NASP project?"

"Yeah." Nick glided his thumb up and under Addy's chin. Right now he wanted to ease her fears, to caress her, to love her and keep her safe. "The guy's trying to play mind games with us, Red. Remember that. If he gets to you, then he's succeeded in what he set out to do."

"Let me have the box, Nick." She pulled away from him, turning toward the counter.

He released her, knowing that all he could do was stand by and watch her confront her past. "I'll have to call Rusty. He needs to know."

Addy's hand hovered over the box. Touching the lid, her fingers trembled. With haste born of fear, she slipped opened the box and stared at the contents. Nestled inside like brittle, golden autumn leaves, the old newspaper clippings lay scattered, mixed with snapshots of her brother. She reached out, but her fingers refused to cooperate. She couldn't touch the items. Tight, choking tears swelled in her chest and burned in her throat.

Nick stood behind her, his big, hard body a source of warmth and comfort. Slipping one arm around her waist, he whispered, "You don't have to do this."

A strangled cry escaped her throat. She balled her hands into snug fists. "This is going to kill Daddy. He never talks about Donnie. Never!"

Forging ahead with all the inner strength she could muster, Addy picked up a photograph of Donnie, dressed in his cowboy outfit and sitting atop his pony. Tears gathered in Addy's eyes. She blinked them away.

"Who would have access to pictures of your brother?" Nick asked.

It took Addy a couple of minutes to understand his question. "Oh, Lord, I don't know. Servants, friends, relatives. Anyone who's ever been at the house. Daddy boxed away all the old pictures years ago, but he kept them in the storage areas above the garage. He even kept all of Donnie's clothes—and all of Mama's things, too."

"That narrows down the suspects somewhat, but still leaves all the major ones. Gerald. Ron. Brett."

Addy picked up a fragile newspaper clipping. The headlines jumped out at her. It was the story of Donnie's murder. A photograph of his lifeless little body accompanied the article. "Oh, God, we can't show these to Daddy!" She handled each article, each picture of her brother, her father, her mother and herself. Her parents' grief-stricken faces had been captured by some over-zealous photographer at Donnie's funeral. Stories of her mother's suicide four years later had made front page news.

The sour, sick feeling began in her stomach. Torturous pounding began in her temples. She swayed slightly and might have lost her balance had it not been for Nick's strong hold about her waist.

Suddenly she pulled away from him, running, running. She made it to the downstairs powder room a split second before her stomach emptied itself. Nick caught up with her in the powder room where she'd knelt on her knees in front of the commode. He grabbed a hand towel, wet it with cool water and bent by her side, laying his cane on the floor as he wiped perspiration from her pale face.

"It's okay, Red. I've seen grown men in the middle of battle react far worse." With tenderness and compassion, he cleaned her face and pushed back loose strands of damp, clinging hair.

"I don't want to relive those days." She accepted Nick's help as he eased her up and onto her feet.

"The person who sent the clippings and pictures knows that. He's counting on your pain and fear as well as Rusty's to get him what he wants."

"Was there a note?" She didn't hesitate to cling, to snuggle, to seek comfort in Nick's arms.

He held her, longing for the power to solve Addy's problems and ease her pain and sorrow. "Yes. I left it in the den."

"What did it say?"

"The same old stuff about bidding on the NASP contract."

"Daddy has to know." She laid her head on Nick's shoulder, closing her eyes, willing herself to be strong and brave. Her father would need her strength. "If only there were some way to keep Daddy from seeing the articles, the pictures of Donnie and Mama.''

"Rusty is going to be able to handle all this old grief a lot easier than he's going to be able to deal with the continued threat on your life." Nick tightened his hold on her, silently cursing the demon whose sick mind was putting Addy in danger. He would not let anyone harm her. No matter what it took, he was going to keep her safe.

"What more can Daddy do? I'm under constant surveillance. You're with me night and day." She thanked the dear Lord in heaven for Nick. All the resentment, the distrust, the uncertainty vanished. Maybe she was a fool. She didn't know. She was certain of only one thing. She was falling in love with Nick Romero.

"Rusty can let me take you away from here. Out of Huntsville to some place no one knows about…where no one can find us." Nick had made that suggestion to Rusty a week ago. He'd told Nick that Addy would never agree. But now, the threat to her life had escalated. Things had changed. With or without her agreement, Addy would soon be going into hiding. He'd convince Rusty that it was the only foolproof way to keep her safe.

"I don't want to leave Huntsville, to run like some scared—"

Nick silenced her by placing his hand over her mouth. She glared up at him, her green eyes vivid with surprise. "You'll do whatever I tell you to do, woman. Understand?"

Addy nodded in agreement, remaining silent when Nick removed his hand. There was no point in arguing for the sake of arguing. Nick's background made him far more of an expert than either she or her father. If Nick said they had to go into hiding, then she'd go.

"You're awfully quiet, Red. Just what's going on in that sharp little brain of yours?"

"I was thinking how lucky I am to have you as my own personal bodyguard."

He stared at her, knowing there was more to her statement than met the eye. Strong emotions vibrated in the air, a pulsating tension between the two of them. She looked at him, her feelings written plainly on her face. Addy McConnell had fallen for him. It was what he'd wanted, wasn't it, for her to care enough to let him be her lover? Becoming Addy's lover could get complicated. Once he'd had her, would he ever be able to let her go?

"Well, I'll be damned," Nick said.

"We both may be damned," Addy said. "But I'm willing to take the risk."

Chapter 8

Nick opened the door and stepped back, avoiding a collision with Rusty McConnell. Addy's father barreled into the foyer like an out-of-control steamroller.

"Where is she?" A splattering of sweat dotted Rusty's ruddy cheeks. His deep baritone voice trembled with anger.

"She's in the den." Nick reached out a restraining hand, grasping the older man by the arm.

Rusty stopped, eyeing Nick with a harsh glare. "Is she all right?"

"Yeah, she's all right...now. But she won't be if you go storming in there and upset her." Gauging Rusty's reaction to his comment, Nick felt him relax slightly, his big, powerful body losing some of its rigidity. "Look, she's worried about you. She's more concerned by how this is affecting you than anything else." Nick released his tenacious grip on Rusty's arm.

"Where's the box?"

"She has it with her," Nick said.

"Dammit, man, why did you ever let her see it in the first place?"

"I didn't want her to see it, but I didn't have the right to keep it from her. She's not a child, and as much as you and I want to protect her, we're not doing her any favors by treating her like one."

"Hell, she is a child. My child! My only child..."

"Granted. But she's also a woman, an adult who's fought long and hard for the right to be treated as one." Nick nodded toward the living room. "We need to talk, just the two of us...alone, before you see Addy."

"Keeping secrets from her?" Rusty asked. "I thought you said we needed to treat her like an adult."

"Addy already knows what I'm going to say to you. I just didn't think it was necessary for her to have to hear it all over again while you and I thrash things out." Nick walked out of the foyer and into the living room, stopping briefly in the doorway to issue Rusty an invitation. "How about something to drink while we talk?"

Rusty grunted, then smiled. "Sure. Scotch. Neat." He joined Nick in the living room, watching while his daughter's bodyguard poured two glasses a third full, then handed one to him.

"Sit?" Nick asked, lifting the Scottish whiskey to his mouth, tasting it, savoring the smoky flavor.

"I know what you're trying to do, Romero." Sitting down, Rusty filled a blue brocade wingback chair with his big body.

Nick didn't respond. He simply stared at Rusty as if he didn't have any idea what he was talking about.

"You want to calm me down before I see Addy." D.B. McConnell took a hardy sip of his Scotch, allowing it to linger in his mouth before swallowing. "Seeing those pictures and newspaper clippings upset her more than she wants me to know. Right?'' When Nick didn't reply, he continued. ''You're trying to protect my daughter from me, aren't you?''

''Look, Rusty, I'm probably overstepping my bounds, but the last thing Addy needs right now is to see you coming apart at the seams.''

''I agree.'' Rusty took another hefty taste of his drink. ''I knew you were the man for Addy the night you threatened to castrate Gerald Carlton, the same night you saved her from a kidnapper.''

''I admit that I care about Addy, that I'll do whatever it takes to protect her, but don't go ringing wedding bells and throwing rice. I've been a bachelor for forty-three years, and I plan on staying one another forty-three.''

Rusty finished his Scotch, set the glass down on a nearby cherry table and stood. ''I like that about you. You're honest with me, and I'll bet you're honest with Addy. That's good enough for me. Don't make her any promises you don't intend to keep.''

Choosing to ignore Rusty's comments, Nick plunged right to the heart of the matter. ''I need to get Addy out of this house, away from Huntsville.'' He set his unfinished drink down beside Rusty's. ''It's the only way I can guarantee her safety.''

''Has she agreed?''

''Yes, she has. Your daughter may be as stubborn as a mule, but she isn't stupid. We're dealing with an unknown quantity here, a guy who's making threats to kidnap— threats to kill—if you bid on the NASP project. If he doesn't know where Addy is, he can't hurt her.''

''I've got a condo in Florida and an apartment outside Washington—''

"And everybody who knows you and Addy knows about the condo and the apartment."

Grunting, Rusty rubbed his chin as he considered other possibilities. "I've got friends and business associates all over, even in Europe. I can call in some favors and have the two of you on a plane to practically anywhere in the world within twelve hours."

"It'll be best if I take Addy someplace that even you don't know about." Nick waited for the lion's roar. He didn't have to wait long.

"What? You can't mean that you don't want me to know where my own daughter is? That won't wash with me, Romero! Wherever Addy goes, I want to stay in contact with her!"

"I've already called Sam Dundee," Nick said. "He's got a place lined up for us. No one except Sam will know our whereabouts. I'll check in daily with him, and he'll relay the message to you. If you need to contact us, then call Sam and he'll get in touch with us."

Rusty paced back and forth in front of the fireplace, his hands balled into fists as if he longed to smash something. "I don't like it...but you're right."

"Then you agree?"

"Yeah. Reluctantly, but I agree."

"Let's tell Addy."

The moment her father entered the den, Addy jumped off the couch and ran to him, throwing her arms around him.

Rusty soothed her, petting her like the child she was to him. "It's all right, baby girl."

"Oh, Daddy, please don't look at the pictures or the articles. It won't change anything. It'll just upset you." She gazed at him pleadingly.

He ran his fingers down her cheek, tenderly grasping her chin in his hand. "I don't need to see them. I'll just take a look at the note."

Addy sighed with relief. Going through the contents of the box had made her physically ill, and even now her mind could not erase the images of those long-ago newspaper articles—articles she'd never been allowed to see when they'd been fresh news. But her father would have seen them all, twenty-nine years ago when Donnie had been kidnapped and murdered, and twenty-five years ago when Madeline Delacourt McConnell had committed suicide.

"Ned Johnson is on his way over here," Nick said.

"You've already called the FBI?" Rusty shook his head. "Do you think there's any way they can trace the box, find out who sent it?"

"It's doubtful. I think we're dealing with a very intelligent person, one who's covering his tracks. I'd bet my life that our mystery man didn't leave any prints on the box or its contents. That's why I saw no reason not to take a look at everything before I called Johnson."

"Even intelligent people make mistakes," Addy said.

"That's what we're counting on." Nick pulled out a sheet of plain white paper from his pocket, handing it to Rusty. "Here's the note that was lying on top of the pictures and clippings."

Rusty released Addy, took the note and read it hastily. "M.A.C. doesn't have to bid on the NASP contract."

"Yes, we do," Addy said vehemently. "No matter who's behind this, Gerald or…or someone else, we can't let them get what they want. Not only will we lose millions, but it could cost hundreds of jobs."

"Your life is worth more than money or jobs," Rusty said.

"My life is safe." Addy turned to Nick, smiling. "Nick and I are leaving Huntsville before daybreak tomorrow, and we're not coming home until M.A.C. has won the NASP contract. Two more weeks and this will all be over."

"If only we knew for sure it was Carlton." Rusty clutched his hands in imitation of a stranglehold, crumpling the threatening letter. "I'd kill that bastard with my bare hands. I should have killed him years ago!"

"If Gerald is behind these threats, then the FBI will catch him." Addy hoped it was Gerald. She'd thought she was long over her hatred and bitterness, but she wasn't. Her ex-husband had put her through three years of agony and stripped her of her dignity as a woman. Death was too good for him!

"When I called Johnson to tell him about Addy's little package, he gave me some interesting information." Nick reached out, taking the badly crinkled letter from Rusty. "Information that possibly links the man who tried to kidnap Addy last Friday night to Gerald Carlton."

"What did Johnson tell you?" Rusty asked.

"The man who tried to kidnap me was named Linc Hites," Addy said. "He worked for a janitorial service that New Age Aerospace uses."

"Damn!" Rusty turned his attention to Nick. "Is there any evidence that Carlton and this Hites fellow actually knew each other?"

"None, but Johnson's keeping tabs on Carlton. If he's our man, then all we need is for him to make one little slip." Nick had gone over the list of suspects time and again. Unless the man behind the kidnap plot was someone unknown to the McConnells, then all the circumstantial evidence pointed to Gerald Carlton.

"Not much can be done without some hard evidence to

back up our suspicions.'' Rusty slumped down on the sofa, his enormous body dwarfing the small couch. ''All right. You and Addy go into hiding. When M.A.C. wins the NASP contract—'' he smiled at Addy, and she smiled back ''—you two come back to Huntsville. The threat will be over. He will have lost and we'll have won.''

Nick wished things were that simple, and they just might be—if the person or persons behind the threats really did want to keep M.A.C. from acquiring the government job and this person or persons didn't seek revenge when things went sour. But what if they did seek revenge, or what if the contract bid was a smoke screen? It never paid to rule out any and all possibilities.

''Let's hope that's the scenario,'' Nick said. ''We'll work under that assumption for the time being.''

''Addy said you two were leaving in the morning.'' Rusty held out his hand and Addy accepted it, seating herself beside her father.

''Yeah. Before daylight.'' Nick picked up the infamous box. ''I'll go wait for Ned Johnson and give you two some time alone.''

''Thanks.'' Rusty put his arm around Addy. She rested against him, her head on his shoulder. ''Oh, yeah, Nick, why don't I send some of Dundee's men with you? They could ride shotgun on your trip.''

''Bad idea,'' Nick said. ''An entourage will call attention to us. A man and woman traveling alone is commonplace. Trust me on this, Rusty.''

Neither man said anything else, but they stared at each other for several silent moments, weighing each other, sizing up one another. Two strong men with the same singular purpose—protecting Addy from harm, no matter what the cost.

Nick turned, leaving the room. Addy had sensed the

unspoken exchange between her father and her…her what? Her bodyguard. Her protector. Her defender.

"He told me he wasn't interested in getting married." Rusty leaned back so he could get a clear view of Addy's face.

"What?" Addy gasped, glaring at her father with startled green eyes.

"I asked him about his intentions," Rusty said with mock seriousness, without a hint of a smile.

"Oh, Lord, Daddy!"

"He said he intended staying a bachelor for another forty-three years."

Addy wondered what Nick had thought of her father's questioning. Had he resented Rusty's interference or had he simply found the notion that D.B. McConnell wanted him to marry Addy amusing? "He told me the same thing."

"The right woman could probably change his mind."

"You hadn't known the man twenty-four hours when you decided you wanted him for a son-in-law. How can you be so sure?" Addy pulled away, giving her father a questioning stare. "You liked Gerald when you first met him, too, remember?"

"Hell, don't remind me! That jerk had us both fooled. He was a charmer. Silver-tongued, smooth and—well, he was a man's man, or at least I thought he was."

"Nick Romero is all those things, too, you know."

"Nick's the genuine article. He's not pretending to be anything he isn't. And he's not pretending his interest in you, either. He knows that I'm aware of how much he wants you, and yet he told me honestly that he isn't interested in marriage."

"Are we both acting like fools again, Daddy, putting so much faith and trust in a man we hardly know, a man who came into our lives because of Dina?'' Addy wanted to tell her father about Dina's real relationship with Nick, that the two had once been lovers, but she didn't want to add to the problems already plaguing him.

''You know about Nick and Dina, don't you?'' Rusty's faded green eyes darkened, his gaze searching her face.

''She told you?''

''Nope. Dina didn't tell me anything, except how fond she's always been of Nick, but I read between the lines.''

''Doesn't it bother you, knowing she slept with her husband's brother?'' It certainly bothered Addy. Every time she thought about Nick and Dina, naked, hot and sweaty, in Nick's bed, she wanted to scratch out the other woman's eyes.

''Dina is very insecure. She thinks money is the answer to all of life's problems.'' Rusty took Addy's hand, patting it gently. ''I know what Dina is, but I still want her. Hell, baby girl, I'm in love with the woman. Besides, I'm not lily-white pure myself. You know that.''

''Then it doesn't bother you, knowing…knowing—''

''When Dina and I make love, I don't waste my energy thinking about who else she's been with.'' Rusty laughed, deepening the heavy lines around his eyes and mouth. ''Damn, this is hardly a subject a man should be discussing with his daughter!''

''If I were your son, you'd discuss it with me, wouldn't you?''

Rusty laughed louder. ''You've got me there!''

Addy joined his laughter. He hugged her to him again. ''Daddy, I think I'm falling in love with Nick.''

''I'm not surprised. There's a chemistry between you two. I felt it the night you met. Romero doesn't know it yet, but I'd bet my last million that he's falling for you, too.''

"I—I've decided to have an affair with him." Addy didn't look directly at her father, uncertain of his reaction.

"Good idea! Try him out and see how he performs." Rusty held back the hardy chuckle straining his lungs.

"Daddy!"

The chuckle burst loose from Rusty, filling the room with his good humor, releasing the tension that hung in the air like a dark rain cloud. "Don't think about the other women he's been with, not even Dina. Those women are a part of his past. You, Addy McConnell, could damn well be his future."

"I hope you're right, Daddy. I hope I have a future—" hastily she added "—with Nick."

He stood just outside the open door of Addy's bedroom, watching while she packed. She was very neat, every item folded and placed with precise care. On top of her slacks, blouses and sweaters lay her lingerie, skimpy little tidbits of silk and lace and sheer nylon in colors from the palest flesh tone to the most lush, vivid purple. He couldn't help but imagine what sort of frothy satin temptations she was wearing beneath her walking shorts and cotton pullover.

The antique grandfather clock in the hallway struck ten times. In less than seven hours he would take Addy away from her home, away from the familiar routine of her daily life. Only four people knew where they were going—the two of them, Sam Dundee and Elizabeth Mallory, the woman who owned the cottage where they'd stay for the next two weeks.

Nick wondered what would happen when they got to Sequana Falls, Georgia. How was he going to spend two weeks alone with a woman he desperately wanted, without seducing her into his bed? He'd never been in this predicament before, wanting a woman who needed more than temporary pleasure from him. Addy wanted him to prove himself to her, and the only way he could bed her and walk away without feelings of remorse and guilt was to give her what she wanted. Somehow, some way, he had to prove to Addy that she and she alone meant more to him than anything else on earth. Since he was fast coming to feel that way about her, he figured there had to be a way to prove it.

Addy's ex-husband had used her and abused her, emotionally if not physically. She was afraid to give herself to another man, unsure of his motives. Because of past experience, she'd come to the conclusion that men who showed an interest in her were after Rusty's money. Hell, he didn't give a hoot about her father's millions. If he'd wanted to marry for money, he could have done so more than once over the years. He bedded women who attracted him, women who turned him on. He had enough money to meet his needs. He neither wanted nor needed more. But he did want Addy McConnell, and he needed her, needed her in his arms, in his bed and in his life, as he had never needed another woman. Once he'd had her, it was going to take a lot of long, slow loving…a lot of hot, wild mating…to get enough of her to satisfy his craving.

"What are you doing lurking out there in the hall?" Addy closed the suitcase lid, zipped it, then set it on the floor beside her bed.

"I wasn't lurking." Nick stepped over the threshold and into her room, instantly feeling as if he'd entered a forbidden zone. "I was just watching you pack. Are you sure you got everything you need in one bag?"

"It's a big bag." She sat down on the edge of her pencil-post mahogany bed. "Besides, you said to pack light."

"I've never needed more than one suitcase." He

glanced at her, noticing how at ease she seemed alone in her room with him.

"You've been traveling most of your life, haven't you?" She crossed her legs at the ankles.

Nick couldn't take his eyes off her legs, her long, slim legs that beckoned for his touch. "I don't own a house or even rent an apartment. I didn't need one when I was in the Navy, and when I was between DEA assignments, I'd either visit my grandmother in El Paso, get a hotel room or stay with my buddies Nate Hodges in St. Augustine and Sam Dundee in Atlanta."

"You've never mentioned Nate Hodges before. How long have you been friends?"

"Since SEAL training in Coronado." Nick's dark eyes glazed over with memory. "We were both a couple of eighteen-year-old half-breeds running from lives we hated, hoping to find something worthwhile. What we found was a living hell in Nam."

Addy wanted to run to Nick, to throw her arms around him and hold him close. She could tell by the tone of his voice, more than the words he spoke, that he was so alone, that he'd been alone all his life—a man always on the outside looking in. She longed to bring him inside, into the warmth and caring in her heart, to show him that he never had to be alone again.

"Daddy was in Korea. He never talks about it. He has this old-fashioned notion that women should be protected from life's harsher realities." Her father had tried, unsuccessfully to protect her mother. Sometimes she wondered if Rusty and Madeline had shared more of the agonizing pain and ugly reality of what had happened to their son would her mother have grown stronger instead of weaker in the years following Donnie's murder.

"Women experience most of life's harsh realities,"

Nick said, leaning against the colonial blue wall near the door. "No matter how much a man wants to protect his women, sometimes he's powerless. I think that's how your father feels now."

"He trusts you to keep me safe." Addy stood up, walking over to face Nick directly. "And I trust you."

Damn, how he wanted to pull her into his arms, to taste her sweet mouth, to feel the sleek leanness of her body. "No need to set your alarm clock. I'll wake you at three-thirty, and we'll hit the road by four." He didn't dare stay near her a minute longer, with those bewitching green cat-eyes of hers casting a spell over him.

When he turned to leave, Addy caught his hand, lacing her fingers through his. "Sleep tight then."

Bringing her hand to his lips, he brushed a feathery kiss across her knuckles. He could feel himself tightening, his whole body preparing for a feast to which he hadn't been invited. "Two weeks, Red, and if we're lucky, this will all be over."

"If we're lucky—" she whispered, then released his hand and stood back, watching him walk out of her room and close the door behind him.

Nick felt like beating his cane against the wall or smashing his fist through a window. He hadn't been this horny in years, and in the past, all it would have taken to ease his pain was a willing woman. This time nothing would give him relief except emptying himself into Addy Mc-Connell's receptive body.

The grandfather clock struck midnight. Nick flipped on the bedside lamp, hauled himself out of bed and slipped into his faded jeans, forcing the zipper up over his arousal. He couldn't sleep. Hell, he couldn't even get any rest. Addy was in the room next to him, probably wearing one of her silky nightgowns and sleeping like a baby. She'd told him that she wasn't any good at sex. He didn't believe it. That bastard ex-husband undoubtedly didn't know the first thing about arousing a woman as sensitive and untried as Addy. If only she'd give him half a chance, he'd prove to her what a sensuous creature she really was; he'd give her unbearable pleasure and teach her how good it could be between them.

Retrieving his cane from where he'd propped it against the nightstand, Nick made his way across the room and out into the hall. Addy's door stood open. They both kept their doors open at night so he could hear every sound. Just in case.

Moonlight poured in through the Federalist-style fanlights above the double French doors that flanked each side of the fireplace in Addy's bedroom. The waxed pine floors glistened in the muted light, and the rich reds and blues in the scattered Oriental carpets gleamed like jewels.

Nick stepped inside. Addy lay in the middle of the big bed, shadows of the crocheted canopy drawing lines across her face. She had neatly folded back the white bedspread, laying it over the patchwork sampler quilt that graced the foot of her bed.

He didn't want to wake her, but he *had* to see her, to look at her. Despite the air-conditioned coolness in the house, Nick felt hot. Beads of perspiration dotted his upper lip and a trickle of sweat ran down his throat, getting lost in the mat of black hair that covered his upper chest.

Without warning, his foot banged into something in the semidarkness. He cursed the object, swearing softly under his breath. Looking down, he saw a brass pot filled with red geraniums near the window. If the damned pecking of his cane hadn't awakened Addy, then maybe his bumbling crash into the flower container hadn't, either.

"Nick?" She sat up in bed, throwing off the thin blue sheet that covered her.

"Sorry, Red. I didn't mean to awaken you. I—I thought I heard something," he lied. "I just wanted to check things out. Go back to sleep."

"I wasn't asleep." She slid her legs over the edge of the bed, allowing her feet to touch the floor. "I'm so restless that I can't sleep."

He took a good look at her then and wished he hadn't. She wore a teal-blue satin chemise that barely touched the top of her thighs. He sucked in his breath, calling on all his willpower not to reach out and grab her. Her curly red hair hung loosely about her shoulders and halfway down her back. Tousled and unkempt, it looked as if some man had been running his fingers through it. Dear God, that was exactly what he wanted to do. But he wouldn't stop with her hair—he wouldn't stop touching her until he had covered every inch of her body and counted every little copper freckle.

"I should go and let you try to get some rest. We've got a long drive ahead of us tomorrow."

Addy picked up her teal-blue lace kimono that she'd tossed across the nightstand. Easing into it, she stood. "Don't go." She took a tentative step toward him. "Stay."

"Bad idea, Red." Nick turned from her, starting toward the door.

"Please, don't go, Nick. Stay and...talk to me." She moved closer, her hand hovering over his back, almost touching him.

Keeping his back to her, he drew in a deep breath. "If I stay, Red, I'm going to do a lot more than talk."

"Oh." She trusted Nick with her life. She had even

admitted to her father that she was falling in love with the man. But was she ready for them to make love?

"It's going to happen sooner or later, but there's no need for us to confront it tonight. There'll be time enough when we're alone in an isolated cabin in the middle of the Georgia mountains." He moved forward, taking a step out into the hall.

Addy followed him, touching his back with the palm of her hand. She felt him stiffen. His naked back was sleek and damp and warm. Her hand burned from the physical contact of flesh against flesh. "Don't leave me, Nick. Stay. Stay and prove to me that—"

"Prove to you that I want you more than I've ever wanted another woman? Prove to you that you're all that matters to me?" He turned around slowly, knowing that once he faced her there would be no turning back, knowing exactly what he was going to do and how he was going to prove himself to her. He prayed that he had the will-power to be the man Addy needed tonight.

She looked at him with big, hungry eyes, the expression on her face a mixture of longing and uncertainty. "I don't want to disappoint you."

He threaded his fingers through her hair, then gripped the back of her neck. "Don't you know that there's no way you can disappoint me? Just be yourself, Addy. Be the warm, loving and sensitive woman you are."

"What if—if—"

He moved his hand down her back to her waist, hauling her up against him. The sound of her indrawn breath when her soft body met his hard arousal fueled his hunger, increasing his determination to give this woman—his woman—unforgettable pleasure. "We're going to take things slow, Red. Slow and easy. I'm going to touch you and you're going to touch me, and we're going to make each other burn.''

Gerald had always been in a hurry to find a quick release, never caring whether or not he gave her any pleasure. ''But you're already aroused. You won't want to wait.''

''That's where you're wrong.'' He touched her lips with his, but didn't actually kiss her. She sighed into his mouth. He drew in her sweet breath, running the tip of his tongue across her bottom lip. ''I've never wanted anything the way I want you. Making love is best when it's not rushed, when you take your time and savor every delicious moment. Especially the first time.''

''No one has ever *made love* to me before.''

Gut-wrenching pain twisted his insides. He vowed that he would never hurt her, no matter how much he had to suffer. He would give Addy what no man had ever given her—*ecstasy*. ''I'm going to make love to you, Red. And you're going to make love to me.''

''But, Nick, I don't know how. What if—''

He kissed her, a gentle yet thorough kiss. Withdrawing his mouth from hers, he said, ''Sometimes it's better not to talk so much. Stop talking, stop thinking and start feeling.''

He walked her, backwards, toward the bed. His big hand never left her waist, his arousal stayed pressed against her belly and his lips kept brushing hers as the two of them moved slowly, inch by inch, making their way across the room.

Nick leaned his cane against the nightstand, then took Addy by the shoulders, carefully sliding her kimono down her arms and off her body. He tossed it to the floor. ''I love the way your body is made, Red. All long and lean and sexy.''

"I'm not—" She saw the look in his eyes, that look that said she'd better not disagree with him. "I've never thought of myself as sexy."

"You're the sexiest thing I've ever seen." He placed his hands on her upper arms, moving his fingers in gentle caresses downward, stopping at her fingertips. Slipping his fingers between hers, he stroked her.

She leaned into him, sighing at the unexpected pleasure his seemingly innocent touch created within her. "Nick?"

He ran his hands up and over her back, pausing briefly before cupping her buttocks. "You've got such a tiny waist and such a firm, tempting little butt."

He'd told her to stop talking and start feeling, but he hadn't stopped talking, and every word he said was driving her crazy. Did he know what he was doing to her? Was he aware of how arousing his words were?

Lowering his head, Nick took one tight, little nipple into his mouth while he continued kneading her derriere. Addy moaned when spirals of heated sensation darted outward and downward, pulling on her femininity, plucking the strings of a heretofore unknown passion. Instinctively, she raised her leg, brushing it against his, rubbing him intimately. He slipped his hand beneath her chemise, touching her stomach, then easing around to cup her naked behind.

For one heart-stopping moment, Nick thought he was going to lose it. All he could think about was ramming himself into her, seeking and finding the sheathing heat of her body, emptying himself and gaining relief for his unbearable ache. "I want to see you, all of you."

When he tugged her chemise upward, Addy placed her hands over his, momentarily halting him. "You'll think I'm skinny, that my breasts are too small, that my freckles are ugly."

"Damn!" Nick spit out.

Addy pulled away from him. He reached out, jerking her to him, taking her mouth with bruising force as he thrust his tongue inside her welcoming warmth. Heaven. That's what it was to be inside her. Sheer heaven. She didn't resist the fury of his kiss or the roughness of his hands as they skimmed her body, finally pulling her chemise up and over her head.

With his lips still touching hers, Nick gave her a gentle shove backward, tumbling her onto the bed. He came down with her, half on top of her, half beside her. "I'm not your ex-husband, Red. I'm no fool. I know that having a woman like you to care for me is worth ten times whatever money your daddy has in the bank."

Tears filled her eyes. She wiped them away with the tips of her fingers. She lay there totally naked, Nick's big, aroused body partially covering her. "Look at me, Nick, and tell me what you see. And, please, don't—don't pretend."

Raising himself on one elbow, he gazed down at her, then swallowed hard. Addy McConnell was as sleek and lean as the most prized thoroughbred. Her arms and legs were long and covered with a light dusting of copper freckles. Her hips flared slightly away from her minuscule waist. Her breasts were small, but high and firm, topped with golden coral nipples. And the hair between her legs was as fiery red as the curls framing her pretty face. "You're beautiful, Addy. I've never seen anything more beautiful."

"Oh, Nick." She reached out, opening her arms and her heart. She believed he meant what he said. He really did think she was beautiful.

"And your freckles are gorgeous. As a matter of fact, I've had more than one fantasy about kissing every freckle on your body." He kissed each one on her face. "You've got a lot of freckles, Addy. It could take me hours to taste all of them.''

She didn't know how long it took Nick to accomplish the task. Eventually she lost track of time, giving herself over completely to the hedonistic upheaval going on in her body. She'd never known that a man could give so freely, titillating a woman with his hands and mouth as if he wanted nothing more than to please her.

Addy's breasts became so sensitized that even Nick's breath on them sent chills of agonized longing through her. When he took her into his mouth, she cried out, writhing beneath him, pushing herself upward, begging for relief from the excruciating pressure building in the core of her body. While he continued to suckle her, he slipped his hand between her thighs. She opened for him. He slid two fingers inside her, testing her. She bucked upward, crying and groaning, pleading with him.

"Easy, Red, easy. I'm going to take good care of you." His fingers sought and found the pleasure point hidden within her.

With a steady, gentle pressure, he massaged her, all the while his mouth tugged greedily on one of her breasts and his thumb and forefinger pinched at her other puckering nipple. He could feel her body tightening. "That's it, Red, let it happen. Don't hold back. Give in to what you're feeling." When the first spasm hit her, Nick increased the speed and pressure of his fingers, bringing her to the pinnacle, intensifying her pleasure. She screamed, her voice a ragged, tormented cry of release. He soothed her trembling body, kissing her closed eyelids, her nose, her open mouth.

When her heartbeat slowed and she was able to breath again, she opened her eyes and looked up at him. "I've never...you made me—oh, Nick.''

He took her mouth as he longed to take her body. But it was too soon. She wasn't ready, despite the fact that he'd helped her achieve her first orgasm. He couldn't bury himself deep inside and take his own pleasure. That was not the way to prove himself to Addy. But, dammit all, he had to take just a little something for himself, enough to keep him from going totally insane.

Lifting himself up, he sat on the edge of the bed and pulled off his jeans. Beneath, he wore a pair of black briefs. Hesitating, he considered the consequences if he went ahead and stripped naked, if he disregarded the inner voice that warned him against such foolishness. With one quick jerk, he pulled the briefs down and off, then turned back to Addy.

She could see him in the moonlight, his big, bronze body poised over her. With more passion than knowledge, she touched him, circling his manhood with her fingers. He throbbed beneath her touch as she moved her hand up and down caressingly.

"Red, honey, you're going to have to stop that... sometime in the next few hours." His voice held a trace of humor.

"You like my touch?"

"Did you like mine?"

"You know I did."

He pulled away from her. She stared at him, puzzled. "If you don't stop, I'll lose it."

"I want you to lose it—inside me."

He thought he'd die. She was asking him to make love to her, completely, thoroughly. "Tonight's for you, Red. For your pleasure. If I take you the way you're asking, then I won't have proven anything to you."

She had to consider what he'd said for several minutes before she realized what he meant; then she smiled.

"You've already proven everything you need to prove to me."

"I've got to prove something to myself." He kissed her savagely, then eased his tongue over her chin, down her throat and across her breasts to her stomach.

"Nick?" She felt the tremors of excitement building again, growing stronger with each swipe of his talented tongue.

"There's so many things I want to do to you, so many ways I want to make love to you." He lifted her hips in his big hands, bringing her body upward so that he could taste her. She tried to pull away. He held fast. "Let me, Red. Please, let me."

She gave in to his plea, never realizing the earth-shattering rapture that awaited her. She became lost in a fog of sensation where the world centered on Nick's mouth and her pulsating flesh. With uncontrollable convulsions Addy's body took the pleasure Nick gave her, rejoicing in each pounding quake of fulfillment.

Afterward she clung to him, weeping warm, salty tears of joy. When he pulled away from her, she reached out, grasping at air. He stood, then picked up his jeans and cane.

"Nick? What are you doing?"

"I'm going to take a shower, Red. I can't stay. If I do, I'm going to ram myself into you so hard, I'll rip you apart."

"Don't leave me. Stay. I want—I want us to really make love. I want you to—"

Nick turned and left the room. Addy lay there feeling satisfied and yet unfulfilled. Why had she ever told Nick that he'd have to prove himself to her? And why was he being so stubborn? The only thing she could figure out was that her father had been right. Nick Romero was falling in love with her and he didn't even know it. No man would put himself through such torment to prove himself worthy of a woman he didn't love.

Addy heard the shower running. She smiled. With a confidence born of her newly awakened feminine powers, she slipped out of bed and made her way down the hall to the bathroom. The door wasn't locked. Obviously, Nick didn't think she'd follow him. But he was wrong.

Moving as quietly as she possibly could, Addy crept toward the shower, eased open the glass door and stepped inside.

"What the hell? Addy?"

Without saying a word, she bent to her knees in front of him. The tepid water poured down over them. Nick reached out, taking her by her shoulders. "Get up, Red. You don't have to do this."

"I want to do this," she assured him, and proceeded to prove to him just how much.

Chapter 9

The hazy, muted light of dawn spread across the eastern horizon like distant candlelight seen through gauze curtains. The hum of the Bronco's motor kept time to the dull drone of the four-wheel drive's big tires as they moved over the asphalt roadway. Nick glanced in his rearview mirror. The nondescript brown sedan was still there. He had first noticed the car when they drove through Paint Rock, a wide-place-in-the-road town not too far outside of Huntsville. It was possible that the driver was simply headed in the same direction they were; it was also possible that he was following them.

Nick heard Addy sigh. Looking down at her head resting against his shoulder, he readjusted his arm that was draped around her. She'd been asleep for the past half hour. She needed rest. Neither of them had slept much last night.

When he thought about what had happened—and he hadn't been able to think of much else—he could hardly believe it. Not only had he made love to Addy more unselfishly than he'd ever made love to any other woman, but he experienced a kind of satisfaction he'd never known. He'd never felt so much like a man, never felt so strong as when he'd brought Addy to completion. Not once, but twice. Her cries of fulfillment had given him a precious pleasure. But when she had come to him in the shower, showing him how much she trusted him, how much she cared for him, he had been humbled and weakened by her generosity and love.

The very thought of her hands circling, her tongue tasting, her lips caressing, her mouth taking, hardened his manhood to an uncomfortable rigidity. Tonight... Tonight they would make love completely. He'd bury himself so deep inside her that he'd become a part of her, and then she would truly be his—his woman, in a way no other woman had ever been.

Just past the outskirts of South Pittsburg, Tennessee, Nick turned the Bronco onto the on-ramp of Interstate 24 and headed straight into the morning sun, which had just appeared, flashing its dazzling golden light like a wealthy woman displaying her array of diamond jewelry. Addy snuggled closer to his side; Nick ran his hand up and down her arm. God, he loved the feel of her. Lean and sleek, yet utterly soft and feminine.

He glanced in the rearview mirror. The brown sedan exited the on-ramp. Only a cherry-red Pinto separated the other car from the Bronco. Still a coincidence? Nick wondered. Maybe, maybe not. He'd wait and see. Before they went through Chattanooga, he'd have to find out one way or the other.

He didn't want to bother Addy with any undue worry, but if he had to make a hasty detour to discern the motive of the sedan driver, then he'd have to forewarn her. Although he'd found out just how strong and resilient Addy

McConnell was, he knew that she had a breaking point. Everyone did. He wanted to get her to Georgia, to their private sanctuary deep in the mountains, where she would feel safe and secure…where they would have two weeks of undisturbed lovemaking.

Addy opened her eyes. Sunshine streamed through the Bronco's windows. She shut her eyes tightly, blocking out the blinding light. When she squirmed against Nick, he petted her, his big hand moving up and down her arm. She sighed, breathing in the clean, masculine scent that was Nick Romero—the man she loved.

Prizing her eyes open a second time, she squinted, then lowered her lids half closed and looked up at Nick, who was totally absorbed in driving. He was a man who concentrated on the task at hand, giving it his complete attention. Last night he had given her his thorough devotion, proving beyond a shadow of a doubt how much she meant to him. Recalling what he'd done to her—for her—sent tingling, reminiscent sensations spiraling through her body. He had made her feel everything, teaching her what a sensuous woman she was, proving to her how wrong Gerald had been about her. Nick made her feel needed… desired…beautiful.

If she lived to be two hundred, she would never forget going to him, slipping into the shower beside him and loving him as erotically as he had loved her. She had acted purely on instinct, driven by desire, prompted by love.

When Nick had reached fulfillment, his body had trembled with the force of his satisfaction. And she had gloried in the knowledge that she had given him pleasure. The experience had been raw, primitive, totally physical. The aftermath had been warm and tender and loving. Nick had dried them both, then walked her back to her bedroom and tucked her in, refusing to stay the few remaining hours of the night in her bed. She'd known he didn't trust himself not to make love to her again and again. It was what she'd wanted, but Nick wanted to wait. Tonight…ah, yes… tonight.

Closing her eyes, Addy slipped her arm around Nick's waist, giving him a gentle hug. "Where are we?"

Squeezing her arm, he glanced down at her, then returned his concentration to the interstate. "Crossing through the tip of Georgia. We aren't far from Chattanooga."

She raised up, moving slightly away from him. He removed his arm from around her and placed his hand on the steering wheel. Stretching, Addy yawned. "I didn't sleep very long then?"

"Less than an hour. You need more rest. You had a busy night last night." His lips curved into a smile as he remembered just what had kept them both so busy. Damn, how he would have liked to pull off the interstate, find a secluded stretch of road and take her hard and fast right there in the Bronco.

Addy saw him smile and felt a staining warmth in her cheeks. She punched him playfully on the arm. "Not as busy as it should have been." She couldn't believe she'd actually said that. What was happening to her? Loving Nick Romero, that was what was happening to her.

"Since we got some preliminaries out of the way last night, I'd say we were both ready to get down to some serious lovemaking tonight."

Addy laughed, the sound light, almost carefree. He'd done that for her, she thought. He was teaching her to enjoy herself, to trust her own instincts and give herself permission to play and have fun.

He hated the thought of having to tell her about the brown sedan, but he had no choice. They'd be in Chattanooga soon, and he couldn't allow the car to continue following them.

Noticing the pensive look on his face, Addy wondered what had caused it. "Are you worrying about your Jag? If you are, let me set your mind at rest. It's as safe as in Fort Knox in Daddy's garages along with his collection."

"Yeah, I'm sure it is."

"Daddy's still bothered by the fact that he doesn't know where we'll be," she said. "I could tell by the sound of his voice when we talked to him before we left."

"I'll call Sam every day, and he'll give your father a report."

"Daddy didn't like it when you suggested that it was best he didn't know too much, that way he couldn't accidentally slip up and tell Dina anything."

"I explained to Rusty why I felt that way." Nick glanced in the rearview mirror. Damn! He would have to make his move soon. "Dina might tell Brett Windsor, and I don't trust the guy. He might not be top on my list of suspects, but he's definitely still on the list."

"I think Brett is sweet—in a little-boy sort of way."

"Red, you don't need a sweet little boy, you need a hot-blooded man."

She ran the tips of her short, neatly manicured fingernails up the side of his neck, stopping to tease his earlobe. "And that's exactly what I have, isn't it, Mr. Romero?"

"Damn right." He clutched her knee, squeezing possessively, then slid his hand between her thighs. He wanted to find a way inside her tan slacks, inside her silk panties, to delve into the hot, moist depths of her body. But now wasn't the time or the place. Reluctantly, he returned his hand to the steering wheel.

"Look, Red, we're going to have to make a slight detour."

"Why?"

"A brown sedan has been following us ever since we went through Paint Rock. I've got to check him out. Understand?" He sneaked a quick glance in her direction. Her smile disappeared.

"Do you think…I mean, could it be…*him?*" Cold, numbing fear clutched her pounding heart and spread icy tendrils through her stomach.

"I don't know." Nick saw the sign that read Tiftonia exit. It would be one of the last exits before reaching downtown. Easing into the turning lane, he slowed the Bronco.

"What are you going to do?"

"See if he follows us."

"And if he does?"

"Confront him."

She sucked in a deep breath, then let out a long, slow sigh. "That could be dangerous."

"It would be even more dangerous to let this guy find out where we're going." Nick exited the interstate. The brown sedan did the same. Damnation!

"Did he follow us?" Addy started to turn her head.

"Don't look back. I can see him in the mirror. He's right behind us."

Nick saw a service station a few yards away. There were no cars around. The place looked deserted. He couldn't tell whether it hadn't opened for the day or if it had recently gone out of business.

Nick whipped the Bronco into the service station, then cut the motor. Opening the glove compartment, he reached inside and pulled out a .38 revolver. He saw the startled look in Addy's green eyes and wished to high heaven he didn't have to put the gun in her hands.

The brown sedan pulled in, parking on the other side of the station.

"Take this," he said, handing it to her.

Addy glared at the gun as if it were a live snake. With trembling hands she reached out, accepting the deadly weapon. "I don't know how to use this thing."

"Don't aim it unless you intend to use it. If your target is at close range, all you have to do is pull the trigger and you'll hit him somewhere. Just keep shooting until you empty the gun."

"Nick, you're frightening me. You're talking like you won't be coming back."

Leaning over, he kissed her forehead, then gave her shoulders a sound squeeze. "This is just a precautionary measure, Red. I'm coming back just as soon as I find out who this guy is and what he wants."

Turning, Nick opened the door. Addy grabbed the back of his shirt. He glanced over his shoulder. "Please be careful," she said.

"Stay in the Bronco and keep the doors locked."

Addy watched while Nick opened the back of the Bronco, pulled his battered suitcase toward him, unsnapped it and reached inside. He pulled out an automatic, and holding the gun in one hand and his cane in the other he approached the parked car. Addy held her breath. Seconds turned into minutes, minutes that seemed hours long.

She saw the car door open and a man emerge. From thirty yards away, Addy couldn't make out his features, but she could tell that he was shorter than Nick, with a stocky build. He hadn't pulled a weapon on Nick. That was a good sign. Then suddenly Nick punched the man in the chest with his cane. Addy's heart stopped. She gripped the heavy gun in her hands, her palms slippery with moisture.

"Dammit, man, I could have killed you!" Nick removed his cane from the man's chest. "Of all the stupid things for Rusty McConnell to do! I told him I didn't want any of Dundee's men following us."

"Mr. McConnell insisted. Hell, Nick, what was I supposed to do? The man is paying the bills, you know. Sam is working for McConnell, so that means I'm working for McConnell."

"Hugh, you should have checked in with Sam before you left. He would have counteracted Rusty's order."

"I'm sorry, Nick. I should have known you'd spot me." Hugh grinned, but Nick didn't. "As a matter of fact, I knew that you were on to me the minute you exited the interstate. That's why I pulled in here."

"There's a lady over there in that Bronco who's scared half out of her mind." Nick slipped the automatic into the back of his pants, anchoring it beneath his belt. "You get on your phone and call her daddy and tell him that his overprotective tactics didn't work, that all he accomplished was to frighten Addy. Then tuck tail and run back to Huntsville as fast as you can."

"Mr. McConnell is going to be madder than hell."

"I'm already madder than hell, Hugh. Who would you rather deal with, Rusty McConnell or me?" Nick spoke the words in a deep, even tone, yet each syllable dripped with menace.

"I get your point, Nick," Hugh said. "I'll call Mr. McConnell and tell him what happened. If he has any problems with my returning to Huntsville, he can call Sam."

"Good idea." Nick turned and walked away, leaving Hugh to jump back inside his brown sedan.

The moment she saw Nick walking toward the Bronco, Addy slid across the bench seat and unlocked the door.

Nick bent down and got inside. Addy had a death grip on the revolver. Prying her hands loose from the .38, he placed it back inside the glove compartment, then pulled her into his arms.

"Oh, Nick—Nick—"

"Shh—shh— It's all right, Addy. Everything's fine."

"Who—who was he?"

"Hugh Talbot, one of Sam Dundee's men. Your father sent him to follow us."

She raised her head, her tear-filled eyes widening in surprise. "But you told Daddy that you didn't want anyone riding shotgun. Isn't that what you said?"

"Yeah, that's exactly what I said, but your old man had other ideas." Damn, he hated the way she was trembling, the way her voice quivered.

She clung to him, seeking comfort and reassurance. "I was so afraid something would happen to you, Nick. I—I couldn't bear it if anything happened to you."

"Nothing's going to happen to me, Red. And nothing is going to happen to you. We're going to the mountains for two weeks of seclusion." He tilted her chin, then gave her a quick, hard kiss. "And during those two weeks, we'll belong to each other, body and soul. I'm going to teach you to laugh and love and enjoy yourself."

"And what am I going to teach you?" Addy stared at him, her face filled with innocence, her eyes as starry bright as an adolescent girl's who'd fallen in love for the first time.

Nick pondered her question. A sharp, foreboding chill raced up his spine. What was Addy McConnell going to teach him? That all women weren't mercenary whores or party-girl blondes who'd slept with more men than they could count? That there were women in this world a man could trust with his heart and count on when the chips were down?

"You're going to teach me how to make you happy, Red, because that's what I want more than anything."

The late-afternoon sun blazed hot and bright, dancing off the hood of the navy blue Bronco. Inside, Nick and Addy remained cool. He watched the road signs while she dozed on and off, fitful in her uneasy sleep. He hadn't been to Sequana Falls in years, not since the summer Elizabeth Mallory had been eighteen, shortly after she'd graduated from college. Sam's young ward was brilliant. Her genius had become apparent at an early age, even before Sam's older brother had married Elizabeth's widowed mother. How old was Elizabeth now? Nick wondered. Twenty-two? Twenty-three? And did she still possess the clairvoyant powers that had driven Sam Dundee to the edge of madness?

Addy had fallen asleep again shortly after they'd exited the interstate and started making their way along the Georgia back roads leading to the mountains. The closer they came to their destination, the cooler the climate. But even at the higher altitude, the July sun proved a relentless adversary. Thank God for air-conditioning. But if he remembered correctly, Elizabeth's great-grandmother's cottage didn't have air-conditioning. Hell!

He saw the sign. Dover's Mill. It wouldn't be long now. Dover's Mill was the last incorporated town before reaching Sequana Falls, which wasn't located on any map. It had been a small settlement deep in the mountains, where a family of Scotch-Irish settlers named Ogilvie had put down roots. Their youngest daughter, Sequana, had married a half-breed Indian. Elizabeth Mallory was their descendant. So in her veins flowed the blood of two ancient peoples—the Cherokees and the Celts.

Addy roused from her brief nap. Rubbing her eyes, she looked like a sleepy little girl. "I can't seem to stay awake."

"Traveling does that to some people," Nick said.

"How close are we to Sequana Falls?"

"Just a few miles."

"Sam must know this Elizabeth Mallory well to ask such a favor of her and to trust her implicitly." Addy rubbed the back of her neck and stretched her long legs out as far as she could in the confinement of the Bronco.

"She was his ward."

"From what I know about Sam Dundee, he doesn't seem the type to take on such a personal kind of responsibility."

"You're right about that." Nick grinned, thinking about his old DEA buddy. Sam Dundee didn't make friends easily. He was a brooding, cynical sonofabitch whose keen mind and sharp instincts had won him the respect of every man who knew him. Few liked Dundee; all feared him. Nick would match his own warrior's skills against anyone's, but in a fight he'd sure as hell want Sam Dundee and Nate Hodges on his side. Luckily for him, the two men were his best friends.

"Why did he?" Addy asked.

"Why did he what?"

"Why did Sam Dundee accept the responsibility of a ward?"

"His older brother, James, married Elizabeth's mother when Elizabeth was just a kid. James and Sandra died when Elizabeth was around twelve or thirteen." Up until his brother's death, Nick had seldom heard Sam talk about his family. But on occasion, usually after several drinks,

Sam would mention Elizabeth. Nick wondered if Dundee had ever sorted out his feelings for the girl.

"How tragic, for all of them."

"Yeah." Nick maneuvered the four-wheel drive off the main highway and onto a stretch of gravel road. "Here's the turn-off to Sequana Falls."

"The road isn't even paved," Addy said, as she felt the jostling movements of the Bronco as it traveled over an uneven assortment of pebbles and rocks.

"This place is totally isolated. That's why it's perfect for our needs."

Addy stared at the towering trees, tall, majestic and ancient, that lined their pathway to Sequana Falls. Sunlight dappled down through the thick foliage, spattering shadows and shimmers across the road. The silence was eerie. After more than five miles, a clearing appeared. A cluster of small cabins lay on either side of them. They passed by, leaving the cabins behind. Another mile into the deep woods, a smaller clearing appeared. Set dead center was a circular driveway in front of an enormous, sprawling, two-story log cabin. A gigantic porch circled the house.

"This is Elizabeth's home." Nick pulled the Bronco up in front, directly behind an old, mud-splattered jeep.

"Where's our cabin?"

"Deeper in the woods, if you can believe it. And Elizabeth refers to her great-grandmother's house as a cottage, not a cabin."

"It's not a cabin?"

"The last time I saw the place it was painted white. It looked as out of place in these woods as we do."

Nick climbed down out of the Bronco. Addy didn't wait for him to make his way around to her side. Opening the door, she jumped down.

"Y'all made good time," a young woman standing on

the front porch called out to them. "Welcome to Sequana Falls."

Addy shaded her eyes from the hazy afternoon sun. Looking toward the sound of the rich, melodious voice, she saw one of the most stunning women she'd ever seen in her life. Elizabeth Mallory's hourglass figure could not be disguised in the faded denim shorts and pale apricot cotton blouse. She was barefoot and braless. Her breasts swelled together like round, ripe melons.

Addy moved closer. Elizabeth descended the wooden stairs leading down from the wraparound porch.

"Elizabeth, let me introduce you to—" Nick said.

"Adeline McConnell," Elizabeth finished his sentence. "I'm so glad you're here, Addy. I hope Sequana Falls gives you the respite from worry and sorrow that you're seeking."

"Thank you." Addy couldn't stop staring at the other woman, whose beauty was almost ethereal. Her light, golden complexion was flawless, her eyes a deep, pure blue and her rich, coffee-brown hair had been French-braided and hung in one long plait to her waist.

"I know you'll want to go straight to the cottage so you can settle in and freshen up." Elizabeth approached Addy, a warm smile of greeting on her lovely face. "But I'm expecting you to share supper with me tonight."

"That's not necessary," Nick said. "We don't want to impose."

"It isn't an imposition." Elizabeth extended her hand to Addy. "It's so seldom we have visitors."

Addy felt the strength in the other woman's grasp as they exchanged a handshake. Elizabeth gazed into Addy's eyes, showing a depth of compassion and understanding that puzzled Addy. "We'd be honored to join you."

Elizabeth released her hand. "That's settled then."

Reaching into her shorts pocket, she handed Nick an elaborately carved antique key. "There's only one path in and out to Granny's cottage. The only way you can reach it is on foot."

"No problem." Nick nodded toward the Bronco. "We packed light. One suitcase each."

"You won't need many clothes while you're here," Elizabeth said, a twinkle of mischief in her big blue eyes.

"I'll have to come down to your cabin once a day to phone Sam," Nick said. "I hope that won't pose a problem for you."

"I look forward to hearing from Sam on a daily basis. He seldom phones and hasn't been here since last Christmas." Elizabeth turned back toward her cabin. "If you'd like, I can have O'Grady bring your bags later."

"Is that old rascal still alive?" Nick asked, remembering the withered old man who must have been at least seventy the last time he'd seen him.

"Not only still alive, but still strong as an ox and stubborn as a mule." Elizabeth's smile created a radiance about her, an invisible but highly sensory light. "He and MacDatho have gone fishing this afternoon."

"Who the devil is MacDatho?" Nick opened the back of the Bronco, pulling forward his tattered leather suitcase and then Addy's expensive paisley-print bag.

"Oh, that's right, MacDatho wasn't born the last time you visited here." Elizabeth paused on the top step, just before reaching the porch. "You remember my German shepherd, Elspeth, don't you? Well, MacDatho is her son, born only a year before Elspeth died."

Nick handed Addy her suitcase, then returned to the Bronco for his own. "We'll head on over to the cottage. I think we can manage these two pieces of luggage. No need to bother O'Grady."

Elizabeth stood on the porch, backing slowly into the cool shadows. "Follow the path behind the cabin. It will lead you straight to the cottage." Opening the front door, she paused briefly. "I'll see you both tonight."

During the ten-minute trek through the woods, Addy and Nick spoke very little. Nick was busy surveying the area, apparently sizing up how inaccessible the cottage would be to any unwanted visitors. Addy spent the time absorbing the beauty surrounding her. She'd enjoyed so many happy hours of her childhood playing on the vast lawns of Elm Hill, but she'd never been in the mountains before, in the middle of the woods.

Addy stopped in her tracks. Nick almost collided with her back. Wobbling slightly, he steadied himself with his cane.

"What's wrong?" he asked.

"Oh, Nick, look!"

He gazed off into the distance, at the small house that looked as if someone had dropped an A-frame Victorian dollhouse in the tiny clearing. The white paint was peeling slightly in spots, giving the structure an antique, weathered appearance. A rickety picket fence enclosed a neat little front yard.

"It's unbelievable," Addy said. "It's like something out of a fairy tale."

"Elizabeth calls it the honeymoon cottage because her great-grandfather had it built for her great-grandmother as a wedding gift, and they spent their honeymoon there and each anniversary for the next forty-some odd years of their lives."

Thoroughly enchanted, Addy walked toward the gate that hung open as if issuing an invitation. "There's something different about Elizabeth. I can't quite put my finger on it, but there's something—she's so serene...so..."

"Mystical?"

"Yes, mystical. You felt it, too, didn't you? What is it about her, do you suppose?"

"You mean you haven't guessed?" Nick followed Addy up the rock walk and onto the porch.

"Guessed what?" Addy paused, setting her suitcase down while she reached out for the key Nick held in his hand.

He gave her the key. "Elizabeth is a clairvoyant."

"You mean she can predict the future?" Addy grasped the key, half doubting, half believing Nick's assessment of Elizabeth Mallory.

"That's only one of her special powers," Nick said. "Just wait until tonight when you get the chance to know her better."

Addy inserted the key in the lock and turned the door-knob. She'd never known a clairvoyant and wasn't quite sure she believed in such a thing, but she knew one thing for certain. She definitely was looking forward to asking Elizabeth a few pertinent questions about the future.

Chapter 10

Cozy and old-fashioned, exuding homey warmth and tranquillity, Elizabeth Mallory's kitchen smelled of cinnamon. Rustic wood blended with creamy beige paint on all the walls, and worn, faded red bricks covered the floor. A humid night breeze fluttered the aged lace curtains at the open windows.

Addy spooned the last bite of apple cobbler into her mouth, the melted vanilla ice cream coating the crust with a milky sauce. "You really shouldn't have gone to so much trouble for us."

"It wasn't any trouble," Elizabeth said, rising from the round oak table, her ankle-length blue skirt swirling around her legs. "Aunt Margaret made the cobbler this morning before she left for Dover's Mill, and O'Grady caught and cleaned the fish."

"I noticed that you still don't have any air-conditioning at the cottage," Nick said, glancing out the window facing the back porch. "You haven't put in any here at your house, either, have you?"

"The cottage is seldom used." Elizabeth sighed, the sound barely discernible, but the dreamy, faraway look in her eyes was quite visible. "It's really a honeymoon cottage, you know. The last honeymooners who used it were my mother and James Dundee."

"I know it's a lot cooler up here in the mountains, but July is hot, even here." Nick wiped a fine sheen of perspiration from his forehead.

"Things will cool off later." Elizabeth began stacking their dinner plates. "It's going to rain sometime after midnight." Placing the dirty dishes by the sink, she turned on the faucet.

Addy stood, removing the used silverware from the dark-blue place mats. "Let me help you clean up. It's the least I can do after you served us such a feast."

Pushing back his chair, Nick stood and grasped his cane from where he'd propped it against the side of the table. "I think now would be the ideal time for me to call Sam and check in."

"Trying to get out of helping with the dishes?" Addy asked, smiling.

"The call should take a while." Nick grinned at both women, who were giving him pleasant but condemning looks. "I'll probably finish up just in time for another glass of iced tea." Not waiting for a response, he left the kitchen, the tapping of his cane as it hit the wooden floor reverberating in the silent hallway.

Addy pulled her cotton blouse away from her damp body, fanning the material against her chest. "I hope you're right about the rain cooling things off."

Elizabeth slipped the glasses and silver into the sudsy dish water. "Here in the mountains rain always brings relief from the heat. It's seldom this humid—only just before a storm.''

''You're sure about the rain, aren't you?''

''I'm sure.''

Addy pulled a glass from its watery bed, enclosing it in a soft, well-worn dish towel. ''Nick said that you were… clairvoyant.''

Elizabeth's laughter was warm and throaty, the utterly feminine sound mesmerizing. Addy stared at the beautiful woman standing beside her and saw the knowledge that lay in the depths of her pure blue eyes.

''Are you curious, Addy? Wondering what I know about you?''

''I'm being rude. Please, forgive me.'' A dim flush of embarrassment colored Addy's cheeks.

''You weren't being rude, just curious. And there's nothing to forgive.'' Elizabeth laid the clean cobbler dish on the drainboard. ''We'll let the rest soak. Why don't we go sit on the back porch for a spell?''

Addy dried her hands and followed Elizabeth out onto the wide wooden back porch, which was simply an extension of the front and side porches. Several sturdy wooden rocking chairs were lined up against the south wall. Each woman sat, rocking her chair toward the center until they faced each other. Elizabeth reached out, taking both of Addy's hands into her own.

''You've come to Sequana Falls for two weeks, to wait out a danger that exists for you in Huntsville.'' Elizabeth smiled when Addy gasped. ''I didn't gain this knowledge from second sight, my friend. Sam filled me in on the pertinent details.''

''Oh.''

''You'll leave here before two weeks,'' Elizabeth said, running the pad of her thumb over Addy's knuckles. ''The reason is unclear…but…your father—your father will need you.''

Addy felt her heartbeat accelerate, wondering if she dare believe this winsome young woman's prediction. "There's no way you could know who—I mean someone is plotting against us…my father and his company.''

"I do not know the identity behind the threats." Elizabeth patted Addy's hand, then gave it a tight squeeze. "I have no control over the knowledge that comes to me and don't understand why some things are so clear in my mind and other things are obscured.''

Addy pulled away, Elizabeth relinquished her hold. "It's a little cooler out here. If only the breeze wasn't so warm and humid.''

"Do you like flowers, Addy? If you do, I'll show you my greenhouse one day while you're here. I grow my own herbs and spices, too, but my prize possessions are my roses.''

"I love flowers, and I'd like very much to see your greenhouse. I'm sure Nick and I will get bored with all this peace and quiet after a few days.''

A shuddering boom of distant thunder echoed in the moonlit stillness, followed by a sharp zigzag of lightning that dimmed the moon's pale glow. Addy looked up. Dark clouds ambled slowly across the sky.

Neither woman spoke. Only the vibrating resonance of the wooden rocker rounds mating with the wooden porch floor broke the hushed silence. Seconds became minutes and the moments floated away like dandelion fluff on a windy day.

Addy's mind drifted, absorbed with thoughts of the hours to come. Tonight she would be alone with Nick. She already knew that she would give herself to him, but what she didn't know was if they had a future together. She wondered if Elizabeth really could predict. Not moving a muscle in her face or neck, she glanced at the other woman.

"You don't have to be afraid of him." Elizabeth's soft voice carried on the nighttime air, like a soothing whip-poorwill's song. "You're right about him, Addy. Nick Romero is your paladin—and you are and always will be his woman."

Addy felt the words surround her heart, freeing her doubts, but before she could reply, asking the questions that filled her mind, an enormous animal came bounding out of the darkness, leapt up the porch steps and made his way to Elizabeth's side. Addy cringed at the sight of the hairy creature, his keen amber eyes glowing, his sharp teeth visible as he panted heavily.

Elizabeth ran her fingers through the thick pelt of black fur, and the huge animal dropped to his haunches, apparently savoring her affectionate touch. "This is MacDatho. He won't hurt you. He knows you're my friend."

"What—what is he? I thought you said he was a dog."

"He's half German shepherd and half wolf." Elizabeth continued stroking her pet, speaking to him in a low, whispered voice. When MacDatho lowered his head to the floor and closed his eyes, Elizabeth turned to Addy. "You love Nick, but he has not yet put the proper name to his feelings for you. He will."

"Are you saying that Nick loves me?" Addy wished she could believe wholeheartedly in Elizabeth Mallory's power to foretell the future. But would she be a gullible fool if she did?

"It is destined." Closing her eyes, Elizabeth began rocking again. "You and Nick will share a life of deep love and commitment. I see—I see little girls."

"Little girls?" Addy scooted to the edge of her seat,

completely ignoring MacDatho when he raised his head, his topaz gaze riveted to her face.

"Yes. Two little girls. Not twins, but very much alike...except— One has fiery hair and black eyes. The other has black hair and green eyes."

"Our children? Mine and Nick's?" Did she dare believe in this voodoo, this witchcraft? With all her heart and soul she longed to believe.

The back screen door opened. Loud, earsplitting thunder rumbled. Sitting up, MacDatho howled at the cloud-obscured moon.

"We'd better head back to the cottage, Red." Nick stepped outside. "I wouldn't want us to get caught in a downpour."

"It won't rain for hours," Elizabeth said. "How was Sam?"

"He's fine. You know Sam, a man of few words." Nick placed one hand on the back of Addy's chair. "He asked about you, Elizabeth."

Addy could actually feel the pleasure radiating from Elizabeth, like heat from a smoldering blaze. She could tell that Elizabeth cared deeply for Sam Dundee. Her certain knowledge of the other woman's feelings made her wonder how much Elizabeth's earlier comments had been based on natural instincts and how much on clairvoyance.

She saw my children, Addy reminded herself. Nick's children. Nick's little girls.

"Sam will call Rusty tonight and give him a report," Nick told Addy. "Daily reports should keep your father content."

Remembering Elizabeth's warning that they would return to Huntsville before the NASP contract was awarded because her father would need them, Addy said, "When you talk to Sam tomorrow, please find out if Daddy's all right. Ask him to tell Daddy to go for a checkup. I'm worried about his heart and his blood pressure.''

"I'll relay your message." Nick circled her arm, urging her to stand. Addy looked up at him. Dark, hot passion blazed in the depths of his black eyes. Rising from the rocking chair, Addy accepted his extended arm, walking with him down the steps and out onto the pathway. Nick hesitated briefly, turning to say good-night to Elizabeth.

MacDatho howled again, his animal moan blending with the symphony of woodland night creatures. Thunder roared; lightning flashed. High atop the southern edge of the great Appalachian Mountains, Addy McConnell and Nick Romero moved toward their destiny. Tonight, the paladin would claim his woman.

The four-room cottage reeked with steamy heat, the humidity so high that Nick and Addy breathed in the heavy moisture. When they stepped inside, a splintering flash of lightning illuminated the living room. Nick took advantage of the momentary light to visibly scout out the kerosene lamp he knew was sitting on a round wicker table. Feeling his way across to the expanse of windows facing the porch, he found the book of matches lying atop the crocheted doily. Removing the globe, he struck a match and lit the wick. A soft, mellow radiance spread over the room with an ivory luster, casting dancing shadows on the earthy-green, antique wicker furniture, the pale creamy walls and the flowered cushions.

Nick looked at Addy standing just inside the doorway. Her topknot of thick red hair had begun to droop, fiery tendrils curling about her face and neck. Dewdrops of perspiration dotted her face, more abundant than the smattering of freckles that covered her nose. Her cotton blouse clung to her, outlining her tiny waist and high, firm breasts. Her billowy tan slacks hung loosely about her hips.

Tall and slender as a reed, Addy moved gracefully across the room. She possessed the very essence of nature—a fiery warmth, an earthy allure. The amazing thing, Nick realized, was that she had no idea how unbearably beautiful she was to him.

Tonight he would show her.

The wind picked up, swaying the treetops, pushing nearby limbs against the windowpanes. Addy and Nick watched each other, like two hungry animals preparing to attack. Sweat trickled down the curve of Nick's spine, his shirt and jeans absorbing part of the moisture.

Just thinking about Addy, just looking at her made him hard. He'd become aroused on the walk from Elizabeth's cabin. It would be so easy to take Addy quickly and ease his throbbing ache. But he wouldn't—he couldn't. Tonight was going to be a first for her, and he intended to make it a night she'd never forget.

He could see the desire in her eyes, and the uncertainty. She wanted him, but lacked the experience to give her enough confidence to tell him so. Before this night ended, Addy would have confidence. He was going to give her that...and a lot more.

Slow and easy. That's how it was going to be—the first time. Addy needed the steady, progressive stimulation to prepare her for the pleasure to come. Even if it half killed him, he was not going to rush this sexual adventure. It meant too much to her, and to him.

Propping his cane against the table, Nick began unbuttoning his shirt. He watched Addy staring at him, her gaze following his fingers as they slipped each button from its hole. "It's so damned hot. This place could use a few fans."

Addy couldn't take her eyes off Nick, off the bare expanse of chest that lay between the two sides of his open shirt. She wanted to touch him. But he was all the way on the other side of the room, and her feet refused to move. "A fan in the bedroom would be good on a night like this."

"All we need tonight is that old wrought-iron bed. It looks pretty sturdy, don't you think? Big enough for two." He tugged his damp shirt off his shoulders and flung it on the wicker rocking chair on his left.

Addy's heart hammered in her chest. The thought of sharing that antique bed with Nick sent shivers of longing through her. "I wonder why Elizabeth has never run electricity out here to the cottage? If she did, she could put in air-conditioning."

"This house is meant for lovers. An isolated retreat used by people who neither want nor need lights or telephones or televisions or radios." Nick ran his hand down his throat, wiping away the perspiration.

Retrieving his cane, he took a tentative step toward Addy. Not moving, she watched and waited. When he was within arm's reach, he touched her, his finger pressing against her bottom lip. She opened her mouth on a sigh. He slid his finger over her chin, down her throat and ever so slowly slipped it inside her blouse. "You're hot, Addy. Hot and sweaty."

"Maybe—maybe I should take a bath. That should cool me off." She gasped when his finger slipped up and down between her breasts, popping open the top buttons on her blouse.

"Maybe you have on too many clothes." He undid the remaining three buttons, then tugged her blouse out of her slacks, easing it from her body and tossing it atop his shirt. "Isn't that better? Cooler?" Her sheer yellow lace bra did little to conceal her breasts, the dark areolae visible, the tight nipples straining against the flimsy material.

She wasn't cooler; she was hotter. Nick's smoldering gaze scorched her. Erratic tingling sensations tightened her breasts almost painfully. She wanted Nick to touch her there, to put his mouth on her, to suckle her. Memories of last night reminded her body of what it meant to be pleasured by a man who truly cared, a man whose only purpose was to give his woman pleasure.

Dropping his cane to the floor, Nick ran his hands up and down her naked arms. She trembled. "Do you have any idea how much I want you?"

"Oh, Nick." She swayed toward him, hoping he would kiss her.

Thunder shook the cottage. Nick jerked Addy into his arms, one big hand splayed against her back while the other sought and found her bra's catch. White, jagged lightning lit up the night sky. The wind's velocity increased, wailing and moaning as it ripped through the trees and whistled along the side of the house. Nick pulled her bra down her arms and off her body, then rubbed his hard chest against her thrusting breasts.

She flung her arms around his neck, savoring the feel of their nakedness as her nipples stabbed into his chest hair. "Oh, Nick, how can you make me feel like this?"

"Like what?" He kissed her neck, his tongue snaking out to taste her. Moving his fingers between them, he undid the front closure of her slacks, then slid his hands inside, scooting her zipper downward several inches. He grasped her hips, forcing her soft delta into his arousal.

"Like—like I'm going to…explode."

Cradling her naked buttocks in his palms, he petted her. "We're both going to explode…over and over again tonight."

Mimicking his actions, Addy loosened his jeans and slipped her hand inside, positioning it over his manhood, touching him through the thin barrier of his briefs. He pulsated with life. "I never knew I could feel like this. That I could want someone so desperately."

"Do you want me desperately, Addy?" His deep voice was as dark and mysterious as the man himself.

"You know I do." She closed her fingers around him.

"Then prove it." Issuing the command, he prayed she would have the courage to obey.

"I—" She started to say that she didn't know how. But she did. Releasing him and stepping away, yet still facing him, she moved backward, her feet edging slowly toward the open door of the bedroom. She stopped in the doorway.

Nick watched her intently, the shadowy darkness from behind her occasionally lit by lightning and silhouetting her tall, slender body. Gripping the elastic of her yellow lace bikini panties, she slid them down her legs, then kicked them aside. She stood before him, beautifully, irresistibly naked. Her willowy body called to him, the fiery curls hiding her femininity, tempting his touch. The look in her eyes promised him unbearable pleasure, and he knew that Addy would never lie to him.

Removing his jeans and briefs, Nick followed her, his gait a slow, heavy limp. Addy walked toward the mullioned door that led to the porch, opening it to stare through the screen door out into the raging night sky.

Nick came up behind her, putting his arms around her and pulling her naked back and buttocks up against his chest and manhood. His big hands splayed across her belly, his fingers inching downward, downward, until they discovered the treasure hidden beneath her curls. His fingers petted her sensitive nub; her thighs opened and she moaned.

"You're wet and hot. You must want me. Do you, Addy? Do you want me?" His fingers played her, strumming her like an untried instrument on which he could make sweet music.

"Yes," she groaned. "Yes, yes."

He bit her neck, then soothed her flesh with his tongue. "Tell me how much you want me." While the fingers of one hand stayed busy at their task below her waist, he raised his other hand to cup her breast, his thumb flicking back and forth over her distended nipple.

Her knees weakened. She leaned back, resting her slowly dissolving body into his rock-hard frame. He throbbed against her. With a strength born of her passion, she pulled out of his embrace, turning slowly to face him. Her hand hovered over his manhood. She looked up into his desire-hot black eyes, knowing that he was hers, that she possessed as much power over him as he did her. The thought exhilarated her, filling her with the glory of her womanhood. Primeval, pagan urges flowed through her. She embodied the strength and power of femininity. Creation and life were hers.

Slowly, sensuously, Addy eased her hot, sweating body away from Nick. Opening the screen door, she walked onto the porch. A fierce, humid wind whipped her hair loose, flipping it around her naked shoulders like flames from a flickering torch. Nick stood in the doorway and watched her, totally mesmerized by her wild abandon.

She beckoned him to come to her. He obeyed. Bright lightning flashed. Sweat dripped from his big body like moisture from an icy glass on a hot summer day. His bare, bronze chest glistened, his small male nipples pebble-hard. Addy watched a trickle of perspiration clinging to his left nipple. She longed to put her lips on him, to curl her tongue around him and lick away that tiny wet droplet.

The moment he was within arm's length, she lowered her head, moving toward his chest. Her tongue flicked out, capturing the drop of sweat from his nipple. Nick moaned, then grabbed her, his mouth covering hers, his tongue thrusting into her in a parody of a more intimate act. She returned the kiss with all the passion, all the untamed longing she felt. Mouths captured, tongues ravaged, teeth titillated.

Nick dropped to his knees, burying his face in the delta between her thighs. He barely felt the warm, hard surface of the wooden porch beneath him. He was surrounded by the smell and taste of his mate—his woman. Running his hands from her hips to her thighs, he spread her legs apart. She swayed. Adjusting his head at an angle, he delved his tongue, seeking out her sweet nectar. He gripped her buttocks to steady her as her legs began to buckle. When she braced herself on his shoulders, he moved his hands around and up to her breasts, taking their soft, smooth weight. The constant pressure on her femininity and her nipples quickly drove Addy over the brink into a shivering, groaning climax. Nick soothed her as he brought her down to her knees in front of him.

She fell into his arms. The hot, damp air did little to cool their heated bodies. Their hands became wet as they touched each other, exploring one another's bodies as if they were new and uncharted territory. Tender kisses turned wild. Lips sought out every inch of slick, fiery flesh.

"I want it all, Nick," she moaned into his mouth. "I need you inside me."

Knowing he could never make it to the bedroom, let alone to the bed, Nick lay back on the porch floor, pulling Addy on top of him. Bracing her hands above his shoulders, she rubbed her body against his. He grabbed her hips, stopping her.

"Open up for me, Addy."

She spread her legs, pressing against his arousal.

"Now take me, Red. Take me!"

She raised her body, positioning herself. Nick grabbed her by the waist, then waited for her agreement.

"Nick?"

"Together, Red. Let's do it together."

And they did. In one swift, synchronized move they became one. Addy flung her head back, her long red hair cascading down her back, feathering across Nick's legs. He thrust up and into her again and again with a savage urgency that almost sent him tumbling over the edge. He slowed the pace, then stopped, allowing her to take over while he reached for her breasts.

The sensations were so intense that Addy couldn't stop herself from increasing the pace, riding him harder and harder until fulfillment burst inside her like a giant balloon of red-hot pleasure. She screamed out, her throaty voice echoing in the darkness, rivaling the resounding booms of thunder. Spasms of ecstasy shook her body; then she collapsed on top of Nick.

He gave her the time she needed to recover from the series of aftershocks that rocked her. She covered his face with kisses. He ached with his need, nearing the breaking point. With three hard, animalistic surges he found his own satisfaction. He spilled his seed into her with powerful, jetting release.

Addy clung to him, crying for joy at the sounds of his loud groans. She was Nick's woman; he was her man. Tonight they had come together, mating like beasts, unable to control their baser instincts. It had been savagely glorious and gloriously spiritual. Despite the very carnality of their lovemaking, their union had created an eternal bond.

Addy knew, as surely as she knew her name, that she would never let Nick Romero go.

Easing Addy to his side, Nick raised up, gazing into the black sky, listening to the sounds of impending rain. "We'd better get inside, Red, before the bottom falls out."

They helped each other to their feet. Nick regretted that he couldn't carry Addy inside. With his bad leg and in his weakened condition, he might drop her.

Sensing his feelings of regret over not being able to carry her to their bed, Addy dashed toward the door. "Catch me!" she teased.

He laughed, realizing that she'd known how much he wanted to lift her into his arms and carry her. He followed her inside. She was bent over, pulling the quilt and top sheet down the antique iron bed that had been painted a dark moss green. Coming up behind her, he rubbed against her, then gave her a playful shove. She tumbled onto the bed and turned over quickly, spreading open her arms. "How long will it be before we can do it again?"

Lowering one knee on the bed, he leaned over her. She stared into his eyes. "I don't think it'll be too long. You wore me out, Red, but parts of my body are still raring to go."

She glanced down at that part of his body and smiled. "Someone told me that men past forty couldn't do it two times in a row."

He came down on top of her, sliding into her wet, tight sheath. "Someone told you wrong."

Chapter 11

Addy awoke to the sound of drizzling rain. Opening her eyes, she looked across the room to the unclosed door leading to the porch. Pellets of moisture had sprayed through the screen, dotting the wooden floor with raindrops. Reaching out for Nick, she found an empty space on the other side of the bed. She rolled over onto Nick's pillow, burying her face in the softness as she breathed in his unique scent that clung to the hand-embroidered case. She cherished every element that made Nick Romero who and what he was, even the lingering smell of his manliness mixed with her feminine fragrance.

Last night had been—magic! There was no other word to describe what had happened or how it had made her feel. Despite the fact that Nick hadn't proclaimed his love for her, not even in the throes of passion, Addy knew in her heart that he loved her. He might not be able to admit it to himself quite yet, but sooner or later he would face the truth. They were meant for each other, destined to be lovers. He was her champion, her paladin, the man she had waited a lifetime to love. And she was his woman, the *only* woman for him.

Addy wondered where he was. When she got out of bed, she remembered that she was stark naked. Smiling, she thought about her clothes and Nick's strewn about in the living room. Glancing across the bedroom to where Nick had placed her suitcase on the small French sofa, Addy debated whether to wrap herself in the lightweight quilt on the bed or to seek out her satin robe. She decided on the robe, quickly making her way across the room to her suitcase. Slipping into the floor-length, sea-foam green robe, Addy began searching for Nick. After a thorough check of the four rooms and bath, she returned to the bedroom and opened the door to the porch. Stepping outside, she felt the cool, misty spray of summer rain.

Nick stood at the edge of the porch, wearing only his jeans, unbuttoned and riding low on his lean hips. His body was coated with a fine sheen of moisture, his thick black hair curling around his neck and ears. He held a large ceramic mug in his right hand as he leaned against the banister railing with the other. He seemed totally absorbed in watching the rain.

When Addy approached him, he turned. The smile that lit his face quickened Addy's pulse. His eyes glistened with the look of beckoning temptation.

"Good morning, beautiful," he said. "You've slept half the day away."

She stood several feet from him, simply staring at him, thoroughly enjoying the sight of his big, bronze body—remembering every word, every touch, every sensation the two of them had shared. "I feel beautiful. You've made me beautiful."

"You were always beautiful, Addy." He put the mug to his lips, downing a swig of black coffee.

"Have I really slept half the day away? What time is it?"

"Almost eleven." He grinned, then nodded to his cup. "I've made coffee. Want some?"

"How did you make coffee? I didn't see anything in the kitchen except an old wood stove."

"Former SEALS and DEA agents are very capable. We're used to surviving under primitive conditions."

"You built a fire in the stove?"

Setting his mug on top of the banister, Nick walked toward her, limping heavily. Every nerve in her body alerted itself to his approach, sending tingles of excitement racing through her.

"I'm good at building fires." Leaning down, he took her lips in a good-morning kiss as passionately sweet and moist as the rainy Georgia day.

He threaded his fingers through the long, silky mane of her hair, cradling her head in his hand, drawing her closer and closer, deeper into his kiss. She skimmed the side of his face, letting her fingers caress his jaw. Gradually, he slowed the kiss, then rested his forehead against hers.

She traced his ear with her fingertips, circling the diamond stud sparkling in his lobe. "When did you get your ear pierced?"

He bit her playfully on the neck as he wrapped her in his arms. "While I was in the hospital. After I nearly lost my leg."

"What made you want to have your ear pierced?" She tongued his ear, then nuzzled the side of his neck.

"My hair got long and my beard and mustache grew, so I looked pretty scruffy there for a while. One of my nurses said I looked like a pirate, that all I needed was a gold hoop in my ear.''

"You're very susceptible to suggestion, aren't you?" She gasped softly when Nick loosened the tie belt on her robe and slipped his hands inside, cupping her behind.

"Very. How about you, Red? Are you open to a suggestion?"

When he pulled her against his arousal, she sighed. "Was she pretty?"

"Was who pretty?"

"The nurse who talked you into having your ear pierced?"

Nick chuckled, sensing Addy's teasing remark displayed a certain amount of jealousy. "She was very pretty. Bosomy and blonde. And she didn't just talk me into having my ear pierced, she actually pierced it herself and supplied the gold hoop." He felt Addy stiffen. She tried to pull back, but he held her tightly. "You asked, Addy, and I told you the truth. I'll never lie to you."

"What—what happened to the gold hoop?" Addy hated the blond nurse and every other blonde who'd ever been a part of Nick's life.

He kissed Addy on the nose. "I gave the hoop back to her when I left the hospital."

"You've known a lot of women, haven't you Nick?" Addy felt a growing sense of uncertainty, wondering if she was a fool to believe that Nick loved her.

"I've never known anyone like you, Adeline McConnell."

"Is that good or bad?"

"Ah, Red, that's good—very, very good." He captured her reply, silencing her as he made love to her mouth with a thoroughness that left her breathless.

Through a hazy fog of passion, Addy realized that Nick

was an expert at changing the subject to suit himself. She pulled out of his arms so quickly that his grab for her missed the mark, allowing her to escape into the bedroom.

Nick watched her disappear into the house, knowing that she was feeling a little insecure. She was new to this business of being a man's lover, new to the joys of sexual pleasure. Addy was the type who'd fancy herself in love, and a woman in love could be less than accepting of a man's past relationships.

He'd give her some time alone, but not too much time. If she started thinking too much, she'd start doubting herself again, and she'd doubt him, too. Finding his cane and their hastily shed clothing on the living-room floor, Nick retrieved his cane and gathered the assorted items. His shirt and briefs. Her blouse and slacks, bra and panties.

A few minutes later, he found her seated at the small kitchen table, a mug of steaming black coffee in front of her. When he entered the room, she glanced up at him.

"I suppose we should try to fix some breakfast." She glanced at the wood stove, which had already heated the room to a toasty warmth.

Leaning on his cane, he stood beside her. "How about a bear claw? There's a fresh pack in the cupboard."

"Fine. They'll taste great with coffee."

Nick pulled the package of danishes from the second shelf, ripping open the plastic and pulling out two of the sticky buns ladened with almond slices. They ate and drank in silence, each sneaking glances at the other.

"What would you like to do today?" he asked.

"What is there to do?"

"Oh, I don't know. A swim in the creek. A hike in the woods."

Addy nodded toward the window. "Have you forgotten that it's raining?"

"I guess we'll have to find something to do inside."

"I suppose so."

Nick pointed his cane at Addy. She stared down at the gold-tipped walking stick. He tapped her on the chest, between her breasts. She swallowed, her heartbeat accelerating rapidly. He ran the tip of the cane down her body, sliding it under her belt, loosening it until the front of her satin robe fell open.

Addy sucked in her breath. The gold tip felt damp and cool against her warm body. Moving the shiny lacquer rod slowly downward, across her stomach, hesitating momentarily at her navel, he positioned it between her thighs, rubbing it against her fiery curls.

"Nick..." Her voice vibrated with the urgency of her emotions.

"This cane was a gift from my friend, Nate Hodges." Nick continued stimulating her with the walking stick. "We were in the SEALS together for ten years."

Addy squirmed in the wooden chair, wanting to run from Nick, from the tormenting rod he'd positioned between her thighs, but she felt trapped by her own sensuality, her own wild desire. "Nick...please—"

"What is it, Red? What do you want?"

Moaning when he increased the tempo with which he was rotating the cane, Addy reached out, grabbing the stick, clutching it in her fist. "I want to take this cane and knock you senseless! You—you know what you're doing to me. You're doing it on purpose."

Jerking the cane away and out of her grasp, Nick smiled, then stood. He held out his hand. "Come on, Red. Let's go back to bed. You can knock me senseless without ever touching this walking stick."

"You're so damned sure of yourself, aren't you?" Addy

glared at him, knowing that she wanted a repeat performance of last night as much as he did.

"I'm sure you want exactly what I want." He took her
hand, tugging until she stood.

"And what do you want?" She refused to budge when
he tried to pull her toward him.

"I want to take you back to bed, drag you beneath me
and bury myself deep inside of you. I want to—" With
one powerful jerk, he brought her into his arms and whispered into her ear, using hot, raw words to describe his
needs, telling her in the most basic words a man can use
precisely what he wanted.

Addy clung to him, her lips accepting his marauding
mouth. Slowly, steadily, they made their way to the bedroom. By the time they reached the bed, both were flaming
fierce and bright, both more than ready to burn themselves
out quickly.

He lowered her to the bed, taking her with a swift, savage lunge that made her cry out from the intensity. Clutching his buttocks, matching him thrusting move for thrusting move, Addy gave herself to Nick, taking from him
everything he had to give. The moment ended almost before it began, each hurled into the spiraling whirlwind of
fulfillment. Breathless, sweaty and totally spent, they lay
side by side in each other's arms, uncaring of the time, the
weather or their whereabouts.

Days passed in a sensual blur of pleasure and happiness,
unlike anything Addy had ever known. She didn't want
her private time with Nick to ever end. Daytime melted
into nighttime, each twenty-four-hour period losing its dis-
tinction as one week ended and another began. Life took
on new meaning, each moment a joy to be shared. They
learned to use the old wood stove together, preparing basic

meals, not once sharing another feast with Elizabeth, although they visited her daily so Nick could check in with Sam Dundee.

They swam in the creek and played under the waterfall. They took long walks in the woods and spent endless hours talking, each totally fascinated by the other, yearning to learn every little detail. At night they sat on the porch, watching the fireflies and listening to the woodland creatures' nocturnal songs.

And they made love—morning, noon and night.

The only reminder of the outside world came when they visited with Elizabeth and made their mandatory phone call. All was well in Huntsville. Rusty's doctor had given him a thorough checkup, proclaiming him as fit as he could be for a man of seventy with a bad heart and high blood pressure. In four days the NASP contract would be awarded. Nick and Addy would leave Sequana Falls. And, hopefully, all danger would have passed.

A pleasant evening breeze rustled through the trees. Addy sat in the small porch swing; Nick sat on the floor, bracing his back against the banister. Twilight descended, painting the sky in various shades of purples, pinks and oranges. As far as the eye could see, vast woodland spread across the mountain, the smell of pine heavy in the air.

"Okay, you left the SEALS after ten years and started back to school." Sitting on one leg, Addy used the toe of her other foot to put the swing in motion.

"Yeah, I was a twenty-eight-year-old college kid." Nick propped his hands behind his head. "I'd decided I wanted to be a DEA agent and I needed more education. That's how I met Sam. He'd done a stint in the marines."

"So you and Sam went to school together, became friends and joined the DEA."

"That's about it. We both fit the bill, had most of the

qualifications. Except Sam didn't speak a second language, so I taught him Spanish. Knowing a second language, especially Spanish, is a plus. And we'd both been in the service and already had some combat training, some knowledge of weapons. That sort of thing.''

"Do you miss being an agent?'' Addy wondered if Nick was the kind of man who simply couldn't settle down, who would always need danger and excitement in his life.

"Sometimes. It's a demanding, stressful job.'' He edged his way closer to the swing, shifting himself slowly across the porch. "They weed out the guys who haven't got what it takes in a fifteen-week training program at Quantico, Virginia.''

"You had what it took, didn't you, Nick? You were physically and mentally a tough guy.''

Rubbing his bad leg, Nick stared at Addy. "Well, that Uzi proved I wasn't as physically tough as I thought I was.''

"Having a crippled leg doesn't make you any less of a man,'' Addy said, tempted to throw her arms around him and kiss away the pain she saw in his eyes. "I've never known anyone who's more a man than you.''

Reaching out, he tickled the bottom of her bare foot. "You're prejudiced, Red. You're only saying that because I'm such a fantastic lover.''

She giggled. "You are so conceited.''

Holding her heel with one hand, he traced the veins atop her foot with his fingers. "You've made me conceited, panting after me all the time, dragging me off to bed all hours of the day and night, groaning and moaning and crying out when you come. What's a man to think, other than that he's a stud?''

Addy twisted her leg when Nick ran his fingers higher,

caressing her calf. "All right, I'll grant that you're a stud—but…"

"But what?" He kissed her ankle, then ran his tongue all the way up her leg to her knee. Brushing aside her billowy cotton skirt, he slid his hand up her inner thigh.

"But you should give me some of the credit. After all, not just any woman could keep a forty-three-year-old man primed and ready all the time."

With both of them laughing, Nick pulled Addy out of the swing and down onto the floor and into his arms. "I think I've created a beautiful, insatiable monster."

"Am I your creation, Nick?" She unbuttoned his shirt and placed her lips on his chest.

Yes, by God, she was his creation. With his patience and tenderness and loving administrations, he'd given Addy the confidence in her own sexuality that she needed to become the woman who'd been buried inside her all her life. With each word of encouragement, with each reassuring, inspiring touch, he'd brought her out of the darkness to which her ex-husband had doomed her. She was his now. His woman…his heart, his soul…his very life.

When the time came, how the hell was he going to be able to take her back to Huntsville and leave her? He'd never been a man for commitments, always moving on when things got too serious. He wasn't the marrying kind, and Addy deserved no less. She'd want marriage and kids, if she could have them, and the kind of love that lasted forever. He didn't know if he was capable of that kind of love, of that kind of lifetime pledge. There was one thing she knew for sure—he hadn't had his fill of Addy, not by a long shot. He was nowhere near ready to give up what they'd found together. Nothing in his life had ever been this good.

"Nick? Nick, what's wrong?" She took his face in her hands, forcing him to look at her.

"Nothing's wrong, Red. Not a damned thing." He buried his face against her breasts, nuzzling her nipples with his nose. "You're my woman, you know that, don't you?"

She sighed, clinging to him, savoring the sheer physical pleasure of being so near the man she loved. "I remember the morning after you rescued me from my kidnapper, you told me that someday I'd become one of your women. Looks like you were right."

"I was wrong," he said, then covered her face with a dozen tiny kisses. "There's never been another woman like you, and there never will be again. You're unique. What I feel for you is different. You're mine—my woman—and I never want you to belong to anyone else."

"Oh, Nick—I love you so much. You must know that. Surely you've guessed." She could feel the rat-a-tat-tat of her heart drumming within her chest. She longed to hear him repeat the words, to vow his undying love for her, but she knew he wasn't ready, that she'd confessed her love too soon.

"Ah, Red. You mean the world to me. I—"

She covered his lips with her index finger, silencing him. "I'm not asking for anything you can't give. You've been honest with me. That's all I ask now and in the future. Don't ever lie to me, don't ever pretend something you don't feel."

"When I'm with you, I don't have to pretend anything. What I feel for you is real. I just don't know if it's love or not because I've never been in love." He kissed the tip of her finger, then drew it into his mouth.

"What about Dina?" Addy hadn't given Dina a thought in days, but she couldn't forget what the woman had once meant to Nick.

"I didn't love Dina, not the way you mean. My teenage male hormones loved her lush, little body."

"I've learned just how powerful sexual attraction can be. Do you think— I mean, is that what you feel for me?"

He pulled her close, pressing her head to his chest. "I've never felt such a strong physical attraction to a woman, but—there's more. A lot more. I enjoy being with you, Red. In and out of bed. I like you. I admire you. And I trust you more than I've ever trusted a woman."

Lying in his arms, Addy smiled. Even if he didn't know it, even if he couldn't bring himself to consider the possibility, Nick Romero *was* falling in love with her. "I trust you, too. Not only with my life, but with my heart."

"If I could ever love a woman, it would be you."

"Is that a promise?"

"That's a fact, Red."

Tender touches and sweet kisses gradually turned to frantic groping and wild, tongue-thrusting lunges. Clothes disappeared and naked bodies appeared. Entangled limbs and damp, moist flesh mated in a savage, mindless dance of pleasure. Man and woman joined. Giving and taking. Finding release. Claiming ownership. Silently professing love in its most elemental form.

Nick heard the loud rapping on the door. Before Addy became fully awake, he'd already leapt out of bed and was feeling around on the floor for his jeans.

"What is it?" Addy asked.

"Somebody's at the front door."

They both heard the voice. "Nick? Addy? It's Elizabeth." Then a mournful wolf howl erupted from Mac-Datho.

"Oh, Nick, something's wrong!" Addy slid out of bed and pulled on her satin robe.

He wrangled with his rumpled jeans, finally getting them zipped. Picking up his cane, he walked over to the door, Addy right behind him. When he opened the door, Elizabeth ordered MacDatho to *stay,* then stepped inside, her flashlight casting a steady stream of light into the bedroom.

"I'm sorry to disturb you so late, but Sam called. He said to call him back immediately. It's urgent."

"Did he say what's wrong?" Addy asked.

"No, he didn't say." Elizabeth reached out, touching Addy's arm, giving her a reassuring squeeze.

"We'll get dressed and come on up to the cabin." Nick held the door for Elizabeth, who stepped back out onto the porch.

"Wait!" Addy cried. Elizabeth stopped. "Do you know what's wrong? Have you felt anything?"

"Your father needs you. That's all I know." Elizabeth turned and left, disappearing back into the woods, the ever-faithful MacDatho at her side.

In frenzied haste, Addy dressed in black slacks and a turquoise cotton sweater. She waited while Nick laced his shoes. "Elizabeth told me the day we arrived that we wouldn't stay here the full two weeks. She said then that Daddy would need me. Oh, Nick, do you suppose Daddy's had a heart attack or a stroke?"

"Don't jump to conclusions. We'll know what's going on as soon as I talk to Sam." Holding his cane in one hand, he offered her the other. "Ready?"

Fifteen minutes later, Addy clutched the cup of hot tea that Elizabeth had handed her the moment she and Nick entered her cabin. Nick had just gotten through to Sam. Three people and one half-wolf dog stood in Elizabeth's living room, waiting for news.

Elizabeth placed her arm around Addy's shoulder. "Drink your tea. It will help soothe your nerves."

"Did you put something in it?"

"It's herbal tea, that's all."

With trembling fingers, Addy put the cup to her lips, sipping slowly. The tea was hot and sweet and soothing.

"Yeah, I understand. When did it happen?" Nick asked Sam Dundee.

Addy handed her cup to Elizabeth, then approached Nick, tugging on his shirtsleeve. "Tell me, what happened?"

Nick slipped his arm around her shoulders, drawing her to his side. "There's no way I'll be able to keep her here," he told Sam Dundee. "We'll head back to Huntsville tonight."

"Nick?" Fear shook her like the impact of a high-powered rifle.

He held her tightly as he continued his conversation. "How's Hester?"

"Is something wrong with Jim?" Addy squeezed Nick's arm.

"I suppose Johnson is at the hospital," Nick said.

"Nick!"

"I'll be in touch as soon as we get there." Nick hung up the phone, turned to Addy, and pulled her completely into his arms. Tilting her chin, she stared up at him. "It's bad, Red. You're going to have to be strong for me and for yourself, but mostly for Rusty."

"Tell me, dammit, just tell me!"

"Your father and Jim Hester had a late dinner meeting tonight. When they returned to the M.A.C. executive offices, they were ambushed."

"Ambushed?"

"Your father's chauffeur-bodyguard was shot. He's dead."

"Alton's dead? My God, he's been with Daddy for years!"

"Jim Hester was shot, too." Addy tensed in his arms. "He's still alive. He's in surgery."

"What about Tiffany? Who's taking care of her?"

"Hester's sister-in-law has Hester's little girl with her."

Addy swayed, her legs buckling under her. Nick steadied her, then helped her to a nearby chair. Bending down on his knees in front of her, Nick prayed she was strong enough to handle the worst news. "The person or persons who shot Alton and Hester kidnapped your father."

"No! Oh, Daddy!" Slouching over, her shoulders drooping, Addy covered her face with her hands. "I was the target! They threatened me, not Daddy! I don't understand this. Why kidnap Daddy?"

"Dina received a call from the kidnapper," Nick said, pulling Addy's clenched fists into his hands, stroking her knuckles, trying to soothe her. "He wants you to withdraw the NASP bid."

"The NASP bid really is what he's after, isn't it? It's not a red herring like you thought." Addy stared at Nick, her eyes overly bright, glazed with anxiety. "It's Gerald. It has to be. But—but he'd know—he'd know I don't have the authority to withdraw the bid."

"Calm down, Red. If Carlton is behind Rusty's kidnapping, we'll nail him. I promise you." Nick couldn't bring himself to tell her that he still doubted the validity of the NASP bid threat, that his gut instincts told him that Rusty's kidnapping had another motive. Someone wanted Addy McConnell back in Huntsville, and they'd used the only conceivable method to ensure her return.

"What if he's already killed Daddy? They killed Donnie. Daddy paid the ransom and they still killed him."

Nick felt her panic. Grabbing her by the shoulders, he shook her soundly. "Don't do this, Red! Don't fall apart on me now."

Elizabeth stepped forward, her clear blue eyes focusing on Addy. "Your father isn't dead." Standing beside Addy's chair, Elizabeth touched her cheek. "Your father won't be killed. You will return to Huntsville and save him."

Nick swung around, glaring at Elizabeth. "She doesn't need to hear this."

"Yes, I do." Shoving Nick aside, Addy stood. "I've got to go back. We need to leave as soon as possible."

Grasping his cane, Nick followed her to the door, but couldn't keep up with her when she broke into a run once she'd entered the yard.

"Addy, stop!" Nick flung open the front door. "Dammit, woman, will you slow down!"

Elizabeth caught Nick by the wrist, halting him. "Keep her guarded, every moment. She's in danger."

"Don't you think I know that!"

"Her enemy is someone she knows."

Nick could hear the deafening roar of his heartbeat throbbing in his ears. "What else? You know more, don't you?"

"He means to kill her." Elizabeth's grip on Nick's arm tightened. "A woman has been helping him, but she doesn't want Addy harmed."

Elizabeth released Nick. They stood for several long moments, staring at each other, Nick uncertain whether or not to believe this woman's soothsaying abilities. Sam had once told him that she possessed unearthly powers, that he'd seen Elizabeth Mallory turn barren soil into flowering life and call the animals out of the forest to come to her and they obeyed. Sam had said that his ward, his brother's stepchild had the ability to see inside a person and predict their future. Sam Dundee had never lied to Nick.

"That's all I know," Elizabeth said. "Hurry and go after her. Now, more than ever, Addy will need her paladin."

"Her what?"

"You, Nick, she will need you, her knight in shining armor. No one else can save her. Only you."

Chapter 12

Nick had broken all the posted speed limits on the trip to Atlanta where a private plane awaited them. They arrived in Huntsville at seven-thirty in the morning, both of them were bleary-eyed and exhausted from worry and lack of sleep. Taking a cab from the airport, they went directly to the hospital. Hot and humid early morning sunshine greeted them the moment they stepped onto the pavement, and one of Ned Johnson's FBI agents, Alan Sturges, met them at the lobby entrance.

"Any word on my father?" Addy asked as the agent whisked them through the lobby and into an elevator.

"Sorry, ma'am, there's no news to report." The young, slender investigator punched in the correct floor, then turned to Nick. "Ms. Lunden is upstairs. We've had quite a time with her. Even Brett Windsor can't do anything with her."

Hell, that's all they needed, Nick thought, an overwrought, hysterical Dina. Addy was close to the breaking point herself; she didn't need Dina's theatrical show of concern sending her over the edge. "What's Dina doing here?"

"She refuses to leave until she sees Ms. McConnell," Agent Sturges said. "She and Windsor have been here since about five this morning."

"Has Jim come out of surgery yet?" Addy asked.

The elevator stopped. The doors opened. The three stepped into the hallway.

"No, ma'am. He's been in surgery for hours. It doesn't look good. He was shot up pretty bad, I'm afraid."

Nick gave the young agent a deadly look, silently reprimanding him for being so blunt with Addy about Hester's condition. "Come on, Red, think positive thoughts."

The minute they rounded the corner that led to the surgery waiting area, Dina Lunden came running toward Addy, tears flowing down her rosy cheeks, her arms spread wide. At the touch of Dina's arm around her, Addy cringed, then chastised herself for being so insensitive to the other woman's feelings. Maybe Dina really did care about her father. If she didn't, she certainly was putting on an award-winning performance.

"Oh, Addy, it's just awful! This shouldn't have happened. If only you had stayed in Huntsville, instead of running off to God knows where and going into hiding." Releasing her tenacious hold on Addy, Dina faced Nick. "It's all your fault. I had no idea when I invited you to my engagement party that you would wind up making such a mess of things."

Brett Windsor came forward, placing a comforting arm around Dina. "Now, Dina, stop talking nonsense. Neither Nick nor Addy could have prevented Rusty's kidnapping."

Dina glared at Brett, her eyes bright and wild. "You

know I'm right, dammit!'' Flinging off Brett's arm, she walked away from him.

Turning to Addy, Brett gave her a gentle hug. "I'm so sorry about all this. Dina's been hysterical ever since she heard Rusty had been kidnapped."

Addy accepted Brett's comfort, thankful that he was around to help keep Dina in check. "You were with Dina when she was told about Daddy?"

"No, as a matter of fact, I wasn't." Brett glanced over at Nick whose dark, pensive stare issued a warning. "I've found my own apartment. I moved out of the mansion three days ago."

"Addy! Oh, Addy!" Janice Dixon ran down the corridor, her blond ponytail flip-flopping up and down on her back.

Pulling out of Brett's embrace, Addy put her arms around Janice. "Oh, Janice, you didn't have to come down here, but I'm so glad you did."

"I've been checking with Dina. She told me what time they were expecting you and Nick to arrive." Teary-eyed, Janice forced a smile. "I—I thought you might need me."

"Of course I need you." Addy hugged Janice with the fierce protectiveness of an earth-mother defending her child. "You're my best friend and favorite cousin."

"Has there been any word on Uncle Rusty's whereabouts? A ransom demand or anything?"

"Nothing new," Addy said. "We're waiting to hear, and praying that Daddy's all right and that Jim survives his surgery."

While the endless minutes turned to an hour and then two, Dina continued to rant and rave, ceasing only when Brett or Nick soothed her. Addy sat with Janice, and Agent Sturges watched over them all.

Ned Johnson appeared in the doorway. Nick rose from

his seat directly across from Addy. He said a silent prayer that Hester was still alive. He might well be their only chance of finding Rusty—if he'd seen the kidnapper's face and could identify him. "Ned?"

"Hester made it."

Addy sighed with relief, tears glistening in the corners of her eyes. When she stood, walking toward Nick, Janice rose and followed her. Nick, who stood in the doorway talking quietly with Ned Johnson, reached out and pulled Addy to his side.

"Look, Red. I'm going in with Ned to question Hester just as soon as he comes around. The doctors say it could be another hour, maybe longer."

"You think he can identify the kidnapper?" Addy asked.

"We're hoping he can," Johnson replied.

"Agent Sturges will stay with you when I go in to question Hester." Nick's big hand splayed across her back. He titled her chin upward, his dark eyes demanding her compliance. "Don't even go to the bathroom unless he's waiting right outside the door. Understand?"

"I understand." She caressed his cheek with her fingertips. "Don't worry about me."

"Brett is taking me home," Dina announced. "I'm simply exhausted." Stopping in front of Addy and Nick, she gave them a heated look. "You will call me the moment you get word on Rusty, won't you?"

"Of course we will," Addy said.

"He's all right, you know." Dina glanced over at Brett, who held her by the arm. "Isn't he?"

"I'll drive her home and stay with her until she calms down. I think a couple of Valium should do the trick," Brett said.

Addy felt a surge of relief once Dina had left. Her father's overwrought fiancée had gotten on everyone's nerves with her moans and sighs, her constant flood of tears and her irrational babbling. Thank the Lord that Brett had been able to persuade her to go home. The FBI was doing everything possible, but Addy knew that a great deal depended on what Jim Hester would be able to tell them about the shooting and her father's kidnapping.

Nick led her back inside the waiting area, sitting down beside her on a vinyl sofa and pulling her into his arms. She rested there, reassured by his comforting strength.

Nick stood inside the ICU cubicle where Jim Hester had just regained consciousness. Ned Johnson, an RN at his side, leaned over Hester's bed and spoke his name.

"Mr. Hester, I'm Ned Johnson. I'm with the FBI. I need to ask you a few questions."

Jim tried to speak, but his voice broke in an awkward squeak when he said Addy's name. He looked up at Agent Johnson pleadingly.

"Ms. McConnell is fine. She's waiting outside, very concerned and eager to see you."

"Alton?" Jim Hester's voice was only a choked whisper.

"He didn't make it," Johnson said. "But the doctors say you're going to be all right. What we need to know in order to find the man who did this to you and kidnapped D.B. McConnell is if you can identify the assailant."

"Mask," Jim gasped. "He wore a mask."

The stocky nurse nudged Ned Johnson out of the way and checked her patient's oxygen supply. Turning back to the FBI agent, she said, "Only a few more questions."

Nick moved to the the foot of the bed. Seeing Nick, Jim reached out. His hand, strapped with an IV needle, trembled. "Romero."

"Good to see you alive, Hester. Addy's been worried sick about you."

"We didn't know…what…hit us," Jim said in a weak, quivering voice. "We drove into the parking lot." He stopped talking, giving himself a much-needed respite. "Before we…knew…what was happening, he opened fire. Shot Alton first…then me. I was on the pavement… couldn't—couldn't get to Rusty."

"I'm afraid that's all," the nurse said. "You'll both have to leave now."

"Just one more question." Ignoring the protective RN, Nick walked around to the side of the bed, reaching down to take Jim Hester's hand. "Can you tell us anything about the man who attacked you, anything that might help us?"

"Mask and hat." Jim squeezed Nick's hand with what little strength he could muster. "Didn't see his face…or hair. Tall. Well-built. I'd say fairly young…by the way he moved."

"Was he driving or on foot? Did you see any kind of vehicle?" Ned Johnson asked.

"That's two questions," the nurse scolded.

"Didn't see a car. Sorry," Jim said.

Nick gave Jim's hand a strong, reassuring squeeze. "Thanks, Jim. You get some rest, and I'll bring Addy in to see you later."

Nick hated hospitals with a passion, especially ICU units. They were an all-too-vivid reminder of his own close call with death, of the endless days and nights he'd lain, helpless and alone. His only link with life had been the pain, which he'd used to push him forward into each new day.

He'd never be the same man he was before Ian Ryker had gunned him down with an Uzi. The doctors had told him that he was lucky to be alive, and he knew they were right. But he'd lost a lot, the proper use of his leg, his job as a DEA agent, his ability to carry his woman in his arms.

Outside the ICU, Ned Johnson gripped Nick's shoulder. "Not much to go on, is it? Whoever we're dealing with isn't taking any chances."

"He's cunning and shrewd, all right, but my bet is he isn't completely sane. He's kidnapped Rusty McConnell and is demanding that Addy withdraw the bid on the NASP contract. Obviously, he hasn't done his homework or he'd know that Addy doesn't have the authority to withdraw that bid."

"He's making mistakes then, isn't he?"

"Let's just hope he makes enough for us to catch him before somebody else gets hurt."

"Ms. Addy McConnell?" A plump, middle-aged woman in a bright-orange sweat suit held the waiting-room phone in her hand.

Standing, Addy replied. "I'm Addy McConnell."

"Telephone call for you."

Addy took the phone from the woman's meaty little hand. "Hello."

"Ms. McConnell?" The man's voice was muffled, sounding similar to the caller who'd threatened her at the day-care center over two weeks ago.

"Yes." Addy's heart seemed lodged in her throat. Her ears throbbed with pressure.

"I know who kidnapped your father."

"Who is this? What do you want?"

Janice rushed to Addy's side, pulling on her arm. "What's wrong? Should I get Agent Sturges?"

Addy glanced out in the hallway where the FBI agent guarding her waited patiently by the door. With a shake of her head, Addy placed her index finger over Janice's mouth.

"I can help you find your father," the caller said.

Addy knew this was the same voice, the same man who'd threatened her before. "Do you have him? Is he all right?"

"I know where he is, and I'll tell you if you'll meet me."

"Meet you?"

Janice grabbed Addy's wrist, shaking her head and silently mouthing the word no. Addy jerked away from her cousin.

"If you'll come to the coffee shop right now, I'll meet you there and tell you who kidnapped your father and where you can find him."

"How do I know I can trust you?"

"I'm your only chance of keeping your father alive. They're going to kill him. It's up to you whether he lives or dies."

Addy swallowed, wishing she could calm the erratic, deafening rhythm of her heart. Clutching the phone, she breathed deeply. "I—I have an FBI agent guarding me. He'll never let me leave the floor without him."

"If you ever want to see your father alive again, you'll find a way. If anyone, and I mean anyone, comes with you, then Rusty McConnell is a dead man."

"How—how will I recognize you?"

"I'll be wearing a Huntsville Stars T-shirt and cap. I'll wait ten minutes."

The dial tone hummed in Addy's ear. "No! Wait—"

Janice whirled Addy around to face her, grabbing her by the shoulders. "What the hell was that all about?"

Addy led Janice to the far side of the room, away from the curious stares of other ICU patients' family members.

"The man on the phone says that he knows who kidnapped Daddy and he knows where Daddy is."

"You've got to tell the FBI and Nick," Janice said.

"I can't do that. He wants me to meet him in the coffee shop. Right now. If anyone comes with me, they'll kill Daddy."

"He's bluffing. If he's in the coffee shop, he can't kill Uncle Rusty."

"He may not be the kidnapper. I think he may just be working for them."

"It isn't safe for you to go down there and meet him alone. He could do anything. He could shoot you right there in the coffee shop." Janice nodded toward the open door. "Besides, Agent Sturges isn't going to let you go anywhere without him. If he did, Nick would kill him."

Addy's instincts warned her that Janice was right. It wasn't safe for her to meet this telephone caller, but if there was even the slightest chance that he was on the level, that he could lead them to Rusty, she had to take the chance, didn't she? If her actions meant the difference between saving her father's life and his death, then she had no choice.

"You can help me," Addy said. "I want you to distract Agent Sturges long enough for me to get to the elevators."

"No, Addy, I won't do it. I don't want anything to happen to you."

Addy took her cousin's face in her hands. Forcing a smile, she tried to sound reassuring. "Look, I won't take any unnecessary chances. The coffee shop will be full of people. And, if I'm not back in a few minutes, then you can tell Agent Sturges where I went. Okay?"

"Addy, are you sure?"

"No, I'm not sure, but I do know that this may be our only chance to save Daddy."

Addy watched while Janice sauntered over to the FBI
agent. No man could resist her cousin's feminine charms.
The woman was lethal. Within minutes, Janice had maneuvered Alan Sturges inside the waiting area and over to
the coffee table, set up and replenished by hospital volunteers for the convenience of the ICU visitors. While Janice poured two cups of coffee, handing one to Sturges,
Addy slipped into the hallway. Taking one last glance
backward, she saw that Janice had her arm laced through
the agent's and was smiling up at him, her hip resting
seductively against his thigh.

Addy punched the elevator down button. While waiting,
she kept checking to make sure no one was aware of her
escape. The elevator doors swung open. Three people dis-
embarked. Rushing inside, Addy punched the lobby button, drew in a deep, courage-seeking breath and said a
prayer when the doors closed and the elevator descended.

Despite the air-conditioned cool of the elevator, drops
of perspiration trickled down Addy's neck. Her palms were
coated with sweat. Her pulse beat rapidly. Her mouth felt
as dry and parched as desert sand.

She knew she shouldn't be doing this. Nick would be
furious when he came out of ICU and found her missing.
God, what had gotten into her, thinking she could rescue
her father, that she could confront a man who could well
be one of the kidnappers? She wasn't thinking straight. If
the man in the coffee shop chose to kidnap her or even
kill her, what help could she be to her father?

Just as Addy made the monumental decision that she
was going to go back upstairs and tell Nick about the
phone call, the elevator doors opened at the lobby level.
Quickly, she punched the ICU floor button. Before the
doors closed, a man entered. With fear racing through her
like molten lava down a mountainside, Addy looked up to

see who was sharing the elevator with her. Recognizing the man, she sagged with relief.

"Oh, thank God, it's you!"

"What's wrong, Addy? You seem frightened."

"I'm all right now. I wasn't expecting to see you." The man reached around Addy, pressing the open button.

"What are you doing? I was on my way back upstairs."

"I'm surprised Nick Romero let you out of his sight."

When Addy tried to press the ICU floor button again, her companion placed his hand over hers, pulling her away from the control panel. Addy glared at him.

"I have a gun in my coat pocket, Addy, and I'm quite prepared to use it."

"You?"

"We'll walk outside together, like old friends, and go to my car. Once we reach our destination, I'll tell you everything you want to know about Rusty's kidnapper."

Addy followed his instructions, cursing herself for being such a fool. Not only had she acted impulsively but she had doomed herself and her father. Icy chills of fear racked her body as her kidnapper opened his car door and gave her a gentle shove. Once trapped inside the moving vehicle, Addy turned her head slightly, watching the hospital until it faded out of sight. The car soon blended in with the afternoon traffic, its two occupants escaping any undue notice as they left behind Addy's protection—Nick Romero and the FBI.

Addy knew her only hope now lay with Nick being able to somehow figure out who had taken her. But would he be able to piece the puzzle together in time to save her and her father? Would he, unlike she and her father, ignore all the circumstantial evidence and go with his gut instincts? Dear Lord, please help him. If ever she had needed her paladin to come to her rescue, it was now.

* * *

Scanning the ICU waiting area, Nick didn't see Addy. Alan Sturges stood by the windows, drinking a cup of coffee and flirting with an overly attentive Janice Dixon. Where the hell was Addy? Was she in the rest room? If so, why wasn't Sturges standing guard outside the door?

Nick marched over to the FBI agent, gripping his shoulder in a vise-like hold. "Where's Addy?"

"Right over—" Sturges's face turned pale, his eyes widening in surprise and fear. "She's got to be in here! I just saw her a few minutes ago."

"Well, she sure as hell isn't here now, is she?" Nick swung the younger man around to face him. "If anything has happened to her, your life isn't worth—"

"It's not Alan's fault," Janice interrupted. "I've been deliberately distracting him. He—he didn't see Addy leave."

Nick released Sturges, then reached out and grabbed Janice by the shoulders. "What do you mean 'leave'? Where did she go?"

"Down to the coffee shop." Tears filled Janice's big blue eyes.

"How the hell did this happen?" Nick's gut tightened into a painful knot. His heart drummed like a roaring tornado. His big hands trembled on Janice's shoulders. "Why would she slip away to go to the coffee shop?"

"A man called."

Hot, acrid bitterness rose in his throat, the physical evidence of a fear too great to be born. "What man?"

"I don't know," Janice cried as Nick tightened his hold on her. "He—he told Addy that he knew where Uncle Rusty was, and he knew—knew who'd kidnapped him."

"Is she meeting this man in the coffee shop?" Perspiration broke out on Nick's face, dotting his forehead and upper lip. He felt the sticky, moist drops of sweat dripping down his back.

"Yes!" Janice's cries grew louder; tears streamed down her face. "I tried to stop her!"

He shook Janice so forcefully that Agent Sturges clamped his hands over Nick's, trying to free the woman from Nick's wrath. Realizing that he was hurting Janice, Nick released her. "Dammit, how could she have done something so stupid?"

Janice sought comfort in Alan Sturges's arms. "She said to tell Alan—Agent Sturges—what she'd done if she didn't come back in a few minutes."

"How long has she been gone?" Nick's voice was a low, deadly growl.

Swatting away a torrent of tears, Janice glanced up at the wall clock. "About—about five minutes."

"Sturges," Nick yelled, "go find Johnson! Tell him what's happened. I'm going down to the coffee shop, and you'd better pray that I'm not too late."

Nick spent the rest of the day in a living hell, fearing the worst and hating himself for leaving Addy in another man's care, even for the few minutes it had taken to question Jim Hester. Someone had timed that phone call just right. Someone had known the minute he'd left Addy. Sturges and Johnson had known, and so had Janice Dixon. Had she been able to contact Ron Glover? Were they the man and woman behind all the threats, behind Addy's attempted kidnapping, the recent shootings and Rusty's abduction? It made perfect sense, didn't it? Glover had been on Nick's list of suspects since the very beginning.

The FBI had set up headquarters at Rusty's mansion, waiting for any kind of instructions from the kidnapper. Thankfully, Dina had slept through the afternoon and evening. Nick had been the one to tell her what had happened to Addy. He'd never seen such sheer horror on Dina's face. Did she really love Rusty McConnell enough to care about his daughter? She sure as hell acted as if she did, as if her own life depended upon Rusty's and Addy's safety.

Mrs. Hargett had been the one to take charge, to prepare sandwiches and coffee for the agents who swarmed over the house like a cluster of drone bees. The housekeeper had also been the one to keep Dina out of the way, soothing her with words and pats and occasional cups of tea that Nick suspected were laced with liquor. By nightfall, Dina was quiet and unobtrusive.

Nick sat in Rusty's huge den, his vision clouded over with memories of the past eight days he'd spent with Addy in Sequana Falls. He heard the agents' voices and saw them moving about the room, but his private thoughts blocked out the reality.

Nothing could happen to Addy. His life wouldn't be worth living without her. If he ever got his hands on the man who'd done this to her, he'd kill him. Slowly. Painfully.

The telephone rang. Every man in the room froze. After an agonizing moment of suspended time, Ned Johnson picked up the receiver.

"McConnell residence."

Nick held his breath, waiting. Silence so profound that they could almost hear one another's heartbeats encompassed the den. Then Johnson said, "What? Is he all right? Where was he found?"

Nick rushed over to Johnson, grabbing him by the arm. "Who's been found?"

Ned replaced the receiver, then turned to Nick. "Rusty McConnell has been found. He's alive and unharmed."

"When? Where?"

"The Huntsville police found him wandering around on the side of the interstate. They thought he was drunk." Ned motioned to two of his agents. "Hankins, you and Murphy go down to the police station and bring Mr. McConnell home. He'll be a little groggy and disoriented. He's been drugged."

"Drugged," Nick said. "If he's been drugged the whole damned time, then he's probably not going to be able to tell us who kidnapped him."

"If the kidnapper let McConnell go, then you can bet your life he didn't reveal his identity."

Within an hour, D.B. McConnell had been brought home, and he'd showered, shaved, eaten and smoked a cigar. No one had told him that Addy was missing, not even Dina, whose tearful reunion with her fiancé had just about convinced Nick of her sincerity.

Nick had stayed out of sight, watching Rusty's home-coming from inside the house while Dina, Mrs. Hargett and half a dozen agents surrounded Rusty on the veranda. If Rusty saw him, he'd ask about Addy. As far as her father knew, Addy was still in hiding, safe and sound.

Ned Johnson approached Nick, who'd found himself a peaceful spot out in the backyard. "McConnell has to be told. I thought you might want to be the one to tell him."

"Yeah, thanks. She was my responsibility, and I let some maniac get to her. If anything happens to Addy—"

"Don't talk like that to her father."

"If anything happens to her, I hope Rusty breaks my damned neck."

"Mrs. Hargett is keeping Ms. Lunden occupied. We've got McConnell in the den." Ned placed his hand on Nick's shoulder. "He can't identify the kidnapper. He didn't see much more than Hester saw, except he saw the gun. A 10 mm., but we would have know that soon, anyway, from the ballistics report on the bullets the doctors dug out of Hester and Alton.''

"Anything else?''

"Yeah. His attacker was driving a dark blue Buick. Rusty got a glimpse of the license plate. He remembered the first four digits. We're running a check now, but don't get your hopes up. You know as well as I do the car was probably stolen.''

"Can you give me a few minutes alone with Rusty?'' Nick asked.

"Sure thing.''

As it turned out, Nick didn't get more than three minutes alone with Addy's father after explaining to him what had happened at the hospital. The telephone rang, stunning everyone into silence.

Ned Johnson motioned an angry and outraged Rusty McConnell toward the phone. "This could be our boy calling.''

Clinching the receiver so tightly that his knuckles whitened, Rusty answered, "D.B. McConnell.''

"You had your chance, McConnell.'' The muffled voice held an edge of sadistic pleasure. "All you had to do was not bid on the NASP contract and Addy would have been safe.''

"Who the hell is this? If you've done anything to harm my daughter, I'll—''

"You'll what?'' The man laughed. "You should have followed instructions.''

"I can still cancel the bid,'' Rusty said. "Is that what you want?''

"It's too late, much too late for Addy.''

"No, no it isn't. Tell me what you want and I'll do it. Just don't hurt Addy.''

"She won't be in any pain. It's going to happen so

quickly, she won't feel a thing. One big boom and she'll be joining her illustrious Delacourt ancestors. Of course, you won't find enough of her to bury in the old family cemetery.''

The line went dead. Rusty cursed loudly, using a string of profanities that would have put the foulest-mouthed hoodlum to shame.

Ned Johnson and Nick jumped on Rusty the minute he replaced the receiver, asking him question after question. Rusty went over the conversation again and again.

Nick knew there had to be a clue in the kidnapper's words, if only he could figure out what it was. As minutes ticked by, slowly but surely counting down the last moments of Addy's life, Nick kept making Rusty repeat every word the caller had said. Finally, Rusty broke under the pressure, turning on Nick. Rusty's big, hard fist made contact with Nick's jaw, knocking the younger man to the floor. Nick decided right then and there that he was glad he hadn't been on the receiving end of Rusty McConnell's wrath when the old man had been a little younger and in his prime.

Dina, who entered the room just as Nick picked himself up off the floor, ran to her fiancé, encircling his thick waist with her slender arms. ''You can't go on this way, Rusty, darling! You must get some rest.''

''How the hell can I rest when some lunatic has my daughter and is planning to…blow…her…up.'' Forceful, manly tears streamed down Rusty's ruddy cheeks and rocked his robust frame. He clung to Dina, who cooed soothing words to him as she stroked his back.

Once again Nick went over the kidnapper's messages, praying that something would click in his mind. *It's too late for Addy. She won't be in any pain. One big boom and she'll be joining her illustrious Delacourt ancestors.*

You won't find enough of her to bury in the old family cemetery.

Nick paced the floor, ruffling his already mussed hair with restless fingers. Again, Romero, again. *One big boom. Delacourt ancestors. Old family cemetery.*

Wherever the kidnapper had taken Addy, he'd planted a bomb. But where had he taken her? And how long before the bomb exploded?

Delacourt ancestors. Old family cemetery. Elm Hill! God, it was a long shot, but what if Addy's kidnapper knew about her mother's ancestral home? Addy had told him that no one had lived there since she and her father had moved out twenty-five years ago.

Nick found Rusty and Dina sitting together on the living-room sofa. Rusty gazed up at him with tear-filled eyes. Addy's father looked every day of his seventy years.

"Where's Elm Hill?" Nick asked. "How do I get there?"

"Elm Hill?" Rusty sat up straight, his tired expression growing alert. "You think he took her to Elm Hill?"

"It's possible. He mentioned her Delacourt ancestors and the old family cemetery."

"The cemetery is on the estate." Rusty jumped up. "I'll go with you and show you the way."

"No," Nick said. "I'm playing a hunch. Addy could be anywhere. You need to stay here by the phone in case the kidnapper tries to get in touch with you again."

"Then take one of Johnson's boys with you."

"If the kidnapper is still there with her when I arrive, I don't want to scare him off. I'll have to go in alone."

Rusty pulled Nick into his bear-like hug, stunning Nick with his affection. "You save our girl."

Nick couldn't reply. He hoped Addy's father knew that he'd do anything for Addy, even die if it was necessary.

Rusty gave Nick instructions on the quickest route out of Huntsville to Elm Hill. Dina, Rusty and Ned Johnson followed Nick outside to his silver Jag.

"Keep in touch by car phone," Johnson said. "I don't like you going out there alone. Anything could happen."

"If I'm wrong about Elm Hill, it won't matter." Nick got behind the wheel, revved the motor and drove down the driveway.

He wasn't a very religious man. Hell, he hadn't been inside a church since his grandmother used to drag him off to Sunday mass. But he sought out God's ear, hoping that The Man Upstairs was listening. He needed a big favor, and he was willing to make any kind of deal necessary. Could he make a deal with God? If he could, he'd promise Him anything in exchange for Addy's life.

Chapter 13

He had stripped Addy down to her black teddy. For a while she'd been afraid he was going to rape her. He had touched her intimately and called her sweet Addy.

Why had she never seen this side of him? Obviously he was a very sick man—a man so obsessed with her father's money that he had already killed two men and was plotting two more murders.

She didn't know how long she'd been alone in the front parlor at Elm Hill. It could have been hours since he'd left. She didn't know.

Straining to see the digital timer attached to the heavy canvas belt he had strapped around her waist, Addy toppled over. Biting down, clamping her teeth to keep from crying, she tumbled around on the dusty floor until she righted herself again, sitting up on her knees. The rope that tied her hands behind her was attached to her ankles.

Even though he had been on Nick's list of suspects, she had never once actually considered him. How could she have been so blind? She and her father had opened their home to him, had accepted him as a part of the family because he was Dina's stepson.

Alone and frightened, Addy went over in her mind everything that happened since Brett Windsor had driven her to Elm Hill.

He had forced her inside the house at gunpoint, made her remove her clothes, and then had run his hands over her with rough, sadistic, sexual pleasure. Closing her eyes, she shut out the dawn light that crept through the tall, bare windows. She couldn't stop herself from reliving those terrifying moments she'd spent with Brett before he'd left her alone to die.

Outside a night owl hooted and a thousand katydids sang in unison.

Brett forced her to her knees, almost knocking her over in his attempt to subdue her. With unnatural strength, he jerked her hands behind her back, binding them securely with nylon cord, then draping the rope over her ankles, effectively hog-tying her.

"Don't do this, Brett." She wasn't too proud to beg; the threat of dying had quickly put her priorities in the proper order.

"Oh, sweet Addy, I had hoped we'd have more time together. I was so looking forward to making love to you." Brett traced the lines of her face with his fingertips. "But that was before Nick Romero had you. I don't want his leavings. Not a second time."

"Are you talking about Dina?" Addy tugged on her wrists. The cord was tight, with very little slack, allowing no chance for escape.

"Did you suspect that we were lovers? Or did Romero tell you?"

"Brett, if it's the money, Daddy will pay you whatever

you want if you'll just let both of us go. You and Dina can fly out of the country with millions." She hoped that she could reason with him, despite his apparent madness.

"I don't want a few measly millions." He carried the battery-operated lantern with him when he moved toward the door. "I plan to have it all. Everything that belongs to D.B. McConnell will be mine and Dina's in just a few months."

"If you kill Daddy and me, Dina won't inherit anything. She—she's not even named in Daddy's will."

"Not yet, but she will be. Once she and Rusty are married."

"Then…you…you haven't hurt Daddy?" An instant surge of relief rushed through Addy. Somewhere in all this craziness there just might be a note of sanity, a ray of hope in the darkness. "Where is Daddy, Brett? What have you done with him?"

"I set your father free only moments before I returned to the hospital and met you at the elevator." Brett smiled at her, his stunning, boyish smile that disguised a sick mind. "I had to kidnap Rusty. You left me no other choice when you allowed Romero to take you into hiding. It was the only way to get you back to Huntsville."

"Why did you have to get me back to Huntsville? I don't understand."

"You're the one I had to kidnap in order for my plan to work. You, Addy, you. Not your father. Rusty's probably at home now, all safe and sound."

Addy sighed with relief. If her father was free, he'd be able to tell Nick and the FBI that Brett was behind all the threats. Suddenly the reality of the situation hit her. Surely Brett wasn't so insane that he would have released a man capable of identifying him. "Does Daddy know that you— that you're—"

"I kept Rusty drugged the whole time. He has no idea who kidnapped him."

"Nick will figure it out. He'll find me, and when he does, he'll kill you. Do you hear me, Brett? Nick will kill you."

Addy called after him, but he didn't reply. She heard his footsteps as he walked out into the foyer and opened the front door. He returned quickly, carrying the lantern and a nylon duffel bag. Bending over beside her, he dropped the bag to the floor.

"Brett, I thought you liked me." Addy had no idea if she could get through to him, but she had to try. What other alternative did she have?

"Addy, sweet, I do like you. I would have made you my wife, if only you'd shown the least bit of interest in me." He unzipped the duffel bag. "I would have allowed you to live another year or so, until I'd disposed of your father and you'd made me your only beneficiary."

"How is killing me now going to get you all of Daddy's money?"

"Once you're dead and Rusty marries Dina, she will, of course, become his only beneficiary." Pulling out a heavy canvas belt, Brett laid it out carefully on the floor. "He will be so overwrought after losing you that Dina will fear for his sanity, but loving him the way she does, she'll be able to persuade him to marry her as soon as possible."

Suddenly Addy realized Brett's diabolical plan. Oh, dear Lord, why had her father fallen victim to Dina's seductive charm? If that woman hadn't wormed her way into their lives, none of this would be happening. And she would never have met Nick Romero, her one hope of survival. "You're going to kill Daddy, too, aren't you?"

"Kill Rusty?" Brett's maniacal laughter echoed in the stillness of the empty parlor. "No, no. Rusty will be so distraught over your death that he'll go into a steady decline—aided by Dina, naturally. After a few months, the memory of how you died will completely destroy your father. He'll probably die suddenly with a heart attack. Of course, if he doesn't oblige us by dying, we'll give him a little assistance. Who knows? Rusty might lose his sanity and put a gun to his head and pull the trigger.''

"Daddy would never kill himself!" Addy screamed, unable to control the rage burning inside her. "Anyone who knows Daddy would never, ever believe his death was suicide."

"That's where you're wrong, sweet Addy." Brett removed something that looked like a small, digital clock from the nylon bag. "You're going to die such a horrible death that—well, there won't be any body to bury, no funeral, no chance to say farewell." Brett dug out a spool of wire, then lifted up a metal box and placed both items on the floor beside the canvas belt.

Sour, salty bile burned a trail up Addy's chest and into her mouth. She thought she was going to throw up. What was Brett going to do to her? *There won't be any body to bury.* "If you were after Daddy's money, why did you demand that he not bid on the NASP contract when you knew it would mean millions in profits for M.A.C.?"

"The NASP contract proved to be an effective smoke screen, didn't it? No one will suspect me in the kidnappings or murders because I would have nothing to gain from M.A.C. losing out on the NASP contract."

"You wanted us to suspect Gerald, didn't you?" Addy glared at her kidnapper, longing for the freedom to attack him, to kick and scratch and hit. Anger welled up inside of her, bubbling like boiling liquid ready to overflow.

"You and Rusty jumped at the chance to condemn Carlton." Brett shook his head, grunting in a mock show of sadness. "Don't you think hiring Linc Hites was a stroke of genius on my part? His only connection to anyone who knew you was to your ex-husband."

"How did you meet Linc Hites?" She wondered how long she could keep Brett talking. She needed time— enough time for Nick to fit all the pieces together.

"Linc and I owed the same man, a rather unsavory businessman, some money. Isn't coincidence a wonderful thing? It brought me together with Linc Hites and brought you together with Nick Romero."

"And it brought Daddy and Dina together."

"Oh, that wasn't coincidence, sweet Addy. That was planned." Brett flipped open the metal box. "I've mapped out everything from the very beginning. When you didn't succumb to my charm, I had to do a little replotting. Simple enough, really—until Romero showed up and thwarted the first kidnapping attempt, then hung around causing trouble."

"Nick's gut instincts kept telling him that something was wrong about the kidnapper's demand. All the while Daddy and I suspected Gerald, Nick wouldn't rule out other possibilities. Sooner or later, he'll figure it out, Brett. You won't get away with this."

"Later won't help you, Addy." Brett's steady, knowledgeable hands worked quickly, removing a small wad of some kind of rubbery substance from the metal box. The glob reminded her of the Silly Putty the children played with at the day-care center. "Romero may think he's a real tough guy, but he's not so smart. Not nearly as smart as I am. And, if by some miracle, he does figure out that Dina and I planned this whole thing, then I'll just have to dispose of one unwanted and unneeded old Latin lover."

"Dina would never let you kill Nick. She loves him."

"I can handle Dina. She may love Romero, but she

loves money even more. Besides, she's as deep in this mess as I am.''

"Does she love money enough to kill for it? To risk the death penalty if she's caught?"

"Dina does what I tell her to do. Ever since my father died, she's depended on me."

Addy watched while Brett turned and came toward her. She wanted to run, but she was hog-tied and could barely move. Cringing when Brett slipped the canvas belt around her, easing it beneath the cord that bound her wrists and ankles, she willed herself to be strong. Now was not the time to panic. She was still alive. Things weren't hopeless. Not yet.

"I admit that I don't especially like Dina, but I can't believe she's capable of murder," Addy said.

"She isn't. Dina hasn't murdered anyone."

Brett clipped the digital timer to the canvas belt, then attached the thin wiring to the fuse he'd fastened to the dab of putty-like substance he'd molded across the belt's metal buckles.

"I had to promise not to hurt you before Dina would agree to help me with the kidnapping attempt," Brett said. "I convinced her that all I wanted was to hold you for ransom. She knows how badly I need money. She's such a sentimental creature. She's really become quite fond of Rusty, you know."

Addy realized that she'd just been wired with a bomb of some sort. She knew very little about such things, but the evidence was there before her, an undeniable fact. Brett Windsor intended to blow her to kingdom come. A surge of pure fear-driven bile filled Addy's mouth. Turning sideways, she threw up, retching until her stomach emptied itself.

Brett took a linen handkerchief out of his pocket and

wiped Addy's mouth, then grabbed the cord that bound her and dragged her into the corner of the room.

"As soon as I set the timer, I'll have to leave to call your father and Romero and give them the sad news." Reaching down, he activated the digital timer. Silently the deadly device began ticking away the last minutes of Addy's life.

Outside a night owl hooted and a thousand katydids sang in unison.

Huddled on her knees, wearing nothing but a black teddy, Addy McConnell awaited her rescue. While time raced by quickly, she consoled herself with one thought. *Nick Romero.*

Nick would find her before the bomb exploded. He had to find her. He was her paladin, her champion. He would never allow anything to harm her.

She knew with a certainty born of her love for Nick and her hopes for the future that she couldn't die. Not now. Elizabeth Mallory had prophesied that Addy would give Nick children. Two little girls. She could picture Nick's daughters. The two perfect angels, one with her flame-red hair, the other with his midnight black. One with her green eyes, the other with his dark brown.

They would name the eldest, the green-eyed brunette, Maria, after Nick's grandmother. And the younger, the brown-eyed redhead, would be called Madeline, after her own mother.

While the digital timing device blinked away the minutes, Addy kept her sanity by planning her future with Nick, by thinking about Maria and Madeline and about what a proud papa Nick Romero would be.

Nick pulled into the weed- and grass-infested circular drive at Elm Hill. The first, tentative rays of sunshine peeked from behind the far horizon. The dawn of a new day was breaking. He prayed that Addy was still alive to greet the morning.

The old antebellum mansion stood as a regal, if somewhat decaying, reminder of a South that had ceased to exist years ago. Like a Southern belle long past her prime, the house sagged with the ravages of time and abandonment.

Nick felt in his pocket for the key Rusty had given him, but when he tried the door it swung open. His heart accelerated at the thought that someone had been there before him. Examining the lock more carefully, he found that it had been jimmied. Addy was here. He could feel her presence.

There had been no other car in the drive and he hadn't run into any traffic on the lonely stretch of road leading to the turn-off. If Addy's kidnapper was still here, he was on foot. Taking no chances, Nick pulled out his 9 mm. automatic. Damn his noisy cane! But if the kidnapper was inside, he would have already heard Nick's car when he arrived. Time was of the essence if a bomb was involved. He hadn't dared waste precious minutes parking farther away and walking.

Making his way into the foyer, Nick waited a few seconds, allowing his vision to adjust to the shadowy darkness inside the mansion. He checked the parlor on the right side. Empty. He turned left. Then he saw her.

Damn! She was half naked, hog-tied and huddled in the corner of the room. Thank God, he'd found her still alive. He wouldn't allow himself to think about what her kidnapper might have done to her. Walking as fast as his slow stride would allow, he crossed the room.

Addy saw the dark figure approaching her. When she'd heard the car, she'd wondered if Brett had returned. Now she knew that Nick had come to rescue her.

"Nick!" she cried. "I knew you'd come."

Kneeling in front of her, he laid his gun and cane on the floor, then ran his hands over her face, cupping her chin in his palm. "Damn, Red, I've been out of my mind!"

He surveyed the situation quickly, able to see the canvas belt attached to her waist. Early morning sunlight illuminated the room with a hazy, topaz glow. Nick recognized the C-4 plastic explosive immediately. God knew he'd seen enough of it in Nam. Although the stuff was deadly, even in tiny pieces, it was one of the most stable explosives around. So damned stable that he and his SEAL comrades had occasionally set it on fire and used it to cook their food. C-4 created an instant hot flame.

And the damned stuff was readily available on the black market, especially in a military town. And Huntsville was a military town. The right person could easily have done the wrong thing, using his position to confiscate C-4 and make himself a nice little profit.

Nick released the catch on his cane. The sharp stiletto blade popped out. With careful manipulation, he removed the knife and immediately began slicing away at the heavy canvas belt. "We've got to get this off."

"How much time do we have?" She stared at him, her gaze locking with his.

He glanced down at the digital timing device. Only minutes remained, but it would be more than enough time for him to cut through the belt, remove it from Addy's waist and get her out of the house. "Plenty of time, Red. Just sit still and I'll have this thing off you in a few minutes."

"Brett Windsor kidnapped me."

"Dammit, why didn't I follow my instincts?" Nick kept his eyes focused on his knife and his hands, on the task of cutting through the belt. He tried not to think about Windsor or what he would do to the man once he'd been caught.

"Brett's insane. He—he planned to kill Daddy, too. Once Daddy and Dina were married, Brett was going to kill Daddy and make it look like either a heart attack or a—a suicide."

Nick cursed the strength of the canvas. His sharp knife had cut through less than halfway. "As soon as I get you out of here, I'll call Ned Johnson. They'll pick up Windsor, and if he's not in jail by the time I get to him—" He heard the floorboards in the foyer creak. Someone else was inside the house. But he didn't dare waste time checking out the intruder's identity. With every beat of Addy's heart, the blinking red timer clicked off another second of her life.

"Nick, it's Brett. He's come back!" Addy cried.

Too late, Nick swung around. His gun lay beside him. Brett Windsor stood in the doorway, the morning sunlight silhouetting his muscular frame.

"Move away from Addy nice and slow," Brett said. "I have no problem with shooting both of you and then letting the bomb take care of the rest."

"Don't risk your life," Addy whispered to Nick, seeing him eye his gun lying a few inches from his knee. "I'd rather die than—"

"Don't talk nonsense," Nick said, his voice so low she barely heard him. "I don't have a life without you, Red."

"Stop whispering and get the hell away from her!" Brett walked into the parlor and pointed his gun directly at Nick's head.

Nick obeyed, standing slowly and walking away from Addy, limping badly without the aid of his cane. He hoped he could find a way to buy them a little time. "Pretty ingenious plan you worked out, Windsor. Get rid of Addy.

Make it look like someone who wanted the NASP contract was the murderer, then once Dina married Rusty and became his primary beneficiary, see that he has a heart attack."

"Gerald Carlton had better hope he has an alibi for the past few hours." Brett laughed, then nudged Nick in the stomach with his gun.

"Where did you park, Windsor?" Nick asked. "I didn't hear you drive up."

"I parked far enough away so you couldn't hear me." Brett grinned, showing his straight, white teeth. "I haven't got time to tie you up, Romero, so I'm going to have to shoot you."

"Yeah, that would be the only smart thing to do. But before you shoot me, tell me how you knew I'd found Addy."

"Dina called me, the minute you left." Brett shook his head and grunted several times. "I hope she doesn't freak out on me. She's upset about all the killing. Dina's such a delicate little thing. I don't know how she would have survived all these years without me."

"Haven't you got that backwards, Windsor?" Nick taunted, wondering if he could rile the other man enough so he'd make a mistake, one that might give Nick the chance to jump him.

"What do you mean by that?"

"You've been living off Dina ever since you went through your share of your father's estate. For months now, Rusty McConnell has been paying your bills."

"He's damned rich enough to pay my bills. He knows I keep Dina happy, and that old fool is so hung up on our Dina that he'd do just about anything for her."

"I doubt he would have welcomed you so cordially if he'd known you and Dina were lovers."

Addy sucked in her breath so loudly that Nick heard her, and knew that Brett had, too.

Brett laughed, his toothy grin sinister in a way that made Addy wonder why she'd never noticed the neurotic glint in his eyes. "Oh, we've all loved her, haven't we, Nicky? That's what she calls him, you know." Brett turned toward Addy, giving her a hasty glance. Nick took a step in his direction. He turned back quickly. "No, you don't!"

"I've known Dina a lot longer than you have," Nick said. "She won't be able to live with herself if you go through with this. She'll break under the pressure."

"That won't be your problem."

All three occupants of the parlor heard the cars drive up, doors slam and footsteps pound on the veranda. Wild-eyed and clearly frightened, Brett grabbed Nick, twisting his arm behind his back and sticking the 10 mm. against his waist.

Dina Lunden ran into the parlor, then stopped dead still when she saw Brett and Nick. "Please, Brett...darling, you mustn't do this."

"What the hell are you doing here, Dina?" Brett asked, his voice shrill.

Rusty McConnell bounded into the room, stopping at Dina's side. "My God!"

"You brought Rusty with you!" Brett screeched. "What were you thinking of? This wasn't part of my plan. None of this was. Everything's going wrong."

"Brett, don't kill anyone else. If you let Nick and Addy go, then Rusty won't file charges, will you, Rusty?"

When Dina turned to him, D.B. McConnell glared at her, then at Brett Windsor. "That's right. I'll see that you're set up with as much money as you think you'll need, and I'll hire a private plane to take you anywhere you want to go."

"I want it all," Brett said, releasing Nick and walking toward Dina, whose arms were outstretched in a pleading, come-to-me gesture. "Dina and I can't live on a paltry six million dollars. I killed once for such a small amount. This time, it'll have to be more."

"Brett?" Dina dropped her open arms. "You didn't kill your father. He—he—Ashley had a heart attack."

"There are ways to fake a heart attack," Brett said.

Nick knew he had a slight chance of catching Windsor off guard as long as Dina kept talking to him. He had to risk it. Now!

Nick jumped Brett. The 10 mm. flew out of Brett's hand and slid across the floor. The two men locked in a struggle of brute strength, fists pounding, knuckles crunching. Brett Windsor was no match for his bigger, stronger opponent. Nick landed one final blow, knocking Brett to the floor.

"Nick, the gun!" Dina yelled.

Then Addy screamed when she saw Brett's bloody hand reach out and grab the 10 mm. from where it had landed on the parlor floor. As if in slow motion, the scene reeled off in front of Addy. Still lying on the floor, Brett turned over, aimed the gun and fired at Nick. Dina ran across the room, her voluptuous body separating the two men. The bullet entered her neck. She fell forward, face down on the floor.

Another gunshot sounded. Ned Johnson stood in the doorway, his automatic in his hand. Brett Windsor lay lifeless, his blank stare facing the ceiling.

Rusty McConnell rushed over, cradling Dina in his arms. Blood gushed from her wound. Nick took a moment to check her condition. Brett's bullet had hit an artery.

"Johnson, get over here quick," Nick said, then rushed to Addy.

While he busied himself cutting through the canvas belt,

Nick heard Dina's dying words. "Oh, Rusty, darling, forgive me. I—I never meant for—"

"Nick, are you all right?" Tears streamed down Addy's flushed cheeks.

"I'm fine, Red." He kept sawing away at the belt. "Johnson, you'd better get Rusty and Dina out of here. Fast."

"We don't have much time, do we?" Addy asked.

"Enough," Nick lied. Two minutes and counting down. The red numerals flashed a warning signal. Sweat coated the palms of Nick's hands.

Ned Johnson picked up Dina's lifeless body. "Come on, Mr. McConnell. Let's get Dina outside and let Nick take care of things in here."

"But Addy—" Rusty said.

"Nick's got everything under control," Johnson assured D.B. McConnell.

"I can't leave Addy." Rusty refused to budge.

Ned carried Dina's body outside, returning momentarily with two young agents who forcefully dragged an enraged D.B. McConnell out of the house.

Only another inch to cut through. Sweat poured off Nick's face. One minute. Fifty-nine seconds. Fifty-eight.

Addy knew time was running out. She said a silent prayer. God wouldn't let them die. Not now when they'd just found each other. "Nick, I love you."

Forty-six seconds. Cut. Forty-five. Cut. Forty-four. Cut. "I love you, too, Red. I love you so damned much." Forty seconds. Cut. Thirty-nine. Cut.

The last thread broke. The belt fell free. Twenty. Nineteen. Eighteen. Grabbing the deadly canvas strap, Nick ran as fast as his bad leg would permit, praying with each faulty step that he'd make it outside in time. If Addy hadn't been hog-tied, he would have left the belt in the house and told her to run. Ten. Nine. Eight.

Reaching the veranda, he raised the belt high in the sky. Five. Four. With all the strength in his arm, he flung the bomb out into the wooded area, away from the house and away from the parked cars. He made it into the foyer when the explosion rocked the house, shattering several window-panes.

"Nick! Nick!" Addy screamed his name over and over again.

Picking himself up off the floor, Nick hurried into the parlor, rushing to Addy's side. He bent down, cutting through the nylon cord that bound her. Pulling loose from the severed rope, Addy fell into Nick's open arms. She cried tears of happiness while Nick covered her face with frantic kisses.

"If anything had happened to you...if I'd lost you." Nick's voice quivered with the strength of his feelings.

Addy reached out, covering his cheek with her hand. She felt the damp stickiness of his sweat, and then she felt something else. Running her fingers upward, she looked at Nick. Tears filled his eyes.

"I'm all right. You saved me." She kissed him and hugged him and kept right on crying.

He held her in his arms, refusing to release her, even when Ned Johnson and Rusty McConnell came into the parlor. He wouldn't even let Rusty touch Addy. He couldn't bear the thought of letting her go. He'd never known what it was like to value someone else's life more than his own, to know that if she died, he didn't want to live, either. Addy McConnell was his whole world, and he was never going to let her out of his sight again. Not for the rest of their lives.

Chapter 14

Addy had not left her father's side since the night Dina Lunden died, and Nick had kept watch over them both. Absorbing everything that had happened and coping with the aftereffects was something the three of them were going through together. Nick hadn't felt such a strong sense of family since he and Miguel were boys. The McConnells had taken him into their lives and into their hearts, and it was just where he wanted to be. But in the aftermath of the horror they'd endured, Nick began having doubts about the future.

He had finally admitted to himself and to Addy that he loved her. And he did. He loved her so much it hurt, but was he good enough for her? Was he worthy of her love and trust? He was a hard-living, cynical, self-centered SOB. She was a gentle, caring, giving woman. And she was a wealthy woman, heir to a multimillion-dollar empire. He had about a hundred thousand stashed away for a rainy day, but he could hardly offer Addy the lifestyle to which she was accustomed.

Guilt riddled his insides like a spray of buckshot. He blamed himself for the nightmare Addy had endured at Brett Windsor's hands. He had suspected the guy was capable of doing practically anything for money, but he'd allowed his past relationship with Dina to blind him to the possibility that she was an accomplice. Damn, he felt like a fool and could only imagine how Rusty McConnell felt. Addy's father had fallen in love with Dina and brought her into their lives. He had to feel guilty as hell.

Nick kept reliving the evening at the hospital when he'd left Addy in Alan Sturges's care. He'd had no idea he was risking Addy's life by trusting someone else to keep her safe. As long as he lived, he would hear Elizabeth Mallory's warning just before he and Addy had left Sequana Falls. *Keep her guarded every moment.* If only he had listened to that warning, Brett Windsor would never have gotten to Addy, would never have put her through a living hell.

When Addy had needed him most, he had let her down. It was his fault that she'd almost died—that she'd come so close to being blown into a zillion pieces. Just the thought of it gave him cold sweats. He should have realized the NASP contract was nothing more than a red herring, which would have ruled out Gerald Carlton. And he should have realized sooner that Ron Glover might be devious enough to plot Addy's kidnapping, but he wasn't smart enough to plan it. If he'd known Janice Dixon better, he would have known she loved her cousin and uncle far too much to have done anything to harm them.

Dina. Damn the woman! And bless her, too. He had to give her credit. When it came right down to it, she hadn't been able to turn a blind eye and let Brett kill Addy. If

Dina hadn't finally admitted the truth to Rusty, then Nick had no idea what would have happened. Rusty and Dina's arrival at Elm Hill, along with Ned Johnson and his FBI agents, had put an end to Brett's evil plans.

And there was one thing Nick knew for sure—he owed his life to Dina. She'd taken the bullet that had been meant for him. Maybe it had been her way of trying to make amends, her final chance for forgiveness. It seemed wrong, somehow, that a woman as vibrantly alive as Dina should have died so tragically. But if she had lived, what would the future have held for her? Prison? After all, she'd been an accomplice to two kidnappings and two murders.

"Almost everybody's gone." Addy stood in the doorway of her father's den. "Janice and Ron are still here, and as usual he's moody and surly."

"How's Rusty? He seemed to hold up all right during the funeral."

"I haven't seen him so unhappy and sad since—since Mother died. It'll take him quite a while to get over Dina, especially her betrayal."

"Rusty's tough. He'll bounce back eventually. Who knows, he might even fall in love again."

"Ginger's with him now. She's fixed him a plate, and they're sitting in the kitchen eating. She cares about Daddy, and—and I think she's good for him." Addy entered the den, hesitating slightly before moving to Nick's side. "Don't you want something to eat?" She slipped her arm through his.

He stiffened. He didn't deserve her love. His stupidity had almost cost her her life. "I'll eat later."

"I know the funeral was as difficult for you as it was for Daddy." Addy ran the tips of her fingers down Nick's arm until she reached his hand. She laced her fingers through his. "Dina was the first woman you ever loved."

He squeezed her hand with such force that she cried out. "I'm sorry." Loosening his grip, he tried to pull away, but Addy wouldn't let go of his hand.

"It's all right that you loved her, Nick. Stop hating yourself because you cared about Dina, because you didn't think she was capable of the things she and Brett did. Daddy loved her. He trusted her. Even I never once considered Dina a suspect." Knowing that Nick was eaten alive with guilt, Addy longed to help him forgive himself for being human enough to make mistakes.

"You'll never be able to forget what happened, and neither will I," Nick said, refusing to look at her, afraid he wouldn't be able to resist the love and understanding he'd see in her green eyes.

"No, we'll never forget, but in time—"

Nick brought Addy's hand to his lips, brushing tender kisses across her knuckles. "I let you down, Red. It was my fault that Windsor got to you. If I had done my job, you would have been safe."

She reached out, covering his cheek with her open palm. "Stop beating yourself up. If anyone is to blame, it's me for being foolish enough to sneak away to the elevator. I realized my mistake on the way down to the lobby, but by then it was too late. Brett was there waiting for me."

Nick jerked her into his arms, his dark eyes searching her face. "When I think about what could have happened."

"It didn't happen." Addy spread her arms around his waist, holding him tight. "You figured out where Brett had taken me. You rescued me, saved me, just as I knew you would. Haven't you figured it out, yet, Nick Romero? You're my knight in shining armor."

"Some knight! I'm afraid my armor is tarnished, Red. You've built me up into something I'm not. You think I'm so wonderful, such a damned hero, when all I am is an over-the-hill ex-SEAL and ex-DEA agent. A guy who's been everywhere, done everything and seen too much of the sick, evil, dark side of life.''

"Why are you doing this? Why are you trying so hard to convince me what a bad guy you are?"

"Because I am a bad guy, Red." Shoving her out of his arms, he turned his back on her. "I can't possibly live up to the image you have of me." He walked toward the windows, stopping to stare sightlessly out onto the lawn. "Remember the man you met at Rusty and Dina's engagement party? You didn't like that man, Addy. You weren't impressed with him at all. Well, I'm still that same man."

"Yes, I suppose you are." Addy couldn't bear to think that she would lose him, but she could feel him slipping away from her. "I was wrong about you, though. There's a lot more to Nick Romero than his Latin lover-boy charm."

"Is there?" Nick had to make her realize that he wasn't in her league. She was head and shoulders above him, a woman who deserved only the best, and he didn't even come close. "You know what my SEAL buddies called me? Romeo. And believe me, I lived up to my nickname."

"I suppose I should be jealous of all those women, and I guess I am a little, but I'm also grateful to them." Smiling, Addy touched him on the shoulder. He cocked his head sideways so he could see her. "All that practice has made you a wonderful lover."

How the hell could she joke about it? He'd thought that reminding her of his past would make her see what poor husband material he'd make. "You just plain refuse to see me as I really am. You've created some fantasy man." He walked away from her. "I'll disappoint you, Red. I'll let you down. I'm no good at this commitment business."

"What are you so afraid of, Nick? Why are trying to put up walls between us?"

"I'm afraid of hurting you. I'm afraid that one day you'll wake up and realize what a mistake you made, that I'm not the man you thought I was."

Addy didn't go after him. She let him walk away, knowing that nothing she could say or do could make him feel any different about himself. Nick loved her as much as she loved him, but he thought she didn't really know him, that she saw him only as her rescuer, only as a lover. How could she prove to him that she knew exactly who he was?

Nick Romero, a flawed and imperfect man with a colorful and slightly unsavory past, was destined to be the father of her children. Somehow she'd just have to convince him that a reformed Romeo would make a faithful husband and an adoring father.

Three days after Dina's funeral, Addy McConnell went home, back to her house in the Twickenham district. Her father and Nick Romero accompanied her.

July had become viciously hot and humid, with heat indexes topping the hundred-degree mark daily. Tempers were short, moods constantly changing. She and Nick had spent little time together. His decision, not hers. He was trying to distance himself from her, to prepare her for his departure.

Addy suspected that today was the day Nick would make an attempt to leave her. But if he thought for one minute he'd ever get away from her, he'd better think again. She wasn't about to lose the best thing that had ever happened to her.

Addy served iced tea in the den. Rusty and Nick sat

opposite each other, the older man inspecting the younger, eyeing him critically.

"You'll be settling down here in Huntsville, won't you?" Rusty asked. "Long-distance romances seldom work."

"Sam Dundee has offered me a job in Atlanta," Nick said.

"Hell, stay on here. Take over as security chief at M.A.C. Tandy McHenry will be retiring in a few months." Rusty puffed on his cigar, then blew smoke rings into the air.

Addy sat down beside Nick on the small sofa. She knew what game her father was playing. It was called "Running Addy's Life."

"Thanks for the offer, Rusty, but—"

"Damnation, boy, quit hem-hawing around." Rusty got to his feet, his ruddy, freckled face flushed with agitation. "You're staying here in Huntsville and marrying Addy, and that's final!"

"Daddy!"

"I hardly think it's your place to decide who Addy marries," Nick said.

"I'm her father, aren't I? Who better to pick out the right man for her?"

"I think Addy should have a say in this. After all, it's her life. If she's as smart as I think she is, she won't saddle herself with a guy like me for the rest of her life."

"You're perfect for her, and you know it," Rusty said.

"That's where you're wrong." Nick stood, facing Addy's father. "I'd wind up disappointing her. I don't know the first thing about love and commitment. Hell, I'm a forty-three-year-old bachelor."

"Boy, do you know how much Addy will be worth

when I kick the bucket? She'll be one of the richest women in the United States.''

"I don't give a damn about your money, about how rich Addy is. If I married Addy, I'd sign a prenuptial agreement. Addy, without one red cent, is worth a king's ransom. She's the kind of woman who's priceless.''

Rusty grinned, his smile lighting his face. "I agree. A man would be a fool to run out on a woman like that, wouldn't he? Especially if the two of them are in love with each other and create red-hot sparks when they're in bed together.''

"Daddy!" Addy jumped up, placing herself between the two bickering men. "I think this has gone far enough. You two are discussing me as if I'm not in the same room, as if I'm not perfectly capable of talking for myself.''

Rusty glanced from his furious daughter to a dark and brooding Nick. Flashing them a brilliant smile, Rusty walked over to the door. "Well, girl, start talking before your man starts walking.''

Addy stared at Nick. He stared back at her. They heard the front door slam and then Rusty's limousine pull out of the driveway. They continued staring at each other.

"I'll go upstairs and get my suitcase. I think that's where your father's new chauffeur put it.'' Nick turned to leave.

Addy grabbed his arm. "I want an autumn wedding. October or early November. It'll take that long to plan the kind of wedding we should have.''

Nick glared at her, disbelief in his eyes. Had he heard her right? Had she said *wedding?* "What are you talking about?''

"I don't want an engagement ring. I'm not much on wearing a lot of jewelry. A simple, wide gold band will be fine.''

"Addy?" He turned completely around, looking her directly in the eye.

"We should go back to Sequana Falls for the honeymoon and stay in our cottage. That's where you fell in love with me, wasn't it?"

"I haven't asked you…we haven't discussed—"

"Nick Romero, if you think I'm going to let you run out on me, then you don't know me very well. I've waited my whole life to love a man the way I love you. I didn't think it was possible. I thought people only felt this way in romance books or in the movies."

"I'm not much of a bargain, Red. I don't know the first thing about being the kind of husband you need."

Addy smiled. "If you run, I'll follow you. There's not a place on this earth where you can hide. You're going to marry me, Nick, and that's final."

How could he respond to a statement like that? Addy was one determined woman. Did he have the guts to take the risk? If he married her, could he keep her happy? "You'll be taking a mighty big chance on me, Red."

"Do you love me, Nick?"

"Do I— Yes, I love you!"

"Have you ever loved another woman the way you love me?"

"No, never."

"Then I'm not taking such a big risk, am I?"

Grinning, Nick lifted his cane, placing it across Addy's back. Taking the ends of the cane in each hand, he pulled her toward him, pressing her against his chest, fitting her body snugly to his. "As long as you know what you're getting."

"I know exactly what I'm getting." She slipped her arms around his neck. "I'm getting the man I love."

* * *

Nick and Addy lay in the middle of her antique bed, their naked arms and legs entwined. Damp with their mingled sweat and the sweet essence of sex, they kissed and stroked and whispered love words.

"Aren't you glad you decided to stay and marry me?" Addy licked the perspiration from his tiny male nipples.

He grabbed her hip in his big hand, pressing her closer to his side. "You're a very persuasive woman, Mrs. Romero-to-be."

"Mmm—hmm. I like the sound of that. Mrs. Romero. Addy Romero." She snuggled against him.

"I suppose you know that you've accomplished an impossible task," he said.

"What's that, taming a wild man?"

Nick laughed, playfully swatting her behind. "No. Capturing the most sought-after Latin lover in the world."

Moving quickly, Addy straddled his hips, tossing her long, flaming hair over her shoulder. "You've accomplished a task just as difficult. You've taught me what real love is all about."

Taking her hips in his hands, he moved her up and down, groaning when he felt a resurgence of passion tightening his body. "And I've also turned a Plain-Jane, frustrated old maid into a beautiful, sex-crazed hussy."

"Why, Nick, what a thing to say! I was never a frustrated old maid, just an unfulfilled woman."

"Woman, I'd like to fulfill you, and soon." He surged up against her, showing her he meant what he said.

"I think we should fulfill each other." She slid down his legs to his ankles, then lowered her body until her breasts touched his thighs. She ran her hands over his calves, caressing him.

"You've never said anything about my scarred leg." Nick threaded his fingers through her hair while she spread kisses over the top of his hairy thighs. "You've kissed it and caressed it, and you act as if it doesn't look any different from my good leg."

Addy's tongue touched him intimately. He groaned. "The scars on your leg are a part of you. When we make love, when I see you naked, I don't think about your crippled leg, except to regret all the pain you must have endured."

"I'm not quite the man I used to be because of—"

"Nick Romero, you're more man with a crippled leg than any man I know with two strong legs. I've told you that before. Weren't you listening?"

She stroked him, pleasuring him with her wanton tongue. "Ah, Addy, you're good for my ego."

"I'm good for *you*, Nick."

He didn't disagree. She moved up his body, straddling his hips again. He thrust himself up and into her, grasping her waist as his mouth sought her breasts. She rode him wild and hard. He gave her a thorough loving, losing control the minute he felt her tighten around him and cry out her release.

In the aftermath of a second heated mating, they lay in each other's arms, listening to the sound of their breathing. Sated and spent, they touched each other with tender weakness.

"I—I lost two babies when I was married to Gerald." Addy's voice sounded loud in the hushed stillness of her bedroom.

"I know." He kissed her forehead. "Your father told me all about it."

"The doctors said I might not be able to carry a baby full term." She took a deep breath.

Nick pulled her close, kissing her with gentle sweetness. "I love you, Addy. You." He kissed her again. "Whether or not we ever have a child won't change the way I feel about you. We're so damned lucky to have found each other. What more could we want?''

"I want to give you children."

"Addy, sweetheart—"

"Elizabeth said that I would have children. Your children." She smiled at him when he stared at her in confusion.

"Elizabeth saw children in our future?" God, he hoped Sam Dundee's little soothsayer knew what she was talking about. If ever a woman wanted and needed children, it was Addy.

"Two little girls, Nick. Maria will be the eldest. She'll be our little green-eyed brunette."

Nick raised up, bracing himself with his hand as he leaned over Addy. "Maria, huh? After my grandmother."

"And Maria's little sister will have my red hair and your black eyes. I want to name her Madeline after my mother."

The conviction in Addy's words made him believe these little girls would be a part of their future. Their finding each other and falling in love had been a miracle. Who was to say that God wouldn't grant them two more miracles? "You know what, Red? I can't think of anything I'd like better than to be surrounded by adoring females for the rest of my life."

"And I can't think of anything I'd like better than being one of those adoring females." She cuddled against him.

"I love you, Red."

"I love you, too." Silently she added, I'll love you forever, *my paladin.*

* * * * *

Silhouette Books presents a dazzling keepsake
collection featuring two full-length novels by
international bestselling author

DIANA PALMER

Brides To Be

(On sale May 2002)

THE AUSTRALIAN
*Will rugged outback rancher Jonathan Sterling
be roped into marriage?*

HEART OF ICE
*Close proximity sparks a breathtaking attraction between a
feisty young woman and a hardheaded bachelor!*

You'll be swept off your feet by Diana Palmer's BRIDES TO BE.

Don't miss out on this special two-in-one volume, available soon.

*Available only from Silhouette Books
at your favorite retail outlet.*

Silhouette®
Where love comes alive™

MONTANA
Bred

From the bestselling series

MONTANA MAVERICKS

Wed in Whitehorn

Two more tales that capture living and loving
beneath the Big Sky.

JUST PRETENDING by Myrna Mackenzie

FBI Agent David Hannon's plans for a quiet vacation
were overturned by a murder investigation—and by
officer Gretchen Neal!

STORMING WHITEHORN by Christine Scott

Native American Storm Hunter's return to Whitehorn
sent tremors through the town—and shock waves of
desire through Jasmine Kincaid Monroe....

Silhouette®

Where love comes alive™

eHARLEQUIN.com

community | membership

buy books | authors | online reads | magazine | learn to write

magazine

♥——————————————————— **quizzes**

Is he the one? What kind of lover are you? Visit the **Quizzes** area to find out!

♥——————————————————— **recipes for romance**

Get scrumptious meal ideas with our **Recipes for Romance.**

♥——————————————————— **romantic movies**

Peek at the **Romantic Movies** area to find Top 10 Flicks about First Love, ten Supersexy Movies, and more.

♥——————————————————— **royal romance**

Get the latest scoop on your favorite royals in **Royal Romance.**

♥——————————————————— **games**

Check out the **Games** pages to find a ton of interactive romantic fun!

♥——————————————————— **romantic travel**

In need of a romantic rendezvous? Visit the **Romantic Travel** section for articles and guides.

♥——————————————————— **lovescopes**

Are you two compatible? Click your way to the **Lovescopes** area to find out now!

Silhouette —

where love comes alive—online...

SINTMAG